Coldiron

by

J.S. Perry

Coldiron

COPYRIGHT © 2024 by Janet Sing Perry

Cover Art by *The Wild Rose Press, Inc.*

The Wild Rose Press, Inc.
PO Box 708
Adams Basin, NY 14410-0708
Visit us at www.thewildrosepress.com

Publishing History
First Edition, 2024
Trade Paperback ISBN 978-1-5092-5549-8
Digital ISBN 978-1-5092-5550-4

Published in the United States of America

Dedication

To my husband Bill, I couldn't have achieved my dream without his love and support.

Acknowledgements

I want to thank the wonderful team of researchers at the Kingdom of Callaway Historical Society in Fulton, Missouri. Barbara Huddleston patiently answered my many questions for years. Also, the wonderful people at Ashe County Historical Society and Ashe County Museum in Jefferson, North Carolina. The Ashe County Library was a wealth of information with wonderful staff. The McKinney Tavern in Rogersville, Tennessee, now Hale Springs Inn, were so kind to let me photograph every part of the Tavern. The staff of H.B. Stamps Library in Rogersville, Tennessee were so helpful and enthusiastic about my book. The staff of the Museum of Middle Appalachia in Saltville, Virginia, were so kind to lead me to books on the history of Saltville and local lore. So many other people helped me along my journey, and I thank them from the bottom of my heart!

A warm thank you to author Candy Simonson for helping me edit my manuscript before submission. She showed me I had the power to split an infinitive!

Thank you to my editor, Ally Robertson and Wild Rose Press! You gave me my chance and I took it!

Many thanks to my family who kept asking: "Weren't you going to write a book?"

Kalteisen

Direct German to English Translation

Kalt-cold
Eisen-iron

Coldiron

Johan Georg Kalteisen, born 3 July 1730 in Goppingen, Wurttemberg, Germany, immigrated to America in 1750 as an indentured servant. He sailed into the port of Philadelphia on 28 August aboard the ship Phoenix. He married Anna Catherine Schumacher in about 1754 in Berk's County, Pennsylvania. By about 1768, they had moved with their three children to Rowan County, North Carolina, near Salisbury. At that time, Rowan County encompassed all western North Carolina. Upon his move to North Carolina, Johan Georg changed his name to George Coldiron.

In 1799, Ashe County was formed from a northwestern piece of Rowan County. George's second son, Conrad, 1760-1835, moved to Ashe County and became one of the first landowners. Conrad was my fourth great grandfather.

Chapter 1

April 22, 1984
Fulton, Missouri

Sarah and Ruth cast sideways glances at each other. The Old North Ward of what was once the Missouri State Lunatic Asylum stood in the distance.

"Are you sure?" Ruth whispered.

Sarah whispered back. "You know I've wanted to see the inside of the Old North Ward since we both started working here in 1960. It was boarded up in 1940 so there was no chance for me to go in."

"If we get caught, we'll not only lose our jobs, we'll also be arrested. Just because we're best friends doesn't mean we'll be cellmates."

Sarah stifled a giggle as she shivered with excitement. "I know, but I've heard so many stories. I want to see inside before it's too late. See the wrecking ball there?" Sarah pointed. "They're using it to tear the building down tomorrow. If you don't want to come, I understand."

Ruth gave Sarah an exasperated look. "No, no, you know I won't let you go in by yourself. You would fall through a floor somewhere." Ruth shook her head with a sigh. "We would never find you."

The four-story building was built in 1851. Dark vacant stares came from the places where the windows and doors were removed. Sarah and Ruth crossed the street and quickened their steps across the bare expanse of ground. The Old North and South Wards were all that was left of the Civil War buildings. New buildings would be constructed when these were gone.

The women hurried around to the front of the building, then up the crumbling stone steps and through the doorway.

Ruth gave a nervous look upward at the twelve-foot-high ceiling where the paint fell in strips. "It's spooky in here, Sarah. See that light socket hanging by a lone wire? Looks like it's about to fall right on us."

Doorways lined the hallway. "C'mon," Sarah urged as she entered the first one on the right. "Look at all these rows of rusty metal beds. I wonder why they didn't take them out when they closed the building?" The walls were painted dark green on the bottom and what was once white on the top. Sarah noticed Ruth biting her nails and realized that Ruth's nerves were working on her. "Okay, let's hurry this up."

They found the stairs at the back of the hallway, and a window at the landing let in a bit of light. The second floor looked the same as the first. The third floor was littered with books and papers. They climbed to the fourth floor, leaving their footprints in the dust.

"Sarah, we're leaving footprints. The owners will know we've been in here. They'll measure our feet and know we left them. They'll put us in jail."

"You're being dramatic. Look, here's a door. I bet it goes to the attic."

Sarah reached to turn the white China knob. The door opened easily and swung inward, silently, almost as if extending an invitation. Steps led to the attic.

"Oh, Sarah!" Ruth grabbed Sarah's arm. "What if there are ghosts?"

"I hope so!" At Ruth's horrified look, Sarah quickly apologized. "No, I'm sorry. A ghost won't hurt anyone, and I have my flashlight." Sarah pulled it from her pocket. She flicked the switch and led the way. The attic was dark, but the rafters were visible because of the small window above the stairs. Sarah's flashlight illuminated the room well enough to show row upon row of high wooden shelves on both sides of the room. The shelves were filled with suitcases and trunks of every imaginable size, covered with thick dust from God only knew how many years.

"Just look at this!" Sarah squealed. "What luck! Let's look at them right quick!"

"Right quick? There must be hundreds of them!" Ruth's voice held a quiver as she waved her hands at the rows of shelves. "Let's move down the row. Maybe the oldest ones are toward the window."

Sarah grabbed a suitcase from the shelf closest to her as she handed the light to Ruth. Sarah worked the leather strap loose from the buckle and opened the sides of the case to peer inside. Her hopes were dashed when she found absolutely nothing inside.

"Oh, dear." Sarah closed the case with a frown.

"Let's open some others," Ruth suggested. Ruth laid the flashlight in the crook of the shelf, placing it so that the beam cast its light down the middle of the rows. "You take that side and I'll take this side." Ruth waved her hands toward the shelves.

"Right, that'll be quicker."

Sarah pulled at a camel-back trunk with chipped black paint in between the wooden slats. Dust-covered straps held it closed. She wrestled with it while Ruth opened a gray grip of some kind. Sarah got the trunk open to find layers of tissue paper on top of what looked like bolts of fabric. She lifted the folded cotton out to find several other pieces just like it. The whole trunk was filled with fabric, nothing else.

"I wonder why it had been stuck up here?" Sarah asked.

Ruth pulled out men's shoes, and belts, lots of belts, nothing else from the grip she held. They went through several more grips and valises; most were empty.

Ruth looked at her watch. "We've been up here for almost an hour. Church will be letting out soon and there'll be more people about. I'm scared." Ruth's voice quavered.

"Let's look just a bit longer, please. I feel, well, I just have a feeling!" Sarah said.

"Your feeling might get us jailed," Ruth sighed in resignation with a shake of her head.

"Okay." She turned around to pull at another grip on the shelf.

Sarah pulled herself up to the top shelf and grabbed hold of the end post that propped up the shelf. Putting her right foot on the bottom shelf, she heaved herself up to grab another suitcase. It was so heavy it fell to the floor with a thud. Sarah knelt and swiped her hand across the top revealing a nametag. Sarah grabbed the flashlight and held it closer to try to make out the name. *S. Coldiron* was written in faded script.

"Oh, my goodness! We have a name!" Sarah gasped and put her hand over her mouth.

"Open it, open it!" Ruth urged.

Sarah unfastened the cracked leather straps holding

it closed and opened the grip with both hands. Wedged in the top pocket was a thin book. *Missouri State Lunatic Asylum* was stamped on the faded cover. Sarah's hands shook as she reverently opened the book and read the faded script.

October 5, 1864, Ashe County, North Carolina

The first thing I needed to do was hide the gold coins where they would never find them. They will follow me and find me and kill me, as they had killed Uncle Prince.

Sarah looked up from the book with widened eyes. "I can't believe it!" She held her breath and repeated, "I can't believe it!" She read on in the journal.

"Sarah, we don't have time to read it now. We have to get out of here!"

"Okay, but I'm taking it! I can't leave it here. I think this is *really* important. There are other papers here too." She closed the case and tried to lift it. "It's heavy but I can carry it. Let's go!"

They stood and looked about them. Cases were strewn all over. "Well, we've made a mess, but we don't have time to put things back. It doesn't matter. They're tearing this place down tomorrow. It seems as if we've been here a very long time."

"We have and we better go. I have the flashlight." Ruth led the way and Sarah carried the case. They hurried down the stairs, their hands sliding down the dusty handrails. Making it down to the first floor, the women hurried toward the doorway. They peeked out and were relieved to find everything unchanged. No one was about, so the journal thieves hurried toward the sidewalk.

"Let's just act as if nothing has happened, as if we don't have a care in the world," Sarah said as she struggled with the large case.

"Yes, let's pretend we don't have a sign on us declaring us thieves and burglars," Ruth whispered with sarcasm.

The women walked along the sidewalk to the Torino without incident. Sarah opened the car door and hoisted the case into the back seat. She hopped into the driver's seat as Ruth went around and jumped in the passenger seat. Sarah started the car and drove slowly away even though she wanted to gun it and lay rubber to get away.

As they sped down Fifth Street, Sarah's mind raced. She couldn't wait to read the journal.

"We need to turn in here if we're going to your house." Ruth pointed to Sarah's driveway.

"Sorry, I was miles away. If you hadn't said something, I would've driven past." Sarah turned into the driveway and pulled up into her carport.

"I hate for anyone to see me take the valise out of the car," Sarah said, eyeing her prized package in the rearview mirror.

"Let's go in without it, pick up a trash bag, and ...no, wait! We can say we got it at a garage sale! Yes, that's perfect!" Ruth said.

"Great idea!"

They got out of the car trying hard to act normally. Sarah looked all around but couldn't spot anyone. The neighborhood was quiet, but then it always was so. Sarah reached into the back seat, and pulled out the valise, and shut the door.

"Let's get inside," Sarah said.

They walked down the rose-bordered walk to the side door of her small white Victorian house. Sarah's house was the last of the old *Asylum Row* houses. The

April sunshine brightened the house and highlighted the wraparound porch and gray trim.

"I left the keys in the car. Crap! I'll be right back," Sarah said.

Sarah set down the valise and Ruth stepped in front of it. Sarah hurried back to the Torino, its dark blue metallic finish gleaming in the sun. She opened the door and reached in to grab the keys. She shut the door softly. No need to advertise their homecoming again.

Sarah rushed back to the house while flipping through the keys to find the right one. Ruth stepped aside and picked up the valise. Sarah opened the door and Ruth followed her into the house. The kitchen was bright, but Sarah turned on the light anyway. Then she pulled down the shade on the kitchen door. Ruth put their treasure on the antique wooden table that had been in Sarah's family for years. The women stared at the cracked brown leather valise.

Ruth spoke in a soft voice, "We already know what's in it."

"I know, but I feel as if this will change us, maybe forever. I have chills."

Sarah reached for the bag and unclasped the leather strap that held it closed. She pulled it open and reached for the journal. Sarah clutched the fragile book and pulled it free.

"What else is in there?" Ruth asked.

Sarah pulled papers from the valise and stacked them on the table. "These look like old invoices. Look, this invoice is for fabric for the sewing room. This one is for thread. Here's a ledger that shows how many garments were made that year. I can't make out the date but it's 18 something. It looks like someone's desk was packed up and put in the valise."

"This gives us more clues, like maybe who S. Coldiron is," Ruth said.

"Let's read the journal first and look at these later. What do you say? We can sit here and read it together." Sarah pulled out a chair.

"No, please. That's so hard to do." Ruth frowned. "Let's do it this way. You read it first. You read faster than I do. Then you can tell me if this is what we think it is."

"Okay, but I need to take you home first."

"No, it's only four blocks. I'll walk. It's a beautiful day. I'll get home in plenty of time to finish my laundry and get ready for work tomorrow. You can call me this evening and we can talk about it. How about that?" Ruth asked.

"Yes, thank you!" Sarah agreed.

Sarah hugged her best friend and opened the door for her.

"Talk to you later. Read fast and let me know."

Sarah watched her friend walk away for a few seconds and then closed the door. She eagerly turned toward the table, picked up the journal and walked to the living room. Kicking off her shoes, she turned on the brass floor lamp. The frosted glass lampshade casts just the right glow to read by. Settling into her favorite chair, Sarah stroked the precious old leather. What secrets did it hold? Holding her breath, she opened the journal to the first page.

Chapter 2

September 28, 1864
Coldiron, Ashe County, North Carolina

It all started with needing salt. The Unionists and Home Guard were a threat, but salt was the key to our survival. Uncle Prince had a plan, and it involved a dangerous trek. But I'd better back up to when the whole thing started.

Prince was tying his old mule, named Mule, to the hitching post when Samantha, Sam to her folks, arrived at the log church at the edge of town. His weathered, bearded face was shadowed by the old slouch hat Sam gave him a few years ago. The wool shirt and homespun britches he wore were threadbare but still had years of wear in them according to Prince.

Sam patted her horse Sugar's mane and then dismounted. As she tied him to the hitching post beside Mule, she stroked his maple-sugar-colored neck and smiled to herself. Sam spoke to her uncle, "You've decided then?"

"We have to go now to get the salt if we're going. It's near about the end of September. I dread this something awful. Let's go see how many have come."

Sam walked into the church where the logs were dark with age. As she sat down, she was glad for the welcome light from the tall windows. She settled her long skirts around her feet to cover her worn boots. Although the pulpit was empty, Sam could still hear Preacher Billings telling everyone how to do right.

Prince sauntered through the doorway and up the aisle. His gaze swung left and right as he passed the nearly empty pews. It looked like God's waiting room! Grandma and Grandpa Coldiron and Grandma and Grandpa Davis were in the right front pew, all aged eighty if they were a day. Prince doubted they could even get on a mule, much less ride for three days going and walk coming back.

Opposite them, in the left front pew, was Shreldi Poole and her husband Wallon. Shreldi's booming voice more than made up for her lack of stature. They owned the general store. Wallon couldn't speak above a whisper. He whistled for Shreldi when he needed to know the price of something. But Wallon did have quite a knack for making bird calls and animal sounds, especially cats.

Fourteen-year-old twins, Cole and Isaac Coldiron, sat tall, trying to look older in their straw hats and homespun. Jim, "Buzzard" Davis, thirteen, sat next to Isaac. Jim went on his first hunting trip and brought home what he thought were two turkeys. When he arrived home and was told they were buzzards, the teasing was merciless, and the nickname stuck.

Deborah Carpenter, Miss Deb, her long cotton day dress neatly folded around her limbs, sat primly at the end of a pew. She tucked a stray strand of hair back into the dark bun at her neck and straightened her back. Her nieces, Hattie, twelve, and Mattie, fourteen, sat with her and gazed around. Mattie spied Isaac in front of them and whispered to Hattie.

Prince pushed his slouch hat up with a forefinger and wiped his brow with the same motion. *The War has thinned us out.*

Prince looked around. "I know you're wondering why I called this meeting. You know we need salt bad. The last shipment that was got in was not doled out to everyone that needed it. That's why we must try to keep this just between us. We don't want nobody knowing what we're about. We're going to have to go get the salt. There is salt to be had in Saltville, Virginia. It's a hard three-day journey by mule just to get there. We'll have to walk back because the mules will be loaded with salt."

"How are we going to pay for this salt? None of us has got any money," Miss Deb asked.

"I got that covered, ma'am, no need to worry about that."

Prince went on. "How many of you has a mule that we can borrow?"

Grandpa Coldiron, Grandpa Davis, and Buzzard raised their hands.

"Okay, I guess I mean how many has a mule and can ride it?"

Buzzard raised his hand and Mr. Davis and Mr. Coldiron half raised theirs.

"Number one," Prince said as he raised his forefinger, "We need more men. No offense, Mr. Davis and Mr. Coldiron, but we need men that can ride."

"None taken, sir. We just came to see what was going on and if we could help. Cole and Isaac can ride our mules."

Miss Deb raised her hand. "My father has a mule that I can borrow."

Wallon stood to speak. "I have a mule and can ride

along. We need salt so bad."

Sam spoke up. "Uncle Prince?"

Prince looked at her and nodded.

"We don't have any more men, none that we can trust anyway. What you need to do is to let us women come along. We can ride as well as any man and we are *here* and the men are not."

"It's just too dangerous, Sam. I can't let—"

"We can dress like men. All of us have some of our menfolk's clothes. We can stuff our hair up under our hats. I've thought about this Uncle Prince. Really, think about it. Remember when we set out for Fayetteville all those years ago? I dressed like a boy because you thought it was safer, and it was. We can do it now. We *have* to do it now. Let's get some food together for the trip. I have those osnaburg bags we can put the salt in."

Prince knew she was right. He really hated it but there was no one else to go.

"All right. Cole, Isaac, Buzzard, Wallon, Miss Deb, get your food together and your mules. You'll join Sam and me. Don't tell anyone where we're going. We don't want to be followed and we don't need any trouble. The Home Guard especially don't need to know anything about this. We'll meet up at Grandpa Coldiron's place at first light. It's right on the trail north."

Everyone nodded their heads in agreement and hurried out.

The sun bathed the morning in a frosty glare as the party set out. They had six mules and Sam had Sugar. Buzzard was there when Isaac and Cole came riding up on their borrowed mules. Miss Deb rode up with Mr. Poole right behind her.

Prince spoke to the group. "We'll ride single file.

Try not to talk. Sound carries here and we need to be quiet."

Prince rode Mule and led them along the path north across the upper edge of the Blue Ridge Mountains. A dense pine forest loomed ahead. The needle-covered path was well-defined even though not as well traveled as the trail south. Isaac brought up the rear.

The party was unarmed except for Prince. He had his shotgun and his LeMat. Sam wasn't exactly sure how he came to have the revolver. She remembered seeing him coming out of the saloon a couple of weeks ago. Sam had met Mrs. Lambeth on the street and noticed that she was impeccably dressed, as always, in gray silk with a matching bonnet. She had her two spoiled sons in tow. Although only seven and nine, both were accomplished liars. Mrs. Lambeth had stopped Sam on the dirt street in front of the general store.

"How's the state of your immortal soul, Miss Samantha?" she asked in her God-and-I-are-one voice.

"Fine, Mrs. Lambeth." Sam gathered her skirts and tried to go on, but Mrs. Lambeth was set on talking to her.

"Have you heard from your brother lately?" She had her head cocked to one side, ready to pounce on any bit of information.

"No, but you know the mail…"

"Of course, of course."

"Mrs. Lambeth, please forgive me, but I need to get on. See you later." Sam rushed on by her, heading up the street. When she passed the saloon, Uncle Prince was coming out. He had a gun and holster in his hands. Sam looked at him with apprehension, knowing his one weakness.

13

"Uncle Prince!"

"Now, don't go giving me the squinty eye! A man has a right to a wee nip at the end of the day. I only had a bit of one…"

"Where did you get the revolver?"

"Darndest thing! I was playing cards with this young gentleman. Yes, indeedy, he was a *southern gentleman,* I could tell. Not from these parts. Plays the lousiest cards; don't know how he gets on. Well, he put his revolver in the pot and I had a ace and he didn't have nothing. So, I won. Gave me the holster, too. Whadda ya think?" He showed her the revolver.

Prince went on. "It's called a LeMat. It's a .36 caliber cap and ball black powder revolver. See this little barrel under here? It is a .20-gauge smoothbore barrel capable of firing buckshot. When you're out of bullets, this holds nine, you can flip this little lever and wham!"

Sugar stumbled on a hidden root in the path and Sam brought herself back to the present. The riding had become so monotonous she couldn't keep her mind from wandering. Uncle Prince had told them to keep their eyes on the mules rump in front of you. Their provisions were strapped to their saddles. All were dressed in their warmest clothes. Their boots were pretty much worn out, but with the War on, there was no way to get any more, even if they had the money. Even though the town had a tannery, there weren't many cattle left to slaughter. Besides, salt was needed to tan the hides.

Everyone kept their thoughts to themselves but everyone was worried, especially Prince.

Sam's thoughts wandered again, this time about her family, her inability to provide food, and her dressmaking business that dried up. No money and nothing to buy if you had it.

Oh! The dresses she used to make! Her favorite by far was the Tyrian purple satin. She got the fabric quite by accident. She and Uncle Prince had made a two-month-long journey to Fayetteville to get supplies. While Prince went to the livery, Sam had gone to the dry goods store to purchase her dressmaking supplies. The store had every imaginable fabric available. She looked longingly at the satin but knew she could never afford it. Her clientele wouldn't be able to, either. The shopkeeper showed her all the pretty calicos and stout cotton muslins. He was a nice man and didn't try to get her to buy things she couldn't afford. Sam had him wrap her purchases and said she'd be back with her uncle to pick everything up.

Sam remembered the event from five years ago when she returned to the mountains and unwrapped the parcels. The purple satin had slid out of the folds of one paper parcel. *I had just started my business then. The fabric was so soft, so smooth.* Sam recalled how she unfurled the satin across her cutting table and stroked it with care. *When Mrs. Gambill had seen the fabric she immediately commissioned a frock with a matching hat. I was glad Mrs. Gambill bought the fabric. She had been so easy to fit and the color was lovely on her as well.* Sam reflected on the memory with a smile and satisfaction in her heart, at first unaware Prince was speaking to her.

"Sam?" Prince brought her back to reality.

"What, I'm sorry, what did you say?"

"You need to pay attention. You were daydreaming. We're coming to the New River. We need to get ready to cross."

The river current was not fast where they were but there were a lot of big rocks below the surface. The drought had lowered the rivers and creeks everywhere.

Prince went to each of them in turn and said, "Let's lead them across. Stay together as best you can. The river isn't but a couple of feet deep here. Keep your provisions dry above all else. We'll move slow."

"Why can't we use the bridge upstream? I haven't heard about it being burned by the Federals," Miss Deb said.

"It's too risky for us. I don't want anyone to know we're here."

Prince narrowed his eyes as he looked into the distance and behind them. *I have to be on the lookout for the Home Guard. I can't afford to lose this money. I don't want them to wonder how I got it and go snoopin' around.*

Prince led the group across. Cole and Isaac crossed behind Prince. Miss Deb was next, Buzzard, Wallon and then Sam brought up the rear with Sugar. Sam knew Sugar didn't like getting his feet wet. She would have to coax him across. "C'mon, Sugar." She patted his neck. "We don't have a choice." Sugar shied a bit, but as always, the horse obliged her.

The little group made it across without mishap. It was only about four o'clock, but the shadows were deep. Darkness would find them soon, and Prince needed to find a place to camp. They rode another mile or so before Prince rode on back to check on each of them. They had made good time with no complaints. "Let's camp here."

"Isaac, would you gather up some deadfall for our fire? Buzzard, you're good at making a campfire, right?" Prince nodded at Buzzard.

"Yes, sir, I sure am. I'll make it up in a flash." Jim was glad to help.

"Cole, I need some help with these mules."

"Yes, sir!" Cole walked behind the mule to unsaddle him.

"Now, Cole, you can't walk right behind a mule like that. It's dangerous."

"Oh, shaw, Uncle Prince, Old Joe won't hurt me."

"Son, a mule will wait his *whole life* just to kick you once. No matter how well you care for it. Now, look out."

Prince spoke to the women who were gathered around where Jim was building a campfire. "Cole, Isaac, Wallon, come over here to the fire. I need to say something."

Prince had their full attention.

"Ya'll did real good today. Tomorrow will be harder because the trail gets a lot steeper from here. It'll be harder to breathe, so it's best not to talk much. As I've said before, sound carries right far here in the mountains. We don't want anyone to know we're here and we for sure don't want anyone to know what we're up to. We just can't trust anybody. Miss Deb, your corndodgers will taste mighty fine. Sam, your coffee, well, what we have been calling coffee, will go right well with them dodgers."

"I have some parched corn and will make us up a nice pot. It will be good and hot." Sam fetched the water for the pot and set it on the fire to boil.

Miss Deb got down her pack and pieced out the cornpone. Everyone handed Sam their tin cup to be filled with the hot brew.

Prince swallowed the last of his coffee and spoke.

"Let's all get settled down and get some shut-eye. Dawn comes early and we need to be ready for it." Prince yawned as he settled himself onto his saddle blanket. He felt for his money pouch. *Lord, please help me keep these people safe so we can git our salt. It'll be a miracle. There is so much that can happen betwix here and Saltville.*

Chapter 3

Sunday, April 22, 1984
Fulton, Missouri

Sarah closed the journal reverently. She ran her fingers over the worn cover. *Until a few hours ago, this had been in a dust-covered valise in the attic of a building that was built 133 years ago. Samantha Coldiron had written this in 1864.* Sarah had sat spellbound for four hours, only getting up once to get a Diet Pepsi. *How will I tell Ruth all of this? Will she think it's real?*

She carried the journal with her to the phone, not wanting to put it down even for a minute. She dialed Ruth's number. "Can you come over?"

"Now?"

"Yes, we need to talk about what I've discovered, and I'm afraid to do it over the phone."

"Okay, I'll drive over right now."

A few minutes later, Ruth arrived and quickened her pace up to the side door.

Sarah saw her coming and opened the door before she got there.

"Well, I can see you're in a fizz! I can't wait to hear this!"

"Let's go into the living room and I'll explain."

Sarah took long, deep breaths to calm herself as she

sat in the wingback chair. Ruth settled herself on the edge of the matching chair, waiting eagerly for Sarah to speak.

"I'll hit the high spots for now and we can decide if we want to pursue this. It's a great story!"

Sarah went on to explain what she had discovered. Ruth sat spellbound for almost an hour. Her ears buzzed with the story Sarah told her.

"I feel really hot and cold at the same time," Ruth said rubbing her shoulders.

"That's just your hot flashes kicking in!" Sarah joked. "No, I'm sorry! I feel the same way. What do you think we should do first?"

Before Ruth could answer, Sarah kept talking. "We need to find out if this is real. To do that, we're going to have to do research. We have to find out if Samantha really lived!" Sarah moved about the room, emphasizing with her hands, chattering all the while. "How to do it? How to do it without letting anyone know why we want to know?"

Ruth nodded her head when she thought it appropriate. "What about—"

Sarah kept rambling. "What if someone finds the money first? Especially if we slip up and someone starts asking questions of us. Do you think it's still there?"

Ruth had to interrupt to get a word in. She waved her hand in front of Sarah. "What about the Historical Society? You told me about a story in the paper about the good things they do for people. I'm sure they can steer us in the right direction."

Sarah's face brightened. "Yes, I'm sure they can. What a great idea!" She lowered her voice and whispered, "We must be careful. If they think we're treasure hunters, they won't take us seriously." She wandered around the room. "We need to ask how we find an ancestor. We have to pretend we're asking about an ancestor, maybe *my* ancestor."

"That's it!" Ruth jumped up from her seat. "To try to find out if she really lived in Ashe County, North Carolina, during the War Between the States!" She clapped her hands.

"Yes, let's see, where's my phone book?" Sarah hurried to her telephone desk. Pulling out the phone book, she ran her fingers down the H's.

"Isn't the name Kingdom of Callaway?" Ruth asked.

"Yes, yes, of course. My brain is swirling around right now, and I can't think straight! I found the number. I'm calling now."

"It's Sunday. They probably won't be there."

"Well, I can leave a message. I bet they have one of those new answering machines. I heard on the news that AT&T made them affordable, and this *is* 1984!"

Sarah dialed the number and both held their breath. "It's ringing!"

It rang three times and was answered by a sweet voice, "Kingdom of Callaway Historical Society, Dolores speaking."

Sarah gulped and cleared her throat and managed to speak. "Yes, hello. My name is Sarah Davis. I wondered if we could come in and ask about how we could find my ancestor. Do you do that?" Sarah was hopeful.

"Yes, we do that. We usually can point you in the right direction. I'm afraid we're closing in a few minutes. We're only open on Sundays from one to five."

"Oh dear, I wasn't aware. Is there any way we could

make an appointment for after four this week?"

"Well, we don't usually do that but—"

Sarah interrupted. "Please, it's so very important. We just want to understand what we need to do. We promise not to take up much of your time."

"Okay, would Tuesday work? What time can you be here?"

"We get off work at four. My friend Ruth will come with me. The address in the phone book says 701 Westminster Avenue, is that correct?"

"Yes, the Tuttle House. You can't miss it."

"Okay, see you at 4:30, if that's all right. We'll have to change clothes, but we'll hurry."

"Yes, see you then!"

They linked arms and danced around the room. Smacked palms and danced in another circle.

"This calls for a cold Diet Pepsi!" Sarah said.

"And a cold Dr. Pepper!" Ruth said.

They floated into the kitchen. Sarah opened the Frigidaire and pulled out the cold drinks. Handing Ruth her Dr. Pepper, she toasted. "To the future!"

"Yes, to the future!"

After a few good swallows, they looked at each other. "This is scary," Ruth said.

Sarah swallowed again and Ruth hiccupped. "Are we crazy?" Ruth's lower lip quivered.

Sarah stiffened her spine. "No, absolutely not! Let's sit down and plan. We must think and think well then plan every step. We can't afford to make mistakes."

"Yes, we need to plan. But we don't have the first idea of what to do. We need to talk to somebody who knows what to do. Do we know anybody?"

"Not that I know of right now. You know my family

doesn't care anything about finding our people. I can't remember Mom saying anything about her great-grandparents. I knew my grandparents on Mom's side but no one else. Nothing but a few names on my dad's side."

"Same here. I thought when *Roots* came out my family might help me, but they weren't interested. I've been so busy working—and you have too— to do much about it," Ruth said.

"Maybe this person at the Historical Society might help us on Tuesday."

"All we can do is hope."

"Let's call it a night for now. You make notes when you get home. I'll make notes on what questions we might ask and how we need to ask them. We can make our plan and change it to suit as we go," Sarah said. "Oh, wait, do you want to read the journal?"

"Not tonight. You've told me what's in it and there's no time tonight. Maybe later." Ruth picked up her keys from the kitchen table and turned to hug her friend. "What a day this has turned out to be!"

"Yes, I think things are going to change dramatically for us!" Sarah predicted.

"Yes, me too!" Ruth said as she waltzed out the door.

"See you tomorrow at work. Will you be in the Big Kitchen?"

"Yes, I hate peeling potatoes!" Ruth said for the thousandth time.

"Me, too! But it beats emptying bedpans!"

Ruth nodded as she got into her old Ford. As always when she turned the key, she said a little prayer. The old

Ford started right up. Ruth waved to Sarah and backed down the driveway.

Chapter 4

September 30, 1864
Mountains of Ashe County, North Carolina

The laurel hells rose on both sides of the trail. Because the branches tore at their legs when mounted, they walked. The morning mist had yet to rise above the bushes even though it was near noon. The narrow trail here wound up in a seemingly endless maze of twists and turns. Breathing came hard at this altitude, so no one spoke much. The cornpone they had for a quick bite before they hit the trail was gone, and everyone was hungry and thirsty.

Sam walked a few steps behind Prince's mule. "Uncle Prince," she called out softly, "how far to water do you expect? We're all near to dying of thirst. Mules need it too."

"Just a bit farther and we'll crest this mountain. When we start down, we'll be in Virginia. About a mile down, there's a good spring. We can stop there. You can tell the others."

Sam turned to Miss Deb. "Pass the word. We'll stop about a mile down."

Everyone nodded, and no one complained. The precious salt was worth whatever they had to endure to get it.

As they rode into Virginia, they saw the lay of the

land. They had not seen a more beautiful sight except for home. The gaps and ridges were various shades of blue in the distance. The mist settled in the valleys like a wispy blanket.

Prince had no other choice than to stop. They were desperate for water but a watering hole can be a great place to get ambushed. The creek rushed with clear mountain water and the trail spread out wide here. A great number of people had been here before. Prince walked his mule over to the edge and let him drink. Prince squinted his eyes up and down the trail.

"Let's all get a drink. Fill your water bags. Miss Deb, see to the cornpone? I know ya'll are about starved. When we get to Saltville, I'll try to get us some side meat. We gotta keep up our strength."

Miss Deb nodded. Holding up her end of the bargain, she opened the saddlebags and handed out cornpone to each one. "Here, Sam, I didn't mean to be stingy with you, have another piece."

"Thank you, Miss Deb. I'm near about starved. We haven't had much to eat lately, and I haven't a store laid up in my belly. I know you and yours have felt the same. Maybe now we'll be able to butcher our hogs and have some meat for the table."

Cole, Isaac, Jim, and Mr. Poole sat down on big rocks as they ate their cornbread.

"Cole, how about you tell me about that 'ere squirrel rifle I heard tell you just got from the gunsmith over to Creston," Mr. Poole whispered.

"Yes, sir! I worked for Mr. Worth for nigh onto six months to pay for that rifle. He had it hid all this time from the bushwhackers and outliers." Cole stopped to take a drink. He bit off another bite of cornbread and spoke with his mouth full. "He needed me to help and I was glad to do it. I helped him with the wagons. The rifle is a .36 caliber. I barked a squirrel the other day—"

"You never neither barked no squirrel!" Isaac interrupted and smacked his brother on the shoulder. "You scared him to death. That's a fact!"

"I did too bark him! I saw the bark fly right off the branch in front of his nose!" Cole shot back and rose to get in his brother's face.

Prince heard the revolver cock a second before he saw the men who rode silently out of the woods and surrounded them. Bushwhackers! Prince cussed himself for not paying closer attention. He counted six mounted men with weapons. He had the Lemat tucked into the back of his britches. If he reached for it, they'd shoot him dead. The shotgun was on his mule.

The man with the revolver eyed the group as he dismounted. "Now, what do we have here? A family reunion? Git your hands in the air where we can see 'em."

Sam looked at Prince with wide eyes. Miss Deb froze and stared at the men. With cornbread still in hand, the boys complied.

"Let's see what ya'll got there to eat. Give it to me!" He grabbed the cornbread from Cole's hand and crammed it into his mouth. The man walked over to Miss Deb and yanked the bag of cornpone from her hands.

"But this is all we have! You can't..." Miss Deb frantically reached for the bag.

"You don't sound like no man." His beady eyes swept down her body. "You a whore? What you got men's clothes on for?"

Miss Deb was petrified of being found out. She tried

to lower her voice. "No, I…"

Sam glanced at Prince with eyebrows raised. He shook his head no. *He would figure a way out. He always did.*

The leader turned to the others. "Lemme see what ya'll got in your pockets. Right now, lemme see." The leader waved his revolver at them.

No one moved until he hollered. "Right now, dammit!"

The boys and Miss Deb showed they had nothing in their pockets. Mr. Poole reluctantly took out his Jews harp, and the man took it. Sam pulled her pockets inside out to show nothing. Prince looked at the men and chewed his lip. He shook his head in despair and let out a sigh as he carefully removed his money pouch.

"Oh!" The big-mouthed leader waved his revolver in Prince's face. "Now, what do we have here?" He grabbed the bag and opened it.

"By Gawd! Silver coins! Look at them purty things!" He held up a coin with a sparkle of greed in his eyes. "We hit the jackpot, boys!"

Suddenly, shots rang out. The leader's eyes darted from the coins to his men, who were already riding away and ducking for cover. Shoving the bag into his pocket, he grabbed for the horse's reins. The horse balked as he missed. "Hold still, you ill-bred nag." The leader found the reins and mounted. "Well, we got your money anyway!" The leader yelled over his shoulder as he galloped away after his band.

Prince and Sam looked around for their savior and saw none. A mule traipsed out of the woods with a peddler attached to him.

"You people all right?"

Prince smiled with gratitude. "Yes, thanks to you! You all by yourself? You sounded like a whole bunch of people!"

"Well, I seed what was what right off. I set my sights on the big 'un but I cain't hit a lick at all. My eyes ain't what they used to be." The peddler had a sheepish grin. "Them bushwhackers git anything from ya'll?"

"My money. We come up here to get... well..." Prince looked at Sam. She knew he didn't want to give away their plans. The peddler seemed harmless, but you never could tell.

Sam went over by Prince. "What're we going to do now? We've come so far."

"Don't you worry, baby girl. I'll see we get what we come after."

"But–" Sam started to argue but Prince held up his hand and gave her a warning 'not now' glance.

"Thank you kindly, Peddler. Might I have your name to put in my prayers this evening?"

"Peddler will do."

Prince faced his people. "Let's get things rounded up. We've got a ways to go yet before we camp for the night. Then it's just a day's ride to Saltville. Everything will be okay, we'll move on."

"But they took our food! How are we going to eat?" Miss Deb asked.

The peddler opened one of his saddlebags and pulled out a bag of cornmeal. "This should make you some meals and maybe you can trade for some more in Saltville."

"Thanks, we're much obliged," Sam said as she took the cornmeal. "If you're ever in Coldiron, back in North Carolina, please stop by and I'll mend your clothes for you."

The peddler looked at his ragged clothing and spoke softly. "Thank ye' kindly, ma'am." Then the peddler melted back into the woods the way he came.

"Now, folks, this is a setback, I have to admit. But we'll soldier on. I've got a plan. We'll get our salt." Prince nodded his head in satisfaction.

Prince checked to see if everyone was mounted, and then he took the lead. Sam followed Prince, then the boys and Miss Deb, with Mr. Poole bringing up the rear. The water bags on each of the mules were fat and the precious cornmeal was safely in Miss Deb's pack.

The little troupe traveled as fast as they could down the mountains and through the valleys leading to Saltville. They came to a stream that ran fast but shallow and would be no problem crossing.

Prince called out to them. "Let's cross and camp on the other side."

They were all too tired to talk, and their movements were slow and deliberate. Even the boys were quiet. Miss Deb got out the cornmeal.

Sam said, "Here, let me." She reached for the bag. "You've cooked all the other meals."

"I need to earn my keep," she said with a bit of defiance.

"Miss Deb, you and your family will have a share of the salt. You've handled your mule and yourself very well." Sam touched her shoulder. "We need you."

Miss Deb started to say something, then stopped, then went on. She hung her head. "Sam, why did that man say I was a whore?" Her bottom lip trembled. "I have never been so embarrassed…"

"Those men are just scunners. No one is going to

pay them any mind and you shouldn't either." Sam hugged her. "Besides, wearing britches doesn't make you a whore."

Sam took the cornmeal and skillet over to the fire the boys had made. She got the coffeepot out of her pack and went down to the creek for water for their pretend coffee. "The cornpone sure would taste better with some salt," she said to herself.

They were all asleep before their heads hit their bedrolls. Prince wanted to stay awake, but his eyes drooped shut. He was exhausted and unused to these long days in the saddle. Thankfully, no one bothered them on this night, and they slept as well as they could on the hard ground.

They rose with the sun and resumed their journey. Used to making and breaking camp now, they felt like seasoned travelers. The terrain smoothed out, and the mules made good time. By late afternoon, they were within a mile of Saltville.

Prince took them off the trail and bade them make camp. He was going into Saltville to look around. "Please let me come with you, Uncle Prince," Sam asked.

"Okay, come on. But you have to do exactly what I say."

"I will. I promise."

Prince and Sam rode out of the woods and down the trail. The trees had been chopped down for miles in this area. The train depot sat to their right. The tracks led away to the grandest sight that Sam had ever seen. Mountains of white salt were everywhere! It looked like snow piled high. The wooden flumes carried the salt water from the salt wells to the furnaces and dripped with salt crystals that looked like icicles. Sam and Prince looked at each other and smiled.

"We made it!" Sam said.

"Stay here by the depot. I'll be back." Prince dismounted and handed the reins of his mule to Sam.

"But, Uncle Prince, we have no money."

Prince looked at Sam, then at the mountains of white salt in the distance. "I'll be back," Prince said again and walked toward what looked like an office.

Saltville, Virginia was heavily fortified. It was a natural fortress with hills and ridges forming circles around the town. As of that afternoon, October 1, 1864, there were only 400 Confederate soldiers guarding the saltworks. Trenches and gun emplacements were all over the hills. Nearly every hill had a lunette or an artillery piece surrounded by earthworks.

Hundreds of wagons waited in line to be loaded with salt. The salt furnaces were laid out in long rows as far as the eye could see. The railroad tracks went northward. To the left, was the Palmer Store. The stables were snugged up close to it and what looked like a large house or hotel could barely be seen in the distance. On the right was another large frame building with several wagons and hitching posts in front of it.

The railcars toward the west were filled with cords of wood to fuel the salt furnaces. In the distance, there were hundreds of little shanty houses all around the furnaces. Saltville was a very busy place and a lot bigger than Prince had mentioned.

Sam dismounted and stood between Sugar and Mule at the side of the depot, where she could see everything that went on. She reached up and snugly pulled down her hat. *So many people! I haven't seen this many people since court day back home.* Sam heard a whistle off in the distance. In a few minutes, a train pulled into the station. She had never seen the likes of such huffing and puffing! She had heard about trains but had never seen one. The big black engine with a huge smokestack that belched black smoke rolled to a stop at the depot. Sugar tried to rear up at these unexpected scary sights and sounds, but Sam stroked his head and held him firmly. Mule just blinked and looked around like he saw big black trains roll in every day of the week.

Sam noticed with concern that the train cars were full of soldiers. *What were they doing there? Guarding the saltworks?* The wooden cars were open at the top with little windows along the side. Sam guessed the soldiers much preferred the openness to the stifling cars at the back of the train. Unless it rained, of course. Sam was amazed at the swarming activity. Gray-clad uniforms were everywhere.

Someone shouted above the din. "Preston's men are finally here!"

Sam's eyes darted here and there, trying to find Prince among the many faces in front of her. She was sure Uncle Prince hadn't counted on all these people or the soldiers.

Meanwhile, Prince walked toward the salt office. He came to a frame house with the words, *Stuart, Buchanan & Company* painted over the door. His eyes cut left and right. He looked through a window. A man wearing spectacles sat at the back side of a large desk. In front of him, men were in line with Federal greenbacks in hand. One man held a small leather pouch to his chest.

Prince had known this wasn't going to be easy. He noticed hundreds of wagons lined up to be loaded with bags of salt. Countless slaves worked to load the wagons. After the wagons were loaded, they were taken to the spur line of the railroad and unloaded onto the cars. The Eastern Tennessee and Virginia Railroad constructed a spur line from Glade Spring to Saltville so they could easily transport the salt from Saltville to supply lines across Virginia.

Prince finally came back and joined Sam. They mounted and headed back to the others at camp. Not a word was spoken the whole trip back to camp. Sam could tell there was a lot on her uncle's mind. She'd seen that look before and it worried her. She knew he was planning something because his lips were moving but no sound was coming out.

The dangerous plan was brewing in Prince's mind: *I know what I have to do, but I have to be fast. The wagon at the end of the row will be the easiest to take. Hopefully, the men will still be at the hotel for breakfast when I come back in the morning. If they come after me, there'll be a fight. I know the odds...and they ain't good.*

Chapter 5

October 1, Saltville, Virginia
The same afternoon

A railroad worker pushed a wooden ramp in place at the rear car and slid the wooden door open. A lean man in a dirty Confederate officer's uniform ducked his head and stepped out. He had a black badge with red markings on his Cavalry hat and on the gray sleeves of his uniform. He reached back through the door to retrieve the reins of his horse. The horse had ridden with him and the other soldiers in the car all the way from Lynchburg, Virginia. His mount was well-disciplined and made no mischief, but he did make a mess. The straw did little to mask the smell.

"Come on, Soldier, let's get out of this hot box."

Soldier eagerly complied and walked down the ramp. His dark coat gleamed in the October sunshine. "That's a good horse," the gray-clad officer said.

At sixteen hands, Soldier was a little above average height for a Morgan. But there was nothing average about him. The officer bought the three-year-old stallion at the start of the war. He was a well-trained Cavalry horse. He had no white markings to give himself away in the dark. Soldier's Morgan temperament was an asset, and the officer trusted him. His stamina was unequaled.

The officer checked his gear. The Spencer carbine

he had found in the Wilderness fight was in its scabbard. His saddlebags bulged with his extra cartridges and his only extra shirt and coat. He lifted his hat, wiped his brow, smoothed his dark hair, and pulled his hat down.

The officer led Soldier and made his way along the train tracks to the depot. He asked a man who was unloading supplies, "Where might General Preston's headquarters be?"

The worker looked up at the man and pointed. "It's that way, sir. East, away from the works. He's at the Palmer Hotel."

****

A couple of soldiers with saddlebags over their shoulders scanned the crowds, glancing from one face to the next. The men walked down the line of salt-filled wagons tethered by the depot. One man glanced over his shoulder, then quickly reached into the last wagon and untied the string holding a sack of salt closed. Reaching into his saddlebag, he pulled out a pouch and stashed it in the sack of salt. He grabbed the string to tie it closed.

The other man grabbed his arm. "Wait, Marcellus, I want you to hide this too."

"Why, Frank?"

Frank handed him a smaller bag. "Just in case they recognize us. I don't want to lose this. I've carried it for three years. I think I recognized an officer at the depot."

The two made note of the faded green paint adorning the side of the wagon. Two new boards were on the same side. Shouldn't be too hard to find later.

****

The cavalry officer searched the depot, hunting for anyone who looked like the men he was after. There were so many soldiers about. He looked across the small expanse to the depot on the other side. A dirty ragged boy stood holding the reins of a beautiful golden-brown horse, an animal not seen much these days. A mule was on his other side.

The officer watched with curiosity as the boy reached up and patted the muzzle of the horse. *Something a little off about him.* The more he studied the boy, he realized the boy didn't stand like a man. *His actions aren't that of a man. Why was this woman dressed like a man? What was she trying to hide?*

An orderly approached the officer. "Sir? The colonel will see you now. It's just up the street a bit."

The officer glanced back at the woman. A man in a slouch hat came up to her and took the reins of the mule. They mounted and rode southeast out of town. The officer walked with the orderly up to the hotel. He tied Soldier to the hitching post, followed the orderly through the doorway and into the room on the right.

The colonel looked up as he laid his pen on the desk.

"Major R.B. Royster, Sir. Just in from Lynchburg."

Chapter 6

Monday, April 23, 1984
Fulton, Missouri

Sarah drove to work Monday morning and yawned all the way. She hadn't slept at all thinking about what she and Ruth would do next.

Sarah didn't hate her job, but didn't like it much either. The kitchen work was hot and backbreaking. What choice did she have? The Fulton State Hospital was the only place to work in Fulton. Her kids were grown and had good jobs as nurses. It would be hard to sell her house and move just to have a different job. Besides, Sarah knew this town. Good friends lived here. Sarah had had this conversation with herself for years. *When you live alone, you cling to what keeps you content, if not happy.*

The first thing Sarah noticed when she drove onto the hospital grounds was the huge wrecking ball already working on the North Ward. Sarah pulled over and got out to watch. Boom! Down came one side of the roof. Sarah watched with sadness as yet another old building was coming down. She was so thankful she had gotten the journal out first!

Not wanting to be late for work, Sarah quickly got back in the car and drove the rest of the block to the Biggs unit where the food service rooms were located.

At least it's April. The kitchens won't feel like ovens yet. It would help so much if there was air conditioning but that won't likely happen while I live and breathe.

Sarah made it through the day and hoped Ruth had had a good day. She drove home and immediately went to the bedroom to make sure the journal was still under her pillow where she'd left it. Sarah grabbed it to her chest, and walked quickly back to the kitchen to get a Diet Pepsi.

She reached into the freezer and pulled out a TV dinner. No cooking tonight! She wanted to read the journal again. Sarah popped the TV dinner into the oven and sat at the table. Her phone rang as she opened the journal. Sarah hurried to the living room to answer it. It was Ruth.

"Can I come over? I just have to talk to you about the journal. We need to talk about our plan."

"Sure thing. I'll pop another TV dinner in the oven."

Ruth knocked on Sarah's door a few minutes later. The sound startled Sarah even though she was expecting it.

"You scared me. I think my nerves are shot and it's only been 24 hours!"

"Yes, mine too. That's why I wanted to talk. Are you sure this lady can tell us how to find out if Samantha was a real person and not a figment of someone's imagination? We *did* find the journal in an insane asylum you know."

"I really hope she can. If she can't, I'm sure she'll know who can. I've never tried to find an ancestor before, which is sad if the truth were told. I don't have the first clue how to go about it. I know the story sounds fantastic, but these things really did happen. The Civil

War happened. I've read a lot of books on this. Granted, some of them were fiction, but very good fiction. The authors researched their information very well."

The timer on the oven dinged and Sarah reached for a potholder and opened the oven door.

"These smell delicious!" Sarah inhaled the scent of turkey and dressing and sighed. She took off the foil tops and put the dinners on the table on top of the potholders.

"You're right! These smell like ambrosia from heaven! I'm starving." Ruth held her face over the dinner and breathed in.

Sarah got forks from the drawer, handed them to Ruth, and opened the fridge to get Ruth a pop. "Let's read the parts of the journal that I marked last night," she said as she sat down. "If all of what we've read in the journal turns out to be true, we will need to ask for time off to go to North Carolina."

"Yes, since vacation time or sick leave is non-existent, it'll have to be without pay." Ruth was wistful.

They talked about the journal as they finished their meal. Sarah wanted to nail down the questions to ask the society lady.

Sarah spoke first. "For one thing, we don't know what questions to ask. All we know is a name and place. We're not even sure it existed at that time."

"Yeah," Ruth nodded. "We can start with that."

"She'll tell us more about how to go about it—"

"And then we'll follow with more questions!" Ruth agreed, interrupting.

"I guess we really can't plan all our questions right now. They'll be based on what she tells us."

"Right, you're right, of course. We'll just have to wing it," Ruth said.

"We just might've stumbled onto something, you know?" Sarah smiled with anticipation.

"Yes, but it scares me to death," Ruth shuddered.

"Me too, but we can't get cold feet before we even start. Can you forget about what we just found? I sure can't." Sarah shook her head.

"No, I can't either. I've not been this excited since, well, forever! I didn't think I would ever get to sleep last night." Ruth rolled her eyes and shook her head.

"Me either. We better get ready for tomorrow. I have a tablet we can use to write our notes. We don't want to try to remember it, we'll be too nervous. Let's meet here as soon as we get off work and then we can drive over to the Historical Society. I have the address written down."

Ruth agreed and hurried home to get ready for work the following day.

Chapter 7

October 2, 1864
Saltville, Virginia
Early morning

Prince left the others with Sam in charge and snuck back to Saltville on foot.

He spotted the wagon he had an eye on the day before. A line of men waited at the hotel to get breakfast. Soldiers hurried toward the north end of town. He headed over toward the wagon with the green paint and untied the mules from the hitching post. Prince hitched himself up onto the wagon seat and backed the mules enough to turn around. He slapped the reins lightly and moved the team away from the depot and down the street. Goosebumps crept over his flesh at the slow pace.

Prince wanted to slap the reins and run, but he knew that would attract attention. The mules made the turn to go back up the mountain and walked on as if they had all day. When Prince got to the small copse of trees where the trail started, he slapped the reins hard. The surprised mules leaned into their traces and the wagon rattled down the road.

Prince's mind was on fire. *Get to the camp and get the salt loaded onto the mules. The sacks weigh 50 pounds, so I'll probably have to load them myself. Hope Sam is ready, I told her to be ready. She'll be ready. I'd better be ready to stand and fight if the wagon owner catches me. Hopefully, it'll be only one man.*

"Salt's here! Uncle Prince is back!" Sam alerted everyone. The others stood beside their mules, ready to load their salt.

Prince rattled up to them and jumped off the wagon. "We've got to hurry!" Prince's deep voice held an edge to it. His eyes narrowed and his nostrils flared as he looked back at the trail.

"Why do we have to hurry?" Miss Deb was worrying the reins she held in her hand, loosening and tightening her hold on them.

"I stole the salt!" Prince said as he jumped down.

"Death's head on a mopstick!" Miss Deb exclaimed as she moved her mule over to the wagon.

"Miss Deb, you keep a lookout while we load the mules," Prince said as he went to the back of the wagon and opened the tailgate. He slid the first bag out and hefted it onto his shoulder. Cole and Isaac ran over to get a bag each and hefted them out of the wagon and onto their shoulders. They were robust boys and helped load the mules directly. Prince wished he had sawbuck saddles for the mules, but he didn't. He had lots of rope, though, and tied the bags tightly and expertly to the saddles. Sugar had two bags roped to his saddle. Each mule had two bags and Prince's mule had three. They had thirteen bags of coarse salt that weighed roughly fifty pounds each.

Prince pulled the wagon off the trail, knowing it wouldn't be going with them. But he hated to leave the mules. *No saddles, but they're perfectly good mules. No sense leaving them here. I'm taking them. Two mules will come in handy at home.* Unharnessing them from the wagon, he pigtailed them to each other and then to his mule. *Don't trust them with a load, so with no load on them, they'll follow just fine.*

"Okay, everything looks good. The mules will walk as fast as you lead them. So we can't walk fast because we'll give out by noon. A steady pace will do it. Sam, you lead us. Miss Deb, you go next. Boys, you get in line and Mr. Poole, you and I'll bring up the rear. Let's step right smart!" Prince looked at the sky and Sam knew he had said a prayer.

Chapter 8

October 2, 1864
Saltville, Virginia
That same morning

Back at Saltville, two men in Confederate uniforms came out of the hotel arguing. The other soldiers were making a beeline north.

A sergeant hollered at them. "Get your butts up to the fort! General Stephen Burbridge and 6,000 Federals are on their way here and ya'll better get to the north of town with the rest of your company!"

Startled, Frank and Marcellus looked at each other. "Damnation! We got to get to that wagon," Frank said. The men ran to the line of wagons and looked up and down. It was gone—as if disappearing into thin air.

"Where's the wagon?" Frank exploded, throwing his hands into the air.

"It was right here last night and this morning. I checked," Marcellus said.

Right then, a rather large man came huffing over as he hitched up his galluses. He looked around. "Where's my wagon? You seen my wagon?" His red face was angry.

"We don't know, and we don't care! Come on Marcellus, we gotta go!"

They hurried away, talking fast. "Frank, we gotta

find that wagon! When Archer gets back, and we don't have that money, he'll kill us. The man that has been following us, you know he'll find us and—"

"Shut up! We're wasting time. We need to find that wagon and find it fast. There are only three roads outta here. From what the sergeant just said, the Federals are coming from the north. So, we can go southeast and southwest."

"We can follow the tracks—"

"There are a million wagon tracks around here, Marcellus!" Frank pointed to the many tracks on the ground.

The wagon owner came over and said, "What wagon you lookin' fer?"

"The wagon with green paint on the side and two new boards on the same side. Why do you want to know for?" Frank spit on the ground and narrowed his eyes.

"That's not your wagon, you puttocks, that's my wagon! Never mind, I know how to find it!"

"Yeah? How can you possibly know that? Wagon tracks all look alike," Marcellus said.

"It ain't the wagon tracks, it's the mules' tracks pulling it. Never mind, get out of my way!" He pushed his way between them and started down the street.

Frank and Marcellus followed the man and pushed him into the alley. Grabbing him by the collar, Frank turned and shoved the man against the wall of the hotel.

Frank pulled his Bowie knife and pressed it against the man's ample middle while his left forearm pressed against his neck. Reddened with anger and exertion, Frank pushed his face within inches of the wagon owner's. "You better tell me right now what you meant by that or I'll gut you where you stand!" Frank's spittle sprayed the other man's face.

"That's *my* salt for *my* store, and you'll not get it!" The wagon owner tried to squirm away from Frank's knife.

Frank pressed the knife harder. What he lacked in stature, he more than made up for in meanness.

"Okay! Okay! Ruby is my lead mule. That's the left one if you don't know. Her left front shoe has an X in the shoe's curve. I had it done that way so I could track her because she loves to run off!"

Frank nodded with an evil satisfaction and then quickly pushed the Bowie knife up to the hilt in the man's gut. The man grabbed at the knife as Frank pulled it out and the blood soaked his shirt. Then he slowly slumped to the ground.

Marcellus grabbed Frank's arm. "Why did you do that? Right here? Right Now?"

"There's people running ever which way. They ain't going to notice. No one cares right now! Look at them! Let's get our horses and get on out of here. Let's check the southeast road first."

Chapter 9

R.B. Royster came out of the colonel's quarters just as Frank withdrew his bloody Bowie knife from the wagon owner's gut. R.B. watched the man slump to the ground as the other two made their getaway. He ducked back into the office and told the colonel he had a change of plan.

The colonel contradicted him. "I need your services right here and right now, Major. Sharpshooters are hard to find, and your skills have preceded you. According to my scouts, General Burbridge is only four miles away."

"All right, let me get my gear and horse, and I'll meet you back here."

R.B. had no intention of letting the men he had chased across Virginia get away. He recognized one of them. Purchasing his supplies the previous night, he was ready to follow them to the ends of the earth if need be. R.B. didn't want to get court-martialed, but General Breckenridge had given him a lot of leeway where pursuing these men was concerned. *Hopefully, I might persuade Colonel Preston to overlook this indiscretion.*

R.B. mounted Soldier and galloped after the two men. They would lead him to the other members of the gang. He caught up with the men just outside of town and couldn't believe his eyes. The men were walking their horses, moving their heads back and forth, staring at the ground as if they were looking for something. *I could take them now, but I need the others.* He stayed back out of sight and watched them for a few minutes. Shaking their heads, they mounted up and headed back toward Saltville. R.B. stayed out of sight, but followed them to the saloon. They tied their horses to the hitching post that already had several horses tethered to it and then walked into the saloon.

R.B. tied up at the hotel across the street. An aide to Colonel Preston ran up to him and said, "Colonel wants you now, sir!"

"G. Rover Cripes!" R.B. said as he followed the aide back to the colonel's headquarters.

Chapter 10

October 2, 1864
Saltville, Virginia
That same morning

"Yankees coming. Ya'll better git where you're a going, real quick." The barkeep informed Frank and Marcellus when they walked into the saloon.

"Yeah, we'll do that." Frank ordered a whiskey. Looking around the room, he found Archer and the others at the back table. He and Marcellus walked over and sat down. "We've had a bit of trouble. We've got to get south of here, quick!" Frank told Archer in a half whisper.

Archer squinted. "Why do we have to do that, Frank?"

"Well, we hid the money in a wagon loaded with salt 'cause we thought that fellar what is always following us was on our trail. Then it was stole, right from under our noses!"

Archer's eyes bored into his. "Why do we have to go south, Frank?"

'Cause we think the man what stole the wagon went that way."

Archer stared at the other men seated at the table. "Yes, Frank, you need to go get the money back. That's our money—"

"It's my money too! I put my life savings in there too."

"Yes, we'll get it all back. But we need to talk a bit about why we're here. I want you to go ask the barkeep to come over here."

"Why?"

Archer's steel gray eyes bored into Frank's weak blue ones. "Because… I said so. Be polite." Archer's voice was icy.

Frank went over to the barkeep and asked him to come over to the table. The barkeep threw his towel over his shoulder and walked over to the table where the five men sat. He looked at the dirty gray uniforms and the threadbare kepis. His eyes settled on the big man called Archer.

"You wanted to see me?"

"Yes. Would you care to tell me your name?" Archer asked.

"Evington, Michael Evington. Do you want a drink?"

"Thank you, Evington. We would all appreciate that very much. Whiskey, please."

The barkeep left them to get the drinks. Archer's men looked at him like he had just sprouted horns. They had never heard him ask for anything, only demand it.

Archer quietly and clearly explained, "We don't want to attract attention. We'll be polite and quiet. Do you all understand?" His beady eyes gave a warning that sent chills.

Marcellus and Frank looked at the others to see their reaction. No one dared to meet their eyes. They all nodded.

The barkeep placed their drinks in front of them.

"That will be a buck and two bits."

Archer handed over the money. The barkeep went back to the bar and made quite a show of cleaning the bar and drying the glasses. All the while, he spied on the men in the corner.

Archer spoke to the men quietly, even though they were the only ones in the saloon. "I don't have time to go over this twice. We're sitting in the middle of a town that has a million dollars in it. The salt office down the street is taking in money hand over fist. There are a thousand wagons waiting at the saltworks to be loaded up. The people buying the salt have greenbacks and gold to pay for it. They don't accept Confederate money."

Archer went on. "There's going to be a battle here shortly. They won't miss us for long. Hell, look out the window. Soldiers are everywhere, but they have a place to go and they're going in a hurry. They're not watching anyone in particular. We need to walk down to that office and take the money. We can get out of town, and no one will notice us because everyone is scared and running home or to the fort."

"Archer, how exactly do you know this? No disrespect, intended sir," Timothy said quickly.

"I looked through the window and saw them doing business. Men are in line with money in their hands. I didn't see anyone in the room guarding anything. I know this is sudden, but there's no other planning needed. We need to take it and run. Try not to kill anyone. We'll walk down there, leading our horses. Tim, I want you to make sure that the horses are still there when we come out. Jerico, you, Frank, and Marcellus come in with me. Just do as I say. This is too good an opportunity to pass up. Do you all understand?" Archer looked at each of them.

Everyone nodded, drained their glasses, and stood up. They tipped their heads toward the barkeep as they filed out. The men took the reins of their horses and walked down the street toward the salt office. There were hitching posts all along the front and sides of the building. Archer and his boys tied up.

Frank and Marcellus slipped the tie-downs off the hammers of their revolvers. Tim and Jerico had their revolvers in their waistbands. Archer nodded to the boys and walked up to the door, opened it, and walked in and the others followed suit.

The office was a lot bigger than it appeared from the outside. The bookkeeper sat at his desk against the back wall in a direct line from the front door. Sunshine from the window backlit him, so Archer didn't get a good look at his face. Big wooden crates filled the corners.

As the men in line to pay turned their heads to see who had come in, Archer planted his feet and drew his pistol. "Everyone put your hands where I can see them. This won't take but a minute unless you don't do as I say. You give me any trouble, well then…" Archer shrugged his shoulders and shook his head. Archer waved his gun toward his men, and they moved to surround the men in line. Then he pointed his gun at the bookkeeper. "Where's your money?"

The startled bookkeeper glanced at the corner crate and pushed his glasses up with a trembling forefinger. Although unnerved, he rose from his seat to stand straight. "It's not my money, and it certainly is not yours. It is Stuart and Buchanon's money." His voice cracked, but he didn't waver.

"Just give him the money, Joe. It ain't worth getting killed over," said Jed, a man in line.

"Jed, I understand, but I just can't—"

The other men in line dropped their money on the floor. "See, we don't care. Let's not get killed over this."

"Well, you had better do it right now. I ain't got all day." Archer took a step toward Joe and poked him in the chest, pushing him toward the crate.

Joe went over to the wooden crate in the corner. He took the front piece off and set it aside. Inside was an iron safe, a little taller than it was wide. On the door was a bronze plaque that was inscribed, "C. Rich N. York, 1843. Salamander Safe." The doorknob had a number inscribed on it.

Joe looked over at Archer and sighed. He turned back to his desk and pulled open a drawer.

"Not so fast, there!" Archer warned and looked to see what was in the drawer.

Joe slowed his actions as he reached in to get the big key. He turned back to the safe, knelt, then slid a small flat piece of metal on the front of the door to the side. He inserted the key in the keyhole and opened the door. Archer's eyes widened at several bags of what was sure to be gold and neat stacks of greenbacks lined the wooden shelves inside. Joe stepped back to his desk while Archer cleaned out the safe.

"Hot damn!" Archer grinned with satisfaction. Only a couple of minutes had passed since they had entered the office. Scanning the room, he waved his gun toward the other men. "Keep your eyes on them, boys, while I get the money."

"You got it, Archer," Frank said. Marcellus and Jerico trained their guns toward the hostages.

The man in front tried to spit his tobacco juice out but was so scared he swallowed it. The others kept their eyes on the robbers holding them hostage.

Archer pulled the greenbacks out and stuffed them into a bag he found in the safe. He couldn't resist taking two bags of coins. He knew they were too heavy to carry long, but he took them anyway.

"Come on boys, let's get out of here," Archer said.

Frank opened the door and looked out. Tim was there with the horses. He holstered his gun and then he, Marcellus, and Jerico walked out. Archer looked back at the men in the room. No one moved. Their frightened eyes betrayed their fear. Joe was still standing behind his desk. Archer shot him in the chest just because he could. Seeing the man crumple didn't faze him and he didn't stay to watch him die. Archer walked out the door and calmly put the money in his saddlebags.

Frank yelled, "I thought you didn't want to kill anybody!"

Archer glared at him and smirked. "Let's go!" The thieves mounted their horses and spurred them down the street toward the depot and out of town.

Chapter 11

Tuesday, April 24, 1984
Fulton, Missouri

Sarah thought work the next day would never be finished. Finally, her shift was over, and she rushed out to get home as soon as she could. Sarah drove home as quickly as the speed limit allowed. She sprinted from the car, opened the house door, and ran to her bedroom to change into jeans and a shirt. Picking up her flats, she spritzed them with Pledge and wiped them dry. As she slipped them on, she heard the kitchen door open.

"Knock, knock!" Ruth hollered.

Sarah bolted from her bedroom to the kitchen. "How did you get here so fast?"

"I changed at work to save time. Let's go! I can't wait!"

They hurried out the door and got into the Torino, and Sarah backed the car into the turnaround. Luck was with them. They breezed through the green lights and made it to their destination by 4:27.

When the women stopped in front of 701 Westminster, they couldn't believe their eyes! The Tuttle House! It was a beautiful two-story house with an attic on the third floor. The clapboard-sided house was a light gray and the gingerbread trim a dark gray. The four turned posts had white, gray, and yellow bands painted around the turnings of the posts.

"Gracious! What a beautiful house!" Sarah gasped in awe. "Let's go in."

They got out of the car and walked up the sidewalk to the porch. They rushed up the steps to the beautiful etched glass double doors. The glass maker had etched the letter "E" in a circle of clear glass on the left door and the letter "T" on the right. The elegant walnut framed doors showed the age of the house. A bronze plaque on the wall beside the door was engraved with the words:

The Tuttle House
Ernest M. and Mary H. Tuttle
1890-1960

"I'm afraid to knock on a glass door!" Sarah's hand hovered in midair.

Ruth looked around for a doorbell. She found a flat, round brass instrument on the lower right with a little knob protruding from it. "Maybe you turn this?" Ruth leaned down and touched the knob.

"Be careful. We don't want to break anything."

Ruth turned the knob, and a ring sounded out, like the ring of a bicycle bell. They stepped back in anticipation, clutching their purses as they waited.

They heard footsteps cross a wooden floor and stop at the door. The right door opened, and a beautiful older lady asked, "May I help you?"

"I am Sarah Davis, and this is Ruth Kincheloe. We spoke to you on Sunday?"

"Yes! How do you do? I'm Dolores Tucker. Please come inside." Dolores gestured with her hands and ushered them through the doors. They stepped over the threshold into the most beautiful room they had ever seen. A crystal chandelier hung from the twelve-foot ceiling. The walnut staircase with ornately turned balusters claimed the left side of the room. Light shone through the stained-glass window on the landing going up to the second floor. Sarah saw a mahogany dining table through a doorway directly across from them. A door to their right led to a parlor with striking period window treatments.

"It's a lot to take in, isn't it?" Dolores asked.

"Yes, it's hard to describe. It's so beautiful!" Sarah couldn't take it all in, and Ruth looked around quickly, knowing that she only had a moment to enjoy this wonderful place.

"So, you would like to find out about your ancestor?" Dolores prodded.

"Yes." Sarah pulled out her notebook. "I would like to take notes. This is so important to us, and we don't want to forget a thing you tell us."

"Okay. Let's go back to the office where we can sit down." Dolores led them across the room and through the door opposite them. "Would you like a tour first, or do you want to get down to brass tacks?"

"Brass tacks, please. The house is beautiful, but I'm sure you want to get home soon. We can come back for the tour on Sunday," Sarah said.

Dolores led them through the period-furnished dining parlor. "I just set this lovely mahogany table for ten." White China and crystal glassware gleamed in the chandelier's light.

"What are you doing, Ruth? You're clutching that purse to your bosom as if it's going to run away!" Sarah laughed.

"No way am I letting it swing and break something," Ruth responded.

They reached the office off the dining parlor, a small room that held an antique desk with two rose-colored wingback chairs in front of it. Shelves full of books lined the walls.

Sarah and Ruth each took a chair, and Dolores sat at her desk in an antique chair that sat on rollers. She folded her hands on her desk and looked at them expectantly through black-rimmed glasses.

"We would like to know how we find a person who lived in 1864 in Ashe County, North Carolina," Sarah said.

"We think she's an ancestor," Ruth said.

"Yes, we do. We, ah, found a letter in my mother's things…"

"Okay. I think I understand," Dolores said.

"We have no idea how to go about finding this out. We're not even sure what questions to ask you," Sarah said.

"Well, there are tax records, census records, and family Bible records you can access. Usually, the county seat, in this case, the county seat of Ashe County, would have most of these records. The county library will surely have a lot of information for you. Library historians can be formidable regarding record keeping! The Civil War was imminent in 1860. It lasted from April 1861 to April 1865. Unfortunately, a lot of these records were destroyed, but hopefully not in your case. The South is very proud of their history, and I'm sure Ashe County will have what you need."

"Okay, let me get this down in my notebook. I can call Information to get the phone numbers and then call when I get home from work tomorrow." Sarah wrote furiously and then asked Dolores. "What exactly is a census record?"

Dolores smiled and nodded. "I love that you're asking questions. It's when the Federal Government takes a count of who and where people live in a certain area at a certain time. Another thing, North Carolina is in a different time zone. If you get off at four, that is five o'clock in North Carolina," Dolores said.

I'll have to take off early to make a phone call, Sarah thought. *It won't go over well with my supervisor. My pay will be docked.*

Dolores noticed Sarah and Ruth's expressions when she explained the time zone difference. "The county offices aren't open on Saturday, but the library is. You can start there if it's a problem taking time off."

"We can wait until Saturday. If we can't get the information on Saturday, one of us will have to take off work to do it," Ruth said.

"We do so appreciate your help today. Especially coming in when you're not open."

"Yes, thank you so much," Ruth added.

"You're welcome, my dears. I'll do what I can to help." Dolores raised her hand. "Wait a moment. I can make the call for you tomorrow, if you agree to pay the society for the long-distance call. How about you call me here tomorrow after work? I'll be here. It's my turn to clean and dust our displays."

Ruth's face brightened, and Sarah was ecstatic. "Yes, of course, we'll pay for it. Thank you so much!" Sarah said.

"I can see this means a lot to you," Dolores said.

"More than you can possibly imagine." Sarah shook her head.

Dolores's eyebrows raised a bit, but she was familiar

with the enthusiasm people had for finding their ancestors once they had the bug. Dolores led them back through the dining room to the large foyer. She opened the door for the ladies and bid them goodbye. "Call me tomorrow," Dolores said.

"How could we forget?" Sarah said with a wide smile of gratitude.

Sarah and Ruth got into the Torino, looked at each other, and grinned. Their quest had started!

Chapter 12

Virginia
October 2, 1864

Sam and the others were on the trail toward home, but home was three days away. Everyone felt scared and no one spoke. Sam knew the salt owner would track them. Her mind spun as they rode. *What would happen when he caught up with them*? The thought caused an icy shiver to run up her spine. *They needed the salt in the worst way. Not sure if that made the thievery all right or not. Nothing makes sense anymore. Nothing is as it should be. We didn't want this war, but we sure have to fight it.*

Sam noticed how Prince turned every so often to look back at the trail. The LeMat was secure in its holster at his waist. She also knew Mr. Poole would shoot if need be. Prince had given him the shotgun to carry.

They walked and walked, leading the animals with their bundles of salt. The sun grew hot, even though it was October. They made it back to the forests by noon and welcomed the coolness.

"Can everyone keep going for a little while longer?" Prince asked.

"Yes, yes!" they all chorused. They knew they were in danger. The more distance they could put between themselves and those who might be tracking them would be for the good.

Suddenly, gunfire was heard in the distance. The frown increased on Prince's brow as he turned to see blue smoke rise from the hills above Saltville. "Keep moving, no matter what," he called out. The mules jerked as loud cannon fire boomed.

Sam wanted to talk to Prince about the cannon fire, but she dared not. He had said to keep moving.

Once they found a bit of grass for the animals and a safe place to stop, Prince called a halt.

"Let's get a cornpone and take a drink. I'm sorry we don't have fresh water. We'll have to make this stop quick."

The animals cropped the grass as the group sat down. After they gulped their late dinner, Prince urged them on. The travelers walked, spurred on by nervous energy. Toward late afternoon, they mounted a hilltop where they could see for miles. Prince saw a break in the woods. "Just a mile or so more, folks, and we can stop. We might've found a shelter for the night."

His words spurred on the foot-sore group and lifted their spirits. They didn't like to camp under the stars, but they would do what they had to do.

Sam spotted the slight path away from the trail and signaled to Prince. The group followed Sam down the path toward an old, partially burned barn at the edge of a small clearing. A small cabin beside it was nothing but charred remains. The tired group eagerly walked to the barn and waited for Prince to catch up.

"Well, what do we have here but a fine castle in which we can rest our weary bodies?" Prince joked as he walked up to the barn.

Cole held up a wooden bucket with a rope tied to it.

"Look here, Uncle Prince, I believe we found a well!" It was indeed a well, and the water was good and cold.

"We'll have to water the mules with the bucket, but that's okay. At least we have the bucket. Let's get to it. Can we do without a fire tonight? It would be best if we didn't advertise the fact that we're here. How much cornpone do we have left?" Prince fired questions left and right, but no one answered right away.

No warm fire tonight, Sam thought. They kept warm from walking during the day, but the nights got cold.

"Uncle Prince, the barn still has hay for the animals!" Sam said as she led Sugar over to the barn stall.

"We've got to unload the animals, or else they'll get sores. We'll have to chance taking the time in the morning to reload them. If we take care of them, they'll take care of us," Prince remarked.

Prince led the mules to the barn, and over to the stalls filled with hay. "Guess the farmers couldn't take the hay with them," he said. "So glad they didn't. This was a piece of luck."

Miss Deb took the sack of food from her mule, went to the edge of the barn, and started making camp. The boys watered the animals that were munching contentedly on the hay. Everyone gratefully accepted the cornpone that Miss Deb doled out. Sitting on the ground as they ate, the twinkling stars shone through the half-burned roof of the barn as darkness set in.

"Let's fill our canteens before we turn in. Always best to have your chores done before bed. That way, we'll be on our way by first light. By tomorrow evening, we'll be done with the second day of our journey. I'm very proud of all of you. You did a right good job today."

"Thank you, Uncle Prince. We appreciate what you did for us today. We know you took an awful chance for us to have our salt. I know we aren't in the clear yet by a long shot, but I feel we're in good hands with you leading us. Thank you." Miss Deb smiled her appreciation.

Miss Deb was downright eloquent this evening, thought Sam. She knew Prince never took praise well. Amused, she watched as he shuffled his feet a bit and looked up at the stars in the sky.

"You're welcome, Miss Deb, and I'm glad that you all have faith. We'll need it," Prince nodded.

"Miss Deb, how much cornpone do we have left?" Isaac asked.

"We have enough for a small piece for our breakfast. Then I'm afraid we'll have to cook some."

"Maybe we can get us a rabbit or squirrel tomorrow. It'll taste right good with salt on it!" Isaac's smile spread all over his face.

That made them all laugh. They had eaten their food with no salt for so long they had forgotten how good salted food could taste. Each one found a soft spot in the hay, settled in, and tried to get comfortable enough to sleep. They were so tired that most of them were asleep within a few minutes.

Prince walked back up the trail a bit and cocked his ear to listen for any noise. Hearing nothing, he went back to camp bone tired and worried. Prince sat down by the edge of the barn, weary to the bone.

From the barn stall where Mr. Poole lay, he saw Prince nod off. He rose and asked to help. Laying a hand on Prince's shoulder, Mr. Poole whispered. "I'll take the first watch, Prince."

"Thank you, Mr. Poole. Wake me in two hours."

Chapter 13

October 2, 1864
Saltville, Virginia
That same morning

Archer and his gang pulled up at the edge of town. "Frank, take Marcellus and Tim with you and take the road that runs southeast. I'll take Jerico with me and we'll go southwest. If we don't catch up to the salt wagon in a couple of hours, we'll double back and follow you. They can't be moving quick."

"What about our share of the money you got now, Archer?" Frank asked.

"You'll get your share of that when I get my share of what you let get stolen."

With hatred in his eyes, Frank glared at Archer for a couple of seconds. "We'll find it."

Frank, Marcellus, and Tim galloped off to the southeast road. Archer and Jerico cantered to the southwest. What Frank hadn't counted on was running into a company of Confederate soldiers at the edge of town. Colonel Giltner and his 4th and 10th Kentucky Cavalry were on their way to reinforce Trimble at the Holston River Ford.

Colonel Giltner halted and accosted Frank and his men. "Where're you going? Where's your company and why aren't you with them?"

"We, we…ah, we got separated in all the fuss. Colonel Preston's men, sir." Frank stuttered and saluted.

"Fall in with us. Preston's men are already at Elizabeth's Chapel," Giltner said.

"Yes, sir," Daniels and his men saluted again and reluctantly fell in behind the company.

****

Archer and Jerico were on the southwest road that led to Glade Spring, Virginia. Gunfire exploded in the distance, back to the north. When they heard the unmistakable sound of countless hooves pounding the dirt, they moved their mounts off the road and hid in the woods.

As the Confederate troops galloped up the road, a captain in the last company saw Archer and Jerico hiding in the woods. He pulled up. The captain's horse pranced and fought the bit as he held the animal in. "Come on out, unless you want to be shot for desertion. This is General John Williams's force from Bristol, Tennessee."

Archer cursed their luck as he and Jerico walked their horses toward the captain. Archer tried to sound apologetic. "In all the commotion, we got cut off from our unit," he whined. "We'll be glad to come with you. We're part of Preston's Virginia Reserves."

"Come along; we'll find Preston's men." The captain watched as Archer and Jerico fell in line with the soldiers. He fell back to observe them but didn't have time to make sure they didn't run off again. The Army of Northern Virginia had its share of deserters.

Meanwhile, Frank, Marcellus, and Tim melted into the rest of the company and fell back as far as they could. The opportunity to desert didn't arrive until late afternoon. As the company fought the battle, they ran back for their horses and skedaddled southeast.

****

Frank and the gang walked along the trail, trying to pick up the prints of the lead mule. But the special tracks with the markings were not to be found. They found wagon tracks, so they mounted and rode away at a fast trot. The trail soon turned steep, and they slowed to a walk. When the ground leveled out again, and they spotted the abandoned wagon ahead. Frank elatedly urged the other men to hurry.

Frank was no tracker, but this was the only trail. He had seen no signs of another side road, so they kept moving as fast as they could. Marcellus and Tim complained they were starving. When they came upon a stream, they pulled off.

"All we got is some jerky. We should have loaded up on supplies," Marcellus said.

"Well, we usually take from the farms as we go, but as you can see, there are no farms around here" Frank's words dripped with sarcasm. "So, shut up and eat your jerky. Water your horses, we need to get back on the road as soon as we can." The others glumly fished around in their saddlebags for their jerky.

Frank thought, *Funny, when Archer isn't around, I can be boss and the others obey.* "Tim, what you got to say for yourself? I haven't heard a word out of you."

"I'm just thinking. Archer didn't have to murder that man. That was pure meanness. They'll hang us now if they catch us."

"They'll shoot us for desertion too, but they can only kill us once. I agree about Archer, but there ain't nothing we can do about it now. We gotta find those bags of salt and our money. Having to stay for that battle cost us."

Frank bit off a piece of the jerky that tasted like shoe leather. "I wonder where Archer and Jerico are?"

"Frank, how come you got that gold you put in the bags? Where did you come by that?" Marcellus scratched his head as he ate his jerky.

"I stole it, fair and square, a long time ago. I've hid it ever since my first days in the army. Matter of fact, that's how I wound up in the army. The Confederate government was closing up the Dahlonega mint in June of '61 down in Georgia. I had worked there the year before doing the sweeps, so I knew where the coining room was. I just happened by and took a pile of them coins right off the table."

Frank bit off another piece of jerky and took a drink. He loved talking about himself. "Now, I had to lay low, so I joined the parade of new soldiers marching down to Camp McDonald. After they about drilled us to death, they put us on a train at Big Shanty. That train took us through Chattanooga, Knoxville, and then Richmond. Rode more than 600 miles to Camp Lee, Virginia. Always meant to desert first chance I got, but then I saw what they did to deserters. So, here I am!"

Chapter 14

October 2, 1864
Saltville, Virginia
That same morning

R.B. came out of the colonel's headquarters and headed straight to the saloon. All the horses that were tied up in front of the saloon were gone, as he figured. He entered anyway, going to the bar to speak to the barkeep. "Have you seen a gang of rough-looking men in here in the past half hour?"

"There were a group of men in here, but they were polite and paid their bill. No trouble," Evington said.

"G. Rover Cripes!" *Where had they gone?* An argument was not something he usually had with a superior officer, and it had cost him this time. Colonel Preston had understood his mission but was not sympathetic to it. Walking out the door, he heard a man hollering in front of the salt office.

"Help! Someone shot a man and robbed us!" The man waved to R.B. to come help. R.B. ran toward him and they went inside. Another man knelt beside Joe and held a rag to his chest.

R.B. checked the man's pulse. "He's gone, sir," R.B. said.

"There was no call for that ratbag to shoot him. He already had all the money. Joe never gave him no trouble at all."

"Do you know the man who shot him?"

"I heard one of his men call him Archer. He was a big fellar. Had three men inside here with him. Don't know 'bout anymore."

I knew it, R.B. thought. He had followed Archer and his gang all summer. They had robbed all along the valley. He was pretty sure two of the gang were in the army and hid out in the soldiers' camp to keep from being found.

"Can you take care of this? I need to get after them." R.B. asked the man called Jed.

"I sure can and will, sir. Please catch 'em."

R.B. ran back to the hotel and asked the aide about the roads out of town.

"Better go south, sir. Burbridge's Federals are on their way here from the north. Be here any minute if the scout's words say true. Two roads south, southeast, and southwest. Take your pick."

Colonel Preston came out of his office. "There you are. We must head out to Elizabeth's Chapel. The Reserves are already on their way. Come on, and no arguments. General Burbridge and his Federal troops are here." The cannon on the north ridge boomed at that moment as if to punctuate his statement.

R.B. hung his head. To leave now would be tantamount to court-martial. He grabbed Soldier's reins, mounted, and followed Preston to the north of town and Elizabeth's Chapel. Archer and his gang would have to wait.

****

The Battle of Saltville raged until late afternoon. Burbridge and his men made a hasty retreat as darkness set in. They left their dead and wounded for the Confederate Army to deal with. The Federals were out of ammunition and knew more Confederate forces were on their way to Saltville. Burbridge wouldn't be there when they arrived.

R.B. sought General Breckenridge when he learned he had made it to Saltville that afternoon. The battle was over. R.B. waited outside of Breckenridge's headquarters.

The aide came out and waved the major in. R.B. saluted and stood ready for orders.

"So, you know these men who have been committing these robberies all summer and using their uniform to get by with it?" General Breckenridge motioned for R.B. to sit down.

"Yes, sir, and now they've robbed the salt office here of more than forty thousand dollars and killed a man in cold blood. I know, considering the battle here, that might not sound as bad, but…"

"I know you've had them in your sights for a while now. Soldiers like them give the army a bad name. I want you to catch them if you can. We'll be here for a while. The saltworks here is vital to the supply lines of the Confederacy and we have to guard it. Take some time. Go after them. You said they went southeast?"

"Yes, sir, I believe so. If they had gone southwest, they would have run into Williams' brigade." R.B. stood.

"Good luck, Major." Breckenridge nodded and returned the major's salute.

****

R.B. mounted his horse and checked his scabbard to make sure his Spencer was secure. He prodded Soldier with his heels and trotted off down the southeast road.

Chapter 15

Wednesday, April 25, 1984
Fulton, Missouri

Sarah called as soon as she walked into the house.

"Kingdom of Callaway Historical Society, Dolores speaking."

"Hi! It's Sarah Davis. We were supposed to call you to see if you had found anything on Samantha Coldiron in Ashe County, North Carolina."

"Yes, I found something I think will make you happy! If you both want to come over, that'll be fine. It would be easier than trying to explain on the phone."

"We'll be right there!"

Sarah called Ruth and told her they needed to get down to the Society. Sarah drove to Ruth's house, and she was standing at the curb. Ruth hopped in the car and away they went.

"I'm so glad Dolores found what we needed. That's a great start." Ruth's voice was confident.

"Yes, I think she can put us on the right track," Sarah agreed.

The ladies pulled up to the Tuttle House and parked. A minute later, they were ringing the doorbell. Dolores let them in.

"Come right on back and I'll show you what I've found."

When they were all seated, Dolores rubbed her hands together. "The county seat is Jefferson, so I called the Ashe County Library. They have a treasure trove of information!" Dolores sat on the edge of her chair.

Sarah and Ruth leaned in with anticipation.

Dolores clapped her hands. "I found Samantha!"

Sarah's eyes widened in excitement. She turned to look at Ruth who was as exhilarated as she was.

"I'm so glad!" Sarah and Ruth said simultaneously. They sat on the edge of their seats anxious to hear more.

"I called this morning and spoke to the librarian, Jane Kemp. She had some time on her hands, so she looked at the microfilm of the 1860 Federal Census. Jane called back this afternoon. The 1860 Ashe County census shows Samantha Coldiron living in Easter Coldiron's household. Hopefully, Easter is her mother, but we can't know for sure from this record alone. She is fifteen years old in 1860. It shows that her mother's occupation was a sugar maker and Samantha's as a seamstress."

Sarah was at a loss for words — a first for her.

"Thank you so much for this information!" That was the best Ruth could do. Those words weren't enough, but that's all she could think of.

"There're a lot more records, but I couldn't keep them on the phone any longer. So, I think this means you found your ancestor!" Dolores clapped her hands again.

Sarah waved her hands in the air. She had always talked with her hands, especially when she was excited, as she was now. "Okay, so if we were to travel to Jefferson in Ashe County, North Carolina, we could find a lot more records? Like maybe where she lived?"

"I asked about that. There are land records at the

Register of Deeds' office that go back to 1799 when the county was formed. I'm sure you can find that out."

"We're so grateful for your help. You've started us on our journey!" Ruth was estatic.

"So, are you girls going to plan a trip to North Carolina soon?" Dolores adjusted her weight in her seat.

"Yes, when we get our wits about us, we'll be able to plan. I think I'm on autopilot," Sarah said with a nervous laugh.

"Well, I understand. Once you have the bug for finding your ancestors, you can't quit. It gets in your blood! Sometimes, it becomes the most important thing!" Dolores said.

"Getting time off is pretty rare, but we'll persevere." Sarah nodded her head.

The girls gathered up their purses and prepared to leave, excitement exuding from their faces. *Samantha had really lived! She was a real person!*

Dolores held out the notes for Sarah, shaking them under her nose. "Don't forget these!"

"Oh, yes, my goodness!" She accepted the notes from Dolores's hand with gentle care and held them to her bosom. "These are so precious!"

The ladies followed Dolores out of the office and back to the doors. "Oh, wait," Sarah said. "What do we owe you for the call? For your time?"

"This is on me! I'm so glad to help new genealogists off to a good start! Please let me know what you find out!"

"We will. Thank you so much!" Sarah giggled. Ruth's feet barely touched the ground as they hurried down the sidewalk toward the Torino. They looked at each other with big grins on their faces. "What say we go to Sonic and celebrate?" Sarah asked.

"I think that would be great! I would love a coney dog!"

Sarah drove by rote, her mind racing. *What to do? What to do?*

"What're we going to do next?" Ruth asked. "My mind is whirling around so fast I can't think straight!"

"I know, I know. Maybe when we sit still, we can think better. Do you want to order and take it home?"

"I feel like celebrating, but I don't think we can talk there. What if someone overhears us? Yeah, we better take it home. It'll still be hot. We can eat the fries on the way."

Sarah felt like she was slowly turning into a skulker, slinking around, and trying to be invisible. They pulled into Sarah's driveway and took their hot dogs inside. Turning on the lights, she set the bag on the table. Ruth reached into the fridge for drinks. They sat down and looked at each other and grinned like schoolgirls with a new secret.

"Well, what do you think? We need to plan. We need to be smart," Sarah said.

"Let's eat and talk. I'm sure we'll have to revise our plans a lot."

"I'll go get a tablet. I think better with a pencil in my hand." Sarah grabbed a pencil and went to her bedroom to get the journal. She was sure they could plan better if they had the journal right there.

"I wish I had gotten a foot-long coney dog. My size tens still fit me nicely. Suddenly, I'm starving and I've already eaten this up," Sarah said.

"You would've been sick if you had done that. Our nerves have been shot for four days. We've been going on nervous energy. You better drink some milk. We don't want to get sick; we have too much to do! Yay! We have so much to do!" Ruth raised her fist to the air.

"Let's plan. First, we need to figure out how much money we're going to need. We have to figure the distance to Jefferson, and I'll figure up how much gas money it'll take. The Torino gets about eighteen miles per gallon. Gas is ninety-two cents a gallon. I wish they would do something about gas prices! Okay. I clear about a hundred fifteen dollars a week. This week is the week to add to my savings account, so I'll have five-hundred fifty dollars," Sarah said.

"I make the same as you do, but I have Stan's social security widow's benefit. That's three-hundred ninety-eight dollars a month. I've saved all of it except for what I had to pay for his funeral. Mr. Maupin was so very nice to make arrangements so I could pay on time. I have almost five thousand dollars in my savings account."

"Ruth, we can't use that money. You need that for your house payments in case you get sick and can't work. If you default, you'll lose your house. You're paying for your kids' college out of that fund. Isn't that tuition due in a couple of months?"

"Well, I can use some of it because this is a glorious cause! Why don't I take out a hundred fifty dollars and you contribute the same? Then we'll see."

"Well, we need to figure out how much money we're going to need first. I'll get a U.S. map so we can see which route is the shortest to Jefferson."

Sarah wrote "map" on her list. "Then, we need to ask for time off. I dread that."

"We never ask for time off. We need to see Mrs. Perkins in the personnel office. She'll tell us who we need to talk to. I can call on my break tomorrow. I hope we don't have to go all the way to the top. People have said Mr. Mayfield is nice, but I don't want to ask the administrator for time off."

"I'm sure we won't have to go that high. Surely there's an assistant," Sarah said.

****

Ruth called Sarah as soon as she got home the next day. "We have an appointment tomorrow at 4:30 with Mr. Dyer in the administration building. Mrs. Perkins was very nice."

"Oh, thank goodness! I got a couple of maps. I'll start mapping out our route. Do you want to come over? I went to the I.G.A. a few minutes ago and picked up some TV dinners. I have a feeling that we're going to be busy planning and won't have time to cook."

"I have extra hamburger. Why don't I make a meatloaf and bring it over? We'll have enough for leftovers. There's nothing like a meatloaf sandwich for lunch, or supper, for that matter."

"Sounds great! I'll get this mapped out and we can talk when you come over."

Sarah figured out the route and was glad that she'd also bought a map of Kentucky, too. The roads were too tiny to spot on the U.S. map beyond the Interstate. The best she could make out, it was roughly 720 miles. She knew they could make good time on the Interstate and the Mountain Parkway, but it looked as if they would have to take a lot of minor roads nearer to Jefferson. The Exon station didn't have a map of North Carolina, but they could surely find one in Kentucky. Sarah figured they would need roughly forty gallons of gas, which equaled about forty dollars, one way.

Ruth arrived with meatloaf and mashed potatoes. Sarah opened a can of peas, and they feasted while they planned. "Near as I can figure it, we'll need about two-hundred thirty-five dollars if everything goes well. So we better add a bit more to be on the safe side. I called Motel 6 in Kingdom City and asked what the average cost for a night was, and they said twenty dollars. I figure four nights in Jefferson, but we don't know what's available there. Hopefully, it's affordable. I'm figuring fifteen dollars a day for five days of food. Do you think that's enough?" Sarah asked.

"Sure, we can eat hot dogs and hamburgers. Egg sandwiches for breakfast. We don't know if the cost of eating in North Carolina is higher than here. We'll have some extra, but we'll have to be very careful. We have to keep in mind we'll have to use some of our savings to live on the week after we get back because we won't get a paycheck."

"Yes, there is that. But what if we find the gold coins? Won't that be a hoot? Will it hex us to hope for it? I think we can hope for it, don't you?" Sarah said, her eyes sparkling.

"Let's keep our fingers crossed. That's the reason for our trip, correct?"

"Yes, of course, but just think! We'll be going right by Saltville, Virginia!" Sarah pointed to Saltville on the map. "Won't it be wonderful to see where Samantha lived and the places she described?"

"That's great! I wonder if it has changed much since 1864?" Ruth put a finger to her lips and grinned.

"We're about to find out, Ruth. I can't wait to see it all," Sarah said as the clock ticked away the hours.

Chapter 16

Virginia Mountains
October 3, 1864

Sam woke first and stretched her tired limbs. Her feet would never be the same. She looked over to see everyone else stretched out every which way. Uncle Prince leaned up against a post and had his eyes shut. Dawn was at hand.

"Morning, baby girl," Prince said with his eyes still closed.

"Morning to you, too."

Prince roused everyone up. "Okay, everybody. Let's get up and get going. It'll be a long day."

Mr. Poole smiled himself awake and stood up to help Miss Deb. The boys groaned and unwound themselves after a minute. Miss Deb got out the cornpone and passed it all around. It didn't take long for them to gulp the food and wash it down with water.

"Let's load the animals and get on the road," Prince said.

As they loaded the animals, Cole noticed one of the new mules was missing. "Uncle Prince, one of the new mules is gone. Rope's chewed through."

"Well, I hate to leave her, but we don't have time to look for her."

Sam headed out with Sugar, and the others trailed

behind them. The sun washed the morning pink, and the valley blushed below. Going down the trail would surely be better than going up.

Prince didn't bother to obscure their tracks or traces of their stay there. He was sure they were being followed and so it didn't matter. There was no place to hide.

They strung out along the trail and tried not to wince as their muscles limbered up. Their feet ached, and they knew there would be no respite until noon. They crossed two small streams and paused long enough for the animals to drink, and then pressed on. No one complained, and no one made any noise.

When they came upon another stream that was bolder than Prince remembered it being, he called a halt. "Ya'll wait a minute until I check this out." He waded out to see how deep it was. The water came up past his knees, but no further.

"It'll be okay. Let's get across. Sam, you lead, and I'll watch the others as they go," Prince said.

Sam led Sugar into the rushing stream and was almost across when Prince urged the rest across. What happened next was so sudden no one had a chance to act.

Now across the river, Sam watched the others cross. Her heart leapt with dawning horror as Jim's mule stumbled. The rope holding the salt came undone. Jim grabbed for the reins but missed. One precious bag of salt slipped from the frayed knots and fell into the creek as the mule righted himself. Jim grabbed for the reins again as the mule picked his way up the bank and out of the creek. As Sam watched the salt melt and the bag flatten, her shoulders sagged with the loss. As it slowly sank into the rocks, Sam let go of Sugar's reins and rushed into the water. Reaching for the bag a few inches below the surface of the water, she heard an unfamiliar sound as the bag hit upon the rocks. *Wait, what's that clinking?*

Retrieving the bag, it felt unusually heavy for an empty bag. Sam opened the sack to find another smaller bag inside. She untied the string that held it closed and stared at the contents. *What's this? Gold coins*! She closed the bag and hurried to Sugar. Her hands shook as she hid the coins in her pack under the skillet.

The others were still crossing the creek and had not seen her open the bag. Sam kept the discovery of the gold to herself and would tell Prince later. She didn't know how the gold coins got into the bag of salt, but she knew the person who put them there was going to want them back. Sam was more terrified than before.

Prince strode over to Sam.

"I'm sorry, Uncle Prince, I didn't get to the bag in time." Sam hung her head in despair. "I tried."

"Sam, you couldn't have kept it from falling. It weighed fifty pounds! Try not to worry about it. It's done. I should have checked the ropes again."

Jim was beside himself, tears coursed down his cheeks. "I'm sorry! I should've gotten to the bag."

Prince put his hand on his shoulder. "Son, there wasn't a thing you could've done either. It was too heavy. You couldn't have caught it without falling yourself."

Prince moved to the others. "Miss Deb, Cole, Isaac, ya'll okay? Mr. Poole, you okay?"

"Just wet and scared, is all," Miss Deb said.

"We're fine." The boys said in chorus.

"Fine, Prince." Mr. Poole whispered and nodded.

Prince checked the ropes on the other bag of salt on Jim's mule. He took the extra bag from his mule and put it on Jim's mule to balance the load. Then he made sure all the other bags were still secure.

"Okay, let's get on. I know you're wet, but your boots and clothes will dry out as we walk. We have about an hour until we need to camp. Then, just one more day till we're home." Prince's words encouraged them and they walked with their heads held high.

Breathing was hard because of the altitude, but they didn't need to talk, anyway. Sam tried to think how she was going to tell Prince about the money. She knew it would worry him more than he already was, but she had to tell him. Where had the gold coins come from? Sam saw Prince keep looking back and shaking his head.

When the sun slanted, and the trail covered in shadow, Prince halted the journey.

Hearing the gurgle of water close by, he signaled to Sam and they headed away from the trail to a small clearing. Prince was glad that the animals had had good forage the night before. There was a bit of grass in the clearing, but the animals would have it gone in no time.

"Let's fill our water bags, unload the animals, then water them," Prince said.

"I can get some cornpone going. Sam, I'll get the skillet," Miss Deb said.

"No!" Sam responded a little too quickly as she rushed toward her pack. "I mean, I'll get it, Miss Deb."

Miss Deb shrugged her shoulders and nodded. She gathered wood and got the fire going. The boys helped Prince get the salt bags and saddles off the animals. They put the piece of burlap that had been covering the bags on the ground, and then placed the bags of salt on top. The boys then covered them with other burlap pieces. They were lucky there had been no rain. Sam filled the water bags and then unsaddled Sugar and led him to the spring. Prince and Mr. Poole hunkered down and Mr. Poole listened intently to what Prince was saying.

"You know what I have to do, don't you?" Prince whispered to Mr. Poole.

"Yes, I do, sir, but I am afraid for you and for us. This has turned out to be so much more dangerous a thing than any of us thought," Mr. Poole whispered.

"Soon as we eat a bite, I'll light out. I need to catch him before he catches us."

Sam looked at Prince and Mr. Poole and knew something was up. She needed to talk to Uncle Prince quickly.

"Uncle Prince, I really need to talk to you."

"I need to talk to you, too, baby girl."

Sam walked over to the edge of the woods, and Prince followed away from earshot.

"Uncle Prince, you're just never going to believe this, but there was something else in the bag of salt."

"What, you mean the one that was lost in the creek?"

"Yes."

"What?"

"Well… gold money."

Prince leaned in close and whispered, "What do you mean, gold money?" His eyes narrowed and his forehead creased.

"Gold coins, a lot of them." Sam showed him the bag.

"Quick, put it away." Prince lowered her hand with his, looking back toward the others to see if anyone had seen her.

Sam quickly stuffed it back into her pocket. "When I picked up the wet sack from the water, I felt something in the bottom. The small bag of coins was hidden inside. I didn't want to have to tell you. It's just added to our trouble," Sam said.

"I know you didn't want to tell me, but I'm glad you did. But now we know for a fact that someone is coming. I have to go back and get them first. You understand, don't you?"

"No!" Sam clutched Prince's shoulder. "Please don't!"

"I have to. I can't let him get to us first. I should've done it yesterday, but I wasn't thinking straight," Prince scowled and shook his head.

Sam could tell that he had thought of something else.

"Sam, what if there's more money in the other bags? We're in more trouble than I thought."

Prince and Sam walked over to the salt bags. "Do you remember which bags were on the second mule?"

"The boys got mine off first and they're stacked on the bottom, I think. They piled the rest as they took them off, so this stack over here, probably." Sam motioned to the pile of bags.

Prince moved the piece of burlap off the first stack and untied the bag of salt. He found nothing but salt in the bag. He untied two more before he found the other bag of money.

"Great horn spoon! Greenbacks, a whole bag of them!" Prince exclaimed as he held the rough sack open.

"Oh, no!" Sam said.

"What're you both cussing about over there?" Miss Deb asked as she mixed water with the cornmeal.

They all heard a pistol cock and jumped at the sound of an unfamiliar foreboding voice.

"Come here, boys, and see the folks who took our cash!" Frank Daniels stepped out of the woods and walked toward Prince.

Sam looked stricken and Prince knew he had waited too long. They spoke all at once. "What're you talking about? We don't have your money!"

Frank walked around Jim, Cole, Isaac, and Mr. Poole, who were frozen in place by the campfire. Passing Miss Deb who was on her knees, cooking the cornpone, Frank walked over to Prince.

"Well, what have we got here?" Frank yanked the bag out of Prince's hand.

"I just found it. I swear. We didn't know it was here until just now," Prince said.

"Where's the other bag, the one with the gold in it?" Frank narrowed his eyes as he gave Prince the once over. Seeing the gun on Prince's side, he took a step closer. "Give me your gun! And don't none of ya try anything!" Frank snarled as he waved his gun at them.

Prince pulled the LeMat from his holster. As his trembling hand held it out to Frank, it slipped and fell to the ground. When Prince scrambled to pick it up, Frank shot him in the chest. Prince jerked back when the bullet hit and landed on his back, clutching at his chest.

Sam screamed and ran toward Frank in fury. With a strong backhand, Frank knocked her down. "I told ya not to try anything." Frank's wild eyes glared at her as she touched her face in pain.

Isaac and Cole scrambled up to help Sam. She sent them a warning look and shook her head. *Don't!* Marcellus and Tim stopped them by pointing their guns at their chests. "Ya'll just stay put," Marcellus warned as he walked over and picked up the gun.

Miss Deb froze, and Mr. Poole looked from Frank to Prince laying on the ground bleeding. He didn't know what to do.

Sam scrambled over to Prince and cried," Uncle Prince! No! No!" She frantically clutched his chest.

Prince tried to talk but couldn't make the words come out. Blood covered his chest. Sam pulled the saddle blanket from the nearby saddle and put it under Prince's head. Then, in a huff of renewed rage, Sam jumped up and flew at Daniels again. "You murderer! We didn't even know the money was there until a minute ago! We gave it back!" Sam tried to hit at Frank's chest with her fists.

Frank pushed her back and yelled at her, waving his gun in her face. "Where's my gold?" Sam stopped short. Then he waved his gun at all of them. He repeated through clenched teeth, "Where's my gold?"

The boys said at the same time, "We don't have it! We don't have it!" They held out their hands.

Frank put the bag of greenbacks inside his vest and walked to the bags of salt. He grabbed one bag of salt and ran his hand down in the bag, spilling some.

"Don't waste it! That'll keep us alive! Why are you doing this?" Sam screamed.

"I want my money!" Frank was adamant. One by one, he untied the bags of salt and with one hand delved into the bags, the other hand gripping the gun pointing toward them.

"We told you! We lost a sack in the river! I'll show you the bag!" Sam ran over to her pack and knelt to pull out the empty bag. "Here's the bag! There's nothing in it!" Sam threw the bag at Frank. As he looked inside, Sam stumbled on purpose getting up, stuck her hand in her pocket and pulled out the bag of coins. *I'll never give him the gold willingly now. He'll probably kill us all anyway.* Rolling over to get up, she slyly stuffed the small bag under her saddle. Then she ran over to Prince and knelt to talk to him. His eyes were closed, and his breathing was slow.

"Miss Deb, do you have any cloth to make a bandage for Prince? I need to stop the bleeding." Miss Deb immediately took off her hat and unwound the scarf that held up her hair. Her long dark hair tumbled around her small shoulders as she handed the cloth to Sam. Sam did the same, and when she undid her scarf, her golden hair flowed to her waist.

"They's women!" Marcellus said to no one in particular.

Sam pressed the cloth to Prince's chest and tried to stop the river of blood that flowed from his chest. Tears flowed down her cheeks. She cast an angry glare at Frank and yelled, "You got your money! Why don't you just leave us alone?"

Frank marched over and grabbed Sam's hair. He jerked her up until they were face to face. "I want my gold!" His breath was fetid.

Sam spit in his face, and he struck her down once more with a hard hand. Sam stayed down and willed herself not to cry as she massaged her bruised face.

Even though guns were trained on them, Cole and Isaac ran to Sam to help her up. Mr. Poole shifted his weight from one foot to the other as Marcellus held his gun to his head.

"Don't move and keep your hands where I can see 'em." Marcellus growled at the man.

Miss Deb sat near the fire and wiped the tears from

her face. She tried to save the cornpone, but it was a charred mess. No one would be able to eat anyway.

"Quit moving! I mean it," Frank said. He walked away from the others and motioned for Marcellus and Tim. "We need to tie them up. I've got to think."

"Frank, we got the greenbacks. We can go," Tim said.

Frank's eyes bored into Tim's and Tim backed away. Frank walked over to Sam and grabbed her bloody hands up and tied them tight in front of her.

"Please don't tie me. I need to see to Prince."

"He's a goner anyway."

Marcellus tied the boys and Mr. Poole while Tim held his gun on them. Then Marcellus tied up Miss Deb. Frank turned and strode over to the bags of salt and paced back and forth.

Kneeling beside Prince, Sam realized he had spoken to her.

"Sam, listen to me." Prince's voice was a faint whisper. "I need to tell you something."

Sam leaned over so she could hear his raspy voice. "Help them …get home. Go to your cabin. Pay close attention. The ridge…behind your cabin… about halfway up… is a cave." Prince gasped and blood bubbled at his lips. "Big tulip poplar… beside the entrance. Gotta search hard to see it. Silver coins…made…"

"What, what do you mean, made?" Sam tried to understand.

"The silver coins to pay for the salt…" Prince coughed. "I coined them…" Blood dribbled from his mouth and ran down his chin.

Sam wiped his chin and snuck a look to see if the

robbers were listening or watching. They were too busy watching Frank sift through the salt bags. "Go on, Uncle Prince," she whispered.

"Everything's there. Get the coins and head out. These men… will track you. I know they will. You must be smart." Prince began to cough up blood again as he clutched his heart. "Do as I say. Please. If you can get away, head out to Missouri …kin there, near St. Louis." Prince labored in his breathing. His skin started to pale. "Ride out the war there." Sam leaned her head on Prince's shoulder. "No…no. I can't go without you."

"I love you, baby girl." Prince coughed and coughed. Blood and sputum covered his mouth and chest. No more words would come. He lay back and the breath slowly left his body.

Sam's shoulders shook as she cried out, "Uncle Prince, don't die! Please don't die!" She hugged his body, buried her face in Prince's shoulder and wept. The boys shook their heads and cried unashamedly. Miss Deb sobbed with her face in her tied hands. Mr. Poole's face fell as he watched his friend die.

Darkness fell on the miserable little group, and the fire did little to chase back the shadows. Marcellus and Tim held guns on them while Frank paced.

"I really need to relieve myself," Mr. Poole whispered.

"Why're you whispering?" Marcellus asked.

"He can't talk, that's why!" Isaac said.

"Don't get smart-mouthed with me, boy!" He motioned to Mr. Poole with his gun. "Go on and do your business. You don't need to be untied to do it."

"Don't try anything or I'll shoot you dead," Tim said.

Mr. Poole sidled off to the edge of the woods to do his business. Just then, a blood-curdling scream rent the air. Everyone jumped as their eyes darted in every direction.

"What's *that*?" Tim asked, crouching and waving his gun around.

Marcellus looked at them all with suspicion while holding his gun steady.

"That there means you gone be panther crap this time tomorra!" Buzzard said with glee.

Mr. Poole calmly walked back to the fire. "Ya'll hear that? We better keep the fire up!" Mr. Poole whispered. Catching Sam's eye, he winked.

Sam knew Mr. Poole was certain to have made the sound. Feigning a scared look, she was glad it had spooked the gang.

Frank went over and yanked Sam from her vigil beside Prince. Standing face to face with the girl, his cold steely eyes stared into hers. "I know you have my gold and I want it. I should just kill you now," he hissed.

The hatred in his eyes made Sam flinch. She pinched her lips together, determined not to answer when her attention was drawn to a unique sound. They all heard it.

Revolvers cocking at the same time.

Chapter 17

October 3, 1864
Southwest Virginia

"Don't anybody move!" R.B. demanded as he stood at the edge of the clearing. Both hands held Navy colts. Tim aimed his gun, but R.B. shot him first. His body slumped over the rock where he sat. Marcellus rolled to get a better aim, but R.B. got him too. Frank used Sam as a shield for a few steps and then pushed her toward the campfire. R.B. couldn't shoot because she was in the line of fire. Frank threw himself over the bags of salt, tumbled and ran into the woods.

R.B. followed Daniels into the woods and then heard a horse galloping off. He hesitated. He didn't want to try to follow him in the dark and decided to wait until morning.

R.B. strode back to the fire and saw the dead man lying on the ground. The others were tied up. These people really needed his help. They all just stared at him with fright written across their faces.

"You going to shoot us too like they shot Uncle Prince?" Sam's voice wavered. *Is he dangerous? He has a uniform on…but then, so did the others. Maybe he only shot them to get the money for himself.*

R.B. holstered his guns. "No, I'm not." R.B. walked over to her and drew his knife.

Just then Sugar knickered and R.B. looked up. He recognized the animal. He looked again at the woman in front of him. The ragged men's clothes. He stared at the dead man on the ground. *This is the woman I saw in Saltville!*

Sam felt weak. *What was he going to do to her?*

"Don't you dare touch her!" Miss Deb was still on her knees but she was furious. Tears coursed down her red cheeks and her voice was hoarse. "We've been through enough!"

"Yeah, you leave her alone!" Isaac hollered and tried to get up.

R.B. looked at the beautiful face of this young woman. "I'm not going to hurt her or any of you," R.B. said softly. "I'm only here to help." R.B. motioned for Sam to raise her hands and he carefully sliced through the ropes binding her. He looked down at the face of the man. "I'm really sorry this happened."

Sam looked up at his handsome face with gratefulness. "Thank you." She stood and rubbed her blood-covered hands together and tried to bring back the circulation.

R.B. went to each hostage and released them. "What's happened here?"

"It's a bit of a story. Thanks for saving us!" Sam looked at him with a shy smile and nodded. She walked over to the stream to wash Prince's blood off her hands.

"Yes, thank you!" Everyone chimed in. They were rubbing their hands together, trying to bring back the circulation. Cole put more deadfall on the fire and they gathered round.

"I wish I could make us something to eat, but that was the last of the cornmeal and I burned it up." Miss

Deb was apologetic.

R.B. went down the path to get Soldier. He came back and tethered him with the other animals and patted Sugar's neck. He rummaged around in his pack and brought out some cornmeal and bacon. "How about this?" R.B. held it out to Miss Deb.

"Oh, my, yes!" Miss Deb was in tears at the sight of the bacon. She took it with reverence and sliced it. They had enough for everyone to have a piece tonight and in the morning for breakfast.

Cole, Isaac, and Buzzard checked on the animals. Mr. Poole whispered a thank you to R.B. and reached out to shake his hand. "I'm Wallon Poole of Coldiron, Ashe County, North Carolina."

"Major R.B. Royster of the 4th Virginia Reserves, Shenandoah Valley, Virginia."

"So glad to meet you, sir."

"I'm Deborah Carpenter, Mr. Royster." Miss Deb said, as she turned the meat and mixed up the cornmeal.

"I'm Cole Coldiron and this is my brother Isaac, sir." Each held out his hand to shake R.B.'s proffered one.

"Buzzard Jim, at your service, sir. We sure do appreciate you saving us." He shook R.B.'s hand gratefully.

Sam came back over and related what had happened when Frank and his devils overtook them.

"What're ya'll doing on this trail, if you don't mind my asking," R.B. said. "Especially you women."

"There were no more men to help us. We need salt. There's none to be had at home. Even the store owners and salt commissioners could not get any over to us in Ashe County. We knew we wouldn't last another winter without salt to cure what little meat we have."

"It's ready. Let's all eat. I'm near starved to death," Miss Deb said as she handed each one a plate with the side meat and cornpone on it. Everyone dug in and there was no noise except for the chomping and slurping of a meal being consumed.

R.B. sat near the fire with the boys. Sam got up to help Miss Deb clean up and took the tin plates over to the stream to wash.

Curious about Sam, R.B. picked Isaac for the impertinent question. "This question might be a little brazen, but I have to know. Does she have a man?" R.B. pointed in Sam's direction.

"Well, I don't know what 'brazen' means, but I'll answer your question anyway." Isaac nodded. "She had one, but he run off at the start of the war. It was all right. She didn't have much use for him, anyway. She was only marrying him cause her mama didn't want her to be an old maid. She was already fifteen then." Isaac was forthright in his analysis of his cousin. "Sam is my cousin. Sam is short for Samantha, Samantha Coldiron."

Sam came back over with a piece of burlap and placed it over Prince's face. She sat down on her saddle and gazed at the fire. R.B. walked over. "I'll help bury your uncle in the morning. Then I'll have to take these two," he motioned to toward the dead gang members, "back to Saltville."

"I appreciate it. I had a run-in with the leader called Frank. To put it mildly, he threatened me and told me he would hunt me to the ends of the earth."

"Why would he say that?"

"Because he thinks we took his gold. It's a story you almost can't believe, and I wouldn't if we hadn't lived it.

A band of bushwhackers robbed us on our way up to Saltville.

Uncle Prince stole the salt because we absolutely had no other way. I'm sorry if that sounds awful. It does, but this war has made things so terrible, it's almost impossible to know right from wrong anymore. It was just an awful coincidence that Frank and his buddies had hidden their stolen money in the bags of salt that Uncle Prince took. We had no idea until right before they came upon us tonight. We gave it back, but he said there was gold in the bags too." Sam left out the part about her finding the gold.

"I've been after this bunch all summer. They robbed people and then a couple of them would hide at the soldier's camp with the money until things calmed down. A private told me about it when he overheard their conversation one night."

R.B. continued. "One other thing, there was a battle in Saltville yesterday. I have to get back. I need to show these men to the private to see if he recognizes them. I don't want to get court-martialed. There are also two other men riding with these men. I have to get them, too."

"We'll be fine. We'll make it home tomorrow unless something else happens. Thank you for the food. We had one meal left, and we burned it up."

R.B. was eager to keep the conversation going with her. He tried to think of something to talk about. "I wanted to ask you about your horse. I saw you in Saltville earlier and recognized him tonight. You were at the depot holding your horse and a mule." *I was so intrigued by you. Wondered why you were pretending to be a man.*

"Yes, we were there. Uncle Prince was trying to get

an idea of how we were going to get some salt." Sam was little sheepish at this. She now knew that Prince was thinking of how to *steal* the salt.

"He's a magnificent animal. You don't see horses like him much." R.B. was matter of fact. "Apart from Soldier, my horse!" R.B. smiled and looked into her green eyes. *I want to brush her hair away from her face.*

Sam looked up in time to see him start to raise his hand to her hair but stopped. She became conscious of her cascading hair and searched around for her hat. She picked it up and put it on. Stuffing her hair under her hat, she answered him.

"Yes, he is! I named him Sugar because he's the shade of maple sugar when you first turn the cake out. We make maple sugar at home in the winter. How he came to be here is quite a story. Back home, there was a man who was very rich and prided himself on his horseflesh. His horses were really beautiful animals and won lots of prizes at the events he took them to in Kentucky. He had an exceptional stallion, a Kentucky Saddlebred, and he rode him into town one day. Uncle Prince's mare was tied up at the saloon and was in season. Mr. McGowan's stallion took advantage and Sugar is the result."

"Where's Prince's mare?" R.B. asked.

"The Home Guard took her from him. He wasn't a match for them and they about beat him to death when he wouldn't let them have her. I keep Sugar hidden as much as I can." Sam tucked another strand of wayward hair behind her ear and gave R.B. a last look under lowered lashes. "We better get some sleep. Dawn will come before we're ready."

When R.B. went to the edge of the woods, Sam took

the opportunity to stuff the bag of coins in her pack. They all bedded down by the fire. R.B. stood watch over them. He had done without sleep before. It was hard, but it was worth it. His gaze rested on Sam as she lay sleeping.

The next morning, R.B. and Mr. Poole carried Prince's body over to the edge of the clearing. Sam covered him with extra burlap. The ground was rocky, and they had no tools to dig with. They piled rocks on the body until he was buried and safe from scrounging animals. R.B. and Mr. Poole piled the biggest stones on top and around the grave.

"Does anyone want to say a few words? If not, I'll go on and have my say," Sam said.

"It just doesn't feel right, leaving him here alone," Miss Deb said.

"He wouldn't mind. Prince preferred his own company above anyone else's, you know that." Sam's smile held sadness. "My uncle was a loner, but he loved us very much. We know Prince was an honorable man. He would help you with anything that was in his power to do. I'll miss him very much. He was more like a father to me than an uncle and taught me so much…" Sam couldn't say anymore as tears streamed down her face.

"Let's recite the 23rd psalm together," Miss Deb said as she bowed her head.

Sam noted the individual voices as they spoke. She could even hear Mr. Poole's hoarse low whisper. R.B. had a deep voice that sent shivers down her back, but she couldn't think about that right now.

R.B. helped them load the mules with their priceless cargo. Sam put Prince's LeMat in its holster and put it over her shoulder. She put the scabbard on Mr. Poole's mule and handed him the shotgun. Mr. Poole would shoot if necessary.

Sam stood in front of R.B. Her eyes were even with the yellow collar of his officer's jacket. The top buttons of his jacket were unbuttoned, and black hair curled out of the vee of his shirt. She looked up at the bluest eyes she had ever seen and smiled. He must have shaved recently because his dark beard was very short.

R.B. held his hat in one hand and smoothed his dark hair back with the other. He stood tall as he looked into her eyes as she spoke.

"Thank you again. We need to be on our way. Good luck to you." Sam wanted to say more, but the words wouldn't come. She looked up at him with a shy smile.

"You're welcome." R.B. searched her green eyes as her cheeks blushed a beautiful pink. *I want to hold her, but I know it isn't permissible. I want to stroke the golden hair she pushed up inside her hat. I know I won't ever see her again! I wish things could be…*

"Oh, by the way, what does R.B. stand for?" Sam asked as she took Sugar's reins from him.

R.B. seemed to consider the request as his forehead creased in thought. Taking in a deep breath, he said, "R.B. will do." He smiled at her look and slapped his hat on his head. He turned to his own horse and mounted. With the dead men tied across the saddles of their horses, he grabbed their reins and set off at a good pace.

Sam watched him go with a strange mixture of exhilaration and sadness, then turned to lead the others home.

Chapter 18

Thursday, April 26, 1984
Fulton, Missouri

Sarah and Ruth were nervous about asking for time off for their grand adventure. But now that they knew Samantha Coldiron was a real person, it was worth it.

The next afternoon, the ladies waited in the outer office of Mr. Dyer, the Personnel Manager of Fulton State Hospital. Pictures of the Fulton State Hospital at various stages of its existence hung on the wall. One showed the austere four-story building without embellishments. The late 1890s picture with the mansard roof, turrets and a cupola, was breathtaking. A large painting on another wall showed the hallway and the grand staircase with tall brass lamps on the newel posts. What a beautiful place the administration building had been. Fire destroyed it in 1956.

Mrs. Perkins' phone beeped. "Mr. Dyer will see you now," she told the ladies as she pushed her dark-rimmed glasses up with a forefinger. She stood to show them the door to Mr. Dyer's office.

Mrs. Perkins smiled at them as she opened the door and motioned them through. Sarah entered first, and Mr. Dyer introduced himself. Sarah had never seen one man with so many teeth in his mouth. She was a bit unsettled, especially since he kept smiling. Sarah wanted to see how Ruth was handling his toothy grin, but she didn't dare look at her. Mr. Dyer motioned to the chairs in front of his desk.

"Now, how may I help you ladies this afternoon?" Mr. Dyer leaned forward with his forearms on his desk and steepled his fingers.

Sarah spoke first, as Ruth had asked her to do. "Well, we need to ask for a week off to go to North Carolina."

"Is there a special occasion, like a funeral perhaps?"

"No, oh dear, does it have to be something special? This is special to us, but it isn't a funeral. We have had no time off since Ruth's husband passed over a year ago, so we thought it would be all right to ask now. This is very important to us. We found family that we would love to meet." Sarah hadn't planned on saying all that and she felt as if she needed to say more but didn't.

Mr. Dyer looked at a ledger. "Well, I see that your attendance records are superb. We appreciate your hard work. But this will leave the kitchen shorthanded."

"Sarah and I realize that, but we can't do anything about it." Ruth knew that fact might keep them from getting the week off, and dreaded what he would say next.

Mr. Dyer studied the ledger and turned a couple of pages. "I will let you both have the week after next off, but then you must be here on Monday of the next week. You understand that, don't you? We won't be able to keep your jobs open if you don't come back on time. We have a waiting list for staff to move to the kitchen when positions open up."

"Yes, we understand, and thank you, sir!" Sarah and Ruth stood up, and both extended their hands, which he shook. They wanted out before he changed his mind. They hurried out the door.

Sarah whispered to Ruth as they went down the hall, "Did you see all of those…?"

Ruth shushed Sarah, "Don't! We're not even out of the building yet!"

The ladies left the administration building with high hopes. They drove to Sarah's as fast as they dared. Sitting at the table with their pop, they planned and dreamed. "Should we leave on Saturday or Sunday? I know that will mean an extra night if we leave Saturday, but we'll need Sunday to find our way around," Sarah said.

"We can't go to the library until Monday," Ruth pointed out. "But, I do think we need to leave on Saturday. That'll give us the extra time we need, as you said."

"So, today is Friday. We have this weekend and all next week to prepare. I'll call Skipper over at Bluff Street Ford to check out the Torino. After the overhaul last summer, it's been running like a top, but I want him to check things out, just to be sure. We'll have time to get everything ready." Sarah had it all planned, and she smiled with satisfaction.

****

Saturday morning, Sarah pulled up to the curb on Fourth Street and cut the engine. She looked to the left and saw Ruth had gotten up from her porch stoop. She picked up her suitcases and hurried toward the car.

"What in the world are you doing sitting in the dark?" Sarah asked as Ruth opened the car door.

"I was waiting for you. You said that you would be here at 5:30 and since you're never late, I closed up the house and waited on the porch. I hate to hurry out of a house. I always think I left something undone." Ruth laid her cases on the back seat and got in the front. "I'm ready. Let's go." The interior light illuminated Sarah's face. Then she looked at Sarah's face.

"Oh, dear, I don't want to hurt your feelings, but, well, did you use your magnifying compact to put your face on this morning?" Ruth asked with a bit of trepidation.

"No, I couldn't find it and supposed I had already packed it. Why?"

"Well," Ruth looked away for a moment stifling a giggle. "You have four eyebrows. That only happens when you're in a hurry and don't use your magnifying compact so you can see."

"Oh, man!" Sarah put her face up to the rearview mirror. "Which ones are the real ones?"

"The lower ones. Here, let me do it," Ruth dug through her purse for a KFC moist towelette. She was always ready for any situation. She dabbed at Sarah's eyebrows and then settled back in her seat. "You really should get glasses, you know!"

"Yeah, yeah, and I should let you color my hair, too. Let's get going!"

"On to North Carolina!" They hollered at the same time. Sarah put the Torino in drive, and they sped off down the street.

Chapter 19

October, 1864
Ashe County, North Carolina

Sam knew her people were upset, and they needed encouragement. "I know this is a horrible thing to have happen to us. Uncle Prince was our lifeline and he would want us to carry on. He was very proud of us because we've risked everything to get our salt and we're still standing. Frank Daniels got away and that means he might come after us. We need to get home as fast as we can."

Sam led the group home. She dared anything else to happen. She knew she would kill anything or anyone that crossed her path to keep her from getting her people home with the salt.

They pushed hard all morning; everyone wanted to get home. They stopped to rest at the New River. They all needed to drink, especially the animals. In the distance, Sam could pick out the mountain where she lived. Just a couple of hours more and she would be home.

Sam double-checked the ropes holding the salt bags on the saddles before moving on. Everything looked good. "Let's go, folks." Everyone got in line, but they were too exhausted to speak.

Sam led them across the river, with Mr. Poole

bringing up the rear. *This is where we crossed six days ago*, Sam thought. *It seems as if it were a lifetime ago.*

It was almost dusk when they entered Ashe County. Grandma and Grandpa Coldiron were the closest, so they made a stop there first. The dogs started barking when they approached the cabin. Grandpa Coldiron came out onto the porch of the cabin. He noticed right off that Prince wasn't with them.

"Whar's Prince?" Grandpa asked as his old eyes searched the road.

Sam fell into her grandpa's open arms and wept, burying her head into his shoulder. "Oh, grandpa! Uncle Prince…is…dead." Sam choked out the words.

Grandpa Coldiron gave the others a questioning look. Pushing Sam away, he looked her over. "Are you okay? Was anyone else hurt?"

"We're all okay." She wiped her tears with her sleeve. "But Uncle Prince. Grandpa, they shot him dead."

His stern look turned to concern, and then fear. "Tell me what happened."

"Well, we got the salt and were coming back with it. Then some wicked men started chasing us." She left out the part about stealing the wagon full of salt or finding gold coins.

"Why were they chasing you?"

"They thought we had stolen their gold."

"Gold? Where on earth would you find gold?"

Sam inhaled deeply. "I need to talk to you about that…later."

"Surely you didn't leave Prince out there, did you? Did you bury him?"

Sam swallowed hard. "We buried him a day's ride

from here. It's a long story. I really need to get everyone home. I'll tell you about it when I get back, okay?" Sam asked with a bit of trepidation.

Grandpa hugged Sam. "We'll talk more tomorrow. You go on home. You're wore out. Be careful."

Sam squeezed her grandpa hard. "Love you, Grandpa." Turning to the boys, she directed them to get a bag of salt. "Boys, just take Grandpa's load of the salt in. It's almost dark, so you may as well go on home." Sam hugged the boys and thanked both for their help.

"It's okay, we're glad to help," Cole said.

Sam led the rest of the group toward Miss Deb's home. Miss Deb's nieces came out on the porch when she helloed the house. The girls hugged their aunt and talked a mile a minute. Sam untied the salt from the saddle.

"Let me do this, Miss Sam. You're plumb tuckered. Me and Buzzard can get home safe after we finish here," Mr. Poole whispered.

"Thank you. I believe I'll go on. I'll divide my bag of salt with Grandpa. I'll come by tomorrow and make sure everyone is safe. You can portion out the salt to your people as you see fit. If you know of anyone who needs this mule, please give it to them. We can't feed it. Thank you very much, Mr. Poole," Sam said and hugged him.

Sam hugged Miss Deb and thanked her, too. She was so tired she didn't think she could get off her horse when she finally made it home. The dark cabin surprised her. The cruel reality washed over her anew. Prince would never be there to light her way again. She didn't have the energy to hate tonight, but she would find it again tomorrow.

Sam unloaded her pack and set the salt on the porch,

then took Sugar to the barn. "Bet you're glad to be rid of the saddle, huh, boy?" Sugar went straight for the pile of hay. Sam wished she had some grain for him. She brushed him down as she thought. *Prince told me about the silver money. Do I dare use any of it to feed Sugar?* The thought scared her because no one had any money. If she showed up with silver coins, people might get suspicious. A person didn't know who to trust. She would decide later. Sam pumped the bucket full of water at the trough. She watered Sugar and then headed toward the cabin.

A musty odor filled her nostrils as Sam opened the door. She found the friction matches on the table and lit the lamp. It did little to dispel the darkness in the room or in her heart. It was cold, but Sam just wanted to get the precious salt inside, wash her face, and hit the bed. She had never been so tired in her life. So tired that she forgot about the gold. Her momma always said things would be better in the morning. *Maybe they will be.* She pulled her boots off and settled under the tulip quilt her grandmother had made.

The sun was up when Sam awoke. She felt disoriented feeling comfortable. Comfort wasn't something she had felt in a while lying on the ground with a rock jabbing into her ribs. Dust motes danced in the sunshine that streamed through the window as she sat up. Muscles were slow to respond. Her nose caught a whiff of something awful. It wasn't the musty smell of the cabin. She sniffed her armpits. *I smell like a goat! Really need to wash up. Now my bed smells goaty too*! Sam sighed. *Now I'll have to wash the bedclothes.*

Sam got out of bed and stretched before she remembered. *Prince. Gold.* She went over to her pack and pulled out the bag. Sam untied the string and poured the coins on the table. She counted fifty coins. One side had a woman's head on it with the date 1861. The other side was marked with a majestic eagle resting on a "D". Beneath the "D" was the word FIVE D. Around the edge were the words: United States of America. There were fifty five-dollar gold pieces! A fortune! She had to find the cave and hide this money.

Sam had to talk to Grandpa Coldiron, but she needed to locate the cave first. Sam built a fire, went out to the well, and pumped a bucket full of water. She put the cornmeal and water in a pot and moved the crane over the flames. There was still a small cake of maple sugar left. She would use it to sweeten her porridge. She had had about a bate of cornpone and this was faster.

While her porridge was cooking, Sam had a good wash and changed into clean clothes. She started to put on her dress but thought twice. Since she was going up the ridge after breakfast, she decided to put on a pair of Uncle Prince's britches. She really loved the freedom britches gave her. Adding a pinch of *salt* to her porridge was pure heaven, and she gulped it down.

Sam filled her small water bag and put the bag of coins in her pocket. Ready to set off to find Prince's cave, she went out the door and looked at the ridge behind the cabin. She and Prince had harvested the sugar maples that covered the ridge ever since she was a girl. Images of stirring the sap with Prince watching her filled her mind.

Sam set off up the ridge. Prince had said to keep straight north from the cabin. As she climbed the ridge, over rocks, around trees, her mind went back to when the Home Guard had busted up her sugar pans before she could hide them. They were going through the mountains in 1862, gathering up every man they could find. *That damn conscription law! No one was safe from it. I've not seen my brother in more than two years because of that law. He had said he would not kill men he had not even met and had had no truck with, bad or good.* Sam had no idea if he joined the Union army. She desperately hoped he avoided the bushwhackers and the Home Guard.

Sam tried to think if Prince had said how long to climb. With all the emotion and commotion surrounding Prince's death, she didn't know if she remembered correctly. *Did Prince say about halfway up? How can I tell when I'm halfway?*

Sam searched for a trail but finally gave up because she realized Prince wouldn't have made one. She now understood his whereabouts when he slipped away for the day. Sam could see the valley below, but couldn't see the cabin because of the trees. Had she moved too far to the left or right?

She stopped and leaned against a rock to take a drink of water. She put the cork back and glanced around. Shuffling her feet, she noted the rustle of dry leaves. Her gaze dropped to the ground and then she looked up. Several tulip poplar trees surrounded her. Some of the dead orange-brown flowers still clung to the branches. *Of course! Look up as you go, silly girl!*

With renewed energy, Sam climbed the ridge. She saw several poplar trees, but none seemed to be as huge as Prince had described. Then gazing straight ahead she spotted the tree. Probably five feet in diameter! Beside it was a large outcropping of rock. Prince specified the entrance was near the tree, close to the rock. Sam walked over to the rocks but couldn't see an opening anywhere.

Sam leaned against the tree and looked down and around. *It has to be here somewhere…* That's when she spied the opening directly across from her. *It's well-hidden. If I hadn't been standing right in front of it…* Sam stepped over some smaller stones and looked down into an opening about three feet wide. The hole was dark so she couldn't tell how deep.

Sam put her water bag down and knelt to brush away the leaves. The opening was big enough to slip down through, but she didn't know what was down there. *Yep, I'm just looking to get snake bit. I wish I had thought to bring a lantern. A cave is dark, for heaven's sake. What if this wasn't the right one? How will I get out? Nope, I'm going back for the lantern and rope. Ain't no way I'm going in there without a light to see with.*

Sam made her way down the ridge just in time to see a rider come into her yard. She couldn't make out who it was, and she was suddenly terrified for her horse. *Had the rider been to the barn?*

"Hey, Miss Sam!" Buzzard Jim said with a wave to her.

"Oh, thank goodness! Hey!" Sam walked into the yard.

"I brung you a rabbit! I snared two and Mama said I should bring you one on account of Prince not being here to cotch you one."

Tears came to Sam's eyes. "Thank you! And we have salt to season it with!" Sam smiled to make up for the tears.

Buzzard cleaned the rabbit and was on his way. Sam was very grateful for the meat. Sam would fry it up when she got back. She had to get back up to that cave and see what was in it. She put her ropes in her pack, picked up her lantern, and set off back up the mountain.

Chapter 20

The trip back up to the tree was quicker this time, since she knew where it was. The tree looked even bigger now. She brushed away the leaves from the opening and tied a rope onto the lantern bail. Sam lit the lantern, lay down on her belly, and lowered the lantern down into the hole. She hung over the edge and looked into the shadows. The drop was only a few feet to the rock shelf. Sam swung the lantern to see if she could see how big the place was. It looked like a room, but she couldn't really tell. *I'm not a coward, but I really hate dark places.*

Sam pulled the lantern back up and got her ropes out to tie one around the tree. The tree's circumference was so large she only had a few feet left at the end. She untied the lantern and used that rope to attach it to the other one and made a good knot. *How to get down and still carry the lantern?* Sam tied the lantern to the end of the rope again and lowered it down. She sat down on the edge and grabbed a twist of rope in both hands and slowly slid down until her head disappeared through the opening.

The lantern cast enough light to see she had to jump only a couple of feet to be on the shelf floor. Sam jumped and was clear of the lantern. The smell of sulfur invaded her nostrils. *Well, that should take care of any snakes.* Untying the lantern, she held it up hardly believing what met her eyes.

Sam was standing on a shelf that had a natural step down into a small cavern about thirty feet long and as many wide. In the middle was a contraption that looked like a sorghum press. There was a long iron lever, about two inches in diameter, that extended out three feet on each side of the big screw in the middle. The screw attached to some sort of device that held it upright. Prince had pegged the device to a square wooden cabinet that was made of thick pieces of wood. Sam walked over to the lever and pushed the long arm away. It moved the threaded bolt up when she turned it one way and moved it down when she turned it the other. There was a small circular indentation on the base where the threaded piece came down.

A tin box lay open on the cabinet with several round flat disks that had no markings of any kind. On the other side of the base, a small basket held silver coins. Shiny new silver dollars! She counted two, four, and...twenty in the basket. *Uncle Prince! What have you been doing?* Sam could hear his voice, "get the money." Now she knew what he was talking about. She picked one coin to examine. The coin was shiny and new, but the date was 1844. On one side, it had a pretty lady sitting on something. On the other side, an eagle held something in one talon, maybe a branch, and the other talon held three arrows. Sam stashed the twenty silver coins in her pocket. Patting her pocket, she smiled. *Thank you, Uncle Prince!*

Sam held the lantern high and scanned the room. A spot of light shone on the floor by the remnants of a campfire a few feet away. Following the beam of light, she saw a small hole about four inches in diameter in the ceiling, like a natural flue. A makeshift crane held a small heavy metal pot. A ladle was on the floor beside it with a few flecks of silver in it.

Sam realized where the source of Prince's income had come from. She had so many questions, but really needed to hide the gold and get out of there. Sam searched for a good spot. She didn't just want to lay the bag on the cabinet and leave. *I need to hide it.*

The base of the cabinet was very heavy. Prince had to have brought the pieces of wood separately and built it here. She knelt and felt along the upper edges of the cabinet from the underside. There were ledges all along the underside not visible from the outside. Sam slipped the bag up under the base and set it on a ledge, satisfied she'd found the perfect spot.

Sam scanned the area and envisioned Prince here working. *Was he always alone? I will never know now.* Walking over to the step, she set her lantern on it and then hefted herself up onto the shelf. She saw the opening about three feet above her head. Sam attached the lantern to the end of the rope again and grabbed the rope to pull herself out of the cavern. It wasn't easy, but she wiggled and squirmed her way out. Pulling the lantern up, she blew it out. She untied the rope from around the tree, coiled it up and put it in her pack. Sam brushed the leaves back around the opening as best she could. *Does anyone else know about this cave? Will I ever be back?*

Back at her cabin, Sam fried the rabbit and silently thanked Jim again. She would keep the gold a secret, at least for now... perhaps forever.

Wash up can wait for later. I need to talk to Grandpa Coldiron and tell him about Frank Daniels and his threats. Sugar greeted her eagerly as she came to his stall. She saddled him and they set off for Grandpa Coldiron's cabin.

As she rode into the yard, she saw it had been newly swept. Trust Grandma Bernice to keep the yards clean, even on doomsday. Sam dismounted and tied Sugar to the hitching post at the edge of the yard. Her grandparents came out onto the porch as Sam limped to the porch and up the steps.

"Land sakes, Girl! You're skin and bones and you're limping!" Grandma said.

"My feet, Grandma, they're a mess. Still very sore; we walked all the way home."

"Let me get you some Porter's Salve. It'll cure anything. Burns, blisters, hemorrhoids, lumbago, you name it. I put the liniment in beeswax and lard and mix it up to make a salve. It stinks, but it works. I'll give you a tin of it."

"Thank you, Grandma. I remember it. It does stink!"

"We just ate dinner, but I can fix you something if you're hungry," Grandma said.

"No, Jim brought me a rabbit. I fried it and put *salt* on it! It was so good!"

Grandma Bernice hugged Sam as they went into the house. "I know, we 'bout forgot how food tastes with salt on it. It's not cold enough yet to kill our two skinny hogs, but in a few weeks, it will be. Thank you kindly for your part in getting the salt. I hate it so much about Prince."

Grandpa put his hand on Sam's shoulder. "We know what it cost to get this salt and we're real sorry. We need to have a service for Prince. The trouble is, the Home

Guard is roaming around again. We don't want no truck with them. I'm afraid if we all gather together, they'll think we're up to something. I've hid the salt and the hogs. I don't want anyone coming around sniffing."

Grandma Bernice brought out the salve and handed it to Sam.

"Thank you, Grandma. I appreciate it. Grandpa, could we go outside and talk a minute?"

"What? Secrets?"

"Not secrets, just advice."

Sam and Grandpa went out the door and down the steps. "Your grandma can hear a gnat fart at thirty paces. Let's go to the creek." They walked out of the yard and sat on a rock ledge near the creek.

Sam leaned over to pick up a stone. Rubbing the smoothness between her fingers, she sighed. "Well, Grandpa, you won't believe some of what I'm going to tell you." Then with skill, she skipped the stone across the water and began to tell him everything except about the gold.

"So, this Frank fellar took what money that was in the bag."

"Yes."

"And everyone saw him take it?"

"Yes. But… well… they think I have their gold."

"Do you?" Grandpa looked away.

Sam got extra quiet as she paused to think. *I can't lie to Grandpa. But if I tell him, he would be in danger if Frank Daniels finds me. He could hurt Grandpa to find out where the gold is.*

She wouldn't look him in the eye either. "Well, Grandpa, yes and no. But no one else knows I have it. I found it in one of the bags of salt. Well, actually, the sack fell into the creek and I picked it up after the salt had melted. The bag of gold coins was inside. Prince found the greenbacks in another bag. All the folks on the trip know about the greenbacks. But we no sooner found them than Frank and his devils surprised us. Prince handed them over to him right away, but got mad when we said that we didn't have his gold."

Sam leaned over to pick up another rock and threw it. "I had it hidden in my pocket. I don't know why I didn't give it back to him. Everything happened so fast! Frank demanded that Prince hand over his gun. Prince accidentally dropped the gun as he was handing it to him. Frank got mad and shot him as he reached down to pick it up. It's all my fault! If I had turned the gold over when he asked…" Sam held her head in her hands and cried.

Grandpa patted her shoulder. "No, no. I'm afraid that gang would've killed all of you anyway if that fellar hadn't showed up to scare them off. Now, about that fellar."

"I've hidden the gold. I won't tell you where. But I'm afraid that Frank will come after me. I won't tell him where it is, he'll kill me anyway. He killed Prince."

"Now, maybe he won't come here looking for you. You said that his gang was dead?"

"Yes, but R.B.—"

"Okay, there's that fellar's name again. What about him?"

"Yes, well, I haven't had the chance to tell you about him. He saved us. He shot the other two men with Frank Daniels, but Daniels got away. I'm all mixed up in my telling this. R.B. said there were more men with Daniels earlier."

"Let me think," Grandpa said. "You said you hid the

gold and don't want to tell me where?"

"I don't think I should. Don't you agree? I shouldn't have told you about it at all, but I couldn't seem to make this story have any sense if I didn't."

"I understand, and I'll pretend I never heard about it. But what do you think you should do? Go away for a while?"

Sam had a quizzical look on her face, as if the thought of leaving was impossible. "Where could I go?"

"We'll have to think on that."

Sam studied her grandfather. "Do you know anybody in Missouri? Uncle Prince said the darndest thing. He said I need to go to Missouri to hide... that we had people there. You know anything about that?"

Grandpa's face had held sadness for a moment, but at the mention of Missouri kin, the sadness vanished. A visible change came across his countenance, one she wasn't familiar with. "Tell you what, let's talk about that a bit later. Let's both think on this. Frank Daniels may find out it's to better leave well enough alone."

Sam nodded. She could sense her grandpa didn't want to talk about Missouri right then. "Okay, I need to check on everyone who made the journey. See if they're all right. I'll stop by this evening."

"Okay, Grandma will have a bite to eat for us. I'll tell her you're coming."

Sam hugged her grandpa. "Thank you so much! You always make me feel better. See you later."

Sam walked back to the yard, swung onto Sugar and started down the trail at a fast trot. Several stops were ahead. Urged on by the eerie feeling of eyes watching her all the way, she heeled Sugar to hurry to her cousin's cabin. She kept close watch of the woods for any movements as she rode.

Cole met her with a big smile when she rode into their yard, but Isaac was nowhere to be seen.

"Where's your mam and pap?" Sam asked as she dismounted.

"Isaac and them went into Coldiron for supplies. Well, to see if there were any supplies that could be had."

"How are you and Isaac?" Sam asked.

"We're fine. We told mam and pap what all happened. They sure are sorry about Prince. I hid the salt until we can butcher our hogs. What you doing here?"

"I wanted to check to see if everyone was all right after our journey. I appreciate all your help. I really do."

"Weren't nothing, ma'am. We was glad to help."

Isaac sprinted into the yard. He was out of breath and it took him a few seconds to get enough air to shout out, "That man! Frank Daniels! I saw him at the general store! He had a bunch of men with him!" Isaac bent over, holding his side while he tried to get his breath.

"What? Are you sure?" Sam's heart went cold.

"Miss Sam, I ain't never gone to forget that man's face, ever. He's here."

"Did you hear anything they said?"

"No, ma'am. I just hightailed it out of there, quick as I could before he saw me!"

Sam couldn't believe it had happened so quickly. Now, she knew what she had to do, but didn't know how to accomplish it. *I have to go. But how and where?*

Chapter 21

Saturday, May 5, 1984
Missouri

Sarah and Ruth drove along Interstate 70, making good time. Close to St. Louis, Ruth waved to the Arch and Sarah's stomach cramped as they drove over the Mississippi river. Sarah loathed driving over large bridges. They took Interstate 64 at St. Louis, then continued on through southern Illinois and a small part of southern Indiana before crossing into Kentucky. Heading down I-64 would take them to Lexington, and then they'd travel on the Mountain Parkway until they arrived in Salyersville, Kentucky.

They took a break for gas eighty miles from Louisville. Sarah observed the gas costing a dollar four a gallon. The Torino had an eighteen-gallon tank, making this fill up more expensive than expected. While pumping gas, she saw a young man on the other side of the pump. His ballcap was inscribed with the words, "*30 minutes of begging is not foreplay.*" Sarah chuckled as she returned the nozzle to the pump. They grabbed a burger at a drive-thru before heading off again.

"When we arrive in Jefferson," Ruth hesitated and then turned to Sarah, "what should we say? Should we just state that we want to know where Samantha lived? What're we going to say to the owners of the land? *If* we find the land."

"I've been giving that a lot of thought. *When* we reach that point, we should be honest. We should let them know what we want to search for. They may lend a helping hand, or they could just tell us to scram. I'm a tad bit anxious, yet I'm certain they'll want to find out."

"Yes, if it were my property, I'd want to at least look. We have the description of the property and how the woods come up behind the barn," Ruth said.

"The description we have is 120 years old. There would be changes in that amount of time. The cabin, for sure, is probably gone. Hopefully, the mountain isn't. We'll just have to do the best we can. Don't worry, this is the part where we *really* get worried about things. We just need to keep our wits about us. The people at the library and Register of Deeds will help us all they can, I'm sure." Sarah pointed a finger at Ruth. "But we shouldn't talk about gold coins or anything like that to them. They won't take us seriously. There will be time for that *when* we find the property."

Ruth quietly nodded.

Sarah had a lot of worries too, but she didn't want Ruth to know. They had made up their minds to come and were on their way. They'd deal with the repercussions of that decision as they came. The Torino purred along at 55 miles per hour. They made good time and were near Salyersville, Kentucky.

"It's almost 3:30 and we'll get to Salyersville in a few minutes. Let's get gas there and go to the bathroom. If there's a restaurant, let's get something to eat. We'll need more energy for this last leg of our journey. We're going to be on some twisty, winding roads, and from the looks of the map, the towns are few and far between.

What do you say?" Sarah said.

"I'm with you, kid!"

The girls pulled into an Exon station and a boy in a Ford hat and overalls came out to greet them. The embroidered name on his shirt was Oliver.

"Fill 'er up?" he asked with an Eastern Kentucky accent.

"You still do that for your customers? I'm impressed, Oliver." Sarah got out of the car.

"Yes, please fill it up." Ruth got out and headed toward the restroom.

Oliver took the nozzle out of the pump, and walked around the car, looking for the gas cap.

"It's under the license plate." Sarah pointed to the back of the car.

"Right, sure!" He nodded as he removed the gas cap and began filling the tank. "This sure is a nice car!"

"Thank you! I bought it new in '68. My first car and I still have it. Had it overhauled a while back and it's still purring along." Sarah patted the roof of the car.

"How fast will she go?"

"Well, I've only had it up to 85, and that scared me. It's my only means of transportation and I can't afford to replace it."

"Yep, insurance companies don't take kindly to racing, I know about that," he nodded.

Ruth came out of the station and pointed across the road. "Oliver, does that restaurant have good food?"

"Yep, pretty good. Thing is, it's the only place around here, so if you're hungry, you better eat now." Oliver chuckled and his homely face lit up.

"Thanks." Sarah handed him the money for the gas.

After he had cleaned the windshield, they pulled

over to the restaurant where several cars were parked. A sign said, "seat yourself" at the door, so they did. Menus were on the tables, and Sarah pulled one out to review.

"Looks like they serve breakfast all day. The special is a dollar ninety-nine, pancakes and bacon. I think I'll have that," Sarah said.

"I think I'll have the scrambled eggs and bacon. It's a dollar ninety-nine too. We had burgers for lunch, so I'll pass on the special of cheeseburgers and fries. I like breakfast for supper, too."

"I need some caffeine, but I don't want to stop in an hour to go to the bathroom. I'll just go for decaf coffee, although it doesn't taste as great as regular."

Sarah and Ruth ordered, and then gazed around at the typical country diner with signed pictures of country music stars on the walls. There were a couple of old guys in the back, dressed in overalls. A couple of teenagers were talking low and holding hands in a booth across the room. Sarah never talked about men to Ruth, thinking the only good man was a dead man. She knew her friend didn't agree. Ruth's husband, Stan, had been a good, moral man who was very good to her. His death of a heart attack at age thirty-nine was a shock to them all.

The waitress brought their food, and it looked delicious. After eating, the ladies jumped back in the car and sped down Rte. 114 to Prestonsburg. Then took 23 & 460 down to Belcher, where they drove across the line into Virginia.

Once in Belcher, they turned onto Highway 80. "It's only 5:30. We've plenty of daylight left. We'll be fine. I'm sure we'll get to Jefferson by dark," Sarah said.

Ruth only nodded saying nothing. In fact, Ruth had said little since they left the restaurant. Sarah gave her friend a slight scowl with a tilt of her head. "You doing okay?" Sarah asked.

"Yes, just a little bit queasy. These roads are so curvy and steep in some places. But I'll be okay. Don't worry." Ruth swallowed hard and closed her eyes.

Sarah drove on and tried not to take the curves as fast, but they came out of nowhere. She had to slow down. "Is the next road 63?" Sarah asked.

Ruth looked at Sarah's notes and said, "Yes, it looks like 80 runs directly to 63. Then we turn south or left. The next town is McClure where we get on 63. I hope there's a sign when we turn. That's always nice."

There was no sign at the T, but they turned left and sped on. When they turned at St. Paul onto Highway 58, the mountains hid the sun. "Well, we'll be fine. We have our map and plenty of gas." Sarah nodded to confirm it.

"Yes, we'll be fine. But we weren't counting on it getting dark so soon." Ruth sat up straighter and patted her face.

"Well, it's not really dark, it's just twilight."

Ruth didn't respond. They saw a sign. Sarah said, "Look, ten miles straight down this road is Abingdon. We'll stop there and freshen up."

"Straight? Straight? Sarah, there hasn't been a straight stretch of road since we left the parkway!" Ruth looked green and put her hand to her mouth. She pointed to the side of the road. Sarah pulled over, and Ruth barely got the door open before she threw up. She felt so sorry for her friend, but what was foremost in her mind was she just threw up a dollar ninety-nine. Sarah rummaged in the glove box for a box of tissues. Ruth got back in and gratefully accepted the wad Sarah handed her.

"I'm sorry, Sarah. I'm making us late." Ruth wiped

her face and blew her nose.

"Nonsense! Don't you worry! We'll stop and get you some saltines and ginger ale, and that'll fix you right up!" Sarah smiled at her friend and patted her hand. Ruth leaned her head back on the headrest and closed her eyes.

When they arrived in Abingdon, Sarah topped off the tank. Ruth bought saltines and ginger ale and brought out a Diet Pepsi for Sarah. She also carried a bottle of Maalox in the crook of her arm.

"Thanks! Diet Pepsi makes everything good again!" Sarah popped the top and took a long drink.

Pulling the Torino into the light traffic, she spotted the Highway 58 sign. As they traveled down the road in the waning light, they saw a road sign: *J. E. B. Stuart Highway*. "Oh dear, did we make a wrong turn?" Sarah worried. A few yards farther down, they saw another Highway 58 sign.

Ruth looked at the map. "I guess they are one and the same. That's so confusing!"

When the rain started, it was fully dark. Sarah squinted to see if they had gone past the turn. Suddenly, something at the side of the road dashed in front of the car and Sarah let off the gas.

"No, no! Crap! A black cat!" Sarah said. "Now we have *that* curse to contend with."

"That's just an old wives' tale," Ruth said with a hint of sarcasm.

"We can't do anything about it now. We just won't think about it."

"According to the map, 58 runs into Highway 16 and we turn south again, or right, so I don't think we passed it." Ruth was optimistic.

They arrived at an unmarked highway. Sarah sat

there with the car running and the wipers moving back and forth across the windshield. Taking a glance across the road, she spotted a two-story home with a double veranda along the front. Light shone from the house.

Ruth reached for the Maalox in the top of her purse. She unscrewed the lid and silently handed the bottle to Sarah. She took a couple of swallows and handed the bottle back to Ruth. Sarah wiped the white ring from her upper lip with a pinch of her fingers. "Dare we risk asking?" she whispered.

Chapter 22

October 1864
Ashe County, North Carolina

Sam urged Sugar to a gallop to get to her grandpa Coldiron's place. A cold sweat had broken out on her brow. *What do I do? What do I do?* She expected to see Daniels around every bend in the road as Sugar galloped through the fallen leaves. *It will be winter soon! Where can I go?* She was unfamiliar with anyone beyond the valley, almost nobody beyond the county. She'd never felt so alone in her life. *If only Uncle Prince were here! He'd know exactly what to do!*

Sam rode into Grandpa's yard, dismounted, and wrapped Sugar's reins around the porch post almost in one motion. "Grandpa! Grandma!"

Sam ran up the steps as they made their way out the door and onto the porch. She hugged her grandma and looked up at her grandpa. He already knew!

"What can I do?" Sam asked.

Grandpa returned her hug and then motioned quickly with his hand. "C'mon. Get inside out of earshot."

Sam inhaled the smell of pumpkin and venison, but her appetite had disappeared. "Oh, Grandma, you went to so much trouble!"

"Weren't no trouble at all. Cousin Brank gave us a

haunch of venison. Now, what's the matter? Your grandpa told me a bit of what has happened."

"Frank Daniels and his gang are in Coldiron. Isaac saw them in the general store. By chance, I was there when he rushed back home and told me. Daniels came here for me. Isaac declared they were all wearing Confederate uniforms. You know what that means!"

"Yes, it means that they can roam free and clear all over these mountains. The Home Guard is around here, too. They don't see eye to eye a lot of the times. Bushwhackers are around too, but no one knows exactly where they are."

"It's obvious that I need to leave. I can't bring trouble to you or anyone else here. But how?"

"Sam, I want you to eat—" Grandpa held up his hand at the shake of her head. "Eat what your grandma has fixed for you to keep up your strength. You just came off a hard trail and you're exhausted. You stay right here until I get back."

"But…where are you…?"

Without another word, Grandpa got his hat and coat and went out the door. Sam watched him go over to the stable and get his mule. He didn't take the time to saddle him, just climbed on and gave him his heels.

Grandma guided Sam to the table. "I fixed everything you like. I wanted it to be like a coming home celebration. You must eat, honey."

Sam went from scared to furious. "How dare those killers come here to our valley?" She paced the floor. "What gives them the right to do that?" She jerked off her hat and flung it on the floor. "Just how dare they?" Sam's face crumpled.

Grandma rushed to hug her. "You've had so much

to bear for so long. I feel awful this had to happen. Why are they after you?"

"It's a long story."

"I want you to settle down and eat. You need your strength." Sitting Sam down in her chair, she gave Sam a loving look. "Another thing, where is the salve I gave you this morning?"

"In my pocket. I'll use it. I know it heals well. But my feet are not worrying me right now." Sam eyed the fixings on the table and Grandma dished up her favorite things to eat. Stewed pumpkin, roasted venison, and onions! She saved the stewed pumpkin for last, to savor it.

"Thank you, Grandma! This was so delicious!" She didn't tell Grandma her nerves were wound so tight that it was all threatening to come back up. She fought the unwanted urge and forced a smile.

Footsteps on the porch alerted them of Grandpa's return. Sam jumped up and ran to the door. Grandpa wasn't alone. A tall, bearded man in ragged buckskins walked into the cabin with him. The stranger removed his well-worn hat and clutched it in his hand. A leather rifle scabbard crossed one shoulder and hung down his back. Grandma gave Grandpa a questioning look.

"Let's sit down and I'll explain. Then Mr. Smith will tell us his plan. Sam, Mr. Smith and I have conversated all afternoon. I've explained your situation, and he's entertained an idea how we can get you away. I'll let him explain his idea."

"I ain't really no explainer, but I'll try. I'm what they call a 'pilot.' I lead men out of these mountains over to Federal-held Tennessee and Kentucky. Stampeders, if you will."

"Stampeders? What in the world are you talking about?" Grandma was incredulous as she gasped with her hand over her heart.

"Yes, ma'am. That's what they're called. Stampeders. I lead them because I know all the trails, hills, mountains, valleys, and rivers in between here and there."

"But—" Sam raised her hand.

"If you would let me finish, please. Your grandpa explained it to me. It sounds like you need to get away for a while. I can guide you out of these mountains to a safer place. It'll be very hard on you. But this war has been hard all along. It makes us bear up under the things that we didn't think possible."

Sam agreed with a nod. "I do need to get away. I don't want to put my family in harm's way. They've already killed my uncle…When do we leave? I need to get ready." Sam's sudden bravado sounded greater than what she felt.

"Good. We have to carry as much food as we can, but not such a load that'll break us before we get down the mountain. I want you to dress as you have here, in britches. Your safety depends on no one knowing you're a woman, you understand?"

"I'll put my hair under my hat, as I've done before."

"No, you best cut it off. We got a fer piece to go. If your hat came off, it would give you away. We're going to join other stampeders and they're all men. I've never brought a woman before and they won't like it I've brought you. But I owe a lot to your grandpa here, and I mean to help. I'm glad your name is Sam. You'll answer to it right enough."

Mr. Smith paused, and no one said a word. "All

right, wear your thickest socks. Make sure your boots fit snug. It'll help with the blisters."

"When can we leave?"

"Tomorra at sundown. I'll be here. We're walking out."

"Sundown? We'll be walking in the dark? What about our horses?" Sam asked.

"Can't hide horses. Horses are noisy and could give us away at any time. We walk out."

"In the dark?" Sam's voice was incredulous.

Mr. Smith leaned over. "Am I hard to hear? Yes, we don't want anyone to see us."

"It's just that, I mean, …how can we see in the dark?" Sam threw her hands up imploringly.

"Just don't you worry. It'll be fine. You'll follow close behind me." Mr. Smith stood.

Sam stood up and looked Mr. Smith in the eye. "Thank you, Mr. Smith. I'll be here and ready." She knew her fate was in his hands. Grandpa wouldn't put her in harm's way.

"Mr. Smith, won't you please have some supper? We've plenty here for once," Grandma said.

Mr. Smith shook his head. "Thank ye, ma'am, but I need to get on." He nodded to Sam. "See you tomorra evening." He went out the door and walked off into the night.

Grandma stared at Grandpa with her hands on her hips. "Benjamin, I've been with you for our entire lives. You've never mentioned this 'Mr. Smith.'"

Grandpa looked at her and lifted his chin. "Well, Bernice, I didn't have to mention him until now. I'm going out to feed the animals. I'll be in directly to have some of this fine supper."

"Grandma, Grandpa, I better get on home. I have a lot to do." Her eyes were bright with unshed tears.

"Sam, how can we help? I hate it so…." Grandma held her hand to her lips and stopped herself. She didn't want to make it worse for Sam.

"I'll be back tomorrow. Don't worry." Sam left to go home and pack. *What could she take with her*? Loneliness kept her company on the way home.

Sam realized she had the whole of tomorrow to get ready. Exhausted, she went to bed. Tossing and turning throughout the night, she finally got up and lit the lamp. Taking it to the loft above, she set it on her cutting table. Spools of thread of every color lay on a shelf. She looked longingly at her Singer sewing machine, a treadle machine with an oak cabinet with three drawers on the left side. Sam had saved her money for a long time to get this machine all the way from Boston. She and Uncle Prince had traveled in a wagon to Fayetteville in 1853 to pick it up. *Uncle Prince had cussed a lot during that journey*, Sam remembered. Getting it up to the loft was an event that caused Uncle Prince to swear it would never move from this spot. It was still there.

Sam picked up her cutting scissors and held them in her hands. She looked into the tall mirror that stood on sturdy legs in the corner. *Might as well get it done*. Sam brushed her long hair and parted it in the middle. Holding the long side strands in her left hand, she cut with her right. It made for a little lop-sided cut, but that didn't matter. Sam looked at the pile of hair on the cutting table and sighed. Her hair now fell just below her ears. Sam looked in the mirror. Tears filled her eyes, but she shrugged her shoulders. *It doesn't matter what I look like*.

Picking up the three hand-sewing needles she had left, Sam carefully pierced a piece of flannel, wrapped them, and put them in an empty matchbox. Then she gathered a couple of spools of thread and put them in the bag.

Downstairs, she laid out her garments for the next day and fished through the bottom drawer for her only pair of wool socks. *Ugh! A hole in the toe. I hate darning.* Sam could sew beautiful dresses, but she couldn't darn a sock without leaving a ridge that rubbed your big toe raw.

Sam lay down again to rest and closed her eyes. *How can I sleep when I'm leaving everything I love behind?* Sam reflected on leaving her home, contemplating the war and all that had been lost. *Surely I could come home after a while…but maybe not. Who was to say? Could I kill Frank Daniels? I want to, in the worst way. But if he has others with him, they could kill me first. Why was the two-hundred fifty dollars in gold so important to him he'd risk coming into mountains he didn't know? He had the sack full of greenbacks. Wasn't that enough?*

Sam dreamed of being shot… of seeing Prince shot again…his blood all over her…

Sam wakes up with a start realizing she had been dreaming. *What time was it*? Light streamed through the windows. *Oh no! I have to get busy*! Sam cooked all the cornpone she had along with a bit of side meat. She baked the sweet potatoes she had left. *How long would it take to get….where did he say we're going?*

It took Sam most of the day to accomplish all her tasks. In the afternoon, she put on Prince's clean clothes and found her warm tan wool jacket with horn buttons and a big hood to cover her head. It had big pockets inside and out. Sam sewed eighteen of the twenty silver dollars into her cloth belt. She planned to give her grandpa two dollars to help care for Sugar. She needed to remember to tell him to come get the bag of salt.

What have I forgotten? The gun! I forgot the gun! Retrieving the gun from under her bed, she noted that it still had eight bullets in the cylinder. They hadn't fired the 20 gauge under the magazine either in the fight with Daniels. *I have no idea what ammunition it needs. Maybe I'll ask Mr. Smith*. Sam wrapped the holster around her hips. She punched a new hole in the belt; it fit reasonably well. Besides the revolver, she had the shotgun. There were four shells left. Rubbing the shells, she could see Uncle Prince's face in her mind. *These were in Prince's pockets*. Sam wiped tears from her cheeks and loaded up her provisions.

Sam filled her water bag and stoppered it. She gazed up the mountain to the ridge where the cave was located. Her gaze drifted to the cemetery where her folks were buried. She knew Grandma and Grandpa would take care of them, but she wanted to see them one last time. She climbed the hill to the graves and looked at the headstones Prince had carved for her mother and father. *Jesse B. Coldiron, Born 1818, Died, 1850. Gone to the Promised Land*. Her mother, *Easter Thomas Coldiron, Born 1820, Died 1863. Loving Mother, Gone to Heaven Too Soon*.

She had no recollection of her father, but her mother and Uncle Prince had taken care of her and her brother extremely well. "Mama, I'm sure you can see I'm in a real fix." Sam looked at the sky, clutching her coat lapels, searching for a response. "I'm alone now, Mama. They killed Prince… I need you, Mama…" She patted the stone. "I love you. Bye." Sam wiped the tears from her face, and trudged down to the barn.

Sam saddled Sugar, really hating the fact that she would have to leave him. But she knew Grandma and Grandpa would take care of him. She had hidden him often from the Home Guard, and he was probably the only good horse left in that part of the country. Walking Sugar out of the barn and over to the porch, she gathered her pack, mounted, and started over the ridge.

Mr. Smith waited in Grandpa's yard, with a rough pack tied to his back. A leather covered canteen hung from one shoulder. His rifle scabbard hung over the other shoulder. Sam dismounted and handed the reins to Grandpa. She had said her goodbye to Sugar on the way over. She couldn't do it again. He led Sugar away toward the barn.

"Would you tell me what provisions you have?" Mr. Smith asked.

"I have a big cake of cornpone, some baked sweet potatoes and a bit of fried side meat. I have needles and thread and some Porter's Salve for medicine. I also have this gun. It's called a LeMat." Sam pointed to her holster.

"Could I see that revolver? Never heard of a LeMat."

Sam handed it over. Mr. Smith rolled the cylinder and counted the bullets. "This all the ammunition you got?"

"Yes."

"You ain't gonna have much of a firefight with eight bullets!"

"I hoped you might help me with that. I don't know about the ammunition. See this lever here? You flip it up and this shoots." She pointed at the little barrel. "It's a little shotgun."

"Well, that'll come in handy, I'm sure!" Mr. Smith smiled as he looked at the gun, then handed it back to Sam. "I'm partial to Griswolds myself. I don't know how long you can carry that on your hips. It'll wear you down. You may have to put the holster over your shoulder. You may as well leave that shotgun here. It's too heavy for you to carry. Say your goodbyes and we'll be on our way."

Sam handed the shotgun to her grandpa. Grandma hugged Sam. "Goodbye Sammy, my girl! We love you and we'll take care of Sugar, don't you worry."

"I love you both so much! Please take care of each other. I hope this war is over soon. I hope so many things!" Sam tried to appear brave, but her fear was obvious. Sam handed her grandpa the two dollars and held her hand up at his protest. "You need it. I wanted to bring the bag of salt, but I couldn't carry it with all of this other plunder."

"I'll go get it directly." Grandpa looked down at the ground as Mr. Smith and Sam walked away. Grandma put her head on Grandpa's shoulder and hugged him close.

****

Sam knew there would be a half-moon later on, but at the moment, it was dark. Mr. Smith and Sam walked down the road and disappeared into the woods. She followed Mr. Smith, who acted as if he had a lighted pathway before him. She didn't know how he did it. Mr. Smith told her later you could see your way if you knew where it was.

Mr. Smith set a good pace, and Sam kept up for the first couple of hours. But then she flagged, and Mr.

Smith railed at her. "Do you want to get out of this or not? 'Cause if you don't, we'll quit right now. I'm not wasting a favor that took me years to pay back. You just tell me now. You want them guys to kill you? They will if they can."

At first, Sam cowered at his words. Everything was so new, she didn't know how to be on a trail. Of course she was tired! But then Mr. Smith's words brought her up short and gave her some energy. Sam stood up straighter. "Yes, I do want to get out of this. I'm sorry. I'll try harder to keep up. But where're we going? You haven't said."

"We're heading west out of Ashe County into Johnson County, Tennessee. We'll meet up with some men going on West. That's why you need to look like a man. We don't need any trouble. Let's go. We got about three more hours before sunup. Then we'll eat and rest."

Sam put one foot in front of the other and kept her eyes on his back. It wasn't freezing, and the constant walking kept her warm. When the moon came out, it illuminated the ridges and Sam could see below her. The faint trail was still dark, but it seemed Mr. Smith could see fine.

Another couple of hours passed, and Sam was about to drop. Her feet were numb and her limbs were rubbery. "Mr. Smith, please! I just need a moment…to rest for a minute." She tried to think of something else to say so he would stop. "I need to do private business."

Mr. Smith stopped and turned halfway around and said, "Okay, don't go off the path. I'll go on a little farther and wait."

Sam was so glad to stop moving. She really had to relieve herself, but was uncertain if she could actually get back up if she bent over. She leaned against a small tree to take the pressure off her limbs. Her breath came in little puffs. After a minute or two, she felt she might be able to do it and get back up.

"Sam! Miss Coldiron!" Mr. Smith whispered furiously. "Where are you?"

Sam rejoined Mr. Smith and looked longingly at the ground. She was so worn out that laying down on the pine needles would be like resting on a featherbed. "I'm here, Mr. Smith. Ready to go on."

Sam rearranged her pack and put her holster over her shoulder. *Mr. Smith was right. I couldn't have held that gun up much longer*. Mr. Smith slung his pack back over his shoulder and started on. *He seems so full of energy. But then, he's used to it, so he could do this forever*. Sam knew, however, she could not.

Mr. Smith finally called a halt as they came down into a valley. Sam could see pink in the sky to her right. "Let's pull up to this little stream, fill up our water bags, and eat a bite. With any luck, we won't be bothered as we aren't on a regular trail. Let's move over to those balsam trees and make a little camp."

Sam gratefully complied. She removed her pack and her holster. She walked over to the stream, sat down, and took off her boots and socks. The wounds on her feet had not had time to recover from the journey to Saltville. The ugly blisters had broken and were stuck to her socks. She peeled them off and stuck her feet in the cold water. The water made them sting at first, but then was soothing.

Mr. Smith moved off to the woods and came back a few minutes later. He sat down and pulled some jerky out of his haversack. Mr. Smith chewed for a while and looked at his charge and shook his head. Sam didn't know he was taking her clear to Kentucky, and he wasn't telling her. "Think ya can make another night of walking?"

Sam limped as she carried her boots and socks back to the campsite, nodding a weak and tired smile. Rooting through her pack, she dug out the salve Grandma Bernice had given her and smeared it thinly on the blisters. Bacon and cornpone came out next. Stretching out her feet on her coat, she relaxed and ate her food.

"We'll rest here till sundown. When you lay down, put your hat over your face so you won't get sunburned. That's good, leaving your feet out in the air. They'll toughen up. I need to go look around, but I'll be right back. You sleep."

Mr. Smith went back up the trail a different way than they had come down. He used his spyglass to scan the mountains behind them and saw nothing moving. He wasn't sure if the others would come on horseback, but they probably would. They wouldn't be worried about Sam doing them any harm. "What could one lone woman do?" he muttered under his breath.

Mr. Smith knew no one back in Coldiron even knew he existed except Benjamin Coldiron, and that man would never tell. He hoped Ben's wife could tell the story convincingly that Sam had left on her own and no one knew where, as they had discussed. He needed to move them deeper into the mountains and off the trail. Few people were aware of this trail, but he wasn't taking any risks. Despite the difficulty of navigating the laurel hells to get to Tennessee, he was determined to keep her safe.

Chapter 23

Saturday night, May 5, 1984
Virginia

"Let's take the risk and ask if this is the right road. We can't afford to take the wrong one. We might've already," Sarah said.

Ruth nodded but said nothing.

Sarah pulled into the driveway and turned off the engine. The rain beat down hard on the windshield. "I'll go and ask. Don't worry, it'll be okay." The rain drenched her the minute she stepped out of the car. A dog started to bark as she ran up to the porch. Sarah didn't see the dog but started back down the steps anyway. But the door opened, and a grizzled old man stepped out.

"What can I do fer ye? You lost?"

"Yes, I think we are. We've been on the road all day from Missouri, and we think we might've made a wrong turn." Rain dripped from Sarah's wet head.

"Ya'll come on in. You look plumb tuckered. Lucinder'll get you some hot coffee."

"We don't want to trouble you."

"You probably won't get where you're going tonight in this rain. Come on in." He motioned to Sarah.

"I'll go talk to my friend." Sarah went back to the car. "They want us to come in. I think it'll be okay." They ran through the rain to the porch where the man held open the door. He ushered them through the door into a large living room. The fireplace popped and crackled.

"Ya'll can go get warmed by the fire. My name is Levi Bare, and this is my wife, Lucinder." He waved his hand at a pretty little woman with gray hair smoothed back in a bun.

"I'll go make some coffee. Be right back," Lucinda said.

"Please don't go to any trouble. We just wanted to ask for directions," Sarah said.

"Have ya'll et?" Levi asked.

"We ate this afternoon, but that's all right. We aren't used to these roads and we're a bit queasy," Sarah said.

"There are some biscuits left from supper. We'll heat them for you, and you both can have some with peach preserves or honey, whichever you want." Levi left to go to the kitchen.

"Oh, Sarah! What have we done? We're in the middle of nowhere with strangers." Ruth whispered as concern constricted her throat.

"They seem like gracious people. I think we'll be okay. Are you feeling better? Your color is coming back."

"Yes, I believe I do." Ruth patted her cheeks as if to feel for a fever.

Levi came back into the living room. "The coffee is hot and the biscuits are warming. Come on into the kitchen."

Sarah and Ruth followed him to the old-fashioned kitchen. White cabinets gleamed from the light over the enamel table in the middle of the room. Lucinda removed a pan of biscuits from the oven and set them on a trivet. Serving two on each plate, she placed them in front of the girls. She quickly set preserves and honey on the table, and then turned to the coffeepot.

Sarah and Ruth sat gratefully. "These look wonderful! Thank you so much! You've just met us, and you treat us like family."

"The Lord teaches us to treat others as we want to be treated. You're lost and away from home," Lucinda said.

"What brings you to these parts, if you don't mind my askin'?" Levi looked them over.

The first test. "We're looking for an ancestor who lived in Ashe County, North Carolina, during the Civil War. The town of Coldiron, to be exact," Sarah said.

"I never heard of Coldiron, but there were a lot of little towns that disappeared after the War."

"We're heading to Jefferson, the county seat. We were told they have records there that might help us," Ruth said as she spooned honey on her biscuit.

"We live here in what is called Volney. You're still in Virginia. But Jefferson is only about 45 minutes from here down 16," Levi informed them.

"Are we anywhere near 16?" Sarah asked.

"Yep, the road right out there is 16. But ya'll needn't get out in this rain. You'll get there way too late. Ya'll don't know the area. Stay here with us. We have four bedrooms upstairs."

"Yes, please stay with us. We know of a nice motel, The Highlander, you can stay in when you get there. But you needn't try to get there tonight," Lucinda said.

Sarah and Ruth eyed one another. *Levi was very sincere with his invitation.* Driving any farther in the rain and on the mountain roads in the dark didn't appeal to either of them. "Okay, thank you! These biscuits are delicious!" Sarah took another bite.

"Ruth, I'll get our bags. No need for you to get any wetter." Sarah went to the car to get their bags. The rain had not let up, and she quickly returned to the house. Lucinda led them up the stairs and showed them the first room. "There are two double beds in here for when our grandchildren come. You can have this room if you like."

"Yes, this will be fine. Thank you." Ruth smiled at her hostess.

"The bathroom is over here. The hot water is a bit fractious, but it will eventually warm up. I'll leave you both to it. We're early risers, so don't worry about waking us. I'll have a good breakfast for you in the morning."

"Thank you again for your hospitality. We really appreciate it."

"You're welcome. Goodnight," Lucinda said.

"Well." Sarah put her suitcase on the far bed and took out her pajamas.

"I'm not sure I can sleep much, but that bed looks pretty inviting." Ruth said as she, too, pulled her pajamas out of her suitcase.

Sarah and Ruth crawled beneath the soft sheets of their beds that smelled of lavender. The beds were extra cozy with the addition of the thick quilts.

"Goodnight, Sarah."

"Goodnight, Ruth. Everything will be all right in the morning."

"Yes, I believe it will."

Chapter 24

October 1864
Johnson County Tennessee

At the end of the second night of traveling, Mr. Smith declared them to be in Tennessee.

Everything looked the same to Sam. On the third morning of their escape from home, Sam lay down and didn't even eat. She was asleep almost before her hand smoothed out her pack she used as a pillow.

Mr. Smith looked down at her and marveled at her spirit. After the first night, she had not complained at all. She followed him and did what he said. She rarely spoke. Her eyes were a little dull, but that was to be expected. He suggested she save her energy for walking, not talking, and she obeyed.

As was his custom, Mr. Smith backtracked to see if anyone was following them. Using his spyglass, he scanned the area but saw nothing that unnerved him. They had made camp in a little copse with hardwood trees all around. While a lot of their brilliantly colored leaves had already dropped, the trees were still far from bare. Mr. Smith plopped down on the ground and chomped on some jerky from his bag. He yearned for a smoke, but was wary of revealing their presence. When he lay down, he was asleep in an instant.

Sam awoke starved. She pulled the last of her bacon

and cornpone from her food bag.

Her stirring about awakened Mr. Smith.

"How're ya feeling?"

"I'm fine. I'm using the last of my supplies. Do you think we might get more somewhere?"

"We're getting close to Trade, Tennessee. We can supply up there. After that, I'm afraid we'll have to depend on the goodwill of people before we reach Kentucky."

"Kentucky?" Sam stared at him with curiosity. A few days before, she would have questioned and argued about the arrangements. But no more, she didn't have the strength.

"Yes, we'll catch up with the stampeders the day after tomorrow. Their pilot knows I'm coming and will wait. I'm afraid he doesn't know about you. We'll need to keep up a pretense about your being a man. You think you can do that?"

"Yes, I can. I have to. I don't want to make any trouble. I appreciate what you're doing for me more than you know. Can you tell if anyone is following us?"

"As far as I can tell, no one is trailing us. We've been very careful. It'll be dark soon. Let's see if we can get a little more sleep. At least the trees still have enough leaves to shade us from the sun. I don't want to hex us, but I sure am glad about the good weather."

"It's been dry all summer and fall. I hope it continues, too."

****

Archer and his men, including Frank Daniels, were indeed following them. Archer had picked up a couple more men since the death of Tim and Marcellus. The gang of five rode their horses down the mountain trails.

One of the new men, Augustus, knew the mountains of North Carolina and East Tennessee like the back of his hand. He was familiar with the trails that would intersect, so they could ride, not walk, to Tennessee and get there much faster.

"Frank, are you sure that kid said that they were going to Tennessee?"

"Yes, he did. I didn't scare him into lying in case that's what you're thinkin'. He just said it, flat out."

"Well, we'll catch them and get our money back. Say again how they took it?"

"They found the greenbacks—"

"All twenty-five thousand dollars?" Archer interrupted.

"Yes, they took all the money. I had to run for my life when that sharpshooter started shooting. I didn't have a chance to get it back." Frank lied through his teeth.

Archer narrowed his eyes at Frank. "I find out you're lying…"

"I'm not, I swear." Frank thought about Archer. *I hid that money so well, no one but me will ever find it. You think you're so tough! I'll show you. Just wish you hadn't found me. I'd be in Virginia right now. It's a wonder you didn't kill me first thing. I wonder…*

Archer and his gang rode on through the trails of Western North Carolina.

****

Mr. Smith and Sam crossed Snake Mountain. Mr. Smith said, "When we make our way down through the gap, we'll be in Trade, Tennessee. We'll supply up there and push on to get to Elizabethton in Carter County. We'll push hard because we need to meet the pilot there

146

the day after tomorrow."

Mr. Smith didn't explain much, so when he did, Sam listened.

"Thank you for telling me. It's hard not knowing where we're going. I was close to forgetting what your voice sounded like." Sam smiled at his reaction. Mr. Smith didn't exactly grin, but his mouth turned up a bit at the edges despite himself.

Mr. Smith led and Sam followed him down the mountain. The terrain was steep, but Mr. Smith followed a trail with switchbacks that wound them down the mountain horizontally. The sun was just peeking over the mountain when they walked into Trade. Sam saw a large building on the left. The sign identified it as the Trading Post and General Store. A post office sat across the dirt street. A large mule with canvas mailbags strapped to his sawbuck saddle stood tethered to the hitching post. Just beyond the post office was a two-story building, and the second-floor balcony held a sign that said "Saloon."

The pair stopped in front of the Trading Post and General Store. Mr. Smith said, "It's best you stay quiet. I'll do the trading. Thank you for the two dollars. It'll buy us some bacon and cornmeal."

Sam pushed her hat until it sat low on her forehead. Her dirt-smeared face disguised her fair skin. She followed Mr. Smith into the trading post. It took a moment for her eyes to adjust to the dimness. Sam looked around as Mr. Smith made his way to the back of the room. Sam gazed longingly at the shelves. She hadn't seen the shelves of Coldiron's general store filled with goods of any kind in years. It was strange to see shelves stocked full. At the counter, the storekeeper haggled with a man for a wolf pelt. A woman behind the counter took jars off the shelves and placed them on the counter for another man. The man pointed to another small bag on the shelf, and she put it on the pile.

The woman behind the counter saw her watching. Sam smiled before she thought about it, and the woman smiled back. Sam quickly averted her eyes, tugged at her hat and moved behind Mr. Smith. Following Mr. Smith's advice, she had put the gun and holster in her bag. She twisted her shoulders to shift the pack and keep the pistol from digging into her back.

At last, it was Mr. Smith's turn at the counter.

"What can I get for you sir?" the storekeeper asked.

"I need a pound of bacon, if you got it and a bag of cornmeal."

"I don't have any more bacon, but a bunch of jerked venison was just brought in."

"Okay, I'll take it."

The storekeeper put the items on the counter. "Can I get you anything else?"

"How much will this cost?" Mr. Smith moved his hand over the 2 items.

"One dollar and fifty cents."

"How much is that can of peaches up there?"

"Twenty-five cents."

"Let's have it then." The storekeeper handed him the can of peaches.

Mr. Smith gave him the two dollars, and he received the two bits in change.

Sam was so pleased when she saw the peaches. She couldn't wait to sample them, and they needed a treat. Mr. Smith gathered the jerky, cornmeal and the peaches and put the items in his pack. Sam took one last glance as they walked out. There were no bolts of cloth to be seen. Just as well.

The pair walked through town to the outskirts, where Federal soldiers had made a small camp. It unnerved Sam to see the Yankees so close. The Union had held Eastern Tennessee since last year. When the conscript law went into effect in 1862, a lot of North Carolina boys made it over to East Tennessee and joined the Federal army. There were no more boys left in the mountains to join anything.

"Let's get on out of town and then we'll find a good place to camp. Too many people to keep my eyes on."

Sam followed him quietly, eyeballing the bulge in his pack she knew was the peaches. She could tell by his expression that he hadn't counted on the Federal troops having a camp here, however temporary it might have looked.

Mr. Smith wound his way down the valley and found a place for them to camp for the day. "Let's save our jerky for when we can't make a fire. We need to cook this cornpone by mixing it with a little water and a pinch of salt. I'll show you after I gather the firewood." Sam gathered more sticks and branches for the fire while he got the fire going. He got out his little pan, shook some cornmeal into it, and mixed it with a little water from his canteen. Then he pinched a bit of salt and mixed it in.

"See, you have to keep it thick so it will stay on the stick, like this." Mr. Smith gathered up a handful and stuck it on the end of a stick that he had in his other hand. "Pat it on and squeeze it so it won't come off in the fire."

Mr. Smith held his corn dodgers over the flames to cook. Sam picked up her stick and gobbed the cornmeal mixture on it. Quite pleased with her handiwork, she held it over the flames. Smelling the delicious aroma of the toasting cornmeal brought a smile to her face. "I bet this would taste even better with a bit of dripping butter on it!" Sam said.

"Yep, I bet it would." Mr. Smith grinned. "I'll cook us up a few of these to take with us. We need to make use of this fire because we may not be able to make one later."

After they ate their corndodgers, Sam pointed to the can of peaches with longing in her eyes. "Don't you think we could open those peaches now?"

"How about we wait until later? We need to sleep for a bit. There's plenty of cover to move in the daylight here. It won't always be so. We'll start down into the Doe Valley in a couple of hours." Sam nodded with disappointment. She knew he knew best but thought that maybe he was just being bossy.

Mr. Smith woke Sam as the sun set. They carefully packed their food and pulled their packs onto their backs. "We'll fill up our water bag and canteen when we get down to the river. It won't take too long to get there."

Sam followed Mr. Smith down through the beautiful Doe Valley of Tennessee. *My feet must be hardening up the constant walking. They don't hurt as much.* Thinking about Daniels and his murdering gang kept Sam's nerves tore up, so she didn't ask Mr. Smith any more questions about being followed.

Dawn was breaking when Mr. Smith pointed. "There's the Doe River. Yonder."

Sam looked ahead and saw the sparkling river curving to the south. "Are you saying we have to cross this river?"

"Yep, we do. Now, the way we usually do it is to strip our clothes off and carry everything over on our heads. That way, we don't have to wear wet clothes. But I'm not sure how we're going to do this now."

Sam stared at the water with fear and looked down at her one outfit. "Are you kidding me? Walk across a river? I've done everything you've told me to do. But I don't think I can do this. I just don't really think that I can." Sam leaned against a rock and put her head in her hands.

"Can you swim?"

"I don't know. I really don't know! Can you show me how to do it?" Sam asked.

"Let's do it this way. I'll take off my outer clothes and put them in my pack. We have to keep our guns dry at all costs and also our coats and boots. I'll strap our packs together and carry them over. The river is low and I'm a tall man. I'll come back for my rifle and you. When the water gets too deep for you, you can hang on to me."

Sam didn't have time to argue about it, which was fortunate. She watched Mr. Smith tie the packs together. Her revolver was in her pack and his revolvers were in his. The Henry rifle was in its oilcloth pouch and stayed with Sam. Mr. Smith took off his buckskin shirt and britches and tucked them under the ropes that held the packs together. He slipped his boots off and tucked them in too. His stained undershirt and drawers were full of holes.

"I need to darn those holes for you first chance we get. I brought my needles and thread." Sam nodded at his small clothes as she handed him her boots.

Mr. Smith nodded. "I'll be as quick as I can."

Sam watched him wade into the shallow water at the bank and slowly make his way out across. The water rose only to his waist until he got to the middle. Then the water rose to his chin. He steadied the packs on his head with both hands and slowly made his way to the bank on the other side. Mr. Smith walked up the bank on the other side and Sam waved to him. He set down the packs and waved back. He moved his arms back and forth to rest them from the strain of holding the pack above his head. "Thank you, Lord! Now, Lord, please help me get her over here," he muttered under his breath.

Mr. Smith waded back into the water and slowly made his way back to Sam. "You should be able to walk until you get to the middle. When it gets too deep, just catch on to my shirt. It'll help you float. It'll be okay."

Sam stared at the water with a new fear emerging and knew without a doubt that she would drown. She had only waded in creeks and had never played or swam as a child in the New River. Sam didn't realize she was so scared of the water. The river was much wider and deeper that the rivers they crossed going to Saltville.

Mr. Smith saw the fear in her eyes as she stared at the water. "Let's go, Sam." Mr. Smith held the rifle with both hands over his head. He stepped into the water to walk a little ahead of her.

Sam forced her bare feet into the freezing water and waded in. She was thankful the river rocks were smooth, so they didn't cut her feet. Soon the water came up to her waist and then her chest. She looked around at the expanse of river. Water was everywhere. Thankfully, the current wasn't strong enough to push her.

Suddenly, Sam's feet went out from under her. "I can't find the bottom! I can't find the bottom!" Sam was frantic, her hands pawing the water.

Mr. Smith's voice was calm. "Sam, just hang on to my shirt. Just like I said. Just hang on to my shirt. You'll float, I promise you. When you do, just move your legs back and forth. See, you're fine." Mr. Smith's soft voice settled Sam, and she floated.

Gunfire echoed as they approached the other side. Mr. Smith hurried out of the river. Sam found her footing and scrambled out.

"Let's get over here behind these rocks." Mr. Smith said as he hunkered down and leaned his rifle against the biggest rock.

Sam's soaked clothes stuck to her. She tried to keep her breast binding from coming loose, but it was impossible to maneuver the wet fabric. She grabbed her boots from the pack and pulled the stockings out of the top of the boots. Impossible to get them over wet feet. Giving up on the stockings, she pulled on her boots and rooted around in the pack for her gun. Meanwhile, Mr. Smith was still in his small clothes but was rummaging through his pack. He grabbed his spyglass and surveyed the north and west to locate the shooters.

"I can see riders in the distance on this side of the river. They appear to be Confederate. Some have gray jackets."

Shots rang out again north of them. Mr. Smith swung the spyglass around. "Federals, looks like several of them. I doubt they've seen us. These rocks are good cover. Let's get our packs and lay low."

Mr. Smith hurried into his clothes and boots. Sam pulled her hat low, pushed her short wet hair back up inside out of her eyes, and sat behind the rock, holding her gun with both hands. Mr. Smith crouched beside the largest rock and got out his spyglass again. The rifle shots were ringing fast and furious now. The Confederates had dismounted and fired too often to be using Enfield rifles. It sounded like Henrys on both sides.

"I don't know why Rebels are coming down this far into Tennessee. Don't they know the Federals control East Tennessee now?" Mr. Smith said to the wind.

"What do we do?" Sam huddled close to the ground, trying to make herself a smaller target.

"Nothing we can do right now. Let's just wait a few minutes and see what happens. We can't run right now. Besides, these rocks are hiding us. They don't know we're here."

The shots died down and finally stopped. Mr. Smith looked through the spyglass again. "I see the Federals riding right for us. There don't seem to be anyone following 'em. I wonder what that was all about. Let's just stay out of sight. Maybe they won't see us."

They heard hoofbeats approach and shouts saying something about getting back to Elizabethton and Andy being hurt.

The hoofbeats became softer and more distant. Mr. Smith raised his head to observe with the spyglass. "There are some Rebels back there. Dang, if they ain't stripping the jackets off some of the dead Federals."

Sam trembled from cold or fright, she wasn't sure. "What do we do? Do you think they're Daniels and his men?"

"Only you can answer that. Do you think you could look through the spyglass and find out?"

Sam gestured for the glass. She put it up to her eye and tried to focus. "I can't find them. How do you work this?"

Mr. Smith reached up and pulled the glass down a bit. "Try now."

Sam moved the glass. "I see them. I don't recognize

any…Wait! Yes, I believe that one on the left is Daniels! Oh God, now what do we do?" Sam returned the spyglass to Mr. Smith with trembling hands.

Chapter 25

Sunday, May 6, 1984
Volney, Virginia

Sarah and Ruth were on their way the next morning by 6:30 after a wonderful breakfast of biscuits and gravy, compliments of Lucinda. She made the best coffee they had ever tasted. Sarah drove the mountain roads and they marveled at the beauy that surrounded them. Even through the light rain, they oohed and ahhed over the beautiful sights seen for the first time.

They had been on the road about a half hour when the clouds cleared. On top of a mountain, looking down over the valley, Ruth pointed to a rainbow which suddenly appeared.

"Beautiful!" Sarah tried to look and keep the car on the road.

"Look, it seems to end right over the road down there." Ruth pointed and shifted in her seat for a better look.

"One of us has to watch the road, you know!" Sarah squinted to get a better look and drove the Torino right through the end of the rainbow!

"Well, nobody is going to believe that! Driving through the end of a rainbow. There was no pot of gold, though!" Ruth laughed.

"I think that takes care of the black cat curse and

then some!" Sarah laughed. Life was good. It wasn't raining, and they weren't lost.

They came into the city of Jefferson. To stay on Highway 16, they turned left, as Mr. Bare had said to do. The ladies drove a mile or so and saw the Highlander Motel on the left. They turned in and pulled up to the red brick office. The motel was situated with a stunning view of the mountains across the road. The rooms were in a line, perpendicular to the road, and the red brick with white trim was neat and pretty.

"It's only 8:00. Should we hold off until a bit later? We don't want to wake anyone up. That's not a good start to our stay. We can go drive around first."

"Yes, come to think of it, we better do that. I'm sure there're a lot of things to see before tomorrow." Sarah pulled the Torino around and back onto the road.

"Let's go to the right, it looks like the town spreads that way. Can you take some notes while I drive?" Sarah asked.

"The notes Dolores gave us are in the glovebox. I'm sure she put the addresses of the places we want to visit on there." Ruth reached into the glovebox and found the notes. "Okay, the library is on Library Road. Well, that narrows it down!" Ruth laughed.

"We need to find a map of Jefferson. I'm sure a gas station has one."

They sped down Highway 16 and stayed straight at the junction to get on Highway 221. They came to a Shell station. It looked deserted but there was an International pickup with more rust than red paint parked beside it.

An old gentleman came out the door and looked them over. Sarah and Ruth got out and walked over to him. He spit in his cup and a bit dribbled down his beard.

"What can I do fer ye?"

"Well, we were wondering if you had a map of Jefferson. We're looking for the library and would like to know how to get there," Sarah said.

"I believe the liberry is closed, ma'am. This be Sunday."

"Yes, I'm sorry. I wasn't clear. We're here for just a couple of days and want to drive around today to find out where the library is," Sarah explained.

"Well, in 'at case, let me tell you how to get thar. I don't have no map to give ye. Now, let's see." He pointed down the street. "You go down this street and turn where the old log barn used to be. Then ya'll come to Jefferson Street. I believe you turn left onta Jefferson. It's down thataway."

"Thank you, we appreciate it, but we don't know where the old log barn used to be." Sarah maneuvered Ruth upwind of the spit cup. No need for her breakfast to be all over the pavement.

He scratched his head in thought. "Okay, I 'member now. E.T. Weaver's Equipment place is there on the corner. Good man. Got good stuff. You turn south and stay on that till you get to Jefferson Street."

"Okay, we're on Business 221 and we stay on this road and it turns left at E.T. Weaver's Equipment place, right?" Ruth asked.

"Yep."

"The library is on Library Road, and it's off of Jefferson Street?" Sarah said.

"Near as I can remember. Yep."

"Thank you for your help. We appreciate it. Mr…" Sarah said.

"Jr., just call me Jr. Glad to help." He spit in his cup

again and walked back into the station.

They got into the car and continued west for a few blocks. "Wait, that sign said the building up there was the courthouse." Ruth consulted the notes. "The courthouse is on Main, so we must be on Main. Great! Let's turn in and see if they have the hours on the door."

They turned into the parking lot of the old courthouse and parked beside a beautiful three-story red brick building with four white columns in front. A fancy brick cupola rose from what looked like the third story and had three porthole style windows. A Terra-cotta tile roof covered the cupola. A sign on the door showed the hours: Open: 9 to 4, Monday through Friday.

Sarah walked over to a white stone monument which stood tall in the front yard. A plaque on the monument honored all soldiers of all the wars up to World War I and World War II. It was erected in 1950. Sarah remembered words from the journal and touched the stone. Ruth came over and touched it, too.

"The war was real, Ruth. Men and boys really fought and died for what they believed in. As best I can remember, this is the first monument to any soldiers I've ever seen. It makes me sad."

"I think this trip is going to open our eyes to a lot of things. We're going to actually find out where Sam lived. It's so phenomenal in this day and age that we can find the remnants of someone's life from a hundred years ago and look at it. I think genealogy is going to become very important over the years. It is to us right now. It might change our lives." Ruth grinned at Sarah.

"Yep! Let's get back in the car and try to find the 'liberry'."

They continued down Business 221 until Ruth

pointed out a sign where 221 turned left. "There's the equipment store, Weaver's, I believe he said?"

"Yes, then we continue to Jefferson Street. I wish he could've told us how far it was."

They wound down through the town and eventually came to Jefferson Street. "Okay. We turn left here," Ruth said. They glanced at the various store fronts along Jefferson Street.

"A cheese factory! I don't think it's open. This is Sunday, but some stores must be open. There are a lot of cars parked along the street. Do you think we better stop and ask about the library since he couldn't tell us for sure?" Sarah asked.

"Let's go on down the street and see what we come to. Wait, we just passed Main again. I'm getting confused. There's State Street. Yeah, let's stop and ask someone," Ruth said.

"Look, there's a church on the corner, Mt. Jefferson Presbyterian Church. It's Sunday and nearly 10:30— time for services. And lots of people. Hopefully, one of them can help us." Sarah pulled into a parking space across from the church.

They got out and walked across the street. A lady parked in front of the church was getting out of her car. A lavender hat and a halo of silver hair framed her face. Sarah moved closer to her, suddenly conscious of her own sweatshirt and jeans.

"Please excuse us, but we're visiting town and don't know our way around. We're looking for the library. Might you point us in the right direction?" Sarah smoothed her sweatshirt down over her hips.

"Of course. This cross street here is Ashe." She pointed to the street sign. "You take this street up a block or so," she pointed, "and you come to Library Road on the right. You can't miss it. But this is Sunday."

"Thank you! Yes, we're trying to find our way around. We intend to go tomorrow. I want to say that I love your hat! The feathers are beautiful!" Sarah said.

"Oh, why thank *you*! No one wants to wear a hat these days, but I have always worn one and I always will, Lord providing, of course. Might I ask your names?"

"I'm Sarah Davis, and this is Ruth Kincheloe, from Fulton, Missouri."

"I'm Mrs. Gambill, Ellen."

"We're trying to find information on an ancestor," Ruth said.

"I love my ancestors! I have a famous ancestor, Martin Gambill. He rode over one hundred miles up and down this valley to tell the people the British were coming. Then they went south down to the Battle of King's Mountain in 1780. Paul Revere wasn't the only one!" She laughed and touched her hat.

"Well, thank you for the story! We had no idea! We'll research it when we get home. Thank you again for your information," Sarah said.

Mrs. Gambill walked on into the church, and Sarah and Ruth walked back to the car.

"I'm so glad we stopped! That's so interesting about her ancestor. Let's go up to the library and see when it opens. Then maybe we better find our way back to the motel and get signed in," Ruth said.

When they found the library, it amazed them at how big it was. The view from the parking lot was breathtaking. Not used to such vistas from every corner, Sarah marveled. "I wonder if the people here realize they live in such an amazing place?"

"I'm sure they do. I know I wouldn't take this view for granted."

Sarah pulled up to the door of the library and read the sign. "Open, nine to five, Monday through Friday, and nine to noon on Saturdays. Great, we'll be here at 8:55 in the morning!" Sarah said.

On their way back, they discovered a grocery store known as the "Food Lion". "What a fantastic name!" Ruth exclaimed. "Why don't we get some bologna and bread? I noticed a picnic table by the office of the motel." They purchased their lunch items and hurried back to the motel.

Sarah parked the car, and they walked up to the entrance. As Sarah raised her hand to knock on the door she read a sign that said, "Come on in." They entered and Ruth dinged the bell. A well-dressed gentleman ducked his head as he came through the doorway to the counter.

"Greetings! My name is Lee Beckworth and I own this fine establishment. How may I help you ladies?" He smoothed the edges of his mustache.

"I'm afraid we don't have a reservation, but we would like to have a room for a couple of nights, if you have any available. Mr. Bare, in Volney, Virginia, told us about your place here," Ruth explained.

"Ah, yes, I have known Levi since we were boys. That was gracious of him."

"He and his wife put us up last night. We had driven all the way from Fulton, Missouri. We were tired and sick, it was raining, and we stopped there. They were so very kind," Ruth said.

"Do you want to pay for tonight and tomorrow night, then?"

"Yes, please. We might need another night or two,

but we really won't be able to tell until we do our research tomorrow. My name is Ruth Kincheloe, and this is Sarah Davis."

"Do you ladies mind to tell me what you'll be searching for?" Mr. Beckworth filled out a form.

"Well, we recently found out about an ancestor, Samantha Coldiron. We want to find out where she lived. We were told by this lady who does genealogy in Fulton how we might go about it at the library and the Register of Deeds office." Sarah explained it a lot better this time.

"Oh, yes! The library! It's a fountain of information, it really is. The head librarian, James McLean, will be the one you want to talk to. You can't miss him. He's bald as an eagle. I'm not being mean, he regularly comments on it himself. I've seen more hair in squirrel gravy than on that man's head!"

Sarah and Ruth laughed. The day was looking up for them.

"That will be forty-two dollars for the two nights, twenty dollars per night, plus tax."

Ruth pulled out her wallet and paid him while Sarah protested. "Sarah, you paid for the gas. I've got this."

"Here's your room key, Number Six. I hope you enjoy your stay. If you need anything, just come back to this office. There are no phones in the rooms. I hope that's all right."

"That's fine. I'm sure the room will be great. There're two double beds?"

"Yes, ma'am."

Sarah and Ruth went to the car and retrieved their bags. Ruth opened the motel room door and looked in to see knotty pine walls and beautiful wood floors. They set their bags on the bed "I get dibs on the bed by the window!" Ruth exclaimed. The bathroom door was open and Sarah called dibs. Drying her hands on the softest towels Sarah had ever felt, she breathed deeply. Everything smelled so clean and was so neat.

"Let's get settled. We can eat our sandwiches at the picnic table and plan our afternoon. Great! Look! There's a little fridge here!" Ruth opened the door and looked inside.

Sarah smiled with relief. *Ruth was definitely feeling better.* "Yes, let's hurry! Ruth, we're here! We made it! And we're alive!"

Putting her food on the picnic table, Sarah settled on the seat. "Okay, this is what we have." Sarah put her potato chips between her bologna and bread and pressed down lightly. "We know Samantha was here in 1860 and was fifteen years old. We know her mother's name was Easter. At least we think it's her mother. She has a brother named Sidney. Dolores said the 1860 census entry was listed on the Old Fields Township, Gap Creek post office page. She also said we need to look in the 1850 census to see if we can find her father's name. We can search the Register of Deeds office for a deed, as deeds usually have the male's name listed."

"I think we have a lot to go on. Let's finish eating and drive around some more. We need to make more notes. We've really been lucky so far." Ruth popped another chip into her mouth.

They both looked at their watches. Twenty hours until the library opened.

Chapter 26

October 1864
North of Elizabethton
East Tennessee

Mr. Smith and Sam crouched behind the rock a few more minutes. "We need to sit tight for now. Maybe they'll go on. We know now they might dress as Federals."

Hearing hoofbeats, Mr. Smith risked another glance. The gang was heading north, riding fast.

Mr. Smith and Sam walked toward where the skirmish took place. Sam couldn't help but look, though she didn't want to. Six bodies lay on the ground. The bright red blotches on their shirts made the ghastly wounds evident. The .44 caliber bullets had torn through muscle and bone with ease. Even in the waning sunlight, they could see all were dead.

"We don't have time to bury them. Maybe the Federals will come back for them. They didn't take this man's jacket, I wonder why." He held it up to Sam, eyeing her stature and then held it out to Sam.

Sam stepped quickly backward with her hands up. "I don't want it. Put it down. It smells awful. Besides, there's blood on it."

"Well, Missy, you just might need this jacket where we're going, so don't be turning up your nose at it. Let's see what else we can salvage here." Mr. Smith hurriedly rustled through pockets and knapsacks. "Here are some crackers, what they call hardtack. We might need these. Looks like the other bunch took everything they had. No ammunition, nothing." He surveyed the area with a side glance. "We got to get out of here."

"Let's at least lay them out—"

"No, we don't touch them. It'll show somebody's been here. With all these hoofprints, I doubt the best tracker could pick out our footprints. I doubt those men following you are any good at anything except killing." Mr. Smith stuffed the jacket in his pack. He handed the hardtack to Sam, who sniffed them before she tucked them in her pack.

"Let's fill up our water bags and get on down the trail a bit. Sundown is about an hour away. We can eat then. There's only time for a brief rest because we have to be in Elizabethton by morning. Travel during the day won't be possible when we're that close. We can wait on Henry until he gets there. We just lost a lot of time."

Sam looked at the dead soldiers. She had packed her feelings way down deep for so long now, she wasn't sure if she still had the capacity to feel anything. It was just something else to survive.

Mr. Smith set a good pace and Sam kept up. She wanted to get out of there as fast as she could. At sundown, Mr. Smith stopped and said, "Let's eat here and rest a bit. It's a secluded place. The trees overhead will protect us from a spyglass view."

Sam didn't waste any time. She got out the hardtack, which was as hard as rocks. "Just how are we to eat these? They'll break our teeth off."

"You soak them in coffee first."

"Well, we don't have any coffee."

"We'll just have to soak them in water. Sprinkle a little of our salt on them. Makes quite a treat, if I remember correctly."

Sam handed one of the pieces of hardtack to Mr. Smith. He poured some water into his tin cup and dipped the hardtack in it. Trying to take a bite, he gritted his teeth. "Well, we might have to soak it a little more."

Sam hid a grin beneath her hand.

"Do we have some corn dodgers left? We could hurry and eat those and then open our peaches! They'll give us the energy we need to push on through the night to make it to Elizabethton by morning."

Knowing the peaches were nigh, Sam made short work of the corn dodgers. Sam dug in her pocket for her knife and jammed it into the can's lid. She worked it around until she could reach in and pull out a half of peach, dripping juice. Before she could help herself, she popped it in her mouth and closed her eyes in ecstasy. "Wonderful! I'm sorry if I was selfish. Have one?" Sam offered Mr. Smith one on the end of her knife.

"Don't mind if I do." Mr. Smith swallowed the peach almost whole and moaned, mocking Sam. He glanced out of the corner of his eye to see her reaction.

"These are the greatest peaches in the entire world!" Sam sighed.

"That's because we're starving. We need to close our eyes for a few minutes until it's dark. Then we'll move out of the Doe Valley down into Elizabethton."

"How do you know the trails in the dark? I can't figure it out."

"When you know the trails well by day, you learn to see them in the dark. You see the outline of the object.

It's something that you learn after some time. It's hard to explain."

Sam lay down and Mr. Smith stood guard and wondered where the scunners were. He dared not try to find them in the dark. It's best he carry on to meet Mr. Jenkins. He would have time to double back when the girl was safe with them. When it was full dark, they traveled down toward Elizabethton and made it by sunrise.

They slept a good bit of the day just east of a large spring in a cluster of woods a bit north of Elizabethton. Then they made their way to the spring where they waited. The sun had just set over the mountains when Sam heard voices.

"Sam, stay here. I'll go meet with Mr. Jenkins and explain things. First, I need to let him know it's us."

Mr. Smith put his hand up to his mouth and made a bird call. Then, a second call, a bit different from the first. The voices stopped. The same call came from the other side of the spring. Mr. Smith strode toward the sound. Sam leaned against one of the big rocks that surrounded the spring. Her pack was at her feet. She really wanted to soak her feet in the cold water, but thought she'd better lie low until Mr. Smith came back.

"Henry, how are you? So glad we could meet up!" Mr. Smith said as a young man walked toward him.

"You're still looking like a young buckskinner!" Henry lied. He took his scabbard strap off his shoulder to shake hands with Mr. Smith. His dark brown hat shaded his eyes, but the rest of his bewhiskered face smiled a welcome. The Navy Colts strapped to each hip showed Mr. Smith that he was indeed still a man to be reckoned with.

"Now, Henry, I need to explain a couple of things." Mr. Smith motioned for him to come away from the other men.

Henry set down his pack and spoke to the other men. "You men set down for a spell. I'll be right back."

From where Sam stood, she heard everything that was said between Henry and Mr. Smith. Good. She wanted to know who was going to decide her fate and why.

"Henry, you'll be surprised at what I'm gonna tell you, but if you would, please let me explain before you get yourself lit up."

Henry narrowed his eyes at his friend, but let him speak.

"I got a woman here—" Henry straightened to his full height and his lips thinned. Mr. Smith went on. "She's in a world of trouble. Some dangerous men think she has their gold."

Henry frowned and put his weight on the other foot.

"See, I told you it was a convoluted story. She says she doesn't have the money, and I believe her. Daniels, the man that thinks she has it, traveled to Coldiron, North Carolina, where she lives. That man threatened to find her and kill her. She wants to get as far away as she possibly can. Maybe even St. Louis."

"St. Louis!"

"Now, I know, we can worry about that later. Right now, she needs to know that you'll take her as far as you can. She's dressed like a man, so she can fit in. Maybe we don't need to tell the others about her being a woman."

"Mr. Smith, I just don't see how it'll work!" Henry glanced in Sam's direction and gave her a once-over.

"She doesn't look like she can stand the trip up to Cumberland Gap, much less St. Louis. I think it's a bad idea."

"Henry, she has no one else to help her and I owe her granddaddy."

Henry shoved his hands in his rough woolen coat pockets and kicked a couple of rocks. "Does she have any provisions?"

"Yes, she does. I'll give her mine too. It won't last but a couple of days, but we always find folks that'll help out."

"If she's going, you have to come along and be in charge of her."

"Thank you, Henry. But I need to double back for a ways and see what I can see. Then, I'll catch up."

"Mr. Smith, you know that's too risky. You come with us now. We'll deal with what comes up later. We're good at what we do. But I admit, I don't like the idea of *knowing* we're followed. We always worry about it, but this. Maybe they won't be able to find us. If they're stupid enough to steal money with the whole Confederate Army around them, they must be plenty stupid. Let's round up everyone. It's almost completely dark now."

"Okay. Her name is Samantha, but she goes by Sam."

Mr. Smith went over to Sam and told her she could go with Henry and the men. She looked over at Henry and nodded, but he turned toward his men and didn't acknowledge. Smudging her face with the mud by the spring was about all she could do besides stay away from everyone except Mr. Smith.

"He knows you're a woman, but he'll go along with

it." Mr. Smith lowered his voice. "Henry won't tell the others about you. We got to keep up and not give him reason to leave us behind."

"I'll keep up, but could you tell me a bit about who they are?"

"Henry Jenkins has been a 'pilot' for over three years now. He's led countless men up to Kentucky. 'Stampeders' they're called. They're men who believe in the Union Cause and want nothing to do with tearing it apart. The men have no slaves. They just want to be left alone, but that's not gonna happen."

Sam nodded her understanding so Mr. Smith went on. "The men with him now are being chased by the Confederates, and there's a reward for their capture. It doesn't matter that the Federals control all Tennessee now. The Confederate sharpshooters are alive and well in East Tennessee, even if their numbers have dwindled. We got to go now."

Henry motioned for all the men to gather round. "Now, men, let's walk. We've got many a mile to cover before sunup. No talking unless you have to and then whisper. Sound travels well in the mountains. These two newcomers are Mr. Smith and Sam."

Henry set out, and the men followed. Sam and Mr. Smith brought up the rear. The going was slow. They picked their way along the rough forest trail, the briars and brambles tripping them up at almost every turn. After about two hours, some men grumbled and rambled on about their need for a rest. Henry ignored the remarks and plodded on.

Sam was glad she had been on the trail for several days. Her legs hurt and cramped, but not as they had at first. Now, she could go on and not embarrass herself or

Mr. Smith by whining or worse, dropping behind. Sam was proud of her silence.

Sam's mind was awhirl even as she put one foot in front of the other. *I don't know what will happen when we get to Kentucky.* Sam thought of her dear grandma and grandpa. *I wish desperately for Uncle Prince to be alive! To have him be here for me and guide me as he always had. He was always there for me, especially after Mama passed.* In her mind's eye, Sam could see her mama now, bedridden, in the cabin's corner, her hair white against the pillow. Mama couldn't get up, but she could still tell wonderful stories.

Sam remembered a particular conversation with Mama about Heaven. Even as a girl, Sam had wondered if there really was a heaven. Mama always said, "Yes, Samantha, it's in the Bible." Sam had asked her that question many times over the years and always got the same answer. Until one day, a day or so before she passed, Sam asked her again to see what she would say. "Mama, you think there really is a heaven?"

Mama wrinkled her forehead and said, "Law, girl! You and the Lord have a fight?"

Sam smiled, lost in her thoughts. Not watching her footing, she tripped over a root. She turned and saw Mr. Smith a little way behind her. The man in front of her stumbled, cursed, and righted himself. Sam knew better than to talk, so she remained silent.

A light rain began to fall, and the wind picked up. Sam put her hat in her pocket and pulled up her hood. After the complaints of needed rest became too many to ignore, Henry called a halt. Sam moved behind Mr. Smith and whispered to him she needed to do some private business. He nodded and stayed put until she returned.

The group had circled around Henry. "You need to ration your food. Try not to eat much. You don't want a heavy belly. We'll rest here for a spell and then move on."

A few men grumbled, but it was generally ignored. Sam and Mr. Smith got out a piece of hardtack and sucked on it. Sam sprinkled a bit of salt on hers, but it made little difference in the taste. They wanted to save their corndodgers as long as they could.

Henry moved among them. "Let's get moving," he whispered. "No talking." They traveled up ridges and down the other side until Sam lost all track of time. Her feet had become leaden, and her breath labored. Heading down the valley, the going became a little easier. Sam was sure she could see a light in the east. *Dawn!*

As they came down out of the trees, Sam could see the valley below. She stopped short in her tracks; Mr. Smith almost ran into her. "Oh, my God!" Sam said. As far as the eye could see to the north and south, a river flowed through the valley.

"What river is that?" Someone farther up the line asked.

"The Holston," Henry said.

Chapter 27

October 1864
North Carolina

R.B. was far behind Sam and the stampeders, just coming down into North Carolina from Virginia. He knew Daniels had joined up with Archer, Jerico and two new men. Tracking Daniels had led him to the other men. They were traveling south on the same path Sam and her people had taken.

Making his plan as he traveled, R.B. thought he would go to Coldiron and try to find Sam. *Why anyone would trust him enough to tell him anything, he didn't know. Yet. Why were Daniels and the others following Sam? They didn't want the salt, only the money. Sam had said that Daniels had the money back. So, what was the deal?*

R.B. stopped for the night, but only made a small fire in the protection of a bunch of rocks. He pulled out his jerky so he wouldn't need to cook. He sat back and gazed into the fire, only to be met by a pair of green eyes.

Chapter 28

October 1864
Eastern Tennessee

Archer, Daniels, Augustus, and the two other men Archer had not seen fit to introduce to the others, camped at the mouth of a small cave on the upper ridge of the Doe Valley.

"Augustus, you need to go out and pick up their trail. You said you were the best tracker in Western North Carolina. Best you start earning that title." Archer told him menacingly.

"It's dark now. I'll pick it up first thing in the morning. You'll see. We'll get them."

"You'd better find them because we're in Union-held territory. I, for one, do not want to go to a prison camp."

"We have our Federal jackets. We can fit in if we come up on any Yankees." Daniels sounded matter-of-fact.

"Well, I'm glad you're so sure of this, but we best come up with a better plan."

One of the two newcomers spoke up. "We think we know who's leading her and where they're going."

"When were you going to let us know?" Archer spat with a frown.

"When we were sure of it." Ed, one of the new men,

scraped his fingernails with a blade. "This path we're taking is used by pilots who direct Unionists to Kentucky."

"East Tennessee is held by the Union now. Why would anyone want to go to Kentucky now?" Archer asked.

"Don't know, but that's where we are."

"Who's guiding her?" Archer asked.

"Could be one of several we heard of. Daniel Ellis or Mr. Smith," Ed answered.

"What you mean, 'Mr. Smith'?"

"Only goes by that. Don't know his first name or if he has one."

Archer shook his head. "Let's get some sleep. Augustus, you take first watch. Jerico, you follow him up. We'll head out at first light."

Chapter 29

October 1864
Northeast Tennessee

"This is the Holston River," Henry informed the men. "We're going on across and will rest on the other side. Strip off your clothes and put them in your pack if you can, your boots too. Wrap everything in a bundle and find a stick or use your rifle to keep it above your head. The river is low right now, so I don't think we'll have any trouble keeping our guns and ammunition dry. Above all else, keep your guns dry."

Sam's heart filled with dread as she looked at the river. *Not again!*

Mr. Smith saw the fear in Sam's face and her shoulders shook. "Now, Sam, this is a wide river, but it's low right now. I doubt it comes up past your waist at the deepest part," Mr. Smith said.

Sam looked at Mr. Smith with trepidation.

"Don't worry. If it gets deeper than I thought, I'll carry your pack."

The men did as they were bid and then sat to get their boots and stockings off.

Sam kept her eyes down and took off her boots and stockings. Most of her blisters had scabbed over but were still painful. Everyone stood up and walked over to the river's edge.

"Let's go— slowly now— don't hurry," Henry said.

Mr. Smith took his boots and jacket off and piled them on his pack. He hurried out of his clothes and poked them into his pack. Sam put her boots into her pack and stood beside Mr. Smith. The bank was littered with rocks, but it wasn't too steep. The men waded in.

A mist formed over the river as the sun came up. The water was freezing but not swift. Henry was in the lead; Sam and Mr. Smith were last. She was glad the water came up past the others' private parts before she stepped in.

Sam felt for her footing before putting her weight down on the smooth and slippery rocks. Mr. Smith walked beside her as the water rose past her thighs. So cold…Sam's head shook, and her teeth rattled. Her arms ached almost immediately from holding her pack above her head.

"It's gonna be fine. You're doing real good!" Mr. Smith said as he made his way through the dark water.

Henry was the first one out. He kept watch over the valley while the others came out of the frigid water, dripping icicles and thankful to be out. Sam was the last to come out of the river. She immediately turned her back on the men when she overheard a young man with a headful of black curly hair.

"I reckon why did he leave his clothes on? Now, he's gonna freeze until they dry."

Sam gathered her things and strode over to Mr. Smith. "You think we can build a fire?"

"I'll ask."

Sam watched as Mr. Smith went over to Henry and posed his question. Henry looked around at the forest at the edge of the clearing and gestured toward the trees.

"Everyone, fill up your water bags and canteens. We'll go over to the trees and make camp for today. Don't eat up all your food. Sleep as best you can," Henry said.

Sam was freezing in the early morning air. She helped Mr. Smith gather up firewood and get a nice fire going. She got out the makings for fresh corndodgers. Patting and squeezing the dough onto the end of their sticks, they roasted their corndodgers in the fire. The hot bread warmed them.

Mr. Smith walked over to the men who clustered around their fire. Sam couldn't hear what they said, but the young curly-haired one reached into his pack and then handed Mr. Smith a small bag. Mr. Smith nodded to the boy and handed him something. He walked back and offered the bag to Sam. "Open it."

Sam gasped. "Coffee! Real coffee!"

"It's already roasted."

Mr. Smith took the bag and laid out a few of the beans on a flat rock. He placed his rifle butt on the rock and slowly rocked it back and forth, crushing the beans into grounds. Swiping the grounds into his hand, he grinned to see Sam already had a pot in her hand. "Let's boil 'em up!"

Taking long sips of the hot brew was comforting. "Almost feels like home, or at least what home used to be," Sam whispered. The hot fire dried out Sam's clothing enough for her to snuggle into her coat and lay down. She pulled her hat over her face and promptly went to sleep.

It couldn't have been more than a few minutes before Mr. Smith's hoarse voice awoke her. "Sam! Sam! Quick, wake up! Riders coming!"

Sam tried to wake up from a deep sleep. Disoriented,

she stumbled while trying to get up. Mr. Smith had already gathered up their packs. "We need to move farther back into the woods. Henry is scouting out the riders. He'll be back directly and tell us what to do."

Sam did Mr. Smith's bidding, and they moved farther back into the woods with their backs to the huge balsam trees. Sam could hear the hoofbeats now as they thundered by at a furious pace.

Henry came up after a few minutes. "Federal patrol. They aren't looking for anyone at that pace. They're headed for somewhere in particular. Let's sleep if we can and we'll head out at sundown."

****

At sundown they started out. They made better time this night, which made everyone feel better about their sore feet. At sunup, Henry told them, "I'm going to risk moving during the day. I know a good man living near here and want to find out if he knows the whereabouts of any soldiers, Federal or Reb. Follow me."

They moved through overgrown fields, over broken-down fences and briefly down a narrow road. They finally came up to an old cabin perched on the side of a hill. The stampeders hid in the woods while Henry approached the cabin.

A little while later, Henry returned to his group and shared what he had learned from the old man in the cabin. "We're almost on the Virginia border. There are several Reb companies just over the ridge. We need to hide out here till dark and then make our way over to Clinch Mountain. We'll have to travel hard through the night. For now, get some food and rest." They all settled into the shadows of the trees, laying low out of sight. Henry stood guard.

After several hours of respite, Henry instructed the group. "It's time. Let's go."

They pushed hard at sundown and came across a stream where they drank and bathed their aching, sore feet and then pushed on through the night. Sam walked on and stared at the back of the man in front of her. They went over flat ground, fields, and hills until all moved by rote.

Fog shrouded the stampeders as morning broke. "We'll stop here until the fog clears," Henry said.

The men huddled in their group, and Sam and Mr. Smith sat at the edge. "We don't have but a few corndodgers left. Do you think we'll be able to get some supplies somewhere? Do you know where we are?" Sam asked Mr. Smith.

"Henry is aware of folks who will help out along the route. I'll talk to him about it."

Mr. Smith walked over to where Henry leaned against a tree. Sam couldn't hear their voices but could tell by the way Mr. Smith stood, he was imploring Henry for some better information. Mr. Smith came back to Sam after a few minutes.

"Well, with the fog, he's uncertain of where we are, and he wants to keep that quiet, but thinks we're close to Clinch Mountain. He knows a family that always helps him with his people, but it has been more than a year since he's come this way. The family may not be there now, what with all the fighting going on around here. We'll just have to wait and see."

The fog lifted as the sun came up over the ridge. The Clinch Valley spread out before them. Henry smiled and shook his rifle in the air. Clinch Mountain was more than one mountain, it was an area, but people called it that. It was a long prominent ridge running from Southwest Virginia almost to Knoxville. "Okay, boys, we're at the base of Clinch Mountain. Are any of you out of provisions?"

Two young men raised their hands. "Well, sir, we didn't have much to begin with, and we are plumb out."

The other two men that came with them at Elizabethton spoke up. "We got some cornpone for today, but not enough to share. We got a handful of meal, that's all."

"Well, I'm sorry but we might be able to get a good meal from a family I know. That doesn't help you today, but if we travel hard all night tonight, we'll get there in the morning," Henry said.

Sam and Mr. Smith were aware they only had enough for themselves for the day. But she didn't say anything, and neither did Mr. Smith. Mr. Smith made a fire and Sam mixed up the last of the cornpone. *What I wouldn't give for a biscuit or a piece of chicken-the thought makes my mouth water, I can near about taste it.*

"Sam, you try to sleep. I'll go over and talk to Henry, then I'll get some sleep too."

Sam pulled her boots and stockings off to inspect her poor feet. There were new blisters on the tops of her toes. Sam smeared some of the salve on them and put her stockings and boots back on. She was worried her blisters might become infected, and intended to wash her stockings as soon as she could.

Everyone was hungry, tired, and sore, but they set out again at dark. It had grown colder, even with the cloud cover. A light snow began to fall around midnight. Sam was warm enough with her hood on, but it was hard to walk with your hands in your pockets on the rough trail. When her fingers became numb, she put them in her mouth to warm them. Mr. Smith spoke now and then as he walked behind her to make sure she wasn't asleep on her feet. Sam felt so grateful to Mr. Smith. What would she have done without him? She hoped she could make it up to him at some point.

The travelers crossed Little Poor Valley, Copper Ridge, Copper Creek and endless hills and valleys toward their destination: the Clinch River. They were almost there by sunup. Sam looked out over the valley and saw a small plume of smoke. She hoped it was coming from the cabin that Mr. Jenkins had spoken of.

"Let's call a halt right here," Henry said. "I'll make my way over to the cabin to see what I can find out. Don't make a fire just yet. Just rest. I'll be back as soon as I can."

"You think them people you spoke of will feed us?" The curly-haired boy asked Mr. Smith.

"I'm sure they will if they can."

Sam watched Mr. Smith pull his rifle scabbard from one shoulder and his pack off the other and then sit down on a fallen tree. "Let's think of what we might get to eat down there. I find it a wonderful pastime," Mr. Smith suggested as he folded his hands in his lap.

"It makes me hungrier to think about it."

"I'm so hungry, it don't matter."

Sam found a log and sat down to wait. The others found a place and did the same. Sam hadn't really looked at the other men in the group. She had tried to keep her distance so as not to invite scrutiny, but from where she sat, she could easily get a look without being noticed. The four men they had met when they had joined up with Mr. Jenkins were dressed in civilian clothes. Their tattered slouch hats and homespun showed years of wear. Two of them looked alike but the other two were big burley men. When one young man gazed her way, Sam quickly looked away.

Although it was only about an hour before Mr. Jenkins came back, it seemed like forever. By his long confident strides, he looked like he had good news. They all gathered round him.

"Good news! The good people say that they will be glad to help us. I told them there were seven of us, but they said they had had a good harvest this year, in spite of the drought. I told them we could pay. If any of you can chip in, they will be grateful. Although you can't eat money, it will help them later on."

They gathered up their packs and made their way behind Mr. Jenkins down the valley to the cabin. Sam could smell the chicken stew from the yard, making her mouth water. Everyone chattered about how they were nigh on to starvin' to death. The man of the house opened the door and bade them come in and get a bite. Mr. Jenkins motioned them on in, and he brought up the rear. Sam knew he had to be as hungry as the rest, but he waited.

"We'll not introduce ourselves, ma'am, if that's all right. Don't want to be subjecting you to any scrutiny later if you understand my meaning," Mr. Jenkins said.

The farmer and his pretty wife nodded, understanding at once. She spoke, "You poor souls ain't the first we've fed in this long war." She had a ready smile that dimpled her plump cheeks. "That old rooster flogged me one too many times and now he's in the pot. Hope you like cathead dumplings with your stew." She laughed. "Help yourselves."

"That smell is enough to bring the angels down to earth, ma'am," Mr. Smith said.

They all gathered with hat in hands around the table. Sam removed her hat, although fearful it would give her away. The farmer's wife gave Sam a knowing look and nodded toward the table, as she set a plate of chicken and dumplings in front of her. Sam sat down, noticing that look in her eyes but didn't think to worry about it.

The men were about to dig in when the farmer began to pray. "Lord, please help these good people on their journey. We ask your blessing on this food and these good people. Amen." Forks flew then!

Sam was so thankful to enjoy such a meal. She didn't care if she ever ate cornbread again. But she had to admit that smelling it baking in an oven was better than burning on a stick over a campfire. There was enough for everyone to have a big plate of chicken and dumplings and good buttermilk besides. There was even a pat of butter to put on the cornbread!

They thanked the good people for their wonderful meal. Sam fished out a dollar from her belt and handed it to the lady. She felt that the meal had saved her today and was thankful. The lady gave her that same look and tightened her lips as she mouthed a thank you.

She knows my secret. Sam fretted only a moment. She trusted the lady would never say a word.

"Let's get on over to the edge of the woods and sleep all we can. I know that a full belly will be a great help in that today," Henry said.

Mr. Smith patted his stomach and smiled at Sam, who smiled back. Sam sat down beside her pack, smoothed it for a pillow, and curled herself into a ball. She pulled her coat over herself tightly and promptly went to sleep.

Late afternoon saw them on the move again. Henry knew they were more at risk in the valleys, but they needed to push on. The prospect of actually seeing their path ahead cheered them all enough for them to press harder to go farther. At sunset, they came to the swiftly running Clinch River.

Henry glanced around to make sure everyone was present. "Hold here for a few minutes; I'll be right back." He walked toward the river's edge and headed north for a bit and found the raft.

Henry walked back to the group. "We're in luck, boys. There's a raft just up the river. How it's still there is a mystery, but I'm delighted to find it. The rope is still tied to a tree on the other side. It's not big enough for us to all to go over at once, but it won't take long to make two crossings."

They gathered up their packs and walked to where the raft lay on the bank. The raft was ten twelve foot long small logs tied together at each end and in the middle. A side iron loop on each end held the rope that was attached to the rope across the river. Henry picked up the long pole that would help push them across the river.

"Okay, who wants to go first?" Henry asked.

The two young men raised their hands. The other two men with them cautiously raised their hands, too.

"Good. Let's get on the raft."

The raft was close enough to the edge for them to take a big step onto it. They sat with their packs on their laps. Henry got on and said to Sam and Mr. Smith, "I'll be back for you directly."

Sam and Mr. Smith watched as Henry pushed the raft along with the pole. The rope holding the raft fast to the crossing rope strained against the current. Sam was terrified of having to cross the river this way— or any way, for that matter. She realized how angry and strong rivers could be.

"I need a private moment, please." Sam told Mr. Smith and then walked into the woods. She fought back nausea. She didn't want to empty her stomach of her precious food. She patted her cheeks and took deep breaths.

Henry made the crossing without mishap and started back for Sam and Mr. Smith. The two settled themselves on the raft, and Henry pushed them back into the current.

"Henry, I can help with the poling, if you need me to. You must be plumb tuckered," Mr. Smith said.

"I'm fine, Mr. Smith, but thank you." Henry looked at lean Mr. Smith with his homespun garments hanging from his bones and shook his head.

The current was strong, but the rope held, and they were safe on the other side before long. Sam got off the raft and looked back over the river. It didn't seem so wide and angry now she was on the other side of it.

"Let's rest a few minutes and fill up our water bags. Then we need to press on."

"How many more rivers do we have to cross, Mr. Jenkins?" John asked.

"Just one more big river. The Powell."

Sam heard but didn't comment. She just wouldn't think about the river but would think about the fact that she got away from Daniels and his gang and hoped they hadn't hurt anyone or stayed in Coldiron long.

Mr. Smith took out his spyglass and scanned the ridges. Sam saw him shake his head, like something was wrong. Then she watched as he went over to talk to

Henry about it. "What do you think, Henry? I didn't see anyone tracking us. That worries me. Are we so clever that we can't be seen or has Daniels lost our trail?"

Henry removed his spyglass from his eye with a worried look on his face as well. "Either they've lost our trail and given up or they're waiting to surprise us. I don't know who they are, so it's hard to cipher."

"From what Sam has told me, they'll kill a body in a heartbeat. That Daniels killed her Uncle Prince in cold blood. I know she's scared and about at the end of her rope. Now we're out of food to boot."

"When we get down to the Powell River, I'm sure we can get a meal. The people I know have lived there a long time. Let's move on. We've got a few miles to make before sunup."

Everyone was hungry and had tried filling up on water. Sam put her pack on her back and with a weak smile said to Mr. Smith, "It'll be fine, I know."

The weary travelers plodded single file, putting one foot in front of the other. The going wasn't as rough as it had been. A full moon helped them find their way. A gray morning dawned when they came down onto a small plateau out of the trees, above a river. Standing there in awe, they gauged the enormity of the river.

Sam followed the men down, but was at her breaking point. *I just can't cross another river!* They were almost at the river's edge when Sam turned to Mr. Smith and screamed, "Please, just kill me! I can't go on, I can't cross another river! Just kill me now!"

Mr. Smith couldn't have been more surprised if she'd bit him. He reached out to pat her shoulder. "I'm not gonna kill you! Now, we can do this!" Mr. Smith spoke in a calm voice, trying to reassure her, as he had done others before her, but she was having none of it.

"Then let me die here! Just leave me here! I don't care!" she cried.

Startled, the men just stared at Sam with her high-pitched voice. Looking at each other with widened eyes and mouths open, they didn't know what to do about this outburst.

"Well, damn, she's a gal! I never heard a man make that kind of noise!" the curly-haired John said.

Sam cried hysterically and held her head in her hands. She crumpled to her knees but couldn't stop crying. Everything had piled up and she just couldn't get herself to stop. Henry strode over and shook her.

"Stop! Right now! Get a hold of yourself. You've just given yourself away." He shook her again.

She looked up at his angry face and started to sob. "I'm sor…ry." Sam hiccupped. She stood up and turned her face away. Because of her outburst, they now knew she was a woman.

Mr. Smith was at a complete loss about how to deal with a screaming woman. Never had to deal with such in all his life. He patted her shoulder again. "It's okay, we'll get along. Try to get ahold of yourself."

Sam wiped her face with her hands then on her sleeve. Squaring her shoulders, she faced the men and apologized in a soft voice, "I'm sorry, I didn't mean –"

Henry interrupted with an upheld hand, then turned and spoke to the men. "Okay, now you know we've brought along a woman and I know you all think it's bad luck. I thought so too. But she's here because she needed my help. Dangerous men killed some of her family and now have it in for her. Just like you all. It's almost the same, so you know how it feels." The curly haired John raised his hand but Henry ignored him.

Henry went on. "We don't have much farther to go. We got to cross this river. No other way." He gave Sam a rugged look. "On the other side, we'll have food and shelter. Now, let's get our gear and get ready. We need to do the same as the other crossing. Put our stuff on our heads and try to keep it dry. She's already seen you in your altogether, so don't get your clothes wet just to prove a point."

"All that screeching has got my nerves all tore *up!*" John said as he picked up his pack.

"She's quiet now. Women do that from time to time. They're known for it." Joe was matter-of-fact.

The river was swift but wasn't running too high. But both Mr. Smith and Henry knew Sam was too short to walk across. Henry nodded to Mr. Smith to get him to come closer and they walked out of earshot.

"We have to have a talk about her when we get to the other side. You know that, don't you?" Henry asked Mr. Smith.

"Yeah, I do." Mr. Smith spat and looked at the ground. He paused a minute in thought.

"Henry, let's do it this way. She can't walk it, it's too deep, and she doesn't know how to swim. She's going to have to hang onto someone. I'm tall enough, I can help her. Do you think you can carry her pack? Maybe one of the others can carry mine? I've noticed a couple of the other packs are almost empty. Can we ask them?" Mr. Smith pleaded.

"Yeah, I'll ask. I'm sure someone'll volunteer."

Henry turned to the men behind him. "Anyone volunteer to carry Mr. Smith's pack over with his own?"

"I will," Joe offered.

Sam took her coat and hat off and put it in her pack. She pulled off her boots and stuffed them in too. Mr. Smith did the same and handed his pack to Joe. "Thank you, Joe." Henry took Sam's pack.

Everyone was ready, or as ready as they would get. The men who wore small clothes left them on but those that didn't were naked. Sam kept her head down, as much for them as for herself. They started across the frigid water. Joe and John waded out and soon the water was up to their chests. Mark and Luke were taller and were farther across before the water reached their armpits. They kept their packs with their rifles above their heads. Mr. Smith and Sam went in next. Sam waded as far as she could and then treaded water and held onto Mr. Smith's shoulder for quite a ways. Henry came in next.

The icy water splashed over Sam's face. Her teeth chattered, and she clutched for Mr. Smith's shoulder but couldn't find it. She instinctively pawed the water and was surprised to find she could still keep her head above the water.

"That's it, Sam. Keep pawing the water and kicking your feet. You'll make it. I'm right beside you." Mr. Smith was still beside her, the water up to his chin. Henry was behind him, packs above his head.

Joe, John, Mark and Luke came out of the river and dropped their packs to the ground. They bent double, panting and wringing their arms to get the feeling back in them. Sam found her footing and then she and Mr. Smith clambered out of the water and collapsed onto the dirt bank. Henry waded out, quickly dropped his bundle and sat down, panting. Then they all laughed, and Sam cried and laughed. They had made it!

Henry stood up. "Let's make a fire. We need to get warm."

Everyone who had stripped got themselves as dry as possible and then donned their clothes. Feeling about frozen, Sam hurried to gather wood to make a good fire. The fire blazed and dried her out. Stockings and boots were slipped on, then her warm coat. Sam was thankful that the sun was out, but it was still cold.

All shared the same fire this day. Everyone was exhausted, and Sam fell asleep. Henry watched Sam with mixed emotions. He motioned for Mr. Smith to come away from the fire so they could talk.

"You know Sam can't make it much farther like this. I've had an idea, but I don't know how you or she'll feel about it. You say she wants to get to St. Louis?"

Mr. Smith nodded.

"Well, we'll be in Harlan County, Kentucky by tomorrow morning, Lord willing. As I said earlier, I know people there and we can get a meal. We can ask if they know a way we might take Sam to the Cumberland River. There're boats on that river that can go clear to St. Louis. Then she won't have to walk anymore."

"I think you know how she feels about water by now. How we going to get her to agree to that?"

"I heard tell those boats are like a floating house. You hardly even know you're on the water. I think if she saw one, she would likely change her mind. She could go a long ways in a short amount of time …to get to her folks in St. Louis."

Mr. Smith thought a minute then nodded. "Okay, we can talk to her when she wakes up. And Henry, thank you."

Henry nodded, and they walked back to the fire and lay down to rest.

Chapter 30

October 1864
Coldiron, North Carolina

R.B. saw the general store not far away on his left as he rode into Coldiron in the early morning. He tied up and walked into the dimly lit store. There were several old men camped around the wood stove. The talk was nonstop, and tobacco juice slid down the side of the spittoon.

As good luck would have it, Shreldi Poole was at the counter and her husband, Wallon, was helping a boy with fishing line and some new fishhooks.

R.B. sauntered over to Mr. Poole. "Might I have a word, Mr. Poole?"

Mr. Poole looked up and smiled but then his eyes got big when he remembered the circumstances of their meeting. No one was supposed to know they had been to Saltville. Mr. Poole motioned for R.B. to come closer and whispered, "Come on out here." He motioned to the adjoining room.

"Mr. Poole, I've come to see about Sam."

"Well, you know, none of us has said anything about our journey. The Home Guard, you know. They would take our salt. We divided it up amongst those that would keep it secret where we got it. We didn't have enough for the store, you understand."

Mr. Poole's whisper was nonstop, but R.B. finally got a word in. "It's okay. I'm not here to make trouble. I won't say a word about how we met or the salt. But I'm glad we met because you know you can trust me. I need to know where Sam is. Have any of you seen the man who killed Prince Thomas? I tracked him and he led me to Archer and the gang he was with when they robbed the salt office. I know they headed south." He paused and looked into Mr. Poole's eyes directly. "Probably straight for Coldiron after Sam."

Mr. Poole shook his head and refused to meet R.B.'s eyes.

"Mr. Poole, please, I'm not here to hurt her. I want to help. But I need to find Daniels and the others. Please, tell me what you know."

"Mr. Royster, we saw Mr. Daniels and his gang. They were in the saloon three days ago. Grandpa Coldiron was heard talking to another person about Sam 'going to Tennessee,' although no one was ever supposed to mention anything about Sam. One of the Lambeth boys may have overheard, and those boys tattle ever thing they know. We're so sorry. We're worried for Sam, sir, very worried."

R.B. tried to be calm, but his insides churned. "Where is Grandpa Coldiron's place? I need to talk to him." *How many days had passed? Three? Four?*

"Take the road heading west out of town, Black Bear Trail. Go about two miles, and you'll see several smaller trails leading away from the main trail. Take the one to the right. It will take you to his cabin."

"Thank you, Mr. Poole." R.B. hurried out the door, mounted Soldier, and took off west at a fast trot. *I have to find Sam and keep her safe. I'll find Daniels and his gang and kill 'em. I don't have to bring 'em back alive. That's going to be too much trouble. I'll get the money and give it back to the salt office, find Sam, and make sure she's all right.*

R.B. found where the trail branched off from the main road. He took the one to the right and hoped he wouldn't come across any bears. There wasn't enough time to tackle a bear. R.B. walked Soldier along the trail covered with October leaves. A creek hugged the trail in most spots but wandered away as it grew steeper where thick forests grew tall. He started down a shadowed grade and thought he heard a voice shout, "get on there." Soldier nickered and tossed his head.

"There, boy, it's fine. Let's go on in." In a small clearing to the right, R.B. saw a cabin with several outbuildings surrounding it. "Hello the house!" R.B. shouted, hoping to alert the household and not get shot.

An old man and woman came out onto the porch. The man must have run his hands through his hair because the silver mass was sticking straight up. The woman wiped her hands on an old apron and squinted to see.

"May I get down and speak to you, sir?"

"Would you care to tell me who you are and what your business is here with us?" Grandpa tried to keep his voice even, though he was leery of the Confederate uniform the man wore.

"I've come to see about Sam, Samantha. I'm Major R.B. Royster, sir."

Grandpa gave a start and looked at Grandma. She imperceptibly nodded.

"I'm dismounting now. I don't want to startle you." R.B. saw no gun but wanted to be prepared. He dismounted, tied Soldier up at the post, and walked over to the porch with hat in hand. He had to gain their trust.

"Sir, I know you have no reason to trust me, but I want to tell you I mean Sam no harm. I came here to…well…, I'm not sure, but I wanted to know if she was safe. Now I've learned Daniels and his gang have found out she's headed for Tennessee. I need to find out where in Tennessee so I can reach her before they do."

Grandpa was taken aback at his revelation and shifted his eyes to Grandma and back to R.B. He ran his hand through his hair and scowled. "Go on."

R.B. continued. "Too many days have passed for me to try to track them. I need to know where she might be headed so I can get there before Daniels. Is she dressed like a man?" He turned his hat round and round by the brim, hoping desperately they would confide in him.

"She told us about you. I recognize you from her description. How you saved them from Daniels and his gang." Grandpa looked at Grandma and she nodded. "Come into the house."

"Thank you, sir."

R.B. walked into the cabin, where Grandpa motioned him to sit in one of the rocking chairs.

"We don't have no coffee, but I can brew you up some ginger tea," Grandma said.

"Please don't go to any trouble. I need to get on the trail as soon as I can."

Grandpa peered at R.B. "She's on her way to St. Louis. Mr. Smith is piloting her through Tennessee and Kentucky. I'm not sure how she's going to get to St. Louis. Mr. Smith thought it best that we don't know all the details. There're trails into Tennessee from here due west to Trade, Tennessee, and the trail winds through the mountains to Elizabethton, Tennessee. The thing about trails is that no good trash follows them too."

"This Mr. Smith— he's a guide, a pilot? You trust him?"

"With my life."

"I'm going to have to try to find them. The trouble is, Daniels is way ahead of me. I'm an excellent tracker and a crack shot. I need to be one step ahead, but I'm far behind now."

"But you're on your own. Don't you have nobody to go with you?" Grandma asked.

"I'm always on my own. Now that I know where they're going, maybe I can catch up. But it would be easier if I had a guide too."

"Son, you can't trust nobody in these mountains. One thing I do know, Mr. Smith will only travel at night and hide during the day. And you're going into territory that is held by the Yankees. You're going to have to be careful." He eyed the sleeves of his jacket.

"I have another shirt, don't worry. I have a Yankee gun, too. That'll help."

"He was bent on getting her to Kentucky first. I'm sorry I don't know how to find her. We was just trying to get her away because Daniels wanted to kill her. We didn't have no time to plan more." Grandpa's eyes watered, and he wiped his face.

"I better be on my way. Thank you for trusting me. Did she live with you?"

"No, she lives over the next ridge, at her mama's place. After her mama passed, Prince stayed with her a lot."

"I would tell you I'd send word, but you know that will be near impossible."

"We'll just pray for your safety and Sam's."

R.B. stood up to leave and offered his hand to Grandpa. They shook, R.B. slapped his hat back on and strode out the door. He mounted Soldier and touched his hat as he left the yard and cantered down the trail. As he came over the ridge, he saw a cabin about halfway down the mountain. No smoke came from the chimney. He rode into the yard and called out. Leaves littered the porch, and the place looked deserted. A large barn was visible nearby. Past the barn, the mountains towered high.

R.B. dismounted and tied up at the post. He went up the steps of the porch and knocked on the door. Turning the knob, he found the door unlocked. He walked into a large dimly-lit room with bedsteads in the left corners. He saw a fireplace in the middle of the back wall and a stove and cupboards on the right. Stairsteps went up the side of the wall to the loft above. "Anyone here?" he called out.

R.B. started up the stairs and paused to listen. Hearing nothing, he went on up to the loft. An iron bedstead was in one corner. A treadle sewing machine was at the top of the stairs and opposite him was a large table. He walked over to the table and saw his reflection in the tall mirror in the corner.

He looked down at the table and reached over to touch a silky pile of golden hair. "She's cut her hair," R.B. said to the empty room. *I remember Mama saying, "A woman's hair is her glory."*

R.B. looked at his reflection again and saw his sharpshooter badge on his hat. *How proud I was when I earned that badge. All the hours I practiced, the tests for distance shooting, the skirmish details I led with the other would-be sharpshooters. That was my glorious moment.* He removed his hat and pulled the red badge off. Carefully, he placed it beside the pile of golden hair.

Then he turned and raced down the stairs and out the door to his horse. He rummaged through his saddlebags to find his other shirt. Peeled off his jacket and wondered. *Should I keep it or throw it away. What if it gets me shot?* He started to pull off the badge on the sleeve, but changed his mind. Rolling up the jacket, he stuffed it in his saddlebag. R.B. buttoned up the coarse shirt and tucked the tail into his britches. The biting wind made him hurry into his other coat. Seeing he left the door open, he ran back up the steps and shut it. Urgency drove him on. Mounting Soldier, R.B. gave him his heels as he hurried westward down the mountain to find Sam.

Chapter 31

October 1864
Trade, Tennessee

After a couple of close calls with bushwhackers, R.B. rode into the town of Trade, Tennessee. Early snow fell the day before but didn't lay, so he hadn't left tracks. The morning sun did little to dispel the chill in the air. R.B. needed supplies and information. By the sign over the door on the frame building to his right, he knew where to get his supplies. Across the street was a two-story building, and the balcony of the second floor had a sign that read "Saloon." Hopefully, he could get a warming drink and some information there.

Several horses were tied up at the saloon and general store. R.B. flinched at the sight of several Federal uniforms among the passersby. He felt as conspicuous as a fly in new milk, although he knew nothing about his appearance should brand him as a Confederate officer.

R.B. dismounted in front of the saloon and tethered Soldier to the post. He saw several other men with gun scabbards hung over their shoulders. R.B. untied his Spencer and shouldered it. He hoped his saddlebags would be safe left on the saddle. People moved along, each with their own place to go. He scanned the street and didn't see any loiterers about.

R.B. stepped through the open double doors of the

saloon and noticed the kerosene lamps on the wall did little to dispel the gloomy interior. He pushed up his hat with a forefinger to survey the room. Tattered civilians stood at the bar to the right of the room emptying whiskey glasses as soon as they were filled. Tables scattered throughout the room were mostly vacant. Directly in front of him to the rear, was a back door. *Always good to know.*

Several men sat around the back table, where cigar smoke hugged the ceiling. It looked to be a somber group. No loud talk, they just sat quietly with their drinks. The men at the bar, on the other hand, were noisily happy about something. One man slapped another on the back and ordered the barkeep to get him another drink.

R.B. walked to the end of the bar nearest the quiet table and asked the barkeep for a whiskey. When the barkeep set the drink in front of him, R.B. asked the location of the livery.

"End of the street, on the left. He don't have no horses left, but he has fodder for yer horse, if that be what yer needin."

"Thank you, it is."

R.B. pondered how he could get information. No one trusted anyone anymore. How could he get directions without giving himself and his mission away? He couldn't just ask if anyone had seen a gang come through. Gangs came through all the time. He certainly couldn't ask about Sam or Mr. Smith by name.

"That'll be two bits." The barkeep wiped the bar.

R.B. laid the money on the bar and sipped his whiskey, or what passed for whiskey.

He could hear some of what was being said at the

table behind him.

"Kentucky…stampeders…pilot…" R.B. perked up and ordered another drink.

A small man with a broad hat was talking. "Now, listen, Coldiron, you said you'd pilot them, and we need you to do it."

R.B. cocked his head to the side to see who answered to the name. A slim man with a slouch hat spoke through his beard.

"Yeah, I did. But you didn't tell me who I'd be piloting till now. I pure and T despise them." Coldiron rose from the table. "I'm going to check on the horses. I need a bit of air." He grabbed his coat from the chair and walked out the door.

R.B. drained his glass and followed him.

Coldiron strode down the wide dirt street toward the livery. R.B. grabbed Soldier's reins and walked him down the street after Coldiron.

Coldiron walked into the livery and spoke to the owner. "Everything okay in here? You see anything suspicious?"

"No, I sure haven't. Been real quiet, in fact. No new customers …" The owner paused when R.B. walked in.

"How much to feed my horse and bed down for the night?" R.B. asked and nodded to Coldiron.

"Two bits for the horse and fodder, two bits for you," the liveryman said.

R.B. fished the money out of his pocket and handed it to the man. The man pointed to the last stall. R.B. nodded and walked Soldier through the livery and down to the last stall. It was warmer here. The place smelled of hay and manure, comforting smells to someone who had spent countless nights in the open.

R.B. cautiously looked around and saw Coldiron checking the saddles and gear of several horses. He stopped in front of a black gelding. The horse nickered and tossed his head.

"Good boy!" Coldiron said as he ran his hands over the horse's head and checked the bridle.

All the other horses were still saddled, and it gave R.B. pause. He left the saddle on Soldier, too— for now. R.B. looked up and caught Coldiron's eye but continued to put hay in Soldier's stall. Coldiron started to walk away. R.B. spoke. "Wait up. Would you mind if I asked you a question?"

Coldiron stopped and turned his tall frame about and looked at R.B. He rested his hands on the butts of the revolvers on his hips. "Round here, asking questions ain't too smart."

"Well, this is important. I've trusted no one for a long time, but now, I feel I need to start with you. What do you say?"

Coldiron looked down and away, rubbing his hand over his face. He eyed the man from head to foot with a slight scowl as he bit his lip. After a pause, he asked. "Okay, what is it you need to know?"

"I heard the man call you Coldiron."

"Yes, I am."

"Would you happen to know a Samantha Coldiron?" R.B. could tell from Coldiron's eyes that he did know her, even though it appeared he was trying to hide it. "I'm taking a chance by telling you this, but since your name is Coldiron, I'm hoping it won't put her in more danger. I'm hunting for Samantha. She took off from the town of Coldiron a week ago. She's being hunted by a gang of thieves who want her dead."

"Why in hell would a gang of thieves be after Sam?"

R.B.'s pulse leaped when Coldiron used her nickname. "So, you *do* know her."

"I'm her brother Sidney."

R.B.'s smile was wide. He held out his hand and Sidney shook it. "We need to talk, but I'm about to starve to death. Is there an eating place here?"

"Yes, there's a hotel here that serves up some pretty good grub. If we hurry, there might be something left."

"Your horses are safe here," the livery owner said as he walked over to a corner to inspect a bridle.

R.B. nodded to him, and he and Sidney left for the hotel, a two-story frame house. A sign that said "Grayson's" hung from the second-story veranda.

"This looks fancy. I probably don't have enough money to eat here," R.B. said.

"Nah, they don't charge but two bits." Sidney shook his head. "Times are hard. They serve stew about every meal and sometimes we even get a biscuit."

"I've not had a biscuit in so long I about forgot what they tasted like."

The men walked in and found themselves in a room filled with tables and chairs. A few men were still at the tables with empty plates. A huge iron chandelier filled with candles lit the room. Muddy footprints marred the floor. A small counter was on the right, with a large ledger open in the center. A rather heavy-set man came through a back door toward the two men carrying a big blue enamel coffeepot.

"Do you have any grub left?" Sidney asked.

"We have a bit of venison stew left. Set yourselves down and I'll bring it out."

R.B. and Sidney made their way over to an empty

table close to the fireplace that took up the entire wall. A fire was exactly what they needed, along with some hot food. R.B. took off his hat and ran his hands through his long, dark hair, and tried to look presentable. He put his hat on the chair beside him. Sidney did the same.

"Been a long time since I used my manners," Sidney said as he smoothed his dark blond hair and black beard.

The man came out with two bowls of stew and a couple of big chunks of cornbread. Steam rose above the bowls as he set the food in front of them. "I'll be back with some coffee."

"Thank you kindly, Mr. Robert," Sidney said.

"Well, the coffee is made from parched corn, but it's hot," Robert said.

R.B. nodded his thanks to Robert as he walked off to get the coffee. The men were ravenous, so there was not much conversation until their bowls were empty. They sipped their coffee from heavy, chipped cups.

"Okay, so how do you know Sam?"

R.B. filled him in on the details that led up to his arrival in Trade. When he got to the part where Daniels killed his Uncle Prince, Sidney's expression changed.

"Uncle Prince was more a daddy to us than an uncle. I've been gone a long time, but always thought he would be there when I went back." He shook his head.

They were on their third cup of coffee by the time R.B. finished his tale.

"Okay, where do I come in?"

"Do you know someone who could give me advice on how best to get to Kentucky? I'm a scout, but I don't know this country. I'm sure there are trails, but ....what?"

Sidney smiled. "Yes, I know someone who can do that. You can trust him, too."

"Can you tell me where to find him?"

"Right here, it's me." Sidney pointed to his chest with his thumb.

"Well, G. Rover Cripes!" R.B. said and slapped his thigh.

"Yes, I'm a pilot for men that want to get to Kentucky. 'Course, since the Federals have been here for a while now, there haven't been too many stampedes lately."

"Stampedes?"

"That's what we call them. Tennessee men that can't fight for slavery stampede up to Kentucky to join the Union. Right now, it's mostly Confederate men trying to get away from other Confederate men who have it in for them for some reason or the other. Rebels don't like it if you decide to help the North, or if they even *think* you're helping the North."

"How long you been doing this?"

"Since the Conscription law in 1862. The Secesh came through the mountains and grabbed up whoever they could. Depending on who was in charge, you either faced being shot immediately or taken away to jail if you refused. I lit out as soon as I knew they were on their way. But, I want you to know, I'm as southern as they come. My people have been here in these mountains for 100 years. I just ain't going to kill other men so rich men can keep their slaves."

Sidney continued. "I was lucky to meet some men who were pilots as soon as I came over. I went with them many times to learn the trails. There were so many at first. We had to keep the number of men in the groups small, so that meant that we had to go on a lot more trips. They needed all the pilots they could get. We traveled

207

mostly at night, walking. You can't hide a horse very well or keep him quiet on the trail. I only have a horse now because I found him. Most other pilots don't have a horse. But like I said, not as many coming over now."

"I need to get Daniels and his gang before they get to Sam. A Mr. Smith was her pilot. You know him?"

"Yes, I do. She's in good hands, but R.B., this trail is very hard, very dangerous. Sam is tough, but she's a woman. She has her limits, as we all do."

"My aim is to get rid of Daniels and Archer. It's my job to get the money back and I'll do that. If I eliminate the threat to her, I can get her back home safe."

"Mr. Smith will probably take her through to Harlan County, Kentucky. He knows people there. That's what I'm thinking. R.B., we're going to have to ride day and night to catch up. You up to that?" Sidney was dead serious.

R.B. narrowed his eyes. "Yes, I am. I'm a scout and a sharpshooter, remember? I've been through four years of war. I'm a Major in the 4th Virginia Reserves. My officer's coat is in my saddlebags. You all right with that?"

Sidney nodded his head. "Yes, I am." He looked sideways at R.B. "You got another stake in this? One you're not telling me?" Sidney smiled at R.B.'s sheepish grin.

"I need to clean up in here, ya'll mind going on out?" Robert asked.

"Sure, we're going. Sorry," R.B. said.

R.B. and Sidney walked back to the livery. "We can supply up in the morning. These guys I'm with, they want me to take someone else, but I'll explain."

"Just give them the barest details. We can't let

anyone else know about the money or Sam."

"Right." Sidney hesitated. "It's good to be able to trust someone again."

R.B. nodded and watched Sidney as he left the livery. R.B. settled in the hay in front of Soldier's stall. He wasn't asleep when Sidney came back a while later. On his way up to the loft, Sidney paused and kept his head down. "What does R.B. stand for?"

"Go on to sleep." R.B.'s voice was low.

Sidney shook his head, smiled, and did just that.

****

R.B. roused first. As he fed and watered Soldier, Sidney came down the ladder.

"Do you think we could get some hot breakfast before we set out?" R.B. asked.

"Yep, it's a long, cold ride to Kentucky and this might be the last we can get for a while. Let's go see if Robert has the fires lit."

They strode over to the hotel and found Robert did indeed have the fires lit and the coffee on. He greeted them as they sat down.

"Ya'll are early this morning."

"We wanted to get here before the rush. Thought if we got here first, maybe you just might have some of those biscuits you make." Sidney squinted up at him.

"Be right out with some." Robert hurried back to the kitchen.

"You mean Robert is the cook?" R.B. asked.

"No, his wife is. We just tease Robert about it ever since we saw him with an apron on."

R.B. smiled. *The last time I laughed with friends was when my best friend and I attended my 24th birthday party at the start of the war.* As R.B.'s thoughts wandered; his smile faded. *Michael is gone. Gettysburg.* He became more somber, then mentally shook himself. *Don't think about it.*

Sidney noticed the change in his demeanor and asked about it.

"Nothing. It's finally good to laugh with someone again."

He and Sidney enjoyed a biscuit with gravy and more parched corn coffee. The dining hall filled up quickly and R.B. and Sidney left for the general store. The shelves had a few bare spots, but the storekeeper had just received a shipment of cornmeal from the mill and several bags of jerked venison. They had no bacon, so they would make do with the venison. R.B. wondered if any of the stores would ever have the stock they used to have. *The smell of new leather...*

Sidney had filled R.B. in on the western route they would take first and then north. They would pretty much follow the Wilderness Road west through Rogersville and turn north at Bean Station. Mr. Smith would have gone through to the Powell River Valley on up to Harlan County. It began to snow lightly as Sidney and R.B. rode out of town. The mountainous terrain ensured them a wide and circuitous route west. They traveled the trails all day and most of the night. They drank at the streams and chewed on their jerky in the saddle to save time.

Chapter 32

October 1864
Harlan County, Kentucky

Henry led them down the last ridge into Harlan County, Kentucky. Dawn was about to break over the mountains. The smoke from the cabin's chimney lay in the valley where the morning mist had yet to rise.

Henry stopped to let the others catch up. "We'll all go down together, but I'll go in and talk to Jeremiah first. Let's go."

Mr. Smith and Sam brought up the rear. Sam had spoken little in the night and Mr. Smith didn't know if that was good or not.

Henry stopped and gave out two whistles, one long, one short, then another long one.

A gray bearded man opened the cabin door and peered out. He spied Henry and smiled as he came out onto the porch. "Come on in! What in the world you doing up here this time of year?"

"Hello, Jeremiah! I have some visitors with me, but could we talk a minute privately?"

"Sure, sure, come on in. Sally just put some coffee on."

Mr. Smith and the others sat down on sizeable pieces of wood that surrounded the wood lot at the edge of the yard. Sam sniffed the air with an upturned nose.

The wonderful aroma of a pig sty filled her nostrils. That only meant one thing: BACON! Looking around, she saw a chicken house off to the side and a barn with a loft faced the cabin.

Inside the cabin, Henry laid out their story as the pair sat in rocking chairs by the fire. "So, Jeremiah, do you have an idea of how we can get her on a boat?"

"Well, the Cumberland River is just over yon hill, but it's not navigable until up near Point Isabell. It's about six hours north of here."

"I knew it was a ways, but I have no idea how to get there. Sam's worn out. I was hoping it was closer."

"Henry, you've been mighty good to me, and I want to return the favor. How about I take her up there? I have two horses that I've kept hid from the Army. They never come down this way much no how. I can take her up and find a way to get her on a boat. We hear tell that the steamboats still come up the river, delivering supplies and taking on cargo to take back down to Nashville and even to the Mississippi. There's a man in Point Isabel who can maybe point us in the right direction."

"That is more than we had ever hoped! Thank you, my friend!"

"Let's get them other folks in here. Sally has been working on breakfast ever since you first showed up."

"Yes, let's get them in here. My biscuits are just about done, and you can smell the bacon!" Sally beamed.

"God in heaven can't eat any better than we're gonna eat!" Henry said.

Jeremiah opened the door and motioned for the others to come in. They all stood and hustled toward the cabin door.

"Joseph, Mark, Luke, and John!" Henry introduced

them as they came through the door.

"Apostles, are ye?" Jeremiah joked.

"We're brothers and cousins." Mark explained as they shuffled around the room.

"This is Mr. Smith," Henry said and then pointed to Sam, "This is Samantha… Sam."

Mr. Smith took Jeremiah's outstretched hand and shook it.

"Surely glad to meet you, Mr. …?" Sam asked. She was hesitant to shake hands. A lady usually didn't do it.

"Howard, Jeremiah Howard."

"There's a washbasin over here in the corner. I know ya'll will want to wash up a bit before breakfast." Sally pointed to the basin.

"Much obliged, Miss Sally. It will be heaven to wash with soap in a basin!" Sam said as she hurried over to the basin. Picking up the small cake of soap, she dipped her hands into the water with a smile on her face. For the first time in two weeks, she dried her hands on a towel.

As Sally stood by the stove, she saw the sawed-off hair, the grimy clothes, dirty hands and face Sam had now washed clean. Sally's heart melted a little. Not blessed with a daughter, she instantly felt a kinship and kindness toward the young woman.

"Thank you for letting me go first," Sam said to the others. "Please, take your turns."

The boys saw no reason to delay their meal by getting clean water, so they used the water in the basin and washed as fast as they could.

"Please, set yourselves down." Jeremiah said as he took his seat at the head of a huge oak table in the middle of the room.

Mr. Smith and Sam sat on oak chairs to his right and the others noisily shuffled around to the empty chairs.

Sally took a big pan of cathead biscuits out of the oven and set it in the middle of the table, and a platter of bacon on one end. Pouring the gravy into a big bowl, she set it beside the biscuits in front of Sam.

Jeremiah gave Sally a smile as Sally settled in beside him. He bowed his head and began. "Dear Lord, please bless this food and the hands that prepared it. Bless these travelers and keep them well on the rest of their journey. Amen."

The hardwood smoked scent of the bacon made tears come to Sam's eyes as she remembered her grandpa's bacon. Taking a biscuit on her plate, she ladled some gravy over it and then passed the gravy down the table. Each person took only one piece of bacon. There was still a piece left when the platter came back around to Sam.

Sally jumped up, got the coffeepot and poured them all a cup of the wonderful steaming brew. Sam expected the raw taste of parched corn, but the taste of real coffee surprised her.

"Much obliged, Miss Sally." Sam expressed her thanks, and the others echoed her.

Miss Sally flashed a smile. "Ya'll are welcome! The Lord has provided for us very well!"

"Miss Sam, I hear you want to get to St. Louis," Jeremiah said.

"Yes…but I don't see how I can get there."

"I've been thinking…, just hear me out and then tell me what you think. The Cumberland River runs through Kentucky, down into Tennessee and back up to Paducah, Kentucky. It's just a bit up the Ohio to the Mississippi, then on up to Cairo, Illinois and from there to St. Louis. I have a good friend that works on the Cumberland. He tells me steamboats come up from Nashville, all the way to Point Isabel, and stop at points all along the way—"

Sam interrupted. "What's a steamboat?" She took a sip of coffee.

"Of course, I'll explain. They're like a floating house on the river. They can be big or small. The steam engines make the steam that powers the boat, that makes it move." Jeremiah nodded and moved his hands in the air.

Sam nodded her head as if she understood but clearly couldn't picture it. She'd never seen a boat of *any* kind.

Jeremiah went on. "The Cumberland starts over here to the east of us, but it isn't navigable until you get up to Point Isabel. Cumberland Falls, big shoals and rocks all the way on this side. I have two horses, so I can take you. We can ride the fifteen or so miles up to Point Isabel. Perhaps we can locate a steamboat that can carry you to St. Louis."

"I've got only a few dollars. I can't pay."

"Bet they would let you work your way. I'm sure there are lots of things you can do. Cook and clean, stuff like that."

"I would like to try, Mr. Howard. Thank you!" Sam's visage looked brighter and her shoulders no longer sagged. She was still afraid but she didn't want to disappoint them. It seemed they had worked between themselves to help her and she should at least try to be grateful.

"Well, that's settled." Jeremiah finished his coffee.

Mr. Smith looked relieved and smiled at Sam.

Everybody cleaned their plates, and then Sam helped Sally ret up the table.

"Jeremiah, we're going to head on out. Manchester is only two hours from here, and that's where these boys are headed. Miss Sally, we thank you for the fine meal." Henry patted his stomach.

Henry and the others put their coats on, grabbed up their packs and went outside. Sam followed to say goodbye.

Sam looked at Henry and smiled. Still not sure of what to do, she stuck out her hand. "I'm so grateful for all your help. I know you didn't want to bring me along with you and I really appreciate that you did."

Henry hesitated and shook Sam's hand. He looked into Sam's eyes and then looked away. "I'm glad we made it. I wish you luck." He turned to Mr. Smith and became matter-of-fact. "Mr. Smith, you coming with us?"

"No, thank you. I believe I'll head on back to Tennessee."

Sam shook hands with the boys and watched them leave with Mr. Jenkins. *So many goodbyes.*

Mr. Howard spoke up. "Sam, you and Mr. Smith are welcome to rest here today. We'll get a good start at dawn. I'm not as good at night traveling as Mr. Smith here, but we'll be there by early afternoon if we ride hard."

"Sounds good to me." Mr. Smith waved his hand over the chunks of wood. "It seems you need a hand splitting this. I'll be glad to help you today."

"Sam, you come on back into the house," Sally said. "You can rest awhile in the loft. No one will bother you there."

Sam nodded and followed Sally into the house. "I couldn't possibly sleep with all this to help clean up." Sam waved her hand at the table.

"Don't you fret none. Here, I have a nightgown you can borrow. Let me have those clothes and I'll wash them, so you'll have some fresh clothes to put on for your journey tomorrow."

"I *am* a bit ripe, that's for sure, but I have a nightgown in my pack. It's just a bit smelly from the journey."

"Give it here and I'll freshen it up, too."

Sam dug in her pack to find the battered nightgown and handed it to her which she exchanged for a fresh nightgown. Sally gestured to the corner ladder leading up to the loft. "There's soap and a towel on the washstand. Help yourself. I'll bring up some hot water."

After a few minutes, Sally poured hot water into a bucket, climbed up the ladder, and handed it to Sam.

"Much obliged, Miss Sally. I'm ever so grateful."

Sam disrobed and handed her dirty clothes to Sally. Pouring some hot water into the basin, she used the soap and a rag to wash the dirt and grime from her body. She turned her head upside down and dunked her head into the water, and then soaped it up. She poured fresh water over it and tried her best to rinse it out. *It feels great to be clean!* Sam pulled the nightgown over her head, settled it in place, and towel-dried her hair as best she could. Crawling into the featherbed, Sam pulled the log cabin quilt up to her chin, nestled herself in, and was asleep before her head settled on the fluffy pillow.

Sam awoke with a start and looked at the ceiling of the loft. She could see the nails that held the shakes to the rafters. Sam remembered where she was and felt a momentary sense of peace lying in the comfortable bed. *I remember now. Uncle Prince, Grandma and Grandpa, and ...R.B. Where was he?* Sam's thoughts paused as she thought of the man with the deep blue eyes. A quiver slithered up her spine as she recalled how he looked longingly into her eyes. Did he get the men back to Saltville? Had he apprehended Daniels yet? How far away was Daniels now? The peace that she felt when she first awoke disappeared with the uncertainty of her fate. A sense of urgency assaulted her. *Where was Mr. Smith?*

Sam got out of bed and saw Miss Sally had neatly folded her clean clothes and placed them at the foot of the bed. She must have been asleep for a long time, so she hastily dressed. She sorted through her pack to take stock. The gun and holster were both accounted for. There was no ammunition for it, but she hadn't fired it. Eight bullets were in the cylinder. The small barrel underneath the cylinder still held the grapeshot. Her brush and the tin of stinky salve from Grandma nestled in the pack's bottom. Her needles and thread were in the matchbox. This was the extent of her belongings. Sam picked up the neatly-folded nightgown and put it in the pack.

Sam scrambled down the ladder and found herself in the big room by herself. She cautiously opened the door and found Miss Sally reaching to open it.

"Goodness, you startled me! I'm not used to anyone but Mr. Howard being around!"

Sam laughed and helped her with the apron full of eggs that she was bringing in. "What time is it?" Sam asked.

"It's coming on suppertime. You had a good sleep."

"Gracious, I've not slept in a bed during the day

since I don't know when. Thank you. I can't seem to say thank you enough!"

"I know you've been through a lot, and I'm glad to help."

"Where's Mr. Smith?" Sam asked.

"He's outside with Mr. Howard."

"I would like to talk to him for a minute, then I'll help you with supper."

"You take your time. I've already got the chicken stew on the stove."

Sam went outside and found Mr. Smith at the woodpile with Jeremiah. "Mr. Smith, might I have a word with you?"

Jeremiah swung the ax down into a big, round piece of wood. "I'm going to go see what Sally has got up to."

Sam put her hands in her pockets and looked up at Mr. Smith with a wistful smile. She wasn't sure what she wanted to say, and Mr. Smith looked a little wary.

"I was just wondering what you were going to do now…um…that your journey to take me away has ended. Do you have any plans? Where are your people? You know, you've never spoken of your people."

"Now, Missy, don't you worry none about me. I have pals I meet up with and a cabin south of Bean Station. With winter coming on, I doubt the Yankees are going to be doing much. This war has to be winding down. It seems there're no more men to replace the South's armies. Lee needs to surrender. I know he won't want to, and the boys sure don't want to, but he'll have to see the light soon. How many more men and boys have to die on both sides?"

"I know. I haven't seen my brother since spring of 1862, when the conscription began. I know I needed to leave home. I don't know where Daniels is, but I feel like he's still out there, hunting for me."

"I know. I wish I could do away with him. I don't know how far behind us he is, or if he *is* behind us. If we can get you on a boat, you can get farther away. Then he may give up. A boat won't leave a trail."

"How big a boat we talking about?" Sam's forehead furrowed because she still couldn't imagine such a thing.

"Don't know, but don't you be worrying about that now. Let's go into the house and enjoy these good people's company."

Sam and Mr. Smith walked into the cabin with their noses to the air at the homey smell of chicken stew and cornbread.

After supper, Jeremiah said, "Well, we better get some shuteye if we're going to get an early start. Mr. Smith, you can bed down by the fire if you've a mind to."

Miss Sally gave Mr. Smith a quilt, and he put his bedroll down on the floor and covered up. Jeremiah and Sally went over to their wrought iron bed covered with Sally's double wedding ring quilt in the corner. Sam climbed up to the loft to the softness of the featherbed.

****

"Miss Sam, it's time to go! You awake?" Jeremiah hollered from the ladder.

"Yes, I'm awake. Coming." Sam put her clothes on in a rush, grabbed her pack, and quickly climbed down the stairs.

Mr. Smith was standing near the door, hat in hand. Sam put on her coat and hat and picked up the water bag she had filled the night before. She pulled her pack strap over her shoulder.

"Sam… good luck to you. I'm sure glad I met you and could return a favor for your grandpa." Mr. Smith couldn't meet her eyes.

Sam hugged Mr. Smith. He hugged her back with his eyes closed tight.

"Thank you, Mr. Smith. I can never repay you for all you've done for me." Biting her lip, Sam tried hard not to cry. She didn't want to embarrass Mr. Smith.

Mr. Smith slapped his hat on his head and walked with them out the door.

Miss Sally had bacon biscuits ready for them to take and cornpone for the journey. Handing the food bag to Jeremiah, she hugged him hard. He gave her a kiss on the cheek.

"I'll be back tomorrow sometime," he said. "I'll stay tonight at Point Isabel with James, if he's still about. Don't you fret none." He and Sally hugged again, and then Jeremiah walked over to the saddled horses.

Sam wanted to wish Mr. Smith a fair journey, but he turned away and walked off toward the south. Sam mounted the waiting horse and wiped her cheeks.

Jeremiah saw Sam's sadness and spoke softly. "Her name is Nell. She's a gentle horse. She's used to neck rein. You'll be fine."

"I'm a good rider. I won't slow us down."

Sam waved to Miss Sally and looked off to the south. Mr. Smith turned to watch her and Jeremiah as they rode off north. *I know I'll never see him again. I have a feeling I'll never see my family again. I'm usually pretty good at not feeling sorry for myself, but I'm awful close now. Mama always taught me it was the unknown that makes us scared. Just go out to meet it, she would say. Face it down and make the best of it. Well…*

Chapter 33

October 1864
Point Isabel, Kentucky

Sam followed Jeremiah up the ridges and down into the valleys. They ate their bacon biscuits about mid-morning and stopped to drink at a stream. Sam dreaded seeing the Cumberland River Jeremiah had talked so much about.

They came out of the forest on a high bluff that afternoon and stopped a moment to take in the magnificent sight. On their right, the South Fork of the Cumberland River tumbled into the Cumberland River in front of them. The trail led down to the river and a landing.

Sam rode up beside Jeremiah with a look of awe on her face. "I've never seen anything like it," she said. "That's a...a... boat?"

Jeremiah nodded. "A steamboat. I've heard about 'em," he said, "but never seen one. Really sumthin' ain't it?"

Sam pointed to the steamboat. "It's huge!! Look! Smoke's coming out!"

Jeremiah laughed. "That's what powers and moves the steamboat."

Tied up at the landing, the white steamboat had the words *U.S. Hospital Ship* emblazoned on the side that housed the paddlewheel. The boat had three decks and a fourth deck, called a Texas, where the pilothouse was located. Solid wooden planks were laid across her starboard deck to the landing. Men carried armloads of wood from the great pile on the bank of the river to the deck of the steamboat. Smoke poured out of the double smokestacks that came up through the hurricane deck. A yellow flag with a green H was flying from the jack staff.

Sam surveyed the scene. Buildings dotted the trail to the landing and many preoccupied people bustled about. Men rolled hogsheads of tobacco out of warehouses and lined them up beside the landing. Wooden crates were stacked on the wharf waiting to be loaded.

Jeremiah and Sam started down the road when Jeremiah recognized his friend. "Well, Mr. Ballou! How are you? It's been a coon's age!"

Mr. Ballou looked up at Jeremiah and grinned. "I'm fine, Jeremiah, I'm fine! Get down and come over to my store and we'll catch up on old times."

Jeremiah and Sam dismounted. "Well, James, before we get too far along in our remembrances, I need to find out some information here for my friend Sam." He nodded in Sam's direction.

James rested his hand on his knobby cane as he looked Sam over. "What can I help you with?"

"What about that boat over there? Do you think it would take a passenger?"

"That's the hospital ship, *D.A. January*. The pilot took a big chance bringing that sidewheeler up here to Point Isabel. Usually just stern wheelers come up this far. Heard tell that he came up here to pick up a *lady* doctor to help at the hospital. You ever heard tell of a lady doctor? Beats all I ever seen. Anyway, I don't know if they'll take anyone, but we'll ask. Hear tell they were going to pull out tonight. The river's going down and they'll get caught at Wild Goose shoals if they tarry much longer."

"I'll go down now, if that's okay," Sam said.

"Let's all go down and I'll see you get to see the person in charge."

James, Jeremiah, and Sam walked to the landing, leading their horses and trying to avoid the bustle of people coming and going to the boat.

"I better stay here and hold the horses. All this going on, I don't know if they'll stand," Jeremiah said.

Sam took her pack off the horse and strapped it on her back. "I'll be back. Wish me luck!" Sam followed James to the stage planks that led onto the boat.

Jeremiah walked onto the boat under a small swinging sign that read, *D.A. January*. The deck floor swayed, and Sam held her hands out wide to steady herself. James walked as if this were a common thing. They proceeded through the open double doors. The first person they noticed was a strapping man with flushed cheeks; Jeremiah stopped him.

"Excuse me, where would we find the person responsible for hiring for the boat?"

"Go on up the next flight of stairs. That's the boiler deck, then go up one more flight of stairs to the cabin deck. The surgeon's office is right by the doors. He's probably the one you need to talk to."

"Appreciate it!"

"Welcome, sir."

James and Sam went on up two flights of stairs to the cabin deck. James opened the door, and they stepped inside. A man with his shirt sleeves rolled up stood to greet them and introduced himself.

"Lewis Rice, I'm the surgeon here. What can I do for you? Don't mean to be rude, but I have a lot to attend to at present."

Sam took off her hat and held it in her hands, turning it round and round. "Sam...Samantha Coldiron, sir." Sam stumbled through her words. "I was wondering if you need someone to help around here. I need to get to St. Louis, and I'm willing to work to pay my way."

Mr. Rice looked her over. "Do you mind if I ask why you're dressed as a man?" He gave a small scowl, but then shrugged his shoulders. "No matter, we need women here as well as men but, in some places, you could be arrested."

"It's been a hard journey, sir. To tell the scriptured truth, it was easier to wear britches."

"We need women to help clean and cook. Several are nursing the sick and wounded. Do you think you can handle that?"

"Yes, sir. I can. I've helped my mama and grandma when they nursed the sick."

"Okay, then. Go through those double doors and ask for Ann. She'll help you."

"Thank you! Is it all right if I go back and say my goodbyes to my friend first? He's waiting outside on the landing."

"Yes, but be quick. I understand that Captain Yore wants to be gone as soon as we can get everything loaded. We're losing the tide."

Sam and James turned and hustled down the stairs and out to the landing. Jeremiah still stood with the horses where they had left him. Suddenly, a long blast, then two short ones rent the air, coming from the steamboat. The horses reared and their front legs pawed the air. Sam and Jeremiah jumped as if shot.

James chuckled. "Just their way of saying they're getting ready to leave!"

"Well, it sure gets your attention, that's for sure!" Jeremiah said.

Sam swallowed hard and squared her shoulders. She knew she had to hurry and say goodbye to Jeremiah and get on the boat.

"I need to get on, Mr. Jeremiah. Mr. Rice was good enough to say I could work my way."

"That's really great news, Sam. You go on and good luck to you!"

"I owe you a lot for bringing me here. Much obliged. You and Miss Sally take good care of each other!" Sam turned and hurried back toward the boat. She certainly didn't want to be left behind. Before going onboard, she looked back and waved to Jeremiah. He waved back and smiled.

Sam gulped hard, took a huge breath, and then disappeared onto the boat.

Chapter 34

October 1864
Rogersville, Tennessee

Two days later, after riding hard, R.B. and Sidney rode into the town of Rogersville, Tennessee.

"We're near froze. Let's go to Roger's Tavern, instead of McKinney's. They don't charge you as much for a bowl of stew and a place to sleep. Of course, it'll be on the floor, but at least it'll be warm." Sidney's words slurred through numb lips.

"Sounds good to me," R.B. agreed with a nod.

"There's a stable behind the tavern. We can tie up there." At the stable, there was just enough light left to find the stalls and pitch some hay for the horses. R.B. took his scabbard and saddle bags off the saddle and shouldered them. Sidney did the same.

"Let's get the lay of the land before we unsaddle. We'd better take our gear with us. We leave it here, someone will steal it, sure enough. People are starving. God, I wish this war would end."

"Amen to that," R.B. said.

R.B. and Sidney walked back around the tavern to the front door and walked in. R.B. quickly glanced around the room. A single door on the opposite side led outside. A crackling fire blazed in the stone fireplace that filled the entire right-hand wall of the single large room.

Age-darkened square logs made up the rest of the room. Tin candle holders on the wall did little to brighten the room. Men filled the tavern, but R.B. didn't see any Federal uniforms. In fact, all he saw were mostly older men in common farmer's clothes.

R.B. and Sidney sat opposite each other at a long table with benches on either side. They both laid their hats on the bench beside them alongside their saddle bags. R.B. slipped his rifle between his knees with the butt on the floor.

A young man in a wool shirt and overalls came over to their table. "Come git a bowl and I'll fill her up with stew. Cornpone comes with it. Two bits."

R.B. and Sidney both fished a quarter out of their pockets and paid him. R.B. hated to leave his rifle but was hungrier than a wolf. He got up to go over to the fireplace where the boy was dishing up the stew. R.B. took the proffered bowl and a hunk of cornpone. "You have anything to drink?"

"Sure, we got whiskey and hard cider. What'll it be?"

R.B. and Sidney both said whiskey and walked over and sat down with their stew and cornpone. The stew was pretty good but tasted like nothing they had eaten before. "You ever taste anything like this?" R.B. stirred his stew.

"Best not to ask; tastes better that way."

The boy set their whiskeys down and said, "That'll be two bits."

"Daggone, I'm not going to have any money left at this rate," Sidney said.

"I'll pay; I owe you."

"You don't owe me, but I'll let you pay." Sidney smiled. They enjoyed their whiskey and the fire.

Someone in the corner began singing "Barbara Allen." A couple of men came in and shuffled to the left and right before they finally sat at the end of their table. R.B. and Sidney nodded to them and sipped from their glasses. The men were already blurry eyed but called for whiskey.

"By God! I'll never…" the bigger dark man slurred, "…play poker again! Lost my shirt, I did!"

"I think they were cheating. But that one big guy, Archer, I think they called him, had one big …" a loud burp escaped his puckered lips, "stack of greenbacks when he sat down. Never… seen the likes of money!" The smaller man hiccupped.

Overhearing their loud conversation, R.B. was immediately on guard. Archer and greenbacks were no coincidence. He was sure Daniels was with him. "You hear that?" R.B. spoke quietly.

Sidney nodded.

The talk at the end of the table continued. "Never going back to McKinney's Tavern again."

"Let's go to the stables." R.B. stood, hitched up his galluses, and pulled on his coat. He slapped on his hat and picked up his rifle and saddlebags.

"Sure hate to miss this fire." Sidney said as he shrugged into his coat and picked up his hat. They walked out into the chilly night and back to the stables. R.B. watched the horses that continued to chew their hay. Nothing seemed to be amiss, so R.B. lit the lantern that hung on a nail. Then he rolled a couple of empty wooden whiskey kegs over for them to sit on.

"We got to come up with a plan." R.B. leaned his rifle against the wall. "We need to go over there and make sure that it really is Archer and Daniels." He leaned toward Sidney, his elbows on his knees.

Sidney leaned in and spoke softly. "Number one, don't you think we need to get the sheriff? I know Elias Beal. He's a good man. What're we going to do when we get over there? Try to arrest them?" Sidney leaned back and crossed his arms. "You know there'll be a fight, they won't come peaceable. You're an officer in the Southern Army. That won't hold much sway over here. We need the sheriff." Sidney smoothed his beard and jutted his chin.

"Those men are murderers! They don't deserve any consideration. They're after your sister and will kill her *and us* if they can. They don't care how. If we involve the sheriff, we'll have to give them a chance to give up, and they might get away."

"But R.B., just how are we going to go about this? We're two and they're five or six."

R.B. reached down and picked up his Spencer. "This makes us even." R.B. smoothed the leather of the scabbard.

"R.B., you're thinking with your heart, not your head." Sidney shook his head. "You sure about Sam? I'm telling you, she won't ever mind what you say. She'll have her own way, no matter. I know!"

R.B. thought of Sam and smiled. "I wouldn't have it any other way."

"Well, anyway, it's dark and—"

"We need to go see if it's them. If it is, we need to follow them. If they stay at the McKinney Tavern, we can't shoot up the place in front of everybody. You know I'd like to just shoot them in their beds." R.B. shrugged his shoulders.

"Well, you can't. I know the McKinney Tavern. It

has three stories and a lot of rooms. We'll need to see which room they go in, wait until they settle down, and then go in after them."

"I know. I shouldn't have said it like that." R.B. was out of patience. "I know we can't risk shooting innocent people. We'll have to get them outside."

"Okay, how about this? Wait until they settle down. They might leave or they might get a room." Sidney squinted in thought. "I'll go in and watch and wait. None of them knows me. I'll see which room they take. I'll go in and wake everyone up by saying the sheriff and two deputies are coming up the back stairs. Better go out the front. I'll wait until they're running down and out and I'll clean up the rear." Sidney nodded in satisfaction at his plan.

R.B. grinned and slapped Sidney on the shoulder. "That's a right good plan. We can't let Daniels and Archer get away. The others don't matter so much. I'm sure Archer has the money on him. Daniels had some too, back on the trail. If we can, we'll get the sheriff involved afterward. Let's go."

R.B. and Sidney gathered their gear and walked back around to the front of Roger's Tavern. Sidney pointed down the street. "Let's go by way of the streets." Sidney shouldered his Enfield. "We don't want to be seen sneaking through the back alley and get shot. People are nervous. McKinney's is just down this street to Main Street, and then to the right, about 100 yards."

They walked toward Main Street. Here and there were oil lamps on tall posts that cast a yellow glow in the night. They made their way to Main and turned right.

"See that big brick building with the balcony? That's McKinney's," Sidney said.

"We're in luck. There's a lamppost right in front. I should be able to see well enough to make out their faces."

Sidney pointed to the building across the street from McKinney's. "That's the Kyle House; you can hole up there, you'll be able to see them come out."

R.B. nodded. "Let's go check their stables. See how many horses are there and if any are still saddled and ready to go."

In back of McKinney's, the stable was a large barn, with stalls that ran the length of the building on both sides. They walked down the middle of the stable and met a stable boy putting his gear away. "Ain't got no more room, sir."

"That's okay, we're just walking a bit, trying to get warm." R.B. and Sidney walked on, and the boy went up to the loft. No horses were saddled. They were full up, like the boy said. The tavern had been very busy tonight.

"Let's go around front. I'll reconnoiter to make sure Archer and Daniels are still there and watch where they go. I should be able to recognize them. If I don't, I'll come get you. We're banking on the thought they'll stay here for the night," Sidney said.

"Hopefully, they will. They've been drinking and gambling. I want to end this now. Here…" R.B. reached out to take Sidney's rifle and gear. "I'll stash this here with mine. Good luck."

R.B. watched Sidney stride across the street to McKinney's, then stepped inside the arched doorway of the Kyle House. He knew it would be a while before Sidney came out. He looked to his left down the street where Sidney said the sheriff and jail were.

Raucous voices greeted Sidney as he walked into

McKinney's. A smokey haze hovered near the ceiling. His gaze swept the room and settled on an empty table in the back, where he could get a good look at everyone. He sat down and watched as a group of rowdies threw their cards down. One man laughed loudly as he raked in the pot. Sidney's ears piqued when he heard their names.

"Archer, you've won every hand for the last hour, don't you think it might be someone else's turn?" a player with a black slouch hat asked.

Archer reached over and lightly smacked Slouch Hat on the cheek. "You need to play better, my friend, play better." Archer's thick lips grinned at the man, but his eyes stayed dark and menacing. "What about you Daniels? You want to win some of your money back?"

Sidney pretended to mind his own business, relieved he now knew what Daniels and Archer looked like. Out of the corner of his eye, he kept watch of the group.

The man to Archer's right picked up his black hat with one hand and smoothed his hair back with the other. He looked down at the pile of money on the table. Daniels pursed his lips to speak to Archer, but decided against it. "It's late, boys, I'm going to bed." Daniels got up from the table.

"Yep, we're moving on tomorrow. Better get our beauty sleep," Archer added.

Archer raked all the money into his hat. The five men followed him as he went out to the hallway where John, the tavern keeper, had his desk near the stairs to the second floor. "What room we got tonight?"

The tavern keeper ran his fingers down the big ledger on his desk. "You'll have to share beds in the common room with a couple of other fellows. The other rooms here are private and are taken. There're three empty beds. That will be a dollar a piece."

"A dollar!"

"Well, sir, you must admit our tavern has the best accommodations around. Clean rooms and breakfast in the morning." A bit of defiance tinted the tavern keeper's words.

Archer grudgingly paid the six dollars, and the men started up the stairs. "Second floor, second door on the left at the top of the stairs." The tavern keeper pointed up the stairs.

Sidney heard it all and watched from the doorway of the tavern room. The tavern keeper had his hair slicked down like he'd been licked to be swallered. Seeing Sidney look his way, he asked, "You need a room? I'm sorry, but I just gave out the last bed. There's Roger's Tavern, just down the street. They might have space, but you'll have to sleep on the floor, most likely. They don't have separate rooms like we do here." He sounded a little smug.

"No, thanks, I just came in for a drink. I'll be on my way."

A feminine voice from the back of the hallway called out, "John, are you there?"

"Coming." John looked at Sidney and turned to go down the hall. Sidney gave him a nod and took a few steps toward the door. When he heard John's footsteps recede down the hallway, he turned back. He quickly took the stairs two at a time and saw the door close on the men who had just made it up the staircase. Sidney walked over and tried the door. It opened. *So, there was no lock on the common sleeping room door.* He opened the door a crack, stuck his head in, saw Archer was taking off his gun belt.

"This room is full up. Go find someplace else," Archer growled.

Sidney saw three beds on the left and two on the right with two men standing beside them. Sidney overheard the discussion between the two men to his right.

"Jasper, we got to get some sleep!"

"Elmer, I know, but we got to hit the grit first light! We got to git home—." Seeing Sidney, the man stopped speaking.

"Sorry to bother." Sidney closed the door. Looking around, he saw another stairway at the other end of the hall. He rushed the length of the hall; his hand skimmed the walnut banister as he went down the stairs. Sidney opened the door at the foot of the staircase and fresh, cold air greeted him. He stepped into the night and walked around to the front of the tavern. Sidney looked across the street to the Kyle House and saw R.B. in the arched doorway. He pulled his coat closed, stuck his hands in his pockets, and walked over to R.B.

"We're set, R.B., I know where they are. They just went up to bed. Second floor, second room on the left as you top the stairs. We can see it from here." Sidney pointed to the lit window on the second floor.

"Okay, I'm set here. I can see the doorway pretty good since the lamppost is close to the door. That balcony casts a shadow, but I can still see well enough to recognize them."

"All right, I'm going back in. I'll shout out 'the sheriff's coming up the back.' They'll run out the front door."

"Got it. Thanks!"

"We'll get'em R.B."

Sidney ran back across the street and around back. He opened the door quietly and slipped up the stairs. He jerked the door open and hollered, "Jasper, Elmer, come on and get up! The sheriff's coming for you! He knows it was you that stole that horse!"

Jasper and Elmer wrestled with the bedclothes, trying to get out of bed. "What? I *knew* it!" Jasper said. "I just knew it!"

Archer and Daniels hadn't fallen asleep yet, so Sidney's words propelled them out of bed.

"Come on, get up!" Archer poked them with his gun. Daniels strapped on his gun and Archer threw his saddlebags over his shoulder. Jerico and Augustus jerked their boots on, and the others followed Daniels. Archer and Daniels ran down the front stairs with the others right on their heels. Sidney was behind them but turned to Jasper and Elmer, innocent bystanders caught up in the trap.

"Don't go that way." Sidney grabbed their shirt collars and held on. "Go down the back way or better yet, stay here."

"Who are *you*?" Jasper pointed his finger at Sidney with exasperation.

"We never neither stole no horse!" Elmer said haughtily and smoothed his lapels. "We've stole a lot of things but—"

"Shut up, Elmer!" Jasper smacked him.

"Just stay here!" Sidney said.

R.B. had got off two shots and knew they both had hit their mark. Archer and Daniels were down, but R.B. couldn't see them.

Running down the stairs, Sidney saw the last four men turn around at the sound of gunfire. Sidney pulled his guns and yelled. "Just stay where you are, or I'll shoot you where you stand!"

R.B. moved down the street a bit and looked back to see two forms lying in front of the inn's door. Shadowed by the balcony, the bodies couldn't be seen clearly. With both guns drawn, R.B. sidestepped across the street, searching for any signs of movement. His pace was calm and deliberate as he moved around the hitching post at the side of the building and could see the bodies. The bigger man's arm moved.

"Don't do it!" R.B. warned, but Archer rolled over and R.B. shot him again. Daniels played dead, but R.B. saw his feet twitch. "I can shoot you again. I don't mind, although I hate to waste another bullet."

Daniels put his hands up and begged. "I'm hit! My leg! Don't shoot! I've got money! I'll tell you where it is!"

R.B. heard the squeak of a door opening behind him and a voice said, "What's going on? I'm coming out, don't shoot!"

First, a lantern appeared, and then a long arm came out the door. A tall, thin man slowly poked his head out and asked, "What's happened here? I'm the proprietor of this establishment."

R.B. ignored the owner's question and spoke to Daniels. "Get up then, but don't try anything."

Daniels tried to stand, but fell back. Blood coursed through the fabric of his britches, soaking his entire leg.

"I'm shot to pieces… get me a doctor!" Daniels whimpered.

R.B. kicked Daniels' gun away and nudged Archer's body with his boot. He didn't move. R.B.'s voice was icy. "You don't deserve a doctor. You murdered a man in cold blood." He looked down at Daniels' leg. "A good man would put a tourniquet on that for you." R.B. stepped away from Daniels and walked over to the proprietor, who watched with wary eyes. "Sorry about the commotion, Mister…?"

"McKinney. John McKinney."

"Major R.B. Royster, 4th Virginia Cavalry. I'll explain all this to you and the sheriff. You got a doctor here?"

"Yes, I'll send my manager for him." McKinney walked back inside.

R.B. looked down and kicked Archer's gun out of reach, just in case. A couple of onlookers had stopped to see what was going on. "Can someone get the sheriff?" R.B. inquired.

"Yes, I'll go get him." One man offered and hurried down the street.

Seeing the wounded Daniels as no threat, R.B. gathered up the weapons and took everything inside. Sidney had the other four men in the dining room, standing against the wall, their guns on the floor. R.B. overheard Sidney's words as he went into the dining hall to set the rifles down.

"Don't even think of trying to get your guns. I would just as soon shoot you right now. I wanted to shoot you in your sleep, but R.B. here," Sidney pointed at R.B. with his guns, "said that wasn't an honorable thing to do. So, here we are!"

R.B. raised his eyebrows at the statement and smiled at Sidney. "I swear, Sidney, you are a good man to have around!"

"Did you get them?"

"Archer's dead, and Daniels' leg is tore up. The

sheriff and the doctor are on their way."

Other people from the inn had gathered on the stairs. R.B. waved his hand toward the stairs. "Would you kind people please go back to your rooms? It's dangerous for you here right now."

The inn patrons turned to go back to their rooms. When someone said the doctor had arrived, R.B. went back outside. He held the lantern while the doctor looked Daniels over.

"Looks like the femoral artery was severed. There's really nothing I can do. He's already unconscious. He'll be dead before we get him to my office, but we can take him, anyway. Anyone here have a wagon we can take him in?" The doctor asked.

"Right here, doctor. I'll help you," someone said. The men put Daniels in the wagon and followed the doctor back to his office.

Sheriff Beal and two deputies came hurrying up. The sheriff was average height but his two deputies were bean poles. The sheriff spread his hands and looked at R.B. expectantly.

"Sheriff, I'm Major R.B. Royster. The dead man here is Archer. I don't know if that's his first name or his last. I'll explain everything, but the rest of his gang are inside. We need to get them out of the inn and put under lock and key."

R.B. followed Sheriff Beal into the dining hall, where Sidney still held his guns on the other men.

"We didn't have nothing to do with nothing!" Jerico said.

"You'll have time to tell your side." Sheriff Beal looked at his deputies. "Cuff them and take them down to the jail. I'll be along directly."

"Yes, sir," one deputy said. Both moved to cuff the prisoners and march them down to the jail. Jerico was heard whining at the deputies.

R.B. nodded his approval as the men left. Putting his hand on the sheriff's shoulder, he asked, "You think we could have some coffee while I explain this situation?"

"I think that would be a great idea!"

"But first, we better get Archer's body. He's going to have a lot of stolen money on him, and we don't want anything to happen to it."

R.B. and the sheriff went back outside where Archer's body lay in a pool of blood on the boarded walk. R.B. dragged Archer's body into the hallway. Mr. McKinney was about to object to the blood being smeared over the floor when the sheriff spoke. "John, could you get a blanket to cover him until we can get his body out of here? I'm sorry about the mess."

"Yes, yes, of course, Elias." McKinney shook his head and walked down the hall.

R.B. and Sheriff Beal went back into the dining hall. Sidney came through the back door carrying a steaming enamel coffeepot.

"Look what I got!" Sidney put the steaming pot on a trivet that was on the table.

"Sidney, where did you get this?" R.B. was wary.

"Don't worry, I didn't make it." His grin was wide. "It's real coffee!"

A young woman came through the door with a tray of coffee mugs. "Here you go."

She set them on the table, bobbed her head at the men, and started out of the room.

"Thank you kindly, ma'am," R.B. called after her as he, Sidney, and the sheriff sat to talk.

"Hell of a night!" Sidney exclaimed. "Hell of a night!"

Chapter 35

October 1864
Rogersville, Tennessee

Sheriff Beal stared into his empty coffee cup and then set it on the table. He had just heard the most incredible story from these two men. Searching Archer's saddlebags, he and RB. had stopped counting at forty thousand dollars.

"So, you see why we needed to search Archer in private," R.B. stated.

"We'll need to get to the bank first thing in the morning. The Bank of Tennessee is the one we need. I've been thinking about how we could let Saltville know about the money. We can't risk sending a telegraph. Someone could intercept it anywhere. I don't even know if the telegraph works all the way to Saltville, anyway."

The sheriff stood and readjusted his hat. "Let's take Archer's body down to the jail tonight and I'll get the undertaker. I have a safe we can put the money in for now. Then we need to put it in the bank. I hate to have to ask it of you both, but can you come guard it? Not that I don't trust my deputies, but this is something we need to keep just between us. I don't know if the men in his gang will tell or not. We just need to get the money in the bank and in their vault as soon as we can."

R.B. and Sidney helped Sheriff Beal load Archer's

body into a wagon and take it to the jail. The undertaker was waiting although no one remembered summoning him. They watched the sheriff put the money in his safe. R.B. and Sidney walked back to the livery behind Roger's Tavern, and retrieved their horses and gear. The jail had a stable right behind it, so they could keep an eye on their horses there.

The next morning, Sheriff Beal brought them breakfast. The men were ravenous and cleaned up their plates in record time. Sheriff Beal opened the safe and took out the saddlebag full of money. "Let's get on over to the bank."

The three men walked down the street to the Bank of Tennessee, another three-story red brick Federal style building in Rogersville. "I swear, this is a fancy bank, not that I've seen that many. Can we afford to put the money here?" R.B. raised his eyebrows.

"R.B., they pay *you* to keep your money here. It's called *interest.*"

"G. Rover Cripes!" R.B. narrowed his eyes at the sheriff in disbelief.

"It's a fact." Sheriff Beal stated with a smile and slapped R.B. and Sidney on their backs.

As the men entered the bank, the sheriff strode over to the barred teller window and asked to see the manager. A well-dressed gentleman came out to greet them and the sheriff asked to go someplace private. They were escorted to his office.

"Sheriff Beal, how can I help you today?" Mr. Rogers motioned for them to sit.

"Sir, we have a story to tell."

Mr. Rogers listened to the story of how they came to have so much money in their possession. "Mr.

Royster, I take it you will want to return this money to Saltville at your earliest convenience?"

"Yes, sir, but I have to find Sam— Samantha, first. I can't afford to have any more time pass. She could disappear."

"Yes, I'm going to help him find her. She's my sister," Sidney added.

"With this war on, you'll have a devil of a time. I wish you luck. One more thing, Mr. Royster, do you understand the Saltville office will probably want to give you a reward?"

"A reward? I was just doing my job."

Sidney expressed himself with open hands. "Wait a minute, R.B. I only have two bits to my name, and I know you can't have much more than that. Mr. Rogers, do you think we might get a few dollars against the amount that you think they might be willing to give?"

"I'm sure we can do that. You both have earned it, risking your lives to get it back."

"You would do us a really good turn, sir. We need supplies in the worst way."

"I'll make out a receipt for you, showing the amount that I'm giving you. That way, you can pay it back in case the Saltville office doesn't give you a reward, but I'm sure they will."

Sheriff Beal witnessed the receipt of the money to the bank and to R.B. and Sidney. They thanked Mr. Rogers for his help and especially for the reward money. Sheriff Beal said he would keep the gang in jail until he could hear from Saltville.

R.B. and Sidney pumped Sheriff Beal's hand. "Thank you, sir, for all your help.

"You're welcome, both of you."

"Not sure how long we'll be gone, but we'll be back. With any luck, you'll be able to tell the Saltville office about the money."

"I'll do my best. Good luck to you both." Sheriff Beal smiled and nodded.

R.B. and Sidney had pocketed fifty dollars each and felt like lords when they went over to the general store to get their supplies. Sheriff Beal had offered one of the gang's horses for them to use as a packhorse, but they had declined. They had to make up for lost time and could go faster without one.

"Well, the sun's shining. You think we might as well get on the road?" R.B. squinted at Sidney.

"Yep, hate to waste this sun. It feels almost warm."

R.B. and Sidney rode west out of town with full packs and in great spirits. They would find Sam. They refused to consider any other option.

Chapter 36

October 1864
On board the D.A. January

Sam ran up steps to the cabin deck and walked through the doors. The stench hit her as soon as the doors closed. Her hand flew to her mouth as she tried not to vomit. A young dark skinned woman with a snowy white scarf wrapping her hair came over to her. A dirty white apron covered her from neck to toes. She carried a tray with small bottles and bandages on it.

"I'm Ann. Mr. Rice told me he just hired another girl to help. I'm truly glad for another helping hand." Ann looked her up and down but didn't mention the britches.

"I'm sorry…" Caught off guard by the power of the stench, Sam made a mad dash out the doors and threw up off the side of the boat. Sam was embarrassed. This was not the right way to start. She wiped her mouth and went back inside.

Ann looked at her with sympathy. "Yep, that's the way most people feel the first time they step foot in here. I know this may be hard to hear, but you *will* get used to it. If you come with me, I'll show you where you can store your pack and then we'll get busy."

"Thank you. How do you ever get used to this smell?"

"The smell is always there, even though we scrub

the floors and air out the wards. When you come into the wards, you'll see why. Come on, this way." Ann motioned for her to follow.

Ann went back through the doors and down the stairs to the boiler deck. She led the way to the right and opened a door to a private quarters' room. A half dozen cots filled the room. Two small clothes chests were on one side of the room. Ann pointed to the back cot. "That one is empty. The bottom drawer on the far chest is empty, too. You can put your pack there and it'll be safe. We're all very respectful of each other's belongings."

"I have some salve I can put under my nose to help with the smell. My grandma used it when she nursed a man with a gangrene foot. We call it stinky salve." Sam explained as she unconsciously pinched her nose.

"That's a great idea. Do you know what's in it? Maybe we can make some. Go ahead, put it under your nose and come with me.

Sam put the salve under her nose, and her eyes blurred. *No matter, maybe I can't smell that awful smell now.*

Sam hurried out with Ann, who marched smartly down the side of the middle deck filled with beds. Ann put her tray on the table and reached down to the shelf beneath to get Sam an apron. "I know this is hard to do on your first day, but we really need you to empty all the bins." Ann handed Sam the apron, and she put it on. It reached her knees and covered her well. "Come on, I'll show you where we keep the big bin that you empty the small bins into."

"What's in the small bins?"

"Used bandages, mostly. When you fill the big bin, take it over to the boiler men, they'll dump it into the furnaces. When you finish here, go up to the cabin deck, the next floor up, and do the same thing. There are a lot more patients up there."

Ann left her and Sam got busy. She started at the back and worked her way down one side of the ward. The bloody bandages were only one smell that assaulted her nostrils. The other was the slop jars under the beds. Large windows were open to let in air, although it was October, but it didn't help much with the smell. Grandma's salve under her nose helped, but the stench was still overpowering in the heat from the boilers.

Sam finished her tasks on the middle deck and tried not to stare at the men in the beds. She took the full bin over to the boilers and a burly man took it and shoveled the contents into the firebox. He didn't look at her, and she kept her gaze down when he handed her the empty bin. She moved on up to the next floor of the boat.

There were four stoves in the ward, positioned at intervals down from the steamboat smokestacks. Sam gazed at the wounded and sick soldiers. Rows and rows of cots lined the room. Bloody splotches at the bottoms or sides of the sheet told which part of the soldier had been injured or was missing. They looked so miserable and sick; it made Sam wince. Her troubles were nothing compared to theirs.

Several women in long aprons administered to the sick. One woman went to a metal canister and pulled a lever. Holding a tin cup under the little spigot that looked like a sugar maple tap, she filled it with water. *I'm so very thirsty. I wonder if I might get a taste of that water.* She walked timidly over to the woman.

"You think I might have a taste of that water? It's looks mighty good."

The woman eyed her up and down. She started to wrinkle her nose but didn't. "Do you know where the kitchen is? I've not seen you around before. They'll give you a tin cup."

Sam shook her head. "I'm new, but if you point me in the right direction, I'm sure I can find it."

"It's over there in front of the wheels."

Sam looked in the direction she was pointing. She guessed the wheels were under the boards built in a great circle and went on through the ceiling to the next floor. "Much obliged."

Sam started to make her way over to the kitchen room. The constant hum of the boat unnerved her, and she hoped she would get used to it. Yet another whistle startled her, and Sam looked around to identify its source. The boat began to move. A bit unsteady on her feet, she put her hand on the wall to steady herself.

"We're just backing out from the landing. Don't worry. It makes you wonder what could possibly come next, right?" A soldier in the bed next to where she stood spoke to her.

"Yes, it surely does." Sam glanced at his bed but couldn't make out where his injury was.

"You'll get used to it. A steamboat is a fine way to travel, no bumping along rutted roads. Doesn't rain on you, and you don't get trampled by a horse trying to get out of the way. It does get hot, but it's still better than a field hospital." The soldier closed his eyes and Sam moved away. She didn't want to get close to anyone, especially a Union soldier.

The boat stopped, and then slowly started moving in the opposite direction. Sam moved over to a window so she could see out. The steamboat slowly made its way down the river. Sam marveled and smiled. *Well, this might not be so bad after all. A lot better than walking to St. Louis.*

Sam moved along the outer row of beds to the kitchen. Several women, Negro and white, bustled about. One woman peeled onions at the sink and the odor was everywhere.

"Could I borrow a cup for some water, please?"

A woman with a calico wrap on her head tilted her head at Sam. "I haven't seen you around before." Her apron strings barely reached around her ample middle. "Here you go. Please bring it back when you're finished." She smiled at Sam as she handed her the cup.

"I'm new, just working my way to St. Louis. Much obliged for the cup." Sam hurried on out of the kitchen. She walked over to the water tank and held the cup under the spigot. Sam turned the lever, as the other lady did, and the cup filled. She looked around the tank to see how it worked. There was a pipe that went into the tank and then the pipe disappeared up into the ceiling. *Well...what about that?*

Nurses bustled about Sam. They handed out medicines and changed bandages. The bins that she just emptied, filled back up in no time. Sam could see there was a system to the way they worked, and she asked one nurse about it.

"These soldiers have been here a couple of weeks. There hasn't been a battle in a while on the Cumberland. There are a lot of small skirmishes and soldiers get wounded. We'll stop at towns along the way back to Nashville to drop off some of the wounded, if they can possibly take any more of them. There are several hospitals along the way, but Nashville has by far the most. The floor below us has the very sick. We try to keep them away from the general wards. We don't want another outbreak of cholera."

Sam blanched at those words. "Is there cholera down there now? I just came from that floor cleaning up bloody bandages."

"Not that we know of right now. Cholera usually comes from bad water. The men down there have been very sick for a long time and we know weak men will take on a fever and it might spread."

"I better get busy, thank you." Sam moved on down the ward and collected the trash from the bins placed beside the aisles. She took the bin down to the furnaces where one of the sweating men there emptied it into the furnace for her.

"Thank you." Sam forgot to lower her voice. The man looked at her, a bit startled.

Hurrying out before the man could say anything, she ran back up the stairs to the cabin deck. Sam's stomach growled. *How could I possibly be hungry after the stench I have endured this afternoon?*

Sam saw Ann working near a sick bed and went to her. "I know this sounds awful, but I'm hungry. Do they have food for us? I didn't think to ask earlier."

"Our bodies want food, even when our minds are saying no. We take turns going to the dining hall to eat. The cook will hit a pot with a big spoon when it's time for us, which shouldn't be too long now. Ann smiled when she heard the pot being struck. "See, right on time. Follow me." Ann walked across to the dining hall and stopped at a washstand that was placed just inside the door. She poured water into the basin and washed her hands and Sam did the same.

A long table with big pots of food on it sat on one side of the room. Cornbread was steaming beside the big pots. Sam and Ann reached for bowls and filled them with hot stew. Sam placed a piece of cornbread in her bowl and followed Ann to the tables with benches placed on either side.

"So, what's your story?" Ann said as she filled her mouth with stew.

"Story?" Sam spoke with a mouthful of cornbread. *So much better than on a stick!*

"How come you here? We all got a story." Ann took a bite of stew, waiting.

Sam studied her food and put the spoon down. "It's a long story, but I'm going to St. Louis. I don't want to go, but I have to." Picking up her spoon, she took another bite. She surely didn't want to get into all her trouble with a total stranger. Ann probably wouldn't believe her, anyway. "How about you? When did you become a nurse on a hospital ship?"

"That's a long story too. We can talk later on tonight if things stay calm." Ann whispered conspiratorially. "You know we picked up a lady doctor and are taking her down to Nashville?"

Sam's voice was soft. "Why are you whispering? I think I heard that, yes. Why is she on this boat?"

Ann glanced around to see if anyone would overhear them. She kept her voice low. "Well, to tell the truth, I don't rightly know. It does seem a bit off somehow. A *lady* doctor, I never thought I'd see it. They usually make a woman be a nurse or an aide."

"Well, I'm glad they came up to get her, otherwise, I wouldn't have had a way to get to St. Louis. Have you always wanted to be a nurse?"

"Law, no! I ran away from a plantation near Nashville and the Union men, they put me in a camp with other runaways. Contrabands, they called us. They asked us to help, so we did. I'm proud to be a nurse. I ain't a field hand no more." Ann pointed to Sam, then to herself. "They even let us eat together here."

Sam looked at Ann and smiled. "Well, I'm a seamstress. I loved making dresses. Not much call for one right now, though." Sam took a last bite of stew.

"Well! We do have something to talk about!"

They picked up their bowls and took them to the big dishpan in the corner. Ann picked up a tin cup, offered one to Sam, and they walked over to the water tank and filled their cups.

"How can it be so cold?" Sam asked.

"There's ice somewhere on this boat. Not sure how the cold water gets here in this tank, but it's really good. The soldiers need to have clean, cold water."

Sam went back to the ward and picked up where she left off. The suffering on the faces of the soldiers melted her heart, even though they were Federal. All her troubles had been with the Home Guard, and she wouldn't call them soldiers.

The *January* moved on down the river with its suffering human cargo. They passed Waitesboro, Creelsboro, and pulled in to land at Burkesville. The wooders were waiting. As soon as the boat nudged the wharf, the men pulled down the stage planks and loaded the wood onto the main deck. It took roughly forty cords of wood per day to power the *January*. Farmers along the river supplemented their income by selling wood to the steamboats. The Federals who ran the hospital ships paid well.

"How many times do we stop during the day?" Sam asked Ann.

"We usually stop four or five times a day, depending on whether there's wood at the landings. Sometimes, there ain't any, so we have to keep on moving."

"You told me the boat moved along about nine miles per hour, I'm not sure what that means, but if we have to stop so many times, how long to get to St. Louis?"

"We move along at night too, unless it's foggy. Then the captain will wait it out. Too many things in the river to snag us. If we move along all night and all day, we'll reach Nashville day after tomorrow. We'll tie up there and see if the hospitals can take some of our boys. We never know when there'll be a battle and we have to have as many free beds as we can." Ann shrugged her shoulders. "So, I'm not sure how long we'll be in Nashville. But the trip over to Smithland doesn't take very long, maybe a day and night, if we don't have trouble. Then we take the Ohio River over to the Mississippi and go on up to Cairo and then Jefferson Barracks in St. Louis."

"Okay, I understand. I'm so glad to help you here. Please don't think I'm ungrateful. I …"

"We'll talk tonight, after things have settled down. Here come the doctors. Let's get busy."

There were three doctors and as many nurses that followed each of the doctors down the aisles of beds. The doctors looked at the wounds and said something to the nurse, who wrote it down in her notebook. Sam went along, emptied her bins, and kept her eyes averted whenever she could. She sighed when the doctor pulled the blanket over one soldier's face and pronounced him dead.

Sam worked hard to keep things neat. The ward was huge, and she counted a hundred beds just in this section. She made her way down to the end of the ward and couldn't believe how many beds there were. Feeling a wind blowing in her face, Sam looked toward the ceiling. A big machine hanging down made the air cooler. She also noticed there were no flies or mosquitos. Sam couldn't believe all the things that made life easier for everyone on this boat. Of course, this was a hospital ship, and the suffering was acute, so she was glad there were some comforts. The heat of summer must have made the wards almost unbearable.

The ladies who helped feed the soldiers moved down the row of beds. Sam's hungry stomach told her it was getting late. Orderlies went down the ward, lighting the wall lanterns. Sam heard someone bang on the pot and watched for Ann. She went into the dining hall, washed her hands, and looked around. She didn't know if she should wait on Ann or get her food. The cornbread steamed, and she longed for some butter on it. *Oh, how good that would taste!* She was amazed the stench hadn't turned her stomach. She got in line and picked up her bowl.

Ann came in as Sam was sitting down; she said she'd be right over. She marveled at finding a woman friend. Ann had showed her nothing but kindness and she nursed white soldiers as if they were her kin.

Ann sat across from her and looked at her bowl of stew. "I hope this is beef. It's the end of the month and sometimes we don't know what's left."

Sam laid down her spoon and frowned at her bowl. Ann laughed gleefully. "I'm just joshing you, girl! It's beef, and it's still good. Did you see the pie they made for us? The cooks here are real good to us."

Sam laughed and resumed her meal. "No, I didn't see the pie, but I'll be glad to have it. I'm starved. But it seems I've been starved for weeks, ever since I left home."

"Where is home?"

"Coldiron, Ashe County, North Carolina. In the mountains."

"Law, you is a long way from home. Why you leave?"

Sam was silent, and kept her eyes averted.

"Never mind, we'll talk after we bed down the soldiers. You go on to our room. You remember how to get there?"

"Yes, I do." Sam's face brightened. "Let's go get our pie!"

Sam made her way down to the boiler deck, which she learned did not have the boilers. Why did they call it the boiler deck when the boilers were on the main deck below? She didn't understand, but wouldn't ask a lot of questions. She opened the door to the quarters and found the room already lit. A couple of women in their nightclothes sat on the beds.

"Sorry, I'm Sam. I just started today. Ann said I could stay here."

"I'm Tennessee, just call me Tenny." She pointed to the woman beside her. "This here is Capitola; call her Cappy. I'm surprised that Ann would let you stay here. Usually, the helpers have to scrounge around for a place to sleep." She eyed Sam's clothing.

"I don't know why. She just said I could. This cot is empty. I really don't want any trouble. I've had a bellyful of that." Sam walked warily over to the clothes chest.

256

"No. No trouble. I used the last of the water. You can fill the jug from the barrel that's around the corner and down the hall beside the water closet."

"Water closet?"

"The outhouse. You mean that you've held it all day?" Tenny's eyebrows raised.

Sam had had so much to do, she hadn't thought about it. "I guess I thought we would use a chamber pot." She reached for the water jug and walked down to the barrel. Sam put the jug down and cautiously opened the water closet door. Inside was a two-seater. Sam shook her head at the presence of an indoor privy. *What in the world was next?*

Sam sat on the cot in her nightgown and looked through her pack. She put her dirty clothes at the end of the bed. Ann opened the door and leaned against the door jamb. Sam looked up at her. "Do we have a place to wash our clothes? I don't have an extra set to wear while these dry, so I need to wash them tonight and let them dry."

"I have an extra dress, but I don't have men's britches." Ann smiled mischievously.

"I don't have a corset, but this binding works pretty well. I was worried that if I put on a corset, they might find me out." Sam explained and the other women perked up at this revelation. "I had to pretend to be a man when we were leaving the mountains. It was too dangerous otherwise."

Ann nodded understanding. "We all have a story and we'll get to know each other. Sam, I'm sure you can wash your clothes in the laundry room and dry them too. It's too late now; you can do it in the morning."

Sam was incredibly thankful to Ann for the timely rescue. She didn't want to go into detail about her circumstances. Sam put her pack under the bed and made sure her gun was still safely there. She had never used it and hoped she wouldn't have to.

Ann got ready for bed and turned the lamp down low. "See ya'll in the morning."

Sam's next day was the same as her first. She knew what to do and did it. That evening when she went to her room, she found it empty. Ann came in a few minutes later. "The other women have the night duties tonight. No one will bother us, so we can talk a bit."

"Thank you for the dress. My clothes are dry, and I can wear them tomorrow. I had forgotten how much of a nuisance a skirt is. I like wearing britches. I'm becoming a heathen." Sam grinned. "I'll wash your dress in the morning. I'm afraid I got it pretty dirty today."

"Yes, girl, I'm sure you will. Now, how 'bout you tell me a little of your story? Maybe I can help if I knows what it is you're running from. I'm scared for you."

Chapter 37

October 1864
On board the D.A. January

Sam felt the need to confide in someone, and Ann had been so nice to her. She was afraid to say everything but would tell her all she could. When she finished her story, Ann squinted at her.

"Well, what about this R.B.? You think you might see him again?"

"R.B.?"

"Yes, R.B. Your voice went all soft when you talked about him."

"It did?" Sam was glad it was dark so Ann couldn't see her blush.

"Yes, it did. Have you ever had a man?"

"Well, I almost did, once, a while back, right before the war started. It turned out he was no account when all was said and done. I don't have much of a story where men are concerned. I've always had too much to do. My papa died a long time ago and I pretty much took care of mama and the farm. We have sugar maple trees. Made a good living…" Sam took a long pause as her mind trailed back, "…before the War. I was a dressmaker before the War. Everything was before the War!" Sam slapped her thigh and shook her head.

"So, you think that this man Daniels is still after

you?" Ann's forehead furrowed.

"I have no reason to think otherwise. I feel like someone is on my trail, always watching. I can't explain it, but that's how I feel. If I can get to St. Louis, maybe I can find my papa's family and hide out till after the war. That's my plan, anyway."

"Tomorrow we'll be in Nashville. We might be there a while, taking the soldiers to the hospitals that can take them in. Then we'll be on our way. Surely, taking this boat will throw him off your trail."

"Yes, I hope so. I'm worn out, talking so much. I feel so much lighter! Thank you." Sam hugged Ann and then settled on her cot. Pulling up the worn quilt, her mind was at peace as she began to doze. *So much better than the ground!*

The next morning, they pulled up to the wharf at Nashville. They had passed into Tennessee during the night. Sam was afraid to leave the boat in case it left without her. She watched the orderlies getting some patients ready to be moved. She had learned from Ann earlier at breakfast that there were several hospitals near the Cumberland. Several of the patients were being taken to Hospital Number Three because it was close to the wharf. Ann said she had been there. It had been the Ensley Building before being converted into a hospital.

Looking out the window, Sam watched the procession of stretchers leaving the boat. She saw the lady doctor speak to Dr. Rice and then shake his hand. She'd seen them talking yesterday, too. Sam liked the way she dressed. Her skirt was short, around knee length with britches on underneath! Sam watched her leave the boat and then a carriage whisked her away.

Sam was glad when the boat left Nashville and was

on its way. Next stop, she was told, was Fort Defiance and Clarksville, Tennessee. Besides wooding up, Sam watched as they took several soldiers into the sick ward on the boiler deck. Not one of them moved or even acted as if they knew they were being loaded onto the boat. Ann had told her they'd take them to the hospital at Cairo. "Until then, we'll try to keep them comfortable."

Leaving Fort Defiance, Sam found herself at the stern of the boat with Ann. Sam pointed to the machine attached to the ceiling. "Ann, what is that?"

"It's called a fan. You notice there're no flies and skeeters down here? The fan moves the air and blows them away."

"It's almost November, not many skeeters right now."

"Not here, but on the Miss'sipi down towards Naw'leans, they's skeeters big enough to diddle a turkey!" Ann quipped.

Sam laughed and ducked her head at Ann's language, then shook her head at the wonders on this boat.

"It's a fact!" Ann laughed, too, and moved on down the wards.

****

At Jefferson Barracks in St. Louis, they tied up alongside the steamboat Sultana. Sam looked out the window to watch the men at the wharf.

"Them's hogsheads of sugar they're unloading."

Sam jumped in surprise as she heard the booming voice of the big man beside her. She had not heard him come up behind her. He made her nervous. Seemed he always watched her when she went down to the boiler deck. Sam hurried away to find Ann. The burly man's intense gaze followed her as she made her way up to the cabin deck.

Sam found Ann. "I have to talk to you." She took Ann's elbow and moved her along. "Now."

"What's going on?" Ann moved quickly and didn't ask any more questions.

Sam spoke as soon as they were in their quarters. "I think I need to get off the boat. Now." Desperation filled her voice. "I think I can find my way now. Maybe I can go to the sheriff's office and—." Sam paced, taking quick peeks out the doorway.

"Why? What's happened?" Ann attempted to calm Sam's pacing by gently guiding her to the cot, but Sam couldn't be stilled.

"That man, the one at the first firebox. He's always watching me, and he makes me so nervous. I'm afraid."

"Maybe we can tell the doctor about him. I wish you wouldn't go. The Federals have St. Louis. You don't know nothing about this place. We going up to St. Louis in a couple of hours. It's just a few miles. I wish you would wait." Ann's voice was imploring. "Maybe you get your family in trouble. We need time to plan on the best way to find your family." Ann clutched Sam's shoulder. "Don't go off this way."

Sam hugged Ann. "You've helped me so much. I thank you and wish you good luck with all that you do. I'll be fine. I'll find someone to help." Sam gathered up her pack and coat. She pulled the gun out and slipped it through a belt loop on her britches. She pulled her coat closed over it. Self-preservation had once again asserted itself in Sam.

Ann could tell her friend was set on leaving and put her hand on Sam's shoulder. "Please be careful. Let me get you some food to take with you." She made as if to leave and Sam stopped her.

"No time, but thank you." Sam made her way down the stairs and out to the wharf. She fastened her coat against the wind that had come up. Making sure her hat was snug, she started walking along the wharf. Every size of steamboat had been moored in a long line at the wharf. Sam kept her head down, trying not to look at anyone.

Then she heard a man's voice shouting at her from behind. Sam turned and saw the man from the boat coming after her. Fear gripped her and she ran, not seeing the tangled rope that lay in her path. Sam tripped and fell, hurriedly scrambled up but the man had caught up to her.

"I got you now! Been watchin' you. You're coming with me!" He grabbed her.

Sam wrenched free and dropped her pack. She made it a few feet and then turned and stopped. The big man's reddened face was dripping with sweat.

"I got you now, girl!"

Sam reached for her gun, cocked it, and pointed it at him with both hands shaking.

"Aw, you ain't gonna shoot me. You ain't got the nerve!" He started toward her.

Sam stood with both arms extended in front of her, clutching the revolver. She leveled the revolver at him and pulled the trigger.

Click.

"Guess you're out of bullets. Ain't that a shame?" The man gave a derisive laugh as he lunged for her.

In an instant, the past few weeks caught up with Sam. The utter losses, the heartbreak, the exhaustion. Sam braced herself, flipped the lever on the LeMat, and pulled the trigger again. The lower barrel of shot exploded, and the man's face disappeared in a red mist. The gun recoiled, and Sam dropped it in her haste to run. She ran down the wharf, past the rows of ships, parting the sea of people as she went. She ran until her sides ached and she was out of breath.

Down the way, Sam spotted a boat with a long line of women on the stage plank. She quietly and calmly stepped in at the end of the line. *Curious.* They were all dressed in the same type of homespun and ragged coat. Sam shuffled on down toward the boat with the rest. She chanced a look down the wharf before she stepped onto the boat. Sam couldn't see anyone running or searching for her or anyone else. She glanced at the side of the boat and read the name *Calypso*. Sam pulled her hat lower and stepped onto the boat.

A woman at the entrance of the boat was looking at something, Sam couldn't make out what, on each person's shirt front. Then the lady made a note on the ledger she held in her hand. The women were then guided through the double doors. When it was Sam's turn, she looked into Sam's face.

"Where's your name tag?"

"My name tag?" Sam asked.

"You're supposed to have your name pinned to your shirt. Where is it?" The lady wasn't happy.

"I lost it. They just told me to get in line," Sam lied.

"Well, there's not a name on here left to check off." The lady looked at her with narrowed eyes, clearly exasperated.

"I just do as I'm told." Sam looked at the women in line in front of her. They simply remained in position, paying no attention to anything. They just gazed blankly at nothing. Sam found it odd somehow.

"Well, you're on your way back to the asylum, so no matter. They'll take care of you."

Sam grew alarmed. *Asylum?*

Chapter 38

October 1864
Tennessee/Kentucky border

R.B. and Sidney had made good time from Rogersville. They hadn't come across anyone except a couple of suspected bushwhackers at Bean Station. They set up their camp a little distance away from the trail in a cluster of trees near the Tennessee/Kentucky border.

"You think we can chance a fire? My fingers are numb, and we need to make some cornpone. We're out of everything else," Sidney asked.

R.B. looked at the sky. "These clouds make good cover. Let's chance it. I won't unsaddle the horses for a while yet, though. Just in case. We haven't seen any soldiers, North or South, for a while. Don't know what that means."

"I know. It's awfully quiet. I'll get the cornpone on. We can't afford for you to make it. I near about threw up last time and we don't have much left."

R.B. smiled but was wistful. "You reckon we'll find Sam?"

"Now, R.B., it's not like you to be down in the mouth. We'll be at old Jeremiah's place come late morning and I'm sure we can find out something. Mr. Smith always stops there."

R.B. and Sidney heard the twigs snap at the same

time and both came up with their pistols drawn. They scurried away from the campfire's light and glanced around.

Someone shouted from the dark. "Hello, the camp!"

"Make yourself known!" Sidney shouted.

"Mr. Smith, from down Tennessee way. Sidney, that you?"

"Well, I'll be booger dogged! If it ain't Mr. Smith himself!" Sidney holstered his guns.

Mr. Smith walked slowly toward the campfire, hands in the air. "Now, don't shoot me. It's been a long day!"

R.B. shook his head in disbelief and smiled at their good fortune. Sidney slapped Mr. Smith on the shoulder. "I'm sure glad to see you! Mr. Smith, this is R.B. Royster."

R.B. held out his hand to Mr. Smith, and he shook it. Then he looked around for Sam. "Where's Sam? Her grandfather said you were the one who led her out."

Mr. Smith looked at Sidney and then R.B. "Well, let me tell you what happened." He inhaled deeply and then let out his breath slowly.

"Is she okay?" R.B. was breathless. "I just need to know that she's okay before you start."

"Yes, she was fine when I left her."

"You left her!?"

"Now, wait a minute! Don't get all ruffled up! She was fine when I left her. We had to change our plans. You think I could sit down while I tell you the story?"

"Yes, I'm sorry." R.B. motioned to the ground. Sidney and R.B. sat down opposite him and eyed Mr. Smith with expectation.

"Well, now Sam just got plum tuckered out. What

with crossing the rivers and walking all the way. We got up to Jeremiah's place, and I asked him if he knew anybody who could get her on a steamboat to St. Louis."

"What!?" R.B. interrupted.

"Henry Jenkins and I couldn't think of any other way for her to get to St. Louis. You know that Daniels and his bunch are after her."

"They're dead. She doesn't have to worry about them anymore." R.B. held his hands out flat.

"What? They're dead? How do you know?"

"Cause I killed them, that's how."

"Good! They needed killing. But now—"

"But now what?" Sidney interrupted.

"Well, by now she's on her way to St. Louis on a steamboat. Jeremiah knows somebody in Point Isabel. That's where you can get on a boat and sail south and west on the Cumberland River."

"Do you know what boat?" R.B. asked.

"I'm sorry, son, I do not. But you can go to Jeremiah's place and ask. I'm sure he's back by now."

R.B. looked at the fire and sighed. Sidney said, "It's a miracle that we met up with you. I know the Lord is looking down on us."

"And shaking his head, probably," R.B. said.

"We were going to Jeremiah's place because I remembered you said you always stopped there. Thank you for risking coming to our fire."

"You're welcome. I'm sure you can catch up with Sam."

"What say we turn in? I'll take the first watch," R.B. said.

"Sounds good to me. I ain't slept peaceful for a while now," Mr. Smith said.

Mr. Smith and Sidney got out their bedrolls and lay down by the fire and promptly when to sleep. R.B. knew he could stay awake all night if need be. He longed to be on the trail straight away, but he knew they had to wait until daybreak.

Dawn came, and it saw R.B. and Sidney on their way north into Harlan County, Kentucky. Mr. Smith headed south. They traveled all morning and came onto the last ridge near noon. R.B. looked down at the cabin. Sidney said, "Something ain't right. I just feel it. There're two horses tied up at the porch."

"We better go down on foot," R.B. said. They tied their horses to a sapling. R.B. unsheathed his Spencer and dug in his saddlebags for more ammunition. Sidney checked his Colts and pocketed more bullets, just in case. Taking shelter among the trees, they descended the ridge and eventually made it to a large boulder near the house.

"You stay here. I'll sidle up to the cabin and see if anything is going on," Sidney said.

R.B. nodded. Sidney made his way over to the cabin. Then, with his back to the cabin wall, he moved as close to the window as he could and drew his gun. He heard voices inside, but couldn't make out what was being said. Sidney chanced a quick look through the window. At the same moment, Sally happened to move toward the table and turn in time to see him.

"I need to go get more water and then go to the privy." Sally reached for the bucket.

Mack, the bigger man with shaggy hair, shook his head and cocked the pistol he held on Jeremiah. "I don't imagine you'll be up to anything, or your husband here will get a bullet. No matter to me. Pete, you go out with her. See she comes right back."

Pete was sullen, but stood, hitching his galluses over his shoulder and adjusting his pants over his fat gut. Sally took her bucket, headed toward the door, and lifted the latch. Pete followed her out onto the porch. Sidney signaled to R.B. that one more was inside and crawled under the porch to wait for Pete to go on down the steps. Sally moved toward the well and set her bucket down. She glanced over her shoulder to determine if Pete was going to follow her. He slouched down the steps and walked a little way out in the yard, his shotgun slung over his shoulder.

R.B. saw Sidney slowly move under the steps, then around and up to sneak to the door. Sidney signaled to R.B. and R.B. shot Pete, and before the sound was spent, Sidney had kicked open the door and moved inside. Jeremiah shoved Mack away and Sidney shot Mack just as his pistol discharged. The shot sent Mack flying backwards, and Sidney's leg gave way beneath him.

R.B. sprinted toward Sally, who ran toward the cabin. They made the porch at the same time and ran through the open door. R.B. saw Sidney was down and bleeding profusely from the wound in his thigh. Sally ran to Jeremiah and hugged him hard.

"Now, Mother, everything's fine. Let's just see to Sidney here." Jeremiah patted her shoulder.

R.B. took off his bandana and tied it around Sidney's thigh. "Now, we don't want to cut off the blood supply completely. It doesn't look to be the big artery, so we're lucky there."

Sidney tried to sit up but R.B. laid a heavy hand on his chest and said, "No, don't try to get up on your own. You're bleedin' pretty good."

Jeremiah helped R.B. lift Sidney and they carried

him to the bed. Sidney groaned and passed out.

"Get his britches off so's I can get to the wound," Sally said.

"You think we need to go get Aunt Sarry?" Jeremiah asked.

"Let's see what we got here first," Sally said. The men tried to get Sidney's britches off, but it was hard to do with him a dead weight.

"They're not budging," Jeremiah said. "What do you want us to do?"

"Here," R.B. pulled out his knife, preparing to slit the seam.

"I don't want to cut them off him. We don't have nothing for him to wear," Sally said. "Let's slide them down. You lift and I'll slide. Hurry, afore he wakes back up." Among the three, they got Sidney's britches off and settled him on the bed. Sally put an old blanket under his leg to save her quilt.

Sally looked at the wound on Sidney's thigh. "Looks like he's lucky. Went clean through, but we need to wash it and make sure there isn't anything in the wound. Since this war started, I've cleaned many a gunshot wound. I hope this is my last."

"Let's get this dead meat out of the house and then you can tell me what happened," R.B. said to Jeremiah. They dragged Mack out of the house and onto the porch. Pete lay where he had been shot. "We're going to have to bury them quick." R.B. glanced around the yard.

"They're scum. Bummers, coming along trying to take everything they possibly can from honest folks. I'm sure glad that you both came along when you did. They would've killed us just for the meal alone."

"I know this may not be the time, but I just can't

hold it any longer. What boat did you put Sam on?" R.B. held his breath.

Jeremiah smiled. "Oh, so that's the way it is!"

"Yep! I don't think I can stand not knowing one minute longer. We met Mr. Smith on the border, and he told us about leaving Sam with you and you putting her on a boat."

"I put her on the *D.A. January,* a hospital ship. James Ballou, my friend in Point Isabel, helped me."

"Do you know where it was bound?"

"Nashville, for sure. They always go on up to Cairo and sometimes to St. Louis. That's where she said she wanted to get to."

"I need to get there and find her."

"Do you know of the men following her?"

"Yes, they're dead. That's a long story." R.B. cocked his head with a "you-don't-want-to-know" look. Jeremiah's eyebrows rose.

The men went back inside. "Do you need anything, Sally? We're going to bury those fellas and get rid of their gear."

"If you would bring me some water." Sally gathered what she needed to clean and dress Sidney's wound.

Jeremiah went to get the water and R.B. stood over Sidney. "You doing okay?"

"Yeah, ...never ...better..." Sidney's eyes were closed, and he winced as he tried to move. "Did...we...get them?"

"Yeah, we got them. We're going to bury them while Miss Sally works you over."

Sally sat down on the bed and handed Sidney a tin cup. "What's this?" Sidney asked.

"White liquor; you're going to need it. I need to

poke around in your wound and it's going to feel like a red-hot poker."

"Do you need us to help?" Jeremiah asked.

"I think I can handle this. I want you to get that scum out of here and buried. We don't have company very often, but if anyone happens by, I don't want those bodies here. I want to forget about it as soon as I can, and I can't do that if their blood is everywhere."

"Yes, ma'am," R.B. nodded as Jeremiah went out the door.

"We'll take care of it, Mother." Jeremiah brought in a bucket of water and set it by the door. "You just take care of Sidney here." He went and gave her a peck on the cheek.

R.B. moved to get the bucket that Jeremiah brought in. He splashed the water over the blood on the floor and handed the bucket back to Jeremiah to go get more. R.B. grabbed the straw broom in the corner and brushed the bloodied water out the door. Jeremiah splashed the rest of the water on the porch and R.B. brushed it away.

"Your momma taught you good! Thank you, R.B.," Sally said as she worked on Sidney. "I'll scrub with sand later. By the way, nice to meet you!"

"You, too, ma'am." R.B. called over his shoulder as he followed Jeremiah to the barn to grab the shovel. Throwing the two bodies over their horses, Jeremiah led the way to the woods. Searching through the men's gear, they found nothing identifiable. Gear was too scarce to throw away, so they brought it back. The horses would be safe until Jeremiah could find a home for them.

Sidney was asleep when they got back. Sally was busy at the stove and R.B. sniffed the delicious aroma of biscuits baking. "We'll just have biscuits and gravy right

273

now. Jeremiah, I need you to go kill a chicken. We need the broth for Sidney, and we'll eat good tonight."

"I hate for you to kill one of your chickens. I know how scarce they are right now. I can go try to kill a rabbit," R.B. offered.

"Son, there's not a rabbit or even a squirrel 'round here. I've had to go deep into the forest to hunt and they're gone, just gone. When it gets a bit colder, I can kill one of my hogs. I've kept them hidden, and I had a good corn crop this past summer, so they're good and fat. I'll go kill that chicken, Mother."

Jeremiah came in a bit later with the chicken minus its skin and feathers. "Sorry about the skin. Had to make a quick job of it. That wind is blowing hard. Might snow."

R.B. looked out the window. He would go in the morning no matter what. R.B. walked over to Sidney, who was now awake. R.B. sat in a chair beside the bed. "Looks like you're going to be in bed for a while. Jeremiah told me which boat Sam got on. I'll go and find her."

"I'm sure I can ride… Just give …" Sidney's breaths came in short gasps. "me a little… time." His grimace and strained voice revealed he was hurtin' bad.

"Now, Sidney, we don't have time and you know it. You stay here and heal."

"Yes, stay here. We'll take care of you and see that you get well. You saved our lives and what we have is yours." Sally's heart was in her eyes. "You saved my Jeremiah!"

"Thank you, Miss Sally." R.B. smiled and nodded.

In resignation and disappointment, Sidney went back to sleep, and R.B. enjoyed biscuits and gravy.

****

R.B. awoke the next morning stiff from the floor, but it would work itself out. A light snow was on the ground as he prepared to leave, but it looked to be a clear day. Sally had packed some biscuits for R.B. He recalled his earlier conversation with her.

"No, I'm not taking your chicken. The biscuits are fine. You need the chicken for yourselves and Sidney. I'll be fine." He had told Sally. "I'll be in Point Isabel this afternoon. Soldier is in fine shape and rearing to go. Thank you for the hay, by the way."

"You're welcome. You talk to James, he'll direct you, I'm sure of it," Jeremiah said.

R.B. walked over to Sidney and held out his hand. Sidney shook it weakly. "Find Sam and… both of you come back safe. We'll go… back to the mountains. This war can't… go on much longer. We'll go back and… make sugar, like in the old days!"

"I don't know how to do that, but I'm sure you and Sam will teach me!" R.B.'s smile was broad and his heart light at the thought.

"Hey, wait… a minute! Before you leave…You… going to tell me… what R.B. stands for?" Sidney's eyes were bright.

R.B. shifted his weight, looked down at the floor, and thought for a minute. He couldn't remember the last time he told anyone. He nodded to Sidney. "It's stands for… Rhadamanthus Bartholomew."

Chapter 39

October 1864
Point Isabel, Kentucky

R.B. made it to Point Isabel by early afternoon. He had pushed Soldier, but Soldier was used to it. He made it to the bluff above the Cumberland River and looked down. His shoulders slumped. Not a single boat was moored at the landing. He made his way down the trail to the river. He determined to ask for Mr. Ballou at the first building he came to. The sound of saws drew him to the back of the building, where lumber was stacked everywhere. He walked around the building and asked the first man he came to about Mr. Ballou.

"He could be in his office, but if he isn't, then he might have gone home."

"Where is his office?"

The man pointed to the building across the yard.

"I'll check the office first. Thanks."

R.B. knocked on the office door and heard someone yell, "Come in!"

R.B. entered, closing the door behind him. "What can I do for you?" The man stood from his desk and reached for his cane.

"Mr. Ballou?"

"Yes, I'm James Ballou."

"Jeremiah Howard told me how you helped

Samantha Coldiron get on board a boat named the *D.A. January*."

"Yes, yes, I did. How is Jeremiah?"

"He's fine, sir. I need to know how to find that boat. Her brother Sidney and I have come after her all the way from North Carolina. Sidney was shot yesterday and had to stay behind."

"I'm really sorry to hear that. Hope he mends quickly." He motioned toward the chair in front of his desk. R.B. seated himself while Mr. Ballou went behind his desk and sat down. Mr. Ballou went on. "Well, I learned the *January* made it to Nashville. It's a wonder. It's a side wheeler and side wheelers don't fare too well on the Cumberland up this far. But I heard the captain needed to get a passenger on board. So, I don't think the *January* will come back up this far again."

R.B.'s shoulders slumped, and he hung his head.

Mr. Ballou continued quickly. "But you can take a cargo boat at one of the other landings on down the river. You can take the ferry here across to the other side and take the road down to Waitesboro. There might be a boat that's going down to Nashville. The cargo boats are big enough to carry your horse, too. Then you can go on down to Nashville and see if the *January* has come back."

R.B. perked up. "Thank you, sir. I'm beholden to you. Is there an eatin' place around here?"

"Yes, just on down the street here. Beard's Boardinghouse. They have food and a place to sleep if you need it."

"Thank you, sir. You don't know how much this means to me."

"I can guess, I can guess." Mr. Ballou smiled and

offered his hand.

R.B. walked out, took Soldier's reins, and walked on down the street. The boardinghouse had a stable beside it. After settling Soldier, he went in for a bite to eat. Only a handful of people were seated at the tables. R.B. made his way to the corner counter where an elderly man was looking at a ledger.

"Do you have meals here?"

"Yes, sir, we do. Beans and cornbread at the moment."

"That'll do me fine." R.B. walked over and sat at a table, leaning his Spencer up against the table.

"Here you go. Will you be needing a room?" The man said as he set the food on the table.

R.B. was uneasy about leaving Soldier. "No, I'll just bed down in the stable. How much for that? I didn't see a stable hand to ask."

"Two bits for the meal, two bits for the stable, and hay for your horse."

R.B. handed him the money and dug into his beans. They were surprisingly good. Since the big bowl was filled to the brim, he ate his fill for once. The man came back to pour coffee in the mug set before him.

"Thank you."

R.B. finished his meal, picked up his Spencer, and walked back out to the stable. Soldier was fine; he felt like a protective father. Soldier had been with him a long time and he was family. After everything that had happened, he didn't want to take a chance on losing him.

Next morning, R.B. was on his way. He had to get to a boat. The ferry ride was an experience he had to pay two bits for. R.B. prayed the boat he was boarding later wouldn't rock back and forth in the current. He made it safely across and then galloped on down the road to Waitesboro. R.B. got there in no time and tied Soldier to the post at the pier. As he started for the landing office, he heard a long whistle. A man came out of the building, shielding his eyes, and looked down the river and smiled. "Steamboat's a coming!"

"Great! How do I get on board?" R.B. asked.

R.B. walked Soldier onto the boat that held stacks of wooden crates and cords of wood. Pigs were in small stalls, on one side. R.B. walked Soldier over to the bigger stalls on the other side and tied him securely.

Not wanting to simply stand around, R.B. asked a burly fireman if he could help load wood. The man had said, "Yes, have at it."

"By the way, what's the name of this boat?" he asked as he helped load wood. R.B. worked up a sweat, and it felt good to be warm.

"We're not supposed to say. See? The name has been painted over." He pointed to the sign hanging from the deck of the stern. "We're a Nashville packet. We have a lot of cargo for the army, if you know what I mean." R.B. didn't, but he acted as if he did.

Two longs and a short whistle alerted the crew that departure was imminent. They moved the stage plank back onto the boat and the boat slowly backed up and then pulled out into the current, headed back down to Nashville. The boat had to make several stops, which grated on R.B.'s nerves. He did what he could to help speed up the process by loading and unloading crates in Creelsboro, Burkesville, and Celina.

R.B. struck up a conversation with one of the crew. "Do you know of a boat called the *D.A. January*? It's a hospital ship."

279

"No, I don't. But there are more than a hundred steamboats on this river. Gunboats, too. When we get to Nashville, you can look along the wharf. A lot of them are tied up in a row all along there."

"Okay, thanks, I will. Do you know when we'll get to Nashville?"

"Depends on a lot of things. We're moving right along, and we normally don't make any more stops, but that can change. We move at night too, so probably day after tomorrow, in the morning."

"I appreciate it. Do you know if the Federals still hold Nashville?"

"Yes, right now they do."

R.B. shook his head. It seemed a long time since he had been a soldier in the field. A long time since he gazed at the smoke from a hundred cannons that lay over the battlefield. The fact that Nashville was in Union hands didn't faze him. He had one mission now, and that was to find Sam.

The night they sat and talked by the fire seemed such a long time ago. They both had been through a lot in the month since then. He could still see her green eyes and the way she looked up at him. He remembered the first time he saw her. Smudged dirty face, ragged clothes. The way she squared her shoulders as he turned to leave them that last day. He carried the memory of her smile with him in his heart.

R.B. anxiously scanned the wharf when they pulled in at Nashville. He asked if he could leave Soldier in the stall for a bit while he searched the wharf for the *January*. Michael, the crewman he had gotten to know, said they would be there all afternoon, so he didn't have to worry about his horse. "I'll make sure no one bothers him."

"Thanks, I owe you," R.B. said.

"No problem, I'm here anyway. Got to guard this stuff."

Unfastening his Spencer from the saddle, R.B. laid it in the corner of the stall next to the wall. He piled hay over it and made sure Soldier wouldn't step on it. Then, he hurried off the boat in search of the *D.A. January*.

R.B. pulled his coat closed and buttoned it. The wind off the river was cold, but the sun was shining. Pushing his hat down, he walked among white and Negro men unloading and loading the boats. R.B. couldn't believe the number of boats tied up along the Nashville wharf. He was about to the end of the line, but next to the last was a huge boat that looked different from the others. The side wheel of the steamboat had "U.S. Hospital Ship" emblazoned on it. R.B. read the name on the sign hanging from the main deck of the stern. *D.A. January!*

R.B. knew the odds of the boat being back in Nashville had been enormous, but here it was. He waited until the plank was clear and he walked onto the boat. He walked through the double doors and asked a nurse where he could find information on someone who had been on the boat.

"Miss Ann, she's on the next deck up. She's a dark skinned woman, a nurse with a long apron. She knows a lot. I just started, so I don't know anyone."

"Thank you, ma'am. I'm obliged." R.B. went up the stairs to the next deck. He walked through the double doors and the stench made him retch. R.B. put his hand over his mouth and nose and looked around. He saw a woman with a white scarf tied around her head, piling bandages into a basket that was on the table.

"Excuse me, ma'am. Might I ask you a question?"

"Sure." Ann said as she kept piling bandages into the basket.

"It's about Samantha Coldiron."

Ann's hands stilled, and she turned. "Let's go out on the deck so you can breathe." Ann left the basket and walked out the doors. R.B. followed and gratefully sucked in fresh air, but the stench was still in his nostrils.

"If you tell me your name, I'll tell you if I can help you or not," Ann queried.

"R.B. Royster, Major." He paused a second. "No, never mind about that part."

"Well, well, you did come after her!" Ann's smile shone all over her face.

"You do know her?" R.B. asked.

"Yes, she was on this boat. She helped us a great deal."

"Can you tell me where she is?"

The look on his face broke Ann's heart. "No, I can't. I'm sorry. We were at the wharf at Jefferson Barracks in St. Louis when she got worried because one of the firemen, that's the men who keep the furnaces stoked, was after her. She said she needed to get off the boat and try to find someone to help her find her family. I asked her to please not go, but she was very stubborn. She said goodbye and got off the boat. I was watching and I know what happened next. That man went after her and she shot him. Then she ran off down the wharf. I don't know where she went after that. I'm sorry."

R.B. was completely broken. He took hold of the ship railing and would have twisted it off if he could have. His heart felt like it was shriveling up inside him.

Just then, a dockworker came over to Ann. "Miss Ann, I knows where she went. I seed her get on another boat." The man smiled hugely, knowing he could help Miss Ann.

R.B. stared at him. "What boat? What boat?" R.B. shouted.

The man was terrified of the white man standing in front of him who was so clearly upset. The man stammered out, "It was the *Calypso,* sir, the *Calypso!*"

A look of terror crossed Ann's face as her hand covered her mouth in a gasp.

"What? Tell me!" R.B. demanded.

"The *Calypso* is a prisoner of war transfer ship."

Chapter 40

October 1864
On Board the Calypso

Mrs. MacGregor escorted Sam and the other women down the hall of the main deck. Sam noticed several women in regular clothes, albeit rags, in the room across from the one they were ushered into. She heard male voices as well but couldn't tell where they were coming from. Mrs. MacGregor informed them, "Sit down in here. I'll be right back."

Sam's gaze swept the room. She didn't know whether to try to escape or not. Surely she was safer here. She could sort things out when they got to where they were headed. Sam tried to look out of the one high, small window that opened out upon the cargo deck. But she couldn't see past the cargo that was stacked there. Sam heard men's voices outside the window, so she moved closer.

"The prisoners are in a room near the stern. They're headed to the State Pen on the Missouri River at Jeff City, Missouri. If we want to break them out, we'll have to wait until they wood up in Washington."

Sam heard the other man huff, but the first man continued.

"I know, that's a pure Union town, but the Federals have control of everything all along the Missouri River.

I can have the boys waiting there, but we gotta decide now. Depends on the current, but they'll probably get there mid-morning in full daylight. So be prepared."

The other man had a very distinctive accent Sam hadn't heard before.

"Ya, we are Union, but some of our families are on this boat. The military does not care who they put in the Gratiot Street Prison. They say they will sort it later. Bah!"

"I'll go tell the boys that we'll have to be ready in Washington tomorrow morning."

Sam now understood she was not only on a boat going to an asylum but there were prisoners of war here as well. One thing she knew, she wasn't going to be in St. Louis and she wasn't going to be able to look for family. Best thing was to stay alive. With a sinking feeling, Sam realized that R.B. wouldn't know where she had ended up. That hurt worse than anything. She hadn't realized how much until now.

Sam kept her head down and listened intently for anything that would tell her what was going on. The lady came back and looked them all over again before she moved down the hall where a man met her.

"Mrs. MacGregor, I am Captain Brandon. I have a favor to ask. I need for you to watch over the women in Room Two. They aren't violent. Just make sure they stay in the room. They've been released from Gratiot Street Military Prison. The provost marshal didn't want them released here where southern sympathizers were on every corner. After we take you and your patients up to St. Aubert Landing, we're transporting the prisoners to Jefferson City. We'll release the other women at Lexington."

"Yes, sir, Captain Brandon. Did you telegraph St. Aubert of our arrival? We hope to have a wagon waiting to transport the patients to the asylum in Fulton."

"Yes, I gave the order."

"Thank you, sir."

Sam kept her head down. She had to keep her wits about her. *Do I want to leave the boat? No. I'm sure they're looking for me for killing that brute, even though he was trying to hurt me. Now, I have two sets of people that're after me. Maybe an asylum would be a good place to hide. I'm not sure what an asylum is, but Mrs. MacGregor made it sound like a home. We'll see.*

The wooden floor vibrated and Sam felt the boat move. No whistles announced their intention of leaving the landing. The boat slowly moved out into the current, headed upstream. Sam looked around the room at the women who were of all ages. All were silent and sat with their hands folded in their laps. The hard benches weren't comfortable, but at least they were off the floor.

Sam spoke to the woman beside her whose name tag read 'Tildy.' "Do you know where we're going?" Sam asked.

The woman put her finger to her lips. "Lady said to be quiet. So, we better be quiet," she whispered.

"Are you scared?"

"No, they said we're going home. They told me that, and I remember home is good." She sat back and looked straight ahead, firmly closing her lips.

Sam realized the woman was simple; they all were. She breathed a heavy sigh.

Mrs. MacGregor came back and said, "Brace yourselves, it'll be a bit of rough going for a few minutes. Turning up the Missouri River from the Mississippi can get a bit scary, but it'll be all right. Captain Brandon knows what he's about."

Sam felt the boat shuddering as they moved out of the current of the Mississippi River into the current of the Missouri. The boat stayed on course and steadily the hum grew fainter. Moving by water was faster than by land, but she still didn't like the water. Mrs. MacGregor wasn't scared, or at least didn't act like it, so Sam figured she had done this before and came out all right.

Sam was starving but didn't dare ask when they might have something to eat. A young man in a Federal uniform came to the door. She figured he must be a guard because he had a rifle strapped across his shoulders.

"Cook says to bring your people down to the mess now." The young man abruptly turned and headed back down the hall.

"Okay, let's all stand up and follow me. We're not going far, just down the hall." Mrs. MacGregor motioned for them to follow her. Everyone did as she asked, including Sam.

As they made their way down the hall, Sam looked for the ladies in Room Two, but they were all gone. She found them a minute later in the mess hall. The ladies were seated at one of the long tables that filled the room. The tables had benches on either side and filled the thirty-foot long room that was as wide as the boat. Mrs. MacGregor ushered her charges along the side of the room. She handed each one a bowl and a spoon. A man dressed in a dirty apron put splashes of beans in the bowls and slapped a piece of cornbread on top.

The beans needed salt, and the cornbread was dry, but Sam and the others were hungry, so they ate. A woman from Room Two asked for another bowl of beans.

"What you think this is, a hotel? One bowl a piece; the men get fed next."

The frail woman sat back down. The hopelessness that came from her eyes was palpable. "It's all right, Mary, I'll share mine." Another woman said to her. "We'll be home soon."

"But we don't know what we'll find at home. The Yankees have taken everything, burned what they couldn't carry and left us with nothing." Mary put her face in her hands.

"We Kincheloes stick together. We'll be okay."

"Thank you, sister. I appreciate that." Mary looked up but didn't look convinced.

After their meal, Mrs. MacGregor instructed the patients to line up in front of a bucket of water. They all took turns having a dipper full of water. Sam saw the water was clear so it was probably not from a river. Thank goodness. She remembered that Ann had told her river water could cause typhoid.

On the way back to their room, they stopped at the water closet, and each took their turn. Sam tried not to breathe in the putrid odor, but it was too powerful.

Back in their room, they settled back in the same places they were before. There was no source of light, leaving the room shrouded in darkness. Sam realized they would have to sleep on the floor where they were but was too worn out to care. They all lay on the floor, heads toward the doorway.

Something woke Sam, but she didn't know what. The room was black but for a slight glow from the window. Sam felt for the bench and crawled up on it and stretched out. She was almost comfortable and at least she didn't have someone breathing their bad breath in her face.

When morning came, Sam wondered what would happen next. They started the day with the same meal they had for dinner, beans and cornbread. The same guard came to the doorway.

"Mrs. MacGregor, we're stopping at Washington Landing in a few minutes to wood up. We'll be about an hour, so if you want to get your people out on the deck for a few minutes, you can. Just keep them to the port side, and they'll be out of the way."

"Thank you, Mr…?"

"Green, Sergeant, ma'am."

"Thank you, Sergeant Green."

The boat steadily made its way to the landing and tied up. One man lugged the heavy stage plank over and dropped it on the landing. Mrs. MacGregor led her group out to the deck and around the corner. A few of the wooden crates were low enough to sit on, but most were stacked high. Sam observed the dock where a large amount of wood was piled up next to the river. Green led his guards out the door, onto the deck, and then onto the landing. He looked around the landing for the wooders. They were nowhere to be seen, although a group of men were striding down the lane from Front Street. Sam could see a church spire in the distance. Everywhere she looked, she saw houses made of brick. A train depot sat a few yards above the landing on higher ground.

"Where've you been? We're on a tight schedule. Load up as quickly as you can." Sergeant Green ordered the men.

A young man dressed as a farmer had a pistol strapped to his side. "We had a delay along the road.

We're here now, we'll get to work."

The soldiers' rifles rested on their shoulders, and their stance suggested utmost boredom. Suddenly, the soldiers were surrounded by the would-be wooders.

One man pulled his pistol. "Put yer weapons down right now and nobody will get hurt."

The men with him pulled their weapons at the same time and trained their guns on the surprised soldiers. One soldier stepped back and tried to run back to the boat.

"Just give me a reason to shoot you, Yankee, just give me a reason!" Sarvis begged.

"Sarvis! Don't shoot!"

"Aw, Stith, he was trying to run." Sarvis lowered his gun and turned to Stith.

"We don't want any trouble."

The soldier had stopped when Stith had yelled and was walking back to the others. He stacked his rifle with the others and moved to stand with the other soldiers. Sergeant Green knew he could kiss his promotion goodbye.

"Stith, what should we do?" Another farmer asked.

"Do not, I repeat, do not hurt anyone. Do not fire your guns. A steamboat landing is an everyday occurrence here. We don't have to invite the whole town down here. Nathaniel, you and Sarvis guard these fine soldiers. Let's go get our boys." Stith strode toward the plank to board the boat.

Stith and a couple of his men boarded the boat, and Mrs. MacGregor took exception. She spread her arms wide to protect them. "Don't you dare hurt my people!"

"We're not here to hurt anyone, just don't get in our way," Stith told her.

Mrs. MacGregor moved as if to protect her charges

further, and her dress hem caught on the edge of a crate. She stumbled and fell, hitting her head as she went down. Sam jumped up to help her. One of the men took it for an act against them and pushed her down.

"I'm only trying to help Mrs. MacGregor." Sam jerked her arm away. She leaned over Mrs. MacGregor. She was awake, but blood streamed from a cut on her forehead.

"I'll go get a towel." She got up and followed the men inside. Stith questioned her.

"I'm just going to get a towel for Mrs. MacGregor." Stith nodded for her to go on.

They had their guns drawn and one fireman waved to them.

"Everybody here is with you, Stith. Ain't nobody gonna say nothing. You go about your business. You might need to go put the captain in his place, though."

"Thanks, Tobias. I owe you." Stith sighed in relief and patted the man on the back.

"Lucas, stay here and guard them, just to make it look good," Stith said.

Sam ran up the steps to the cabin deck to look for something for Mrs. MacGregor. Stith hurried up to the pilothouse and met the captain coming down.

"What's going on? Why isn't the wood being loaded?" the captain asked.

"We have a slight change in plan." Stith pointed his gun and motioned for the captain to come on down the stairs. They went down to the boiler deck and off the boat.

Captain Brandon looked around at the sight of the subdued soldiers being held at gunpoint. "You have just cost me my contract with the State!" He shook his finger at them all.

"Awe, button it up and stand over there. We'll be gone in a minute." Stith motioned with his gun. "Come on, Lawler. Let's go see about our southern boys." They went back onto the boat and walked down the corridor, looking to the left and right. They came upon the women in Room Two.

"Are you prisoners? Do you want to come with us? We're getting the prisoners out of here."

"Are you out of your mind? We just survived six months in Gratiot Street Prison. We won't survive trying to get away from here. Besides, they're taking us home." Mary's voice quivered.

"You believe those Yankees will do as they say?" Stith asked.

"We have to take our chances. We're in no shape to run, and they know that."

"Okay, whatever you want; we didn't know you were here. I'm sorry we can't help you."

Stith and Lawler went on down the hall and found the prisoners. They looked so frail and ragged; it would be hard for them to walk out on their own. The rescuers assisted the prisoners to stand and helped them down the hall and out into the sunshine.

"Back on the boat. Move!" Stith said to the soldiers. He pointed to Nathaniel and Sarvis and said, "Come with me. We need to lock them up."

The soldiers, with their hands high, made for the boat.

Stith pointed to his men. "Okay, the rest of you, follow the plan. We'll meet you in a few minutes."

Stith, Nathaniel and Sarvis marched the soldiers and the captain to the room where the prisoners had been.

Stith closed the door and put the lock on it. It didn't matter if any of them had the key; the hasp was on the outside. That should hold them for a while.

Stith and the others came back out on deck and Stith looked at Sam. She held a towel to Mrs. MacGregor's head. The patients stood there with blank stares at Mrs. MacGregor. Then they looked at the man holding the gun. Not comprehending, they looked like they wanted to speak, but all stayed quiet—except for Tildy.

"That wasn't nice, and now Mrs. MacGregor is hurt." Tildy said, shaking her finger at him.

"We're sorry, and we're leaving." Stith motioned for Nathaniel and Sarvis to come with him. "We need to meet the others in the alley behind Clayton's store. They can't wait long. There were more of them than we realized. We don't have enough horses for everyone."

"We'll sort it when we get up there." Sarvis was matter-of-fact.

Stith turned to Sam. "Do I have your word you won't help the soldiers get out?"

"You do. I'm a Southerner, same as you." Sam raised her chin in defiance. "This war has torn up my life, and I *will not* help a Yankee. I'm going to help Mrs. MacGregor with the others here and mind my own business. You better hurry."

Stith studied her briefly. He could tell she was proud. "Thank you. Good luck to you." He strode off toward Front Street to catch up with the others.

Chapter 41

October 1864
On board the Calypso

Sam gathered the ladies and ushered them back to the room. She lent her support to Mrs. MacGregor as she made her way back to the bench.

"Thank you. Wait, I still don't know your name. I know you didn't come with the other patients from the women's prison. I appreciate your help." Mrs. MacGregor's voice held concern, nothing else.

Sam's shoulders sagged, but thought she had to be honest. She took a deep breath. "My name is Samantha Coldiron. Please don't turn me out. I…I have no place else to go. I have a question too. If these women are patients, why were they in a prison?"

"We'll talk later. Don't worry. I'll explain. I need to clean up."

"I'll bring you a clean towel and see if Cook has something to give you for the pain."

"Thank you." Mrs. MacGregor leaned her head against the wall.

Sam walked down the hall and stopped at Room Two. "Are you all okay?"

"Yes, we couldn't go with them. We're sick. The Yankees are taking us home. We have to believe they'll do as they said they would. Is Mrs. MacGregor hurt bad?" Mary asked.

"No, but her head is bleeding. I need to find some clean towels and maybe some medicine."

Sam walked down to the mess hall. Cook was nowhere to be seen. She saw a doorway at the side of the room. Walking over, she looked in and found bags of beans and cornmeal. There were several bottles on the shelf. Sam picked up one and read Laudanum on the label, the next, Quinine, Paregoric, Morphine powder. She didn't understand what these medicines were. No willow bark? Sam didn't see anything that would help her friend. What she needed was some good white liquor, but she didn't see a jug anywhere. She picked up a clean towel and some bandages.

Sam walked back to the room where Mrs. MacGregor and the others were. An enormous crash startled her. She ran to look out into the hall. The door to the prisoner's rooms had burst open and the soldiers fairly flew out of the room running to the front of the boat. They grabbed their weapons that had been stacked on the landing and looked up at the Washington waterfront. There was no movement they could see.

The firemen rushed back up on deck. "Are they gone? We need to get this wood loaded up and get out of here!" Tobias panted.

"I give the orders around here!" Captain Brandon pointed to Sergeant Green. "You all help them get this wood loaded up. We don't have the manpower to follow them. I'll send a telegraph to let Jefferson City know. Do any of you know where the sheriff of this town is located?"

Sergeant Green spoke up. "The Provost Marshall, Colonel Eitzen, controls this area. At least he did. I'm not sure now. He's never long in one place. They do have a sheriff, August Brinsick, but I haven't met him, so I don't know what he looks like. Sir, if I may, those prisoners won't get far. They were sick. Gratiot Prison is so crowded with sick, we needed to move some to the Jeff City pen. They probably won't live long, anyway."

"They still broke out, and that is a blot on my record. Captain Bryan will have my head. Jonas, go up to Front Street and try to find the sheriff. If you can't find him, we'll send a telegraph to Jefferson City."

Jonas, the chief mate, ran up the lane to Front Street. The soldiers and the firemen loaded the wood onto the boat. A few minutes later, Jonas came rushing back down from Front Street. He held his side until he could get his breath. He hesitated before speaking to Captain Brandon. Jonas looked at the sky and shrugged his shoulders.

"Well, speak up! What did you find out?" Captain Brandon bellowed.

Jonas spoke as fast as he could. "The telegraph and ticket office were burned a few weeks ago by Price's Army. Price is still rampaging over the countryside. The sheriff's also a doctor, and he left a note on his door saying he's out delivering a baby." Jonas backed away from the Captain as he delivered the undesirable message.

From where she stood, Sam heard the whole conversation. She had never heard so many swear words come out of anyone's mouth, especially without taking a breath. When the captain was out of swear words, he took a deep breath.

"Let's get the rest of this wood loaded," he said through clenched teeth. "We'll steam as fast as we can to

St. Aubert. If the lines are down here, they probably are down all along the river. No use wasting time stopping in Hermann. We have enough wood to get to Jeff City. We'll just get the women to St. Aubert, and then go on to Jefferson City and make a report."

"Sir, will we take the other women to Lexington?" Tobias asked.

"We'll see what happens at Jeff City."

"Sir, we still need to see if we can raise a posse to get the prisoners back. Like I said, they can't get far," Sergeant Green said.

The captain was clearly out of patience. "You go right ahead. But the people of this town have just been raided. They'll not want to go anywhere and leave their families. This boat is leaving. It's up to you whether or not you come with us."

Sergeant Green looked resigned and waved to his troops to come back on board.

Captain Brandon stomped on board and hollered to anyone who would listen. "Cook, Cook! Where the hell are you? Make some coffee!" He stomped up to the pilothouse.

Cook, hiding in the privy, opened the door, slipped out and hurried down to the mess.

Sam went to Mrs. MacGregor and sat beside her. "Can I get you anything?

Mrs. MacGregor smiled. "A cup of water would be good."

Sam went to the mess and asked for a cup. Cook handed the tin cup to her and went back to his pots and pans.

The patients sat quietly but eyed Sam as she handed the water to Mrs. MacGregor. Sam saw how the women watched longingly as Mrs. MacGregor drank. She went back to the mess and picked up the bucket and dipper and brought it back to the women. When they all had a dipperful, Sam brought it to the other women in Room Two.

"Thank you. What's your name?" Mary asked.

"Samantha Coldiron. Yours?"

"Mary Lewis Kincheloe. Do you think they'll still take us to Lexington?"

"The Captain, Mr. Brandon, said he would see. I'm sorry. I hope they do."

Sam went back to Mrs. MacGregor. The boat was moving along at a pace faster than Sam had felt before. Maybe it wouldn't be long now.

"Mrs. MacGregor, would you tell me now about how you're here with these women?"

"I work at the State Lunatic Asylum in Fulton, Missouri. Three years ago, in October 1861, we had to send the patients home because we no longer had funding. The city diverted the asylum tax to the military. Counties fell behind in their payments and families no longer sent money for their relatives' care. The administrator, Mr. Smith, sent out a notice for the families to come get their family members, but few came. We had to take them home and to hospitals that could accept them. They sent these patients to St. Vincent de Paul Catholic Church in St. Louis. They were good enough to take them in as they have a hospital of sorts."

Sam nodded her understanding as Mrs. MacGregor went on.

"The Federals occupied our asylum for a year or so. When they left, we were able to get a portion of the asylum ready for patients. The state is paying us again so we can afford to keep our people. I came to St. Vincent's to get the patients who were sent here. I had a roster of their names. Yours was not on it." She smiled at Sam.

"I came to this boat quite by accident. But I'm very glad I did. Men are after me but, I was only defending myself. I…"

Mrs. MacGregor patted Sam's hand. "You can tell me later. It's no matter right now." Mrs. MacGregor's Scottish brogue was soothing to Sam's ears.

The *Calypso* steamed up the Missouri. They passed Hermann, Missouri, and finally made it to St. Aubert Landing. Clouds were gathering on the horizon when they tied up at the landing.

Mrs. MacGregor asked the captain about their wagon.

"I'll see about your conveyance myself. I'll be back shortly." Captain Brandon went out to the landing. The wind came up and his cap almost blew off. The soldiers came out on deck and asked if they could be of assistance.

"I gave an order for a telegraph to be sent to the authorities here in St. Aubert. I now know that they probably didn't receive it. We need to see if we can get these women to safety."

"There's a telegraph office here, just up the road. I'll go and see what can be done," Jonas offered.

"Thank you. Please be quick about it."

Jonas hurried off the boat and up to the shack. He was glad to find it occupied. A young man was lighting the lantern on the wall. "We need to find a wagon to transport some patients up to Fulton. Do you know anyone who can do that for us? It's very important.

These people have been through a lot."

"I have a horse hidden a little ways down the river. I would offer to go to St. Aubert and see who can be found, but I can't leave this building unattended. It would cost me my position."

"I'll run back and tell the captain what's going on and see if I can stay here for you. I'll be right back."

Jonas ran back to the boat and explained and then ran back to the shack. The man had put on his coat. "The captain said I could stay while you go. Thank you, ah, what is your name?"

"Joseph, Joseph Lawler. I'll be back as soon as I can."

****

Joseph's old horse had but one gait— slow, but it was easier than walking. A wagon and mule team were tied up in front of the saloon. Recognizing the team, Joseph pulled up. He went into the saloon and looked around. He spotted the wagon maker, Mr. Allen, at the bar talking with the barkeeper.

"Mr. Allen, sir, might I have a word?"

"Joseph! What are you doing away from your post at this time of day?" Mr. Allen asked.

"Well, I've come to ask a favor of you, sir."

"Let's sit and talk about this favor." Mr. Allen walked to the nearest table and motioned for Joseph to do the same.

"Sir, this won't take a minute to ask. Sir, the captain of the steamboat, *Calypso*, has asked if you could possibly use your wagon to transport some women patients back to Fulton. He had telegraphed, but he didn't know the lines were down. Might you help? These ladies are tired and scared and need to get to a dry and safe place. Might you help, sir?" Joseph talked fast while turning his hat round and round in his hands.

"It's getting ready to storm, don't you think it best they stay on the boat for now?"

"They have no accommodations on the boat, sir. They slept on the floor last night."

"Well, let's try to get the canvas over the wagon." Joseph and Mr. Allen went outside to the wagon. "Help me put the bones up. They fit in these pockets on the side."

Joseph and Mr. Allen worked to put on the frame for the canvas and then unfolded the canvas top. It popped and buckled in the wind, but they secured it over the frame in short order.

Mr. Allen climbed onto the wagon and reached for the reins. "Come on, mules!"

Joseph rode alongside the wagon back to the landing. Mr. Allen got down and tied the mules at the post. Captain Brandon walked out to meet him.

Joseph introduced them. "This is Mr. Allen."

"Captain Brandon of the *Calypso*. Thank you for coming to these women's rescue. I'm sure the state will reimburse you for the trip."

"I'm sure they will, but it might take some time!" Mr. Allen laughed. "Let's get the women on the wagon. It's going to storm, and we need to get on the road. It'll be way after dark when we arrive, and the road is pretty bad."

Chapter 42

October 1864
St. Aubert Landing, Missouri

Mrs. MacGregor came out on deck and was introduced to Mr. Allen. "I'm so glad to see we have transportation. It's been a terrible day. Thank you so much for helping us."

"That's fine, ma'am. Let's get loaded up. We need to make some time."

Mrs. MacGregor ushered the women out on deck and down the plank toward the wagon. Mr. Allen helped them up. There was no place to sit except on the floor of the wagon. "If I had known, I would've put some hay in the wagon. It'll be rough."

"We'll be fine." Mrs. MacGregor turned to Captain Brandon. "Thank you for all your help."

"I'm sorry about all that has happened today and the fact the telegram didn't go through so they would know you're coming."

"Well, that couldn't be helped. We'll make do." Mrs. MacGregor nodded at the captain.

Captain Brandon helped Mrs. MacGregor up beside Mr. Allen. She pulled her bonnet strings tighter against the wind as Mr. Allen slapped the reins and said, "Come on, mules!"

Sam was glad to be on dry land again. The canvas

flapped over their heads but stayed securely tied. Mrs. MacGregor said it was fourteen miles to Fulton, but they were going at a snail's pace! It would take a while to get there in this wagon that was shaking her to her bones.

Cook had fed them before they left the boat. He had watered down the bean soup, and there was only a small piece of cornpone for everyone. Sam was proud of the other women. They sat stoically and tried not to bounce into each other. No one said a word. It was a little unnerving.

As soon as it began to rain, Mrs. MacGregor climbed into the back. She settled herself in and gave Sam a weary smile. The rain dripped off Mr. Allen's slicker and the brim of his hat.

In spite of the jolting ride, Sam, as well as the others, kept falling asleep. They arrived at the asylum around midnight. All things considered, Mr. Allen had done a superb job getting them there. Mrs. MacGregor hustled them inside. Sam glanced around; the place was huge. Mrs. MacGregor didn't want to wake the entire place, so she led them up the grand staircase to the second floor. She walked down the corridor and went through a doorway leading down another hall. Sam became hopelessly lost. Mrs. MacGregor took them into a room with several rows of small wooden beds covered with blankets and a pillow.

"Now, we'll clean up in the morning. Let's get our shoes off and slip under these nice, warm blankets." Everyone did as she asked, and Sam settled down under the blankets, falling asleep immediately.

****

Sam awoke at dawn with light streaming through the tall windows. She sat up and noticed Mrs. MacGregor was lacing her shoes. "I'll get you some clean clothes. I know you want to dress as a woman now. Think there's even a corset around here somewhere. We'll have to look around for shoes, but we can clean your boots up for now. After breakfast, I'll take you to meet Miss White. She runs the sewing room. I'm sure they'll let you work there. We need all the hands we can get." Mrs. MacGregor spoke fast to ease the worried expression on Sam's face.

"Thank you! I'm so grateful to you for all you've done for me! Are you sure they won't turn me out when they find out about me?" Sam worried the blanket in her hands, twisting it in her eagerness for answers.

Mrs. MacGregor's face gave the indication she wasn't sure, but she didn't voice it. "Let's get you cleaned up."

Sam felt almost human again after a bath and a clean dress that almost fit her. She tightened the belt and ran her hands down the skirt's dark cloth. Her hair wasn't long enough to put in a bun, so she smoothed it back and tried to pat it into place.

"Here, I have a net that you can use to keep it back. You need to look tidy for Miss White." Mrs. MacGregor handed Sam a black hair net crocheted from fine thread.

Sam had never worn a hair net so wasn't sure how to put it on. She twisted it round and round.

"Here, let me." Mrs. MacGregor said and reached over to tie it up, tucking in stray strands of hair. She tried to make sure Sam's ears were covered. "There, that will do. Let's go eat breakfast. I'm hungry, and I know you are too."

"Where is everyone else?" Sam asked as they walked down a corridor.

"I took them down to breakfast while you were washing up. We'll see them in a minute."

Sam went down the stairs with Mrs. MacGregor and walked into a huge room filled with tables and benches. The hall was full of men and women of various ages seated at the tables.

"Let's go get our breakfast," Mrs. MacGregor said as she walked over to the front of the room. The workers filled Sam's plate with bacon and eggs and something they called porridge. The porridge Sam knew didn't taste anything like it, but it was sweet and hot. She feasted a bellyful!

"Let's get on over to the sewing room. I'm sure you're anxious to get this over with."

Sam nodded, not able to say anything.

Mrs. MacGregor led the way through yet another hallway, down through another corridor. Sam noticed a door with sunlight streaming through the glass panes. "Mrs. MacGregor? Might we see the outside before we go on? I couldn't tell anything about this place last night."

"Of course, we can take a minute." They walked outside where the sun shone brightly on the white stone of the four-story building. "This is the back of the building, but you can see the middle part here and the north and south wings. We're standing where the administrator's office and the various other offices and quarters are on the second and third floors. The north and south wards house the patients. Now, we better go back in and get some things done."

Sam followed her back in and was amazed at how big the rooms were. She had seen some sights on her journey away from home, that was for sure. Sam followed Mrs. MacGregor down a couple of corridors to what she learned was the sewing room. Light shone through the tall windows. There were shelves filled with bolts of cloth on both sides of the room and along the back on both sides of the door. Several ladies were hard at work, sewing at a large table. Sam could see a sewing machine in the next room. Her palms were clammy, and her stomach rolled.

Mrs. MacGregor spoke to a tall woman with her hair severely pulled back in a bun. Her dress was as severe as her demeanor. She held a ledger of some sort in one hand and a pencil in another. "Miss White, this is Samantha Coldiron. She would like to work here in the sewing room."

Mrs. White looked her over, and Sam quailed. "So, you say you can sew?"

Sam closed her eyes for just an instant. She could see the purple satin unfurl across her cutting table as she shook it out. Sam straightened her shoulders and nodded slightly.

"Yes, ma'am, I can sew."

Chapter 43

Monday, May 7, 1984
Jefferson, North Carolina

Sarah and Ruth stopped at Hardees for a breakfast sandwich on the way to the library. Hardee's had a special, two sausage and egg biscuits for 99 cents. They were ecstatic about saving money for breakfast. Now they could have a better lunch. They pulled up to the library at 8:55 a.m. and observed a lady unlocking the door. The amateur sleuths, with notes and tablet in hand, hurried up to the door. They explained to her what they needed. The lady directed them up to the second floor. "Mrs. Kemp is who you need to see. She's been doing genealogy for thirty years."

"Thank you!" Ruth said.

Sarah and Ruth hurried up the stairs and over to the counter. A lovely older lady was busy stacking books on the desk.

"How may I help you?"

"Are you Mrs. Kemp?" Sarah asked.

"Yes, I am."

Sarah hurried to explain. "We're here from Missouri to find out about my ancestor. Dolores Tucker from the Kingdom of Calloway Historical Society called for us week before last about Samantha Coldiron."

"Yes, I remember. I was the one who looked up the

census for you. Nice to meet you. Could you both come over to my office for just a moment?"

Sarah and Ruth gave each other a sideways glance but followed her to her office. Sarah was hoping for a magic bullet.

"Sit down for just a moment, please." Mrs. Kemp gestured to two chairs in front of her desk. "I can tell you're both ecstatic. It's written all over your faces. But I want to share something that I figured out a long time ago. You must be slow and deliberate when you look through old records. One can't scan quickly. You'll overlook vital information if you hurry. I'll help you learn how to use the microfilm machine." Mrs. Kemp let that sink in. "Now, which census did you want to look up today?"

Sarah folded her hands in her lap and looked at Mrs. Kemp. "First of all, thank you for calming us down. We need to go back to Missouri in the next couple of days, or else we'll lose our jobs. That explains why we appear to be in a hurry because we are. We appreciate your help very much. Could we look at the 1850 census? We want to find out if Samantha's father was in the household. That way, we can find the deed at the courthouse and maybe find out where they lived."

"Well, you're in luck! We have a book compiled by Danny Miller on the 1850 census that you can look through. You won't have to look at microfilm. The 1850 census is special because it's the first census listing the household members by name, as well as the head of household. The index in the back lists all the people from the census alphabetically."

"Wonderful! That'll save us a lot of time! What about the 1870 census?" Ruth asked. "We decided we needed to see the 1870 census too. We want to find out, if we possibly can, if R.B. did return with Samantha and live here. We thought the 1870 census will tell us that."

"No, we don't have that one yet. Mr. Miller is currently working on compiling the 1860. I don't know if he plans to do an 1870 abstract. We can look at the microfilm for that year."

Mrs. Kemp led them out to the reference section of the library. She found the 1850 census book for them and handed it to Sarah. "I'll go over and get the 1870 microfilm ready for you."

Sarah eagerly opened the book to the index. Ruth looked over her shoulder and then sat beside her. Sarah read out loud while she ran her finger down the page. "Let's see, Cockram, Cocram, Colbert, *Coldiron, 30-33-59.* Okay, so Coldirons are listed on pages 30, 33 and 59." Sarah thumbed through the pages to page 30. She found James and Nancy, yet there was no one called Easter and no children were documented. Sarah flipped to page 33. Jesse B. Coldiron, 32, and beneath his name was *Easter, 30*! Underneath Easter was Sidney, 10 and Samantha, 5.

"Oh, Sarah! We found them!" Ruth had tears in her eyes.

"Yes, we did!" Sarah hugged her friend and whispered, "We need to quiet down. We're in the library."

A lady walked by and said with a grin, "We get that a lot!"

Sarah wrote everything down and then looked for Mrs. Kemp. She was walking toward them and motioned for them to come over to the microfilm machine.

"I've put the reel in for you. You turn this little

crank, and you can see what's on the film by looking at the screen here." She pointed to the screen. "You're in luck. John H. Carson could write legibly, while so many others could not. He was the Assistant Marshall of Ashe County in 1870. He's the one who conducted the census." She turned to go. "One more thing. You'll have to go through each page because the entries are not in alphabetical order. The census taker started at the beginning of a road and worked his way down it, stopping at each house. The people you see listed lived next door to each other."

"Thank you very much." Sarah sat down in front of the screen. "I'll take the first turn, Ruth. It looks like there's a lot of pages to go through."

"I'll watch you and look too, although you have to have your face pretty close to read it."

Sarah read the top of the page:

"Page one, Chestnut Hill Township, County of Ashe, State of North Carolina, enumerated by me this day, 20th of June, 1870. John H. Carson, Ass't Marshall. Written on the top left of the page was "Post Office: Jefferson."

The first household was Stamper, E.C., 61 years of age, male, white, farmer. Value of Real Estate, seven-hundred dollars, Value of real property, three-hundred thirty-three dollars, born in North Carolina. He was a male citizen of the United States.

"Well, I think we need to just look for the name of Coldiron, don't you think? Better not take the time to read everything," Sarah suggested.

"Yes, maybe that'll be best. All the other stuff is so interesting, though," Ruth said.

Sarah looked down through the page looking for the

name Coldiron. "Oh no! Ruth, I should have been looking for the name Royster, too! What if they did come back and got married? I've wasted twenty minutes!"

"Sarah, be calm. Remember what she said. Let's wind it up, start over, and look for both names. Do you want me to do it for a while?"

"Yes, please. I'll go to the bathroom. We should take turns more often, so we don't get a headache and can keep a clear head."

Ruth looked up as Sarah came back and sat down beside her.

"Sarah, the thing about the 1850 census book we looked at is that it doesn't show the township or the post office. On the 1870 census, it gives this information. This will narrow down where they may have been living."

"Yes, I'm glad we decided to look at the 1870 census." Sarah took over again at 11:30. Ruth needed a walk. "I'll walk around downstairs for a few minutes."

"Okay, I'll come get you if I find something" Sarah rubbed her temples. Then she slowly turned the crank and tried not to hurry through the pages. At 11:45, Sarah was staring at the record, but had been hunting for it so long she almost didn't recognize it. The entry read: *Royster, R.B., 34, male, white, farmer and sugar maker.* Underneath R.B.'s name it read: *Samantha, 25, female, white, sugar maker and housekeeper*! Listed beneath her name it said, *Prince, 4, male, white!*

Sarah was white lipped when she motioned for Ruth to come over. Ruth started crying. She couldn't help it; her nerves were so shot. Sarah hugged her friend.

Sarah started writing everything down as fast as she could but had to keep wiping tears so she could see. Mrs. Kemp came over to them and smiled. "Success, I would guess!"

"Yes, yes, I can't believe it!" Sarah's face was flushed, and she waved her hand to cool it.

"Do you want me to print out that page for you? That way, you'll have it exactly as it appears on the page. It's 10 cents a copy."

"You can do that? Yes, please!" Sarah hugged Ruth again.

Sarah's hand trembled when Mrs. Kemp handed her the copy. "Thank you so very much for your help. You don't know how much this means to us." Sarah gave her the dime and picked up their papers.

They floated down the stairs and out to the car. The sun was still high in the sky, and the car hadn't moved. Everything looked normal outside, but Sarah and Ruth had been altered forever. As if in a daze, they strolled to the car and climbed in.

"Well, it seems as if a long time has passed since we walked through the library door this morning. What say we go get something to eat? My head is spinning, and I need a Diet Pepsi in the worst way." Sarah rubbed her eyes.

"Yes, I believe we've earned it. I want a Dr. Pepper!" Ruth massaged her temples.

"Let's go back the way we came, so we don't get lost. Let's just stop at the first place we come to. I'm pretty sure we can find the courthouse now." Sarah was confident. "With the information we just found, we're sure to find out where Samantha lived."

Chapter 44

Monday, May 7, 1984
West Jefferson, North Carolina

The women had no time to waste. Because the diners were packed, they had to go all the way back to Hardee's to get a sandwich. They hurried back down Main Street to the courthouse. Pulling into the parking lot, they got out of the car and dashed in.

Entering a wide hallway that ran the length of the courthouse to the double doors at the back, they saw a beautiful oak staircase winding up to the second floor on both sides of the entrance. The hallway had multiple oak doors, each featuring a glass transom. The hallway was vacant, so Sarah and Ruth entered the first doorway on the left. They were in luck; it was the Register of Deeds office. The ladies walked up to the first desk.

"How may I help you today?" a lovely older lady asked. The nameplate on her desk read "Ellen McAlister."

"I'm Sarah Davis, and this is Ruth Kincheloe. We have some information on an ancestor and wanted to see if we might find out where they lived here in Ashe County."

"Are you here to do a title search?" Ms. McAlister asked.

Sarah looked at Ruth with surprise. Ruth said, "No

one has mentioned a title search to us. We don't know what that is. We wanted to find the deed, so we could find out where the property is located."

"Yes, that's a title search. We can't do that for you. But," she said hurriedly because of the pained look on their faces, "we can do it this way. I'll show you the index books and how to look for the names. Come this way."

Ms. McAlister led them through the doorway to the records room. It was like walking into a giant safe because of the thick metal door. Rows upon rows of huge deed books lined the walls, each set in its own little cubby hole. At the end of one row there was a stack that read *Index.* The Index books were labeled *1799-1822, 1822-1870* and so on.

Ms. McAlister explained as she pointed out the books. "Each Index book has separate tabs for each letter of the alphabet. The entries are listed by surname then given name. But the names are not in alphabetical order. For example, all of the A's are together, B's and so on. They're listed according to grantor. Grantor means they're selling the property."

Ms. McAlister pointed to the next ledger. "This is the Indirect Index, those are listed by grantee."

The women gave her a deer-in-the-headlights look. She hurried on. "But we won't go into all of that right now. You can just go to the tabs you need and look through those pages for the names."

"The Index books will have the book and page number on it out to the side of the name in the next column. Come get me if you find a name and I'll get the correct book to look up the deed. If you have questions, please ask one of us. We're glad to help."

"Thank you so much for your help. This is the first time we've done anything like this," Sarah said.

Sarah and Ruth put their purses in a nearby chair and went over to the daunting stack of ledgers. Sarah reached for the 1799-1822 Index book in the bottom cubbyhole and pulled it out. "May as well start at the bottom," she said as she lugged the huge ledger to the table. Ruth did the same with the Indirect Index book with the same dates.

Sarah opened the ledger and looked at the entries. A few were very easy to read while others were written in a scrawl that was almost impossible to decipher. Sarah slid her fingers down the "C" section and was disheartened when there was no Coldiron listed. Same thing for the R's but she didn't expect to find the Royster's yet.

"How are you coming, Ruth?"

"Nothing. Maybe I'm not looking correctly."

Ruth went to ask for help. "Ms. McAlister, might we ask a question?" Ms. McAlister followed Ruth back into the deed room.

"We know the Coldiron's lived here, but we're not finding any pages with their names on it. Are we looking correctly?" Ruth asked.

"They might have been renting property. Also, if the property was inherited, the heirs didn't always record that transaction at the time. Sometimes, they didn't record the purchase or the fact that they were bequeathed the property until they sold it."

"Oh no! That would be like looking for a needle in a haystack!" Sarah moaned.

"Yes, sometimes. That's why title searchers make a good living." Ms. McAlister smiled encouragingly.

"You should take a look at the next book. See what you can find."

They took the next Index book, *1822-1870*, and pored over the pages together. The same for the Indirect Index for the same years. Then they took the Index book with the dates *1870-1889*, to the table. On the second page of the R's they found *Royster, R.B.* as grantor and in the space for grantee was written "*procession of land,*" Book U and page 585. Under Title of Instrument, it said "Procession."

Ruth ran to get Ms. McAlister. "We found something, we found something!"

Ms. McAlister hurried back to the deed room. She looked at the entry that Ruth's finger was on. "Okay, let's look in Deed Book U and see what we find."

Retrieving Deed Book U, she turned to page 585. There, in flowing script, was the description of the property. "Procession of lands known as the R.B. Royster property." It did not, however, give the location of the property, just a description, which was followed by fifteen poles and such. But at the bottom of the deed, there was a plat drawn out of the property, showing the property was in the shape of a triangle. It also listed who owned the land adjacent to the property. The name Muckleduff was written on the top line of the drawing and McGovney on the bottom, but they couldn't make out the name on the short part of the triangle.

"You're in luck! We hardly ever find a plat on the deed." Ms. McAlister was astonished.

"But what is "procession?" How're we going to know where to look for the property? It doesn't show any roads or anything." Ruth's voice rose a notch with every word.

"Procession means they're making sure of their boundaries. If there were any roads, they would probably be changed by now. *But* we can look for it because of the property's unique shape on our old plat map. It will just take a little time."

"Do you have time to show us that? It's almost 3:30." Sarah was hopeful.

A pretty woman in a navy pants suit came through the door and walked around to an empty desk. The nameplate on the desk read "Cherrie Jones." She put her purse down and came over to the group. "What ya'll got going on over here?" Cherrie looked at the ladies in expectation.

"Well, we just found an old plat map. The property is uniquely shaped, which should help us locate it on our big plat map," Ms. McAlister explained.

"Let me see." Cherrie walked over to the deed book. "I know that piece of property. Mr. Muckleduff, who is a descendant of the first Muckleduff here in Ashe County, just sold that piece of property that's adjacent to the one in question. I can look in the files to see where it's located, and, in turn, find the property you're hunting for. How's that?"

Sarah clapped her hands, and Ruth nodded vigorously. Cherrie went over to a cabinet and pulled out a file. She shifted her focus to the plat map and traced it with her finger. She stepped back to the file cabinet and took out another file.

"Okay, here it is. That property is registered to a William R. Royster, 620 Bland Road, Jefferson."

Sarah and Ruth started dancing. "I feel good, na-na-na-na-na-na-na!" Sarah smacked her hands over her head. "Yep, so good!"

Ruth was crying and jumping and hugging everybody.

Sarah was beside herself. "Could we please borrow a phone book?"

Chapter 45

Monday, May 7, 1984
Jefferson, North Carolina

The ladies in the Register of Deeds office offered the use of their phone, but they declined because they didn't want to talk about it in front of them. They drove to the pay phone in Hardee's parking lot. Sarah dialed the number with shaking hands. It rang four times and then a deep voice answered.

"Hello?"

"Hello. My name is Sarah Davis. My friend Ruth is with me. We've traveled all the way from Missouri to Jefferson. We just spent the day in the library and the courthouse looking up records. Are you William R. Royster?"

"I am."

"Well, this would be so much better if we could talk in person. We've found an ancestor here and would like to talk to you about it if you have time."

"I'm sorry I can't right now. I have plans for this evening. But if you want to come by in the morning, I'll be here."

"Yes! That's great! What time?"

"I'm an early riser. Is 8:00 too early?"

"That's fine. Would you give me the directions to your home?"

Sarah wrote as he spoke and repeated it back to him to make sure she had it right. To get lost now would be a catastrophe. She hung up the phone and rested her head against it. This endeavor had become so important, the most important thing actually. *Just don't mess this up now, Sarah.*

Sarah got back into the car and beamed at Ruth. "We can meet him in the morning at 8:00. I wish we could have gone this evening, but the sun is already on the other side of the mountain and he's busy. I told him where we were staying, and he said it would take about twenty minutes to get to his place. So, I guess we have time to have a nice supper. Let's go down to that nice diner, Hometown, was it?"

"I believe it was. We can brainstorm on our strategy for tomorrow when we speak to him. We can't mess this up now," Ruth said.

"I was saying that very thing to myself just a minute ago!"

Sarah and Ruth had a nice sit-down dinner and made it back to the motel before dark. Showered and in their pajamas, they talked into the night. Since neither could rest, they waited until the sun came up.

Sarah awoke with a start at the buzzing of the unfamiliar alarm. She couldn't find a button to make it quiet. It was the old-fashioned kind with a bell that rang incessantly. She finally found the button and shut it off.

Ruth sat up, trying to get out from under the covers. "Well, that was quite a wake up. I guess we did fall asleep after all."

The pair hurried to get ready and left about 7:15, figuring in extra time in case they got lost. That gave them a good forty-five minutes to be there by 8:00. They followed Mr. Royster's instructions exactly. Sarah's last notation was of a dirt road. There was no sign on the road, but Sarah knew it had to be the right one. "Well, at least all the other roads were marked. This is the only road to the right, so it has to be the correct one. We'll take our time. We still have ten minutes."

Sarah slowly drove the Torino down the lane. The morning was bright and there wasn't a cloud in the sky. A large two-story log house sat at the end of the lane. Maple trees surrounded it and a rail fence separated the yard from the driveway. Two red barns sat in the distance behind the house with mountains rising steeply behind them.

A man came out of the house and walked toward them. Sarah caught her breath. She had never seen a man as handsome as he. She immediately sucked in her stomach and wished fervently she had let Ruth color her hair. The man took off his hat, and the sun shone on his full head of wavy silver hair.

"William Royster, ma'am." Mr. Royster smoothed his full silver beard with one hand.

Sarah looked up into his cobalt blue eyes. "Sarah Davis and this is Ruth Kincheloe." She extended her hand, and he shook it and then turned to Ruth to do the same.

"So glad you could make time for us, Mr. Royster," Sarah said calmly, even though her heart was beating like a sledgehammer.

"Bill, please. Let's go to the porch. We can sit and talk."

"Yes, that's a great idea." Sarah and Ruth walked toward the porch as Bill extended his hand for them to go ahead.

Sarah sat down in one rocker and Ruth did the same.

"May I get you some tea? Unsweet is all I have. I can add some sugar. Is that okay?" Bill asked.

"Yes, unsweet is fine," they answered, even though they never drank it.

"I'm so nervous!" Sarah whispered to Ruth when Bill had disappeared through the doorway. She kept rearranging her collar and putting her hands flat on her lap.

"Me too, but we're here now. We have to be strong and articulate." Ruth patted Sarah's hand. "Try not to be nervous."

Bill came out with their tea on a tray and set it on the small table in front of them. He handed the tea around and sat in the chair opposite them. "Well, it's nice to meet you ladies, but I must admit I'm mighty curious about why you're here. I don't get much company out here. I'm sort of off the beaten path."

"You can say that again," Ruth blurted out and then looked sheepish.

Bill's smile was so quick, Sarah almost missed it. She guessed a smile was something that was a stranger to his face.

"Okay, Mr. Royster—Bill—" Sarah smiled and went on. "There's only one way to start, and that's to just start. We really hope that you don't think we're crazy. The past month has been very different for us. Well, I mean... so much has happened since we found Samantha's journal," Sarah said.

Something flickered in Bill's eyes when she mentioned Samantha, but it was gone in an instant. Sarah explained everything that had happened since they found the journal. Bill listened intently and didn't interrupt.

When Sarah stopped, Bill leaned forward with his fingers steepled together.

"I'm going to be honest with you right off the bat. There's no need for anything else. I found that cave when I was a boy. I found Prince's smelter, his press and the dyes. I found the silver blanks he hadn't made into coins yet. I know all about the counterfeiting, but I've said nothing about it to anyone. I didn't and I still don't want anyone to know about that. I—"

Ruth interrupted, "But, the journal also said she hid some gold coins."

"It was silver that I found. Uncle Prince was smelting ore and coining silver. I don't know anything about gold coins."

Sarah heard the reference to "Uncle Prince" and her heart leapt.

"Let me get the journal and you can read that part. Then you'll see what we're talking about." Sarah hurried to get the journal out of the car. She handed the journal to Bill. "See, I have it marked."

Bill read the page. "I've been over that whole cave several times. I've never come across anything like this. I would tell you if I had. Really." He closed the journal. That seemed final.

Sarah stammered, "W-Would you consider letting us see the cave?"

"It's a hard climb up there. I haven't been up there in almost thirty years. It really is too dangerous. I'm sorry." Bill spread his hands in a definite no, even as he said the words.

Sarah bit her lip and Ruth put her fingers to her lips, trying not to cry.

"Is it the money that you're after?"

Sarah felt so dejected that she couldn't be insulted. "No, I guess the quest to see if the remnants of Samantha's life were here is what we wanted to find most. We don't think that fifty gold coins are worth a fortune or anything. We've researched and studied and looked for so long it seems as if she's family now." Sarah took a deep breath to keep her voice even. "Did she exist? Did she ever come back? Did R.B. find her and bring her back home? We were hoping to find that information, and we did. I guess we'll have to be content with that. Sorry to have bothered you. We'll leave now." Sarah awkwardly tried to smile.

All three of them stood.

"Thank you for your time." Ruth walked down the porch steps.

Sarah looked up at him. "Yes, thank you."

Bill hung his head and toed the ground. He started to speak then thought better of it.

Sarah and Ruth got into the car. Neither said a word until they were on the black top headed toward the Highlander. "Do you want to get on the road as soon as we get back? It's only 9:30. We didn't tell Mr. Beckworth we would stay another night. We might as well make some progress toward home." Ruth's voice was soft. She didn't want to make Sarah cry or let herself either.

"I am just so disappointed. I really thought we would find out *something* about the gold. It didn't occur to me to ask Mr. Royster how he was related to Samantha. I wonder if he would've told us."

"He seemed like a private kind of man who doesn't give much. He looked sad to me." Ruth paused as she thought out loud. "Maybe he thought it wasn't any of our business."

Silence filled the car as Sarah drove. Neither had anything to say. Sarah pulled the Torino into the space in front of their motel door. "I'll tell Mr. Beckworth we'll be on our way," Sarah said.

"I guess you were unsuccessful in your research. You look pretty down in the mouth, I'd say," Mr. Beckworth observed.

"Well, we were successful in a way. But we didn't find out everything we wanted to know. Thank you for a very pretty room. We've enjoyed it immensely."

"You're welcome! You both come back and stay anytime."

Sarah walked up to the room and started packing. Ruth had cleaned up the bathroom and made sure they hadn't left anything on the shelves. Sarah shrugged her shoulders and looked around the room. It felt as if they were leaving home. Sarah sighed and walked out the door to the Torino. She gazed across the road at the beautiful mountains.

"Sarah! Sarah! Telephone! It's Mr. Royster!" Mr. Beckworth shouted from the office.

Chapter 46

Tuesday, May 8, 1984
Jefferson, North Carolina

Sarah and Ruth drove back to Mr. Royster's house as fast as they dared. Bill was waiting for them at the door.

"Thank you for changing your mind." Sarah smiled up at him.

Bill looked down for a second and then widened his eyes at Sarah. "Come in; I want to show you both something." He held the door for them to come inside.

The women entered the great room of the log house. The kitchen was to the right and a rock fireplace encompassed the left wall. Directly in front of them was a staircase that led to a loft. Bill gestured toward the oak table that was surrounded by chairs. On the table was a garment, laying on sheets of yellowed tissue paper.

"It's my great grandfather's Confederate officer's uniform. Major R.B. Royster, to be exact."

Sarah and Ruth stared in amazement. The gray wool was weathered, and the brass buttons had darkened with age. The collar and cuffs were a faded yellow. With their hands behind their backs, they leaned close so they could see every detail.

Bill explained. "The gold braid trim on the sleeves was called 'chicken guts.' There are three braids that denote Major. The black and red badge on his sleeve was a sharpshooter's badge."

"We read about it. It's so great that you still have it," Ruth marveled.

Sarah hesitated. "What made you change your mind about us?"

Bill looked at her with that intense blue gaze that made her stomach knot and quoted Clint Eastwood, "Everybody's got a right to be a sucker once."

As she gazed into his eyes, Sarah's heart thundered so loudly that it echoed in her ears. All she could think of to say was, "*Two Mules for Sister Sarah* is one of my favorite movies!"

Ruth just smiled, clasped her hands behind her back and rocked on her heels.

Bill held her gaze a couple of seconds before he averted his eyes and said, "Okay, let's get going. We have a climb ahead of us. I have a jug of water and my Mag Lite. I don't know what we'll find at the entrance to the cave, so I'm bringing my rope. Did you bring your jackets?"

"Yes, they're in the car."

Bill held the door for them, but then stopped them with a hand. "I want to tell you both that if we find anything, it'll be yours. No matter what we find. I just wanted to make sure you both know how I feel about it."

"But that won't be fair. Surely, we have to divide it. We've been prepared to divide it," Sarah argued.

"Well, I've told you how I feel, so let's get going."

Sarah offered to carry the flashlight, but Bill had it clipped to his belt which held quite an array of things. One looked like a knife pouch and some other gizmo in a leather case. He led the way behind the house and up to the trees that covered the mountain.

"Just follow me. It's going to get steep pretty fast. Just try to plant your feet as you climb. It's going to take almost an hour to get there."

They climbed silently. They used what breath they had just to breathe. They all shed their jackets after a few minutes and tied them around their waists by the sleeves.

Bill stopped for a drink. "You all doing okay down there?"

"We're... fine." Sarah's words came out as gasps.

"You need a drink? The spout lifts, I don't have cups. I've wiped off the spout." Bill handed Sarah the red and white Igloo jug. Sarah drank deeply and handed the jug to Ruth. "That's the best water I've ever tasted." Ruth handed the jug back to Bill.

"Mountain water, there's nothing like it!" Bill turned around and started back up the mountain. After ten minutes or so, they came to a small clearing. Sarah turned around and saw a vista spread before her. The mountains extended as far as you could see. The valleys were saturated with deeper hues than the ridges, and everything was enveloped in a blue haze.

"This is the most beautiful place I've ever seen," Sarah said in awe.

Pride rang through Bill's deep voice. "The Blue Ridge mountains are the most beautiful mountains, at least according to me and the people who live around here. The blue mist you see gives them their name."

After a brief rest, they continued their trek up the mountain. Sarah noticed enormous trees that had orange blossoms on them. "Bill, what are the trees with the orange flowers?" Sarah asked.

"Tulip poplar trees."

"Oh!" Sarah's enthusiasm piqued. Her voice raised a notch in excitement. "Sam hid the money in a cave that was hidden by a massive tulip tree."

"Yep, that's where we're going. It won't be long now."

Sarah and Ruth panted and followed Bill blindly up the mountain. They stopped when he stopped. He looked around. Sarah gave him a questioning look.

"Just getting my bearings. Don't worry. It's been a while, but I know where it is."

Bill climbed a bit farther west, and they followed. Sarah looked up when he said, "I believe it's just over here." Sarah and Ruth followed his gaze upward as he pointed. The Tulip tree *was* massive. The tree's branches provided a vast canopy of orange blossoms over their heads. Fallen blossoms furnished a beautiful orange ground cover.

"Oh my goodness! It's here, just like Sam said!" Sarah's face glowed with amazement.

Bill's smile transformed his countenance. "Yep, right here. This tree is probably more than 400 years old." He moved around to the other side of the tree where the boulder still guarded the entrance; there was still a dark space on one side. Bill swiped away layers and layers of leaves from the opening, got down on his hands and knees and looked into the dark crevice. He pulled out his flashlight and flicked it on. He lay down flat and leaned over with the flashlight, casting the beam about.

"I can't tell how far it is to cave floor, but if I remember right, it's not far."

"In the journal, it said it was just a few feet. Sam had tied a rope around the tree and lowered herself down with her lantern," Sarah said.

"Yes, that's what we better do. I'll go down first," Bill said.

"Yes, I vote for that!" Ruth said. They all laughed. "I'll just stay up here and keep watch."

"No one knows we're up here," Bill said.

"Exactly. Someone needs to stay here and go for help in case this goes wrong, plus…"

Bill held his hand up to stop her. "I understand. That's a good idea." It was obvious that no matter what, she wasn't going down into that cave.

Clipping the flashlight back onto his belt, Bill tied his rope around the immense trunk of the tree. Then he pulled a couple pairs of gloves out of his pocket and handed a pair to Sarah. "These might help." He sat down at the edge of the opening, grabbed the rope with both hands and eased down, flipping the rope as he descended. His head disappeared and then he hollered out. "I'm on the shelf! There's another ledge that leads down into the room. Sarah, I'm going to let go of the rope. You pull it up and then let yourself down."

Sarah pulled up the rope and tried to figure out how she was going to lower herself down without falling in altogether. She put the gloves on, sat down, and wrapped the rope around her right hand and while holding onto it with her left. She scooted over the edge and leaned into the rope as it took some of her weight. The rope took more of her weight as she started down. Her arms started to weaken. *This is a lot harder than I thought. I don't have the arm strength like Bill.* As her muscles began to quiver, Sarah broke out in a sweat. *Oh, no! I'm slipping.* As she lost her grip, Sarah frantically grasped at the rocky ledge, but could do nothing but fall. With eyes squeezed tight, she braced herself for the hard impact.

Landing squarely on top of Bill, she scrambled up. He had broken her fall as they tumbled on the rocky ledge. Looking up, she saw she'd only fallen a couple of feet.

Hearing the commotion, Ruth rushed to the edge and hollered down, "You guys okay?"

Bill laughed as he quickly scrambled to get up. "No broken bones!" he shouted. Then looking at Sarah, his voice held concern. "You okay, Sarah?"

"Yes, are you? Oh my, I'm so sorry! My weight slamming you to the ground couldn't have been pleasant!" Sarah laughed self-consciously as she picked herself up and dusted off her clothes.

"I'm fine." Bill grabbed the flashlight and cast its beam around the cave. Sniffing the air, a slight frown crossed his brow. "There must be a sulfur vein around here."

Trying to calm herself, Sarah took a whiff and nodded. "Yes, in the journal Sam said she smelled sulfur and was glad because she figured that drove out the snakes."

"I don't see any evidence of snakes." Bill jumped down to the cave floor and turned to help Sarah down. She took his outstretched hand and jumped down.

"I'm kind of scared. I want the gold to be here so badly." Her words sounded a lot calmer than she felt after holding Bill's hand.

Bill moved the flashlight beam settling on the big iron press. Sarah couldn't believe it. *I am actually standing in the exact cave in North Carolina that I read about in a journal! A journal I found in the attic of an insane asylum in Missouri!* Her excitement made her giddy.

"Sarah, you go on and look. If it's there, I want you

to find it," Bill said.

"Okay, I will." Remembering how Sam had described where she put the gold, Sarah knelt and reached up to feel under the wooden cabinet. Finding the ledge, she moved her hand around the ledge all along the side and down toward one end. She shifted position and felt along the other side when she nudged something. Her heart skipped a beat when she felt along the contours of it. *Could it really be true?* Sarah's breath quickened as she grasped the fabric and pulled it down into the light. It was a thick cotton bag. Sarah squealed with joy. "It's here, I found it!" Shifting her weight to get up, she laid the bag on the cabinet. Bill held the light as she pulled off her gloves and opened the bag. She tipped it and watched the gold coins slide out in a pile.

"Oh, God! Oh, my! I can't believe it!" Sarah jumped up and down.

"Did you find them?" Ruth hollered down into the cave.

"Yes, yes! We did!" Sarah squealed.

Bill was grinning from ear to ear as he shook his head in disbelief. "Let's get these back in the bag and get out of here. We can look at them down at the house," Bill said.

"Great idea!" Sarah scooped up the coins and put them back into the bag.

"You'll have to put the bag in your pocket. My pockets aren't big enough." Sarah handed him the bag.

Bill pushed the bag down into the big pocket on his pants leg and pushed the Velcro flap down to secure the bag. "Ready now. Let's go. You go first and I'll help you up," Bill directed.

Sarah moved toward the ledge, and Bill helped her

up the step. Sarah grabbed the rope. "I didn't realize how much strength it took to hold your weight. The movies make it look so easy."

"Your feet can help you climb. It's a matter of leverage. Just try to walk up the wall. Ruth will be there to help you out."

Sarah grunted and pulled and tried to pull herself up. Bill helped push from behind, which made them both laugh. Eventually, Sarah made it out. Bill climbed out easily and stood to brush himself off. Everyone was grinning with victory and congratulated each other.

Ruth's eyes sparkled with curiosity. "Could I see them?"

Bill stooped to open his pants pocket and pulled the bag out.

Ruth peered inside. "I just can't believe it! We found them!" Ruth danced a little jig, and they all laughed.

"Let's look at them down at the house. I don't know about you all, but I'm starving!"

Bill put the bag back in his pocket. He loosened the rope from the tree and coiled it up and put it back around his neck and shoulders.

"Now, going down can be just as tricky. We'll stop when ya'll need to stop. Plant your feet, especially in the leaves. You'll slide if you don't."

The trio made their way down the mountain. The sun was shining, and it was a glorious day!

Chapter 47

Tuesday, May 8, 1984
Jefferson, North Carolina

Finally reaching the bottom of the mountain, the weary but happy trio dropped gratefully onto the chairs on the porch. Feeling parched, Bill offered to go in and get tea for everyone. The ladies followed him inside, offering to help. Bill set out glasses and then opened the fridge. Sarah sneaked a peek and didn't see a Pepsi or a Dr. Pepper one. Bill poured their iced tea, and they went out to the porch.

Ruth released a huge breath after taking a long drink of her tea. "Finding treasure is hard work." Bill and Sarah gave her a comical look and then they all laughed.

Bill pulled at his beard as he thought. "What we need to do first is find out how much these coins are worth. I do a bit of coin collecting and I have a person I trade with down in Asheville; Les Stevenson has a rare coin shop and I trust him. I know he'll do you right."

"Do *us* right, you mean. We have to share this equally. Really, we must. We can't take all the money. The coins might not be worth much— and then, they might be worth a lot. But, I think we must agree first that we share equally, no matter what," Sarah said.

"Yes, I agree." Ruth was adamant.

Bill was reluctant to agree. "Okay, but they would

still be there if you both hadn't come along."

"Well, first, we need to get something to eat. I'm starving. Why don't we zip into town? We know where Hardee's is, so we probably won't get lost." Ruth smiled.

"Why don't I make us some supper? The meat is already thawed and I can put some fries in the oven. I'm not a great cook, but I can do up a burger. How about it?"

"Okay, as long as we can still get back before dark. We can help," Sarah offered.

Sarah volunteered to set the table. "Do you have paper plates? No use making dishes to wash if we don't have to."

"No, I'm afraid I don't. The plates are up in the cabinet over the sink."

As Bill prepared the burgers, Sarah got the plates and Ruth set the tea glasses beside each plate. Ruth looked in the fridge for mustard and ketchup and set them on the table. It didn't take long for the meal to be cooked and they sat to eat.

"I'll say grace." Bill bowed his head. "Lord, thank you for this food and thank you for new friends. Amen."

"Amen," Sarah and Ruth said together.

"These are delicious!" Sarah said as she bit into her burger. "Thank you. I don't know when we've had someone cook for us. It's been TV dinners for us for a long time. We were so jumpy about the journal and getting ready to come here, we had no appetite."

"Yes, these are absolutely delicious!" Ruth was equally enthusiastic.

Bill grinned. "I'm really glad. It seems no one likes bear meat anymore!"

Sarah tried hard to swallow. Ruth laid her burger on her plate and looked at it solemnly.

Sarah finished swallowing and looked at what she had in her hands.

Bill laughed and smacked the table. "I'm just joshing you! It's beef!"

Ruth and Sarah looked at him ruefully but finally smiled. "I can't tell you how glad I am that I just didn't eat a piece of bear!" Sarah said and laughed. Ruth gave in and laughed too.

"How did you come to find the journal again?" Bill asked, wanting to keep them talking.

"Sarah wanted to go into the old North Ward of the asylum in Missouri before they tore it down. We went up to the attic, and the rest is history!"

"Well, it wasn't easy. We wanted to see if Samantha had been a real person or if this was written by someone who had made up the story. We didn't have the slightest clue how to go about it. Mrs. Tucker at the Kingdom of Callaway Historical Society helped us get started. We came here and the wonderful librarians at the Ashe County Library helped us. Then the ladies at the Register of Deeds office helped us find you. It was nothing short of a miracle, really, when you think about it. If that lady, Cherrie, hadn't come in when she did, we would still be looking."

Sarah thought a minute. "Wait a minute…you mean you didn't know about the journal—or about any of this?"

Bill hesitated. "No, I didn't know about *that* journal." He changed the subject.

"When do you all have to be back?"

"We have to be back at work on Monday or we'll lose our jobs," Ruth said.

"Why would you lose your jobs?"

"We work at the State Hospital, the same one that used to be named the Insane Asylum. We started at the bottom, scrubbing floors and emptying bedpans. Now we work in the kitchen. There is a long line of staff who are waiting for our jobs if we don't show up. They're not the best jobs in the world, but they're our jobs, and we need them," Ruth said.

"Well, tomorrow is Wednesday. I'll pick you both up at the motel, say seven? It's a three-hour drive to Asheville from here. By the way, I better give Les a call right now. We want to make sure he'll be there." Bill went over to use the phone on the desk in the corner. Looking up the phone number in his diary, he dialed and waited. Sarah and Ruth listened to his side of the conversation.

"Yes. Hello, Les, this is Bill Royster. How are you today? Good, good. Listen, I'm coming down with a couple of friends tomorrow. Will you be there? We have something very important we need you to examine. Yes, good. Okay, we'll be there around ten. We'll leave here at seven. Yes, thank you, Les. See you tomorrow."

Hanging up the receiver, Bill turned to the ladies with a grin. "I guess you heard. He'll be there."

They finished their meal, and the girls offered to clean up. "No, you just get on back to your motel. That way, you'll get back before dark. I'll clean up here."

"Oh, dear! We forgot to tell Mr. Beckworth we needed to stay another day..." Sarah was worried. "... or two."

"I'm sure Mr. Beckworth will understand. We'll pay him when we get back," Ruth said.

"Do you trust me to keep the coins in my safe and bring them with me tomorrow?" Bill asked.

"Of course, we do! Thank you! We certainly don't have any safe place to keep them," Sarah said.

They got into the Torino and drove down the bumpy lane back to the black top.

"Sarah, I just can't believe that we *actually found* the coins. What if they're worth five-hundred dollars apiece? I just figured it out in my head. That's twenty-five thousand dollars!"

"I know! I've been figuring it out too. We've tried not to speculate on what we'll do with the money for fear of hexing ourselves. But now that we've found them, what do you want to do?" Sarah giggled like a schoolgirl.

"I want to buy a new car. My old Ford has been faithful, but I pray every time I try to start it. Maybe we'll have enough for me to buy it new. How about you?"

Sarah patted the dashboard. "Don't you worry, Betsy, I'm not trading you! I would really like to have a new heating and cooling system for the house. My window air conditioner makes so much noise I can't sleep. That's what I want to do."

Silence loomed between them a moment while they daydreamed of bright futures. Then Ruth bit her lip and dared to broach the question she'd been aching to ask.

"What do you think of Bill? I'm not trying to pry. You know that's not my style. But I've never seen you interact with a man before. It was different today. Like maybe he was nice, and you might like him? Hmmm?"

Sarah thought for a minute. She hadn't thought of a man in such a long time. She didn't go anywhere where she might meet someone, mostly because she just wasn't interested. But, she had to admit that being near Bill made her feel something she hadn't felt for a long time. "Well, I just met him, and he seems very nice." Sarah tried to describe how she felt. "I do like talking to him. We'll just see. We live 750 miles from each other, so I don't think anything can come of it."

Ruth picked up the tremor in Sarah's voice. "Okay, I won't say anything else. Forgive me if I made you feel uncomfortable. You know that wasn't my intention."

"Of course! It's just different for us to have this kind of conversation." Sarah was at a loss as to how to continue the conversation, so she didn't.

They made it back to the motel, and Mr. Beckworth said it was fine for them to stay longer. They counted their pennies and paid for another two nights, which made them very nervous regarding money. They got ready for the next morning and then went to bed. Since they hadn't slept much the night before, they were exhausted and exhilarated at the same time. Sarah set the alarm, and they lay down, falling asleep almost instantly.

The pair were ready by 6:30 the next morning. It hadn't crossed their minds to think of what to do for breakfast, but they could get something along the way.

At seven, there was a knock on their door with a deep voice calling, "Room service!"

"What in the world?" Ruth opened the door. Bill stood there with a Hardee's bag in his hand.

"We can eat in the car. You don't mind if we take my car? There's plenty of room for all three of us." Bill pointed to a red and white 1957 Ford Fairlane Skyliner. "You're not the only one who loves old vehicles!" Bill said to Sarah. "She runs like a top and gets good gas mileage, so we'll be okay. It has a retractable hardtop, but we'll leave it up for now."

Sarah gazed at the car, and then at this handsome man who stood before her. Her heart ached with a longing she didn't know she could possess. She wondered if he felt it, too.

Chapter 48

Wednesday, May 9, 1984
Jefferson, North Carolina

Bill opened the passenger car door and pulled the back of the seat forward. Ruth hurried to get in the back seat so Sarah would have to sit in front with Bill. Bill motioned for Sarah to get in and then closed her door. Sarah was at a loss. No one had ever opened a car door for her before. She got in and Bill closed her door. Sarah turned around and raised her eyebrows at Ruth. Ruth simply smiled and nodded.

Bill got in and started the car, while Sarah handed the breakfast sandwiches around. "I don't want to get crumbs on your beautiful red leather seats." Sarah wiped her crumbs off and put them into the bag.

"No matter, it'll clean up." Bill pulled out onto the black top. "We'll take highway 194 out of town down to Boone. I'm afraid there's no quick way to get anywhere. There's been talk of several highway widening projects, but they're not a reality yet."

The trio sped down the highway and the talk was lively. "So, you're a descendant of Samantha and R.B.? Have you always known that?" Sarah asked.

"Yes, oral history and our ancestors have always been important to our family. My late wife did a lot of research on my family as well as hers."

"I'm sorry about your wife." Sarah went quiet. She wanted to ask more about his ancestors, especially Samantha, but it didn't seem the right time. Maybe later he would volunteer more information.

"Thank you. It happened a long time ago."

"My family never talked about their history or ancestors. Maybe they didn't know about them. That's why Sam's story has been so interesting to me. Do you have children?"

"I have twin boys. They're men now, actually. I'll always think of them as boys, I guess. Rhady is twenty-four and a newly minted lawyer in Raleigh, and Bart is an accountant in a CPA firm in Winston-Salem. How about you, Sarah?"

"My son D.J. and daughter Leigh are both nurses, one in Springfield, Missouri and one in Wilmington, here in North Carolina," replied Sarah. "Ruth's kids are still in college in Columbia, Missouri."

Ruth quipped from the back seat. "Yes, I'm proud of them. They're not sure what they want to do, but it's early days."

They sped down the twisty, steep road. "Not a lot of guard rails around, I see," Ruth commented. "You can see the road down below. Will we eventually get down there?"

Bill laughed. "Yes, these switchbacks are designed to get us down the mountain gradually. Otherwise, it would be a straight shot and a lot more dangerous."

The road gradually smoothed out a bit when they came to highway 19E. They drove through the small towns of Spruce Pine and Burnsville. They turned onto 19-23 at Mars Hill and sped onward through Weaverville to Asheville.

"I'm really nervous about this. Should we just bring in one coin to show him?" Sarah asked.

"Yes, I think that would be best. We can trust Les. We'll show him one. When he gives us a quote, then we'll tell him how many we have. It might overwhelm him to dump the bag out right away." Bill's eyes twinkled.

Bill turned the car onto Market Street, and they pulled into a parking space in front of an old-fashioned store front. "Stevenson Rare Coins and Jewelry" was painted in gold letters on the glass window of the big oak door.

Bill reached into the glove box and took out a blue zippered bank pouch. The old cloth bag was tucked safely inside. "Maybe we better bring in the whole pouch. I don't want to leave this in the car. Would that be all right with you both?"

"Yes, I didn't think of that and am glad you did. I'm not used to having a bag of gold coins in my possession." Sarah was still astounded by that fact.

Bill opened the door for them, and they all trouped inside. Glass counters surrounded them, and the gilt chandelier cast a lovely glow over the room. At the sound of the door tinkling, a dark-haired gentleman came through a doorway at the back.

"Hello, Les! It's good to see you again." Bill shook Les's hand. "These are my friends Sarah and Ruth."

Les shook hands all around. "How may I be of assistance, Bill? It's been a while," Les said.

"We have something for you to evaluate. An old coin—." Bill reached into the pouch for the coin. "Actually, an 1861 coin."

"Let me get my magnifying glass." Les walked

around behind the counter.

"The good thing is, you can see the markings very well without it," Bill said.

Picking up the coin, Les held it to the light. The passage of time hadn't dulled the brightness of the coin. It shone in all its glory in the chandelier's light.

"Oh, my! This is fine! A fine specimen!" Les brightened with excitement. "Let me get my book."

Les laid the coin on the counter and hurried over to a corner desk where he picked up a black book. He flipped through the pages as he walked back to the counter. Les looked at the page and then at the coin. Then he looked at the coin and then at the page. His green eyes twinkled.

"This is a significant find! Do you have any idea what this is?" Not waiting for them to answer, he went on.

"This is from the Dahlonega, Georgia mint. Many people might think the "D" means Denver mint, but the Denver mint didn't start making coins until 1906. The Dahlonega mint only made coins from 1838 to 1861. There were only about 1500 five-dollar half eagles coined there. This coin is in mint condition and probably has never been circulated. It's in too fine a shape to have been in pockets for very long. It would be great if we had the provenance."

Sarah cleared her throat. "We're pretty sure we have that." Sarah's voice quavered in her excitement. "Um-mm…Do you have any idea how much it could be worth?"

"It says in my book here, which is the newest edition, that this is worth eighteen thousand five-hundred dollars, maybe more, since it's uncirculated."

Sarah grasped the edge of the counter, her knees wanting to buckle. Ruth put her hand over her mouth to stifle a squeal. Bill was grinning. Sarah's and Ruth's faces beamed at each other as they hugged. "Oh my God! Great God Almighty! I just can't believe it!" Sarah said. Ruth was speechless.

"Les, you aren't going to believe this, but we have fifty of these," Bill informed him.

Les was astonished. "Are you kidding me? Where on earth did you find these?"

"Well, that's a long story, and we'll tell you about it. But first, what's the next thing we need to do?"

"Well, the first thing we need to do is put them in my safe. We can't have them sitting out here on the counter. I'll make out the receipt for you. I need to call my bank to be sure, but I think I can offer to buy all the coins from you."

Bill jotted down a couple of numbers on a pad. "But that's nine-hundred twenty-five thousand dollars!"

"Yes, isn't that grand?" Les was jubilant. "I'll have the best collection ever to offer!"

"What would be your percentage for doing that for us?" Bill asked.

"I usually ask ten percent. Is that acceptable to you? Let's see, that would be ninety-two thousand five-hundred dollars. Would that still be acceptable?"

Sarah couldn't think. She looked at the ceiling, and then at Ruth. From Ruth to Bill, then to Les. She simply couldn't imagine that kind of money. They had never in a million years thought the coins would be this valuable. "Yes, yes, of course! Whatever you think best. Bill trusts you, so we trust you. Thank you!"

Les made his call and came back beaming. "We're

all set. Let's get down to brass tacks, so to speak. We'll sign this contract, so you'll be secure in putting your coins in my safe. I'll go over to the bank and sign some paperwork. How do I make out the check?"

"Divide it three ways. Although we can't travel with that kind of money all the way home, even in a check. What do you suggest, Mr. Stevenson?" Sarah asked.

"How about we do it this way? I'll give you each a thousand dollars to open an account here. You can open your accounts while I go to my bank. Then come back here, and I'll give you your checks and you can deposit them in your new accounts. That's pretty safe."

"I already have an account here with NationsBank. I can take the ladies there to open their accounts," Bill said.

Bill handed the bank pouch over to Les, and he took it back to his safe. When he came back, he handed Bill the contract, and all three signed it. Les tore off the original and handed it to Bill who passed it on to Sarah. Les kept the carbon copy. He gave each of them an envelope. "Here is your thousand dollars. Okay, let's get to it," Les said.

Bill, Sarah, and Ruth walked out of the shop and stood in front of the car. Sarah rubbed her temples. It felt as if her head was going to explode. Ruth's smile was wide. Bill couldn't stop smiling and shaking his head.

"The NationsBank is just around the corner. We can walk if you like. It's hard to get parking here on Market Street," Bill said.

"Yes, that's fine. Maybe we can clear our heads while we walk," Ruth said.

The trio walked around the corner and down to the NationsBank. The Buncombe County Courthouse, built between 1924 and 1928, was directly across the street from the bank. Beside it was the pink domed City Hall building, built in 1928.

They went into the bank, and Sarah and Ruth sat down to open their accounts while Bill waited patiently. "We're opening our accounts with cash, but we'll be back shortly with a large check to deposit. We live in Missouri. Will that be a problem?" Sarah asked.

"Not at all. We have branches in Missouri. Let me make a copy of your licenses and we'll be finished in a jiffy."

"Let's keep some of the cash, don't you think? We might need some more on our way home." Sarah wondered what it would feel like to not have to worry about money. She couldn't fathom it. Ruth didn't answer her. She seemed a million miles away. Sarah prodded her with an elbow.

"Yes, yes, good idea! Sorry, I was picturing a red Ford Mustang in my carport." Ruth grinned and wiggled in her seat.

As they walked back to the coin shop on Market Street, Bill pointed out the Jackson Building on Pack Square, built in 1924. "There are a lot of beautiful old buildings here." They walked in and Les was at the counter, smiling.

"You all have made my day, you know that?" Les spread his hands wide.

"We feel pretty much the same way!" Sarah and Ruth agreed. "We're on Cloud 9 with no rain in sight!"

"Now, will you tell me where you found them?"

Sarah looked at Bill and he nodded.

"Well, you won't believe it, but we found them in a cave on Bill's property. His ancestor had hidden them there in 1864. We found a journal that she wrote when she fled the county and ended up in Fulton, Missouri. That led us to Ashe County and Mr. Royster here," Sarah said.

"That is a fantastic journey! May I tell that story?" Les rubbed his hands together and his eyes gleamed with anticipation.

Sarah and Ruth looked at each other and shrugged. "Yes, we guess so. We're leaving in the morning for home. We've not thought that far ahead. Bill, what do you think?"

"Well, we won't have the coins on our person for anyone to steal. Les, are you worried about that?"

"Are you kidding? The more publicity, the better. I've always wanted a one-of-a-kind collection, and now I have it!"

"Who are you going to tell?" Sarah asked.

"I've already told my financiers about the coins. I think it's a fantastic story and want to share it. If you're all sure?"

They all nodded. "You have our permission."

Les handed them their checks. He had deducted the thousand dollars he had already given them and the checks were made out for two-hundred seventy-six thousand five-hundred dollars each! They still couldn't believe it!

They all shook Les's hand and left. Bill drove them around to the bank and once more they walked in with money. The teller's eyes were enormous as she read the amount. Nevertheless, she handed Sarah her receipt and Ruth stepped up to the window. The teller handed her the receipt and smiled at them. Bill was next, and he pocketed his receipt.

"Yay, it's a grand day!" Ruth waved her receipt in the air.

The trio walked out of the bank and got into the Fairlane. "I think we better have some lunch before we start back," said Bill. "I'm starving now that it's over. We can go right down College Street to a great little diner that's been around since 1969, The Med. It's next door to Kress's Department Store, another unique building. You'll love the food. What do you think?"

"Yes, that's fine with me." Sarah said. "Ruth?"

"Yep, I'm starving now too!"

Bill drove the Fairlane down College Street and found a parking space in front of the restaurant. "This is a bone fide miracle, finding a parking spot on College!" They all laughed.

"Maybe today *is* our day for miracles..." Sarah thought out loud.

Bill held the door for the ladies and ushered them in. They seated themselves in a booth and looked at the menus. Right away Ruth knew that the print was too small for Sarah to read; she saw Sarah squinting. She didn't want her friend to be embarrassed in front of Bill. "Look here, Sarah, your favorite! They serve breakfast all day!"

Sarah knew what Ruth was doing, and she was grateful for it. "Well, I have to admit, Bill, that I need glasses. I'll get them as soon as I get home."

Bill pulled his glasses out of his pocket. "Well, at least two of us can read the menu!" They laughed again and turned to the menus.

"What's a grit?" Ruth asked.

Chapter 49

Wednesday, May 9, 1984
On the road back to Ashe County, North Carolina

Bill drove while Ruth and Sarah held their own thoughts. It had been quite a day. Sarah couldn't think of much to say. Anything she considered talking about was about when she got home. She would do this, or she would do that. Sarah wanted to convey her thanks to Bill for everything, but a thank you just wasn't enough. The fact he had allowed them on his property and had led them to the coins was such a tremendous act of generosity. She was without words to express her thanks because it had changed all their lives forever.

Bill pulled up to the Highlander Motel and parked beside the Torino. Turning off the ignition, his eyes met Sarah's. "Well, you have had an adventure for sure. Thank you for your time and effort to come all this way. To tell you the truth, a mere 'thank you' just doesn't do this justice. I've been trying to think of what to say, but I don't know what to say. But I thank you for your tenacity and courage to follow through when you found the journal."

Sarah was so glad his thoughts mirrored hers. "Thank you for letting us all share equally in the treasure. Few would have done that." Sarah didn't know what to say, either.

Bill got out of the car and went around to open Sarah's door, but she had already opened it. Seeing him stop short, she quickly shut it. His mouth curved into a smile as their eyes met again. Bill opened her door, and Sarah got out. Then he pulled the seat forward for Ruth.

Ruth got out and held her hand out to Bill. "Thank you so much for everything. I'm going on in. Sarah, take your time!"

"You're welcome." Bill shook Ruth's hand and then turned to Sarah. "Say, I know you both need to get packed. But…well… can I have your phone number?" Sarah smiled and nodded. She reached for a page of her notes, wrote her number on the bottom, tore it off, and handed it to Bill.

"I *will* call you. I'll let things settle down for you and then I *will* call you. And you have my number, if you're ready before I call. Be safe." Bill turned to get in his car.

Sarah hesitated. "The name in the phone book said, 'William R. Royster.' What does the 'R' stand for?"

Bill turned back to her, smiled and said, "Rhadamanthus."

A word about the author...

Janet Perry is a Civil War historian, reenactor and seamstress. She grew up in Missouri but spent thirty years in the mountains of North Carolina researching the rich folklore of the beautiful Blue Ridge Mountains. Janet lives with her husband on a century old farm in South Central Missouri. Follow her on Facebook as Janet Sing Perry.

Thank you for purchasing
this publication of The Wild Rose Press, Inc.

For questions or more information
contact us at
info@thewildrosepress.com.

The Wild Rose Press, Inc.
www.thewildrosepress.com

www.ingramcontent.com/pod-product-compliance
Lightning Source LLC
Chambersburg PA
CBHW072312020726
47501CB00002B/480